sweet water

Also by Christina Baker Kline

FICTION

Desire Lines

The Way Life Should Be

Bird in Hand

Orphan Train

NONFICTION

The Conversation Begins: Mothers and Daughters Talk About Living Feminism (coauthored with Christina Looper Baker)

Child of Mine: Original Essays on Becoming a Mother (editor)

Room to Grow: Twenty-two Writers Encounter the Pleasures and Paradoxes of Raising Young Children (editor)

About Face: Women Write About What They See When They Look in the Mirror (edited with Anne Burt)

sweet water

A Novel

CHRISTINA
BAKER KLINE

wm
WILLIAM MORROW
An Imprint of HarperCollins*Publishers*

HarperCollins books may be purchased for educational, business, or sales promotional use. For information, please e-mail the Special Markets Department at SPsales@harpercollins.com.

A hardcover edition of this book was published in 1993 by Aaron Asher Books, an imprint of HarperCollins Publishers.

FIRST WILLIAM MORROW PAPERBACK EDITION PUBLISHED 2014.

Designed by C. Linda Dingler

The Library of Congress has catalogued the hardcover edition as follows:
Kline, Christina Baker, 1964–
Sweet water/Christina Baker Kline.—1st ed.
p. cm.
"Aaron Asher books."
ISBN 978-0-06-019033-0
I. Title.
PS3561.L478S93 1993
813'.54—dc20 92–54717

ISBN 978-0-06-236100-4 (pbk.)
14 15 16 17 18 OV/RRD 10 9 8 7 6

To D.K. and Beth,
who helped me find my way

The past is never dead. It's
not even past.

—WILLIAM FAULKNER

But in order to make you understand,
to give you my life, I must tell you a story—
and there are so many, and so many.

—VIRGINIA WOOLF,
THE WAVES

sweet water

part one

I used to want to forgive, but now all I want is to be let alone. I don't have forgiveness left in me. My forgiveness ran out with her blood on that long backwoods stretch of highway when he crawled away in terror that he would be found out. He left her to bleed to death because he could not bear to watch his own life's blood draining into that red Tennessee dirt; he could not accept that a life he made he had also destroyed. He could only think in the think-speak of whiskey that no one must know, and he gathered up the shards of the bottle, searching for them in the darkness, the smell of burning rubber. He clasped the jagged pieces against his shirt, cutting himself on the glass, and crawled with them far out into the cornfield on the right side of the road, where he dug a hole with his fingers and buried them as deep as he could, which wasn't deep enough.

He lay there in the trampled corn until his mind started to search through the debris of drunkenness and work itself back into logic and he realized in the lightening darkness, the shadowy cornstalks starting to emerge around him, that he was in it deep. So he dragged himself out of the field on his hands and knees at first and then staggering to his feet, not so much from the whiskey now but in the clearing consciousness of accountability, and made his way back to the scene of the crime. When they found him he was leaning, sobbing over our daughter, dirt all over his hands and knees and sweat tears blood on his face, and he was saying, "Sleep now, Ellen—sleep. We'll wake you in the morning."

I never really knew my mother's father. So when I received the message on my answering machine from a magistrate at the Sweetwater courthouse asking me to attend the reading of his will, it was as if I'd won a prize in a contest I couldn't remember having entered. I sat in my Brooklyn apartment in the fading afternoon light, listening to the soft drawl of the voice on the machine several times while I tried to figure out what it meant. Then I called my dad.

"Hi, honey," he said. "Well, I'll be damned." He was silent for a moment. "Of course you know there's no need to go down there. They can send you the details of whatever it is the old buzzard's left you."

"I didn't even know he died."

"Elaine sent me the obituary last week." His voice sounded tired. "I guess I should've called you."

"But what does it mean?" I said. "Why would he leave me anything? He never even so much as wrote me."

"Oh, it's probably something of your mother's he's been hanging on to all these years. Some keepsake."

"Why now, though? What good did he think it would do?"

"Who knows why anybody does anything? Maybe this is his way of apologizing. To be fair to the guy, Cassie, it couldn't have been easy for him. I'm sure he's been carrying around a lot of guilt for a long time."

I laughed dryly. "Never stopped him from drinking."

I could hear my dad draw a deep breath. "That's just what Elaine says, but then, she was never his favorite kid. Look, Amory Clyde had a hard life. And the drinking he did after the accident was different. It was his only way of dealing with it. I don't think it's for us to judge."

I sat there fingering the dial on the telephone. I tried to remember my mother's face, but all my memories seemed to be derived from snapshots. I could see her in a lime-green dress and black shoes, short dark hair and red lipstick. She was holding me up, pressing our cheeks together, whispering through smiling teeth, "Smile at the camera, honey." Another time, I vaguely remembered, we had gone to the zoo. I was wearing white tights and a tan corduroy dress and holding a blue balloon. When I pointed at the gorillas and made a face, she scratched her head like an ape and pretended to peel a banana.

"I've got to go, sweetheart," Dad was saying. "Susan's out there in the kitchen by herself. She's getting so big I want to keep her off her feet as much as possible these days. But if you come into a fortune, don't forget who raised you."

"You mean Mrs. Urbansky?" I smiled into the phone.

"Hey, you hated her guts, remember? You told me she used to make you floss until your gums bled. She made you swallow Listerine every time you brushed your teeth."

"Did I tell you that? I really must have wanted to get rid of her."

After he hung up, I rested the receiver on my shoulder for a moment. As long as I held on, there'd be a connection between us; if he picked up the phone again, I'd still be there. I imagined him going back and chopping onions, whipping eggs for a soufflé, laughing with Susan in the kitchen as people waited for their food. Sometimes all I wanted to do was go home and live above the restaurant again, waking to the voices of deliverymen in the street below, drifting to sleep at night amid the smells of lemon chicken and fresh bread.

The receiver started to beep in my hand, and I replaced it on the cradle. It was too late to call the magistrate today; I'd have to do it tomorrow, from the gallery. I wondered if I should try to call my grandmother but almost immediately thought better of it. What could I possibly say to a woman I hadn't seen since I was three?

I tried to conjure images of my grandfather, of what my grandmother's voice sounded like, the shape of her body. I could dimly recall a powdery smell and soft, dry skin. The only thing I knew with certainty was that one Easter, right before the accident, they gave me a doll that blinked, with hair that grew. The doll had been as big as I was. It was still around somewhere, locked in the musty attic of my dad's house.

I leaned over and picked up the phone again, dialing my friend Drew's number. "You know what to do," his tape-recorded voice announced.

"It's me. I've either inherited a plantation or a lock of my dead mother's hair. Call if you want to celebrate."

My voice, talking to a machine in an empty room, sounded strangely hollow. All at once I realized that I was sitting alone in the dark. I wondered idly where Drew was, then remembered that he was at some Sotheby's function in the city. The apartment was hot and sticky. I got up and started unlocking windows, hauling up the heavy wooden frames and releasing into the room a cacophony of city sounds. The smell of burgers drifted over from across the street, and feeling a stab of hunger, I realized I hadn't eaten anything but an apple since morning.

I could have called someone to meet for dinner, but I didn't feel like it. I went into the bedroom and curled up on the futon, one part of me burying everything and the other part excavating, dredging up faces and smells and sounds. My grandfather had died and I never loved him, never even knew him. It didn't matter. I didn't care. My mother was dead and now he was dead too, and so everything was finished. There was no one left to blame. I lay under the darkness as if it were a blanket, a churning sea, trying to forget and trying to remember, until I drifted into sleep.

* * *

After my mother died, my father used to tell me the story of my name.

He told me that Cassandra was a princess from the land of Troy, the beautiful daughter of a proud king. That she had special powers: she was a visionary, she could see into the future. That she was wise and knowing, nothing ever surprised her. And she always told the truth. Then he'd look at me intently and say, "We had a hunch you'd be something special."

When, in the fifth grade, some too-smart kid on the playground told me the details of the story—that everybody thought Cassandra was crazy, that she was stabbed to death by the wife of her two-timing lover—I demanded to know how they could have named me after a lunatic with a curse hanging over her head.

We were driving home to Brookline after one of our afternoons at the Boston Aquarium. It was raining; the loose old wipers swished and slapped against the windshield.

My father looked at me. He pulled on the tufts of his beard like he always did when he didn't know what to say. "We never thought of it that way," he said. He adjusted the knob for the wipers, trying to speed them up. "Maybe we should have. I don't know." He moved his shoulders up and down in a shrug.

"Can I change my name, then?" I asked.

"To what?"

"Sandra." I had thought about it. It seemed like a good compromise.

"You're serious about this."

"She was *murdered*, Dad. Nobody believed a word she said."

"But they were wrong, Cassie," he insisted. "She was the only one who knew what was going on."

I sighed and leaned back against the cool vinyl. "Nobody believed her, so what good was that?"

He drove for a while, adjusting the wipers again, fiddling with the rearview mirror. "'Sandra.'" He said the name as if he were holding it out and inspecting it. "I'm not sure I can get used to it."

"How about Ann?"

He put his big, warm hand on my cold knee. It felt as large and leathery as a gorilla's. "You have to understand, Cassie, we were very idealistic. We thought the truth was the most important thing." He paused. "'Cassandra' was your mother's idea."

There was nothing I could say to that. I looked at my side window, at the spots of rain slanting against it and running down in a sheet.

"She loved you very much, Cassie," he said in the stillness. "And I do too. You know that, don't you?"

My father didn't normally say things like this. I knew how difficult it was for him. I felt a lump in my throat and fought to keep from crying, angry at myself for giving in.

"Okay," I said in a hard voice.

"Okay what?"

"I know."

"You know what?"

"I know you love me," I said, my voice muffled against the glass.

"Good," he said, tugging at his beard. "Good."

I didn't want to feel sorry for my dad, but I did, and I felt even sorrier for myself. I stared out at the gray streets, the shiny cars, the muddied puddles and potholes. My breath fogged the window.

After a few minutes I could feel him looking over at me. "Don't you think it's interesting—," he began. I turned to him. "Not to change the subject, but don't you think it's interesting that all those swimming mammals evolved from the same group as bears?"

"You mean walruses?"

"The whole bunch of them. Walruses, sea lions, seals. They're called Pinnipedia. 'Fin feet.'"

"Pinnipedia," I said. We were back on familiar territory. "They even look kind of like bears. When you think of it."

"They kind of do," he agreed. "And you know, another thing. It's very easy to tell their age. Their teeth have rings, like a tree trunk. One ring for each year."

"Really?"

"Really. Some of them even live to be forty. They must have *enormous* teeth."

The rain was lighter now, only sprinkling. He turned the knob, and the wipers ground to a halt diagonally across the windshield. We stopped at a red light, and my father yawned and stretched.

"Cassie, it's up to you, I guess," he said. "You can change your name if you want. It's your decision."

I sighed again. My breath made a big, soft-edged circle against the window. I reached up and erased it with my index finger. "I guess Cassie's okay," I said. "For now."

"All right."

"I might want to change it later."

He nodded. "Later would be fine."

When my mother died, my dad was a junior faculty member in the anthropology department at Boston University, but after the accident he didn't want to teach anymore. A year later he opened the restaurant, Grasshopper's, in Brookline. With the occasional help of Mrs. Urbansky, a shrill, fastidious woman with a mania for oral hygiene, he raised me in the little apartment upstairs. When I woke in my bed with nightmares, he was there to soothe me. He took me to antiwar demonstrations in Cambridge and interpreted the Watergate hearings—with a lot of yelling at the television—as we watched them together in the restaurant the summer I was ten. He might have been overbearing if he hadn't had the restaurant, which kept him busy enough to give me space. I always had the feeling that he was scared of hurting me, and that he wanted me to like him. It made us afraid to tell each other too much. We awoke anxieties in each other with our too-careful dance around the edges of truth, our shared memories of pain.

We almost never talked about my mother. Over the years I picked up bits and pieces about her—her favorite poet was William Carlos Williams, she loved Brahms, her favorite color was midnight blue—but I was always afraid of pushing too far, of being too demanding. It wasn't until Susan moved in that I felt I could bring up some questions I'd been saving for years.

"You still miss her, don't you, Dad?" I asked one time when he visited me at college. It was a bitter-cold Parents Weekend in the fall, and we were sitting in the dark-paneled student pub, drinking coffee.

"I still think of her," he said.

"It's been hard on you."

"Harder on you, not having a mother. I mean, I've got Susan."

"But you didn't, for a long time."

"I didn't," he agreed.

I wrapped my hands around the paper cup and leaned over it, blowing holes in my coffee. "Is Susan very different?"

He sat back. I could tell he felt uncomfortable talking about it, even now. The question hung in the air between us. "She is," he said finally. "Well, in some ways. Major ways. But there's something—I don't know what it is—something about her that every now and then reminds me of Ellen"—he looked up; he had never used her name like that with me—"reminds me of your mother. It's not the way she looks, or an expression, or anything like that. I guess it's a spirit or something." He pulled at his beard.

"I don't remember very much about her," I said.

"What do you remember? I mean, I was never really sure."

I tried to think back. When I was little, five or six, I used to go home after school and sit in the window overlooking our narrow, busy street, waiting for her to come back. One day, I was certain, I'd recognize my mother's shining dark hair among the crowds at the end of the street, weaving and bobbing purposefully toward the restaurant. As she got closer, I was sure I'd see her thin, bare white arms, her lime-green dress, the slant of her cheekbones.

"I'm not sure I remember anything."

While we were talking, the lights had come on in the pub, and the sky outside had darkened like a stone dipped in water. I sipped some coffee, burning the tip of my tongue, and blew into the cup again.

"I've often wondered what kind of a mother she would have been. A pretty good one, probably." He paused, considering. "But you know, Cassie, I think both of us have built up this memory of a woman who was close to perfect, and she wasn't that. She was unpredictable. Moody when you'd least expect it. And she would've hated living in that tiny apartment above the restaurant for however long it's been—twenty years? She'd probably have gone crazy. But maybe I wouldn't have quit teaching if . . . Who knows?" He looked over at me. "And maybe it would've been better to get out, anyway. It's such a day-to-day life."

"That's not true, Dad."

"You would have loved her, though," he continued. "I mean, I know you do, but if you really knew her . . . " He squinted, as if concentrating on an object across the room. "She was captivating, Cassie. Here I was, this boy from New Hampshire. I had never met anybody so passionate about so many things. Her feelings were so strong it scared me sometimes. And she didn't do anything by halves. In her mind, you were either with her or against her. If you weren't with her, you were against her." He shook his head at the memory. "I was entranced."

"I'm not so sure we would have gotten along," I said.

He looked at me, distracted. Then he reached over and grasped my hands. "Oh, no, you would have! I know you would have. It's hard to get across the whole picture of who she was. She was . . . " His voice trailed off. "You know, I don't think either of us were ready for it when she got pregnant. It took us some time to adjust to the idea. But as soon as you were born, all that changed. We used to take you everywhere in this little papoose carrier—museum tours, hikes in the country, concerts in the park. You just became a part of our lives together. And she cared about you intensely. When she died I felt so sad that she would never get to see you again. It just didn't make any sense. And I couldn't quite believe that you and I would have to go on living, without her."

He wasn't talking to me any longer; he was looking off in the distance. He didn't say anything else about her and I didn't ask. The pub was warm and intimate, and it was so cold outside I didn't want to leave. We just sat there drinking coffee until the staff turned up the music and dimmed the lights, getting ready for a different crowd.

He called me Clyde, as if his public name was my private one, as if none of who I was before was worth saving. At the time, through the thick haze of love, I thought it was because he wanted me so badly that he wanted all of me; he wanted to define me as his own, as him. Now I know he just wanted his appropriation of me to be the only proof of my worth.

In those first days of marriage, as my belly swelled with the child we had made not in love but in heat, we looked at each other and discovered strangers. After the shock of coming face to face with each other, hour after hour, day after night, we began to construct a way to define ourselves as part of each other. Almost without my realizing it, this came to mean that both of us defined me as part of him.

"Constance Clyde," he whispered that first night as he unbuckled the belt of my going-away dress in our little room in the Sewanee Inn. "Constance Clyde. Constance Clyde," as he lifted my skirt. By the time Horace was born, Amory was saying, "What's for dinner, C. Clyde?" "C. Clyde, where'd you put my coat?" But soon enough it was just Clyde, and nothing else. I kept thinking that someday it would shrink to C; and then after a while, maybe so I didn't even notice, I would have no name at all.

Sitting in the studio, on the kickwheel, I watched my foot as it pumped hard, then lifted. The wheel flew, specks of dried clay becoming a soft blur. I put my heel against the wheel to slow it. The clay pieces I'd finished were awkward and ungainly, misshapen bowls and off-center urns scattered on newspaper around the floor. I was determined to get the next one right.

In the evenings and on weekends, whenever I could, I came to NYU to work with clay. In college, when I was learning to use the equipment, everything was free; now I had to pay to use the space. "When you start to work with the kickwheel you're going to feel overwhelmed," a teacher had explained one September day long ago. "Try not to think about it. The brain can be a potter's worst enemy." She had put her hands out in front of her like brakes. "Don't feel you have to learn everything at once. Take your time. Experiment a little."

Ever since I was a little girl I had wanted to be a sculptor, maybe because I knew that my mother had been an art teacher before I was born. In elementary school I used to go home with my best friend, Dee Dee Harrison, in the afternoons. Her mother was a sculptor; she had a small studio in what had been a closet off the kitchen. Dee Dee and I would color or paint on construction paper at the kitchen table while Mrs. Harrison worked in the room next door. One day we came home with a story about a sculpting project we'd been assigned in art class: we were supposed to mold one of three Disney characters and then paint it to look like its cartoon self. Mrs. Harrison was furious. "What kind of learning . . . Our tax money going to waste . . . ," she ranted, pacing around the kitchen. When she calmed down she said that since the school wasn't going to teach us to sculpt, she would do it herself.

The clay was cold and hard to the touch, and smelled of deep dirt on autumn mornings, of damp leaves at the bottom of a pile. When I squeezed it, it molded to my hand. When I took my hand away, it retained the imprint of my fist. When I started working with clay, I felt I had control over something for the first time in my life. That first day, and for a long time afterward, my awkward fingers could not manipulate the clay into the shapes I envisioned. But every time was new, and each piece had potential—and someday, I knew, I would make my imagination manifest, for everyone to see.

Now, on the wheel, I kneaded a lump of clay until it was silky and supple, and set it in the middle of the plaster bat on top of the revolving wheelhead. Holding my hands steady, I worked the clay into a concave shape. When I first started on the large wheel, it was like learning to ride a bicycle; I was clumsy and slow. I couldn't keep up with the ceaseless turning. But once I mastered the movement it began to feel natural to me, and I could work fast. Carving a curve into the clay on the wheel was like taking a swift, smooth turn on a bike around a narrow bend: the way your body and mind lean into the curve simultaneously, as if one with gravity; the way you feel lifted up, as if on wings.

As I learned about throwing clay, I taught my hands how to move in to center it, how to glide up the sides of the bowl to cut the excess or save a weak rim. The process became intuitive; my mind threw out messages, and my hands worked them into the clay, responding to unplanned patterns and rhythms. Working with clay, I decided, was like being in a relationship: as you move with and against it, as it moves with and against you, you put part of yourself into it and it takes on part of you and supports you. That's why you have to work quickly; you need to do it, as my teacher said, without thinking too much.

I could feel the energy in the air, my energy, as I worked through the afternoon, my mind racing beyond thought. When I looked up I was surprised to find the daylight faded, the room dark and quiet, the flowing shapes in front of me the only signs of turbulence.

There was a time before all of this when I was young and Amory touched my body as if it were a shrine. When I was beautiful, or thought I was because he thought so. When we shared secrets instead of hoarding them. When we stayed together not because of the children, not because of the past, but just because. When, if I had danced, we would have danced in step.

There are so many ways to tell this story.

This is the story I told my children.

The first time I ever saw your father he was playing the piano at a party in Chattanooga. He was tall, even sitting down, with large ears and great big watery-blue eyes. I had never met a man who could play the piano, and I was impressed. Everyone was singing along. I even remember the song; it was "Mood Indigo."

Your father looked up, across the crowded room, straight into my eyes, and smiled at me. And then he sang the words directly to me: "You ain't never been blue 'til you've had that mood indigo." My girlfriends pushed me forward, and I mouthed the words back at him, and soon we were singing it together, as if we were the only people in the room.

When the song ended he asked my name and I told him it was Constance Whitfield.

"That's a very pretty name," he said. "Mine's Amory Clyde. How do you like it?"

I told him it was real nice.

"Good," he said. "I'm glad you like it, because it's going to be yours someday."

Four months later, we were married in a small Baptist ceremony in my parents' house at 11 Edgeley Drive in Chattanooga. My dress was silk, simple and white, with embroidered rosebuds and silvery beads, and it came almost to the floor. Your father wore a blue suit with a black tie. Your aunt Clara was maid of honor, and she wore a rose-colored dress with matching ribbons. Granddaddy Whitfield gave me away. For our honeymoon, we went to Atlanta. I'd never been there before. We stayed at the Sewanee Inn, and when we got there your father carried me across the threshold into a room that was filled with flowers, top to bottom. There was a piano in the lobby of the hotel, and that night your father started to play and people gathered around. It was just like being at that party where we'd first met, except that now I had a wedding band on my finger and our smiles weren't shy anymore. We sang "Mood Indigo," and everybody moved aside. I harmonized, singing soprano to his strong alto, and at the end everyone clapped. When we got back to our room, we found a bottle of champagne chilling in a bucket of ice, compliments of the hotel. And the next morning they served us breakfast in bed.

Ellen would ask, "Was he handsome, Ma?"

"I thought he was the most handsome man I'd ever seen."

"Was it love at first sight?" This from Elaine.

"From the moment I saw him."

"Would you do it again?" Horace wanted to know.

"I can't imagine life without my three beautiful children," I'd say, and that would be the end of the story.

This is the story I told my father.

I met Amory Clyde at a piano recital he was giving. Afterward, he walked me back to the gates of the college and asked if he could see me again. From then on, one thing just seemed to lead to another.

* * *

This is the story the family Bible tells

Amory Vincent Clyde, born January 27, 1913. Constance Winn Whitfield, born October 14, 1917. United in Matrimony September 22, 1937. Horace Whitfield Clyde, born March 15, 1938.

This is the story I tell myself.

The dance hall was dim and smoky, like a grainy photograph. Tricia and Marie, my roommates from the teachers college, had persuaded me to come, though I'd told them I was not allowed to dance. The week before, they'd convinced me to climb through a trapdoor to the roof above our bedroom in the women's dormitory, which was guarded like a citadel, and smoke cigarettes. The first time I inhaled, I felt my stomach flip with nausea, but I didn't choke. Soon we were going up there every night.

The night we went to the dance hall, we waited until all the lights in the dormitory were out and then escaped down the fire stairs. We'd brought high-heeled shoes in a paper bag, and Tricia had rouge and lipstick, which we applied squinting into the circular mirror of a compact under a streetlight. The three of us entered the hall as though we were on a mission. The few cigarettes we'd smoked outside in the dark had made me heady.

When I first saw Amory he was standing at the bar with a drink in his hand. His hair was golden, wavy and long in the front, and his fingers, wrapped around a whiskey glass, were narrow and delicate. He didn't look as if he had done a day's work in his life. I liked that about him. He was talking to a woman with her back turned to me. When she took out a cigarette he set down his drink and produced a silver lighter, flicking it with one hand, cupping the flame with the other. He was smooth, I could see: smooth bordering on slick

When he started playing the piano I felt something ignite in the pit of my stomach. His playing was butter on corn. I felt myself swaying to the music, almost dancing, and the thrill of taboos breaking one after another was like fireworks in my head. A song I didn't recognize turned into "Mood Indigo," and suddenly I was humming along and then singing, and then, somehow, standing at the piano with him, looking into his cloudy blue eyes.

I always get that mood indigo
Since my baby said good-bye
In the evening when the lights are low
I'm so lonely I could cry . . .

When the song ended we were staring at each other. He picked up his drink, took a swallow, and said, "You've got quite a voice."

"Thank you." I leaned a little closer to the piano. "Where'd you learn to play like that?"

"Oh, here and there." He ran his fingers up and down the keys. "Do you play?"

"Used to," I said. "But then, everybody takes lessons, I guess."

He laughed. "Maybe where you're from. What's your name?"

I told him.

"Pretty name for a pretty dame."

I blushed. Part of me wondered how many times he'd used that same line; but a bigger part of me didn't care.

"I'm Amory Clyde," he said, extending his hand. When I reached out to shake it, he held mine tight. "I hope you like my name, Miss Constance Whitfield, because someday I'm going to give it to you as a present."

That night, behind the dance hall, I was kissed for the first time in my life, by a man I had known less than two hours. He touched my breast beneath my thin polka-dotted dress, and I, intoxicated by his whiskey breath and virtuoso hands, did not even try to stop him. His tongue moved inside my mouth as softly as his hand caressed my nipple. All the while, he moved his thin, lithe body against mine in precisely the kind of dance that the Baptists tried so hard to prevent.

To his credit, when I found out three months later that I was pregnant, Amory asked me to marry him on the spot. My father was enraged and then heartbroken that I could not be married in Chat-

tanooga's largest Baptist church, to which our family belonged. He hadn't liked Amory from the beginning. With his delicate bones and sensitive mouth, his cigarettes and indolent smile, Amory struck my father as a dilettante and a dandy. But above all else my father believed in respectability and family honor, so the wedding was held in the front parlor of our enormous house. My mother cried through the entire ceremony.

After Horace was born, my father sent Amory to Baton Rouge to learn how to run a cotton mill so he could eventually expand my father's dynasty to Sweetwater, Tennessee. I moved into a lonely house with too many windows that had been built for us on the outskirts of town. A man named Jeb Gregory came out a few times a week to tend to the garden and fix up the place, and his daughter Lattie, who was fifteen, lived with me while Amory was away.

As the months went by, I met the ladies of Sweetwater, especially Bryce Davies and May Ford, who welcomed me into their circle. I'd get Jeb to take me into town for bridge and tea parties and other things that ladies do. Bryce and I became close friends; she'd drive out to my house with Taylor, her little girl, and they'd stay all day. We'd sit on the porch drinking lemonade, and in the afternoons we'd put the babies to bed and have long talks in the summer heat. She had straight black hair, which she wore up on her head, and she confessed to me that she was part Cherokee. She said I was the only person she'd ever told. Her husband was working at Daddy's mill down in Athens, but when Amory came back in the fall he would work for him.

That time when I was alone and missing Amory, receiving each letter as if it were a priceless treasure, rocking Horace to sleep on the wide, cool porch and watching summer fall into autumn, jeweled vistas turning almost perceptibly into colors of blood and flesh: I think now that that time may have been the best and sweetest of our marriage.

The woman from the Sweetwater courthouse said she thought I could get good money for the land.

"That's a pretty piece of property your granddaddy's left you. Developers have been itching to get their hands on it for years," she said. Her name was Crystal. Her voice was slow and sweet. "We're not exactly a booming metropolis, but people come and go."

"What's the house like?"

"Well, it's not much to look at, but the location's great. About five minutes outside of town, running parallel to the highway. Easy to get to. That's why I say you won't have any trouble getting rid of it. They can chop it into three or four subdivisions, pave roads all through it, and even the farthest houses won't be more than ten minutes from town.

"But I don't imagine you'll get much for that old house. They'll probably tear it down and start from scratch. Too much of a pain to work around it. I'll tell you what, though, you ought to get somebody to help you if you've never handled land before. You'll get swindled if you're not careful."

It was quiet in the gallery, a typical weekday morning. A blond, Nordic-looking couple in their thirties were the only visitors. I smiled at them politely, cradling the phone on my shoulder with my chin, and wrote down the names Crystal was giving me. To my surprise, the list included my uncle Horace, a local real estate developer.

My grandfather had left me sixty acres. *Sixty acres*—I couldn't even visualize it. The land stretched across my imagination like a continent, a universe of dying grass and scrubby hills, with an old abandoned house at the center. Crystal, who seemed to know everybody, told me that Clyde, my grandmother, hadn't wanted to live there. She thought it was inconvenient, too remote and old-fashioned. She lived in a modern housing development closer to town, with electric garage doors and access to cable TV. Horace and Elaine, my mother's siblings, lived with their spouses near shopping malls. Their children were grown and out of the house.

"I wouldn't call your uncle first on this one," Crystal was saying. "To be honest with you, it was a surprise to everybody that old Mr. C. left you that land. Not that you don't deserve it, seeing as you're Ellen's daughter and all, but I think people had just plain forgot about you."

In his will, my grandfather had said he wanted to leave his three children sixty acres each but since my mother was dead her share would be passed on to me. From what I could get out of Crystal, it seemed that Horace and Elaine had thought it would be theirs to divide.

It occurred to me that I had absolutely no idea what the property was worth. Thousands of dollars? Five, ten, fifty? Crystal said she had no idea either. She gave me a name to call for an estimate. "And after you talk to him, take some time to think it over," she said. "You don't have to decide what to do right away. That land ain't going nowhere."

When I hung up the phone, the blond woman looked over at me. "Such an interesting collection you have here," she murmured, tapping one long fingernail on the wall next to a dark abstract acrylic. "Vietnamese. Quite unusual, no?"

I handed her a flier about the artist, and she rolled it up and used it to point out features of the painting to her friend.

I looked around the gallery. The place seemed absurdly small, despite all the work Adam and I had put in trying to make it feel larger: eggshell walls, track lighting, bare, polished pine floors. Geometrically arranged paintings and drawings, each separately lit, lined the walls. The current exhibit—attenuated wire sculptures that resembled cyclones—hung from the ceiling on long wires or rested on butcher-block pedestals we had retrieved from a defunct meat-packing plant. Brochures were stacked on an old wooden desk near the entrance next to an open guest book and cards that read:

Rising Sun Gallery
Contemporary Vietnamese Art
304 Hudson Street, NYC
Adam Hemmer, Owner

with the hours and a phone number.

In the seven years I'd known him, Adam had always wanted his own gallery. In college he studied Asian languages and art history; his mother was a collector of Vietnamese art, so he had a ready field of interest. When he came into some family money in his early twenties, all the groundwork had been laid.

I was with him from the beginning. The two of us spent countless hours finishing the floor and arranging the lighting and seeing to hundreds of details. On opening day we worked through the early hours of the morning, completing final touches as the opaque slice of sky outside the window became transparent: gray, then misty yellow tinged with rose. At five o'clock, as the sun was edging around the corner of the building and spilling in shards across the canvases, over the sculptures, he reached for me in the stillness and we made love for the first time, on the hard wood floor. I remember the smell of paint and polish, the sounds of us echoing in the high-ceilinged room. I thought at the time it was like making love in a church.

That was a long time ago. I can barely recall, now, what drew me to him in the first place. I think it had something to do with the fact that unlike most of our friends, he had a plan for himself and seemed bent on achieving it. He was witty; he was smart. And working for Adam, I knew, would be valuable experience. When it got so that we were barely communicating except to talk business, I repeated those words to myself—*valuable experience*—like a mantra.

Somewhere along the way, I suppose I must have fallen in love with him. When he reached for me that first time, that early morning in the gallery, it seemed inevitable. The air around us had been charged for weeks. And for a while he was so sensitive to me, so gentle, that I confused the touch of his fingers with love, though a whispering voice in the back of my head warned me not to trust him, even then. So when I found out that he had been seeing other women, I was devastated at first and then philosophical, as if they too were somehow inevitable.

I continued to work with him and even, occasionally, to sleep with him. But as time went on I began to feel a strange silence breeding inside me, a void as tangible as anything I could devise to fill it. I could feel it hollowing against my ribs, inching higher and higher, corroding into itself like a hill of sand.

The blond couple signed the guest book before leaving. I could hear them conversing in some guttural language as they clomped down the stairs to the street. At the bottom of the stairs they paused, letting somebody in, and I cocked my ear to listen. This was what I liked least about being in the gallery alone: you never knew who might be on the way up; you just had to wait, defenseless.

It was Adam. "Oh, hey," he panted, coming into view. He was lugging a large canvas. "Help me here. Meet Veronica." He tilted his head toward a tall hazel-eyed woman following behind him. "She's cataloguing this stuff."

"Don't get up. I'll help him," she said in a posh English accent.

Adam raised his eyebrows at me. "Did that couple buy anything?"

"No. They looked around for a while, though. They took a card." I pretended to straighten some papers on the desk. "If you don't need me, I've got some errands to do."

"Well, actually—"

"Let her go," Veronica said. "I'm happy to stay."

I smiled evenly at her. "Great." I went back into the office and got my bag. When I returned, Adam and Veronica were deep in conversation about the oil painting propped against the wall.

"I think it's quite marvelous, really," Veronica was saying, nervously glancing at Adam. She waved her hand in front of the canvas. "All that . . . movement."

"You think?" He sounded dubious. He was silent for a moment, his hand on his chin, and then he said, "No. It hesitates. Nok could *see* it, but he couldn't *do* it."

"Hmm." She stepped back, squinting.

"Maybe he should've settled for being a gallery owner, then," I said.

Outside, the West Village was crowded with people heading for lunch, meetings, health clubs. Despite the heat, the air was damp. As I walked along the mazelike dead-end streets, I thought about the winding streets of Venice I had wandered the summer before; there were so many of them, and they all seemed to lead nowhere. But in New York, unlike Venice, people walked with a sense of purpose. They had appointments to keep, problems to solve, deals to make. Just thinking about it made me tired.

I drifted up Hudson Street, buying a salad from a Korean grocery along the way, heading toward the concrete playground where Hudson and Bleecker intersect. A homeless woman followed me, and I gave her my change. After that I was approached three or four times, and every time I turned away I felt a part of me harden and steel itself. This happened every day, and every day the process was the same.

I felt that familiar hollowness, the gnawing space inside me that seemed to be growing. I thought about the gallery, the flawed painting, Adam's hand on Veronica's back.

All at once I was overcome with anxiety at the narrowness of my routine. My days had become numbingly predictable. Every morning the clock struck seven and the alarm drove me toward it—back to the city, into each day, the minutes ticking one after another, time that loitered but wouldn't stand still. Up and showering, soap, shampoo, orange juice by the sink, scanning the paper for fatalities in the neighborhood, hesitating over my umbrella—would it rain? Applying lipstick, nude, the color for summer, at the mirror in the hall. Locking the door behind me once, twice, three times. Swinging shut the iron gate out front, walking in the sun or wind or rain and descending into darkness, tokens, the smell of urine. On the subway folding screens—the *Daily News,* the *Times*—hid blank faces the shades of New York: boredom, mistrust, ennui.

As the clock struck nine we'd be open for business, for pleasure. Hot Brazilian coffee and bagels delivered by Julio, tip included. Inventory. Phone calls. Mail: exhibition at the Sonnabend Gallery, opening at Elena's; the Philadelphia Museum requesting a piece for its collection, but the artist and his work were nowhere to be found.

Time would speed up for a deadline, quickly slow down again: the clock would strike one and it'd be time for lunch. Adam seducing a collector on the phone in the office, me eating turkey on rye, reading the *Voice.* As the day heated into afternoon, Adam might leave for a late lunch with a dealer, and suddenly the gallery would be full: twelve Japanese tourists who speak no English and want to take pictures of the pictures; a couple with three little children; two skinheads who tell me they're from Milwaukee. A headache pounding against my brain. Three o'clock. Four. Adam would return smelling of bourbon and cigarettes.

Evening overpowered afternoon. Long shadows would fall across the butcher block as we shuffled papers, locked the office, straightened the desk. At seven the street was eerily deserted, trash dancing across the gutter. At eight I'd be in the White Horse Tavern with Drew, nursing a seltzer with lime.

The silence consumed me like a parasite, making me high-strung and nervous. Nothing was happening. Tomorrow would be the same. In the bar I'd eat a bowl of olives and watch the lights come on. Nine o'clock. Ten. Then we'd be out on the street: perhaps now it was raining. I wouldn't have my umbrella. My hair would be plastered down in strips around my face. The rain would be soft, radioactive, bringing the refuse of the city back to itself. We'd split a taxi to Brooklyn, and Drew would tip the driver. It would already be tomorrow. I was almost twenty-seven. The silence whispered in my head. Other faces in other taxis turned and looked at me, and I looked back; I saw myself. The silence grew.

At the park I slipped off my shoes and sat on a bench with my knees up and my arms wrapped around them. All of SoHo and all of the Village probably didn't amount to sixty acres.

I was never good at much besides being a teacher, but I was real good at that. When I married Amory I couldn't cook to save my life or anyone else's, and I didn't like to clean. I was not adept at organizing bridge or fixing the house for Christmas. My children were always a kind of mystery to me.

But when I was inside those four walls of a classroom, with a book or a piece of chalk in my hand, I knew exactly what to do. I knew that I could get up there in front of the class and for fifty minutes I could be whoever I wanted; I could tell them almost anything, and they'd believe me. And then they would disappear, melt away until the same time tomorrow, when they'd be sitting there the same as today, waiting for me to start telling stories. I taught English; all of it was stories. I heard that behind my back they took to calling me Miss F'rinstance because I told stories about everything.

I'd only been inside a few classrooms on my own when I had to pack my bags and leave the college, but I had the thrill of it in my blood and truly thought I'd be coming back. Amory seemed to be enough for a while; we'd be eating supper or lying in bed and he'd listen to my stories and laugh at the punch lines. But soon he got busy, and whenever I started to tell one he'd act irritated, get a glaze over his eyes, and that took the fun out of it. Then I tried with the children, but at first they were too young, and when they were older they acted like I was just rambling. Like they were impatient to get away.

Both of my brothers in Chattanooga finished college, and they sent me books to read, thick hardback books with small type, not those paperbacks with the bosoms and burning houses on the covers. Real books. Oh, I read the other stuff too, when my attention was short and the babies sapped my energy. I took words when I could, any words; I wasn't picky.

Words never came easy in our house. I'd fight for them, coax, plead. I kept a dictionary in the front room by the Bible, and if I ever heard a word I didn't know, I'd write it down on a napkin or a scrap of paper and save it to look up. I taught the children to do that too, but Amory didn't set a good example, and Ellen was the only one who stuck to it. She mined words like gold.

"The sky is iridescent, Ma," she said once when she was five, and Amory turned on me in a rage: "What the hell are you doing, teaching that girl to talk so we can't even understand her?" He knew, of course, exactly what I was doing.

I don't read much anymore, and I keep my stories to myself. But even now the smell of chalk makes me dizzy, and the feel of a new book makes my heart drop.

Afterward, except for our breathing, there was silence in the small room. It was almost dark. I lay without moving on the damp cotton sheet, staring at the outline of a framed museum print. Four flights below, the noises of the city blended like an orchestra. I strained to hear each instrument: the rumbling of heavy trucks and buses, the muffled hum of cars, the blare of horns and the faint wail of a distant siren. I studied a crack in the wall, watching how it splayed into branches across a corner of the ceiling.

"Christ, Cassie," he said. "You might have feigned a little interest."

I inhaled thin, cool air from the air conditioner in the window above, its breeze mingling with the smell of our sweat. Flecks of light fell into the room, sprinkling the white sheets and my bare, pale arms. Moving my fingers, I watched the light slide over them like mercury.

"I've decided to leave," I said.

"What are you talking about?"

"I'm going to Tennessee. I wanted to tell you first, before you heard it from anybody else."

He sat up and looked at me, rubbing his short dark hair with his hands. When I reached over to touch his shoulder, he flinched as if an insect had landed on him.

"Look, I'll help you find someone for the gallery," I said. "I won't leave until you've got somebody trained."

He swung his legs over the side of the bed and reached for his striped boxer shorts on the floor, putting them on in one fluid movement.

"Adam—"

"It's a big gamble," he said, standing up stiffly, his eyes flat and expressionless. "Good luck."

"What are you saying?"

"I'm not saying anything. You're taking a big risk, that's all. I admire you for it."

"What's so risky?"

"Well, this is it, right? Make it or break it. What if it turns out that all that talent you've been keeping on a back burner isn't there?"

"That's not the point. That's not why I'm going."

"Oh, really?"

"I just need to get away. It's not a matter of proving anything."

His mouth turned up at the corners. "Look, Cassie, I'm sure you know what you're doing. It's just that usually when people pick up and move they're either going toward something or running away."

"It's not like that."

"You sure?"

"For God's sake, Adam, if you're not going to even try to understand—"

"I am trying. I just think you need to be certain that you're doing the right thing. For yourself, I mean."

I drew back. "I wasn't really asking for your approval. I just wanted you to know. For the gallery."

Adam picked a T-shirt off the floor and turned to leave the room. I watched him make his way down the narrow hall, switching on the light with his shoulder as he veered into the living room at the end. After a few seconds I could hear a canned voice talking about the Yankees. I sat against the headboard, dragging the sheet up around me.

After a while I began to get dressed, gathering my bra and underwear and large brass earrings, which were scattered around the room. In the smattering of light from the window, I groped for the black dress and slingbacks I wore to work, then shook my hair over my head, combing through the tangles with my fingers. I wiped the mascara from under my eyes. Trembling a little, I went down the hall to the living room.

"Is three weeks' notice enough?" I asked Adam's back.

He kept his eyes on the TV, now tuned to *Jeopardy.*

"Hollywood Romance for six hundred, Alex."

"This famous couple's romance ended tragically when she died in a plane crash in 1942."

"Gable and Lombard," Adam said.

"Who are Vivien Leigh and Laurence Olivier?" said the contestant.

After a few moments an ad for dishwashing detergent came on. "I assume you can let yourself out," Adam said.

I paused for a second, examining the front door. "Actually, I never did figure out how to undo all these locks."

He stood up, as if with great effort, still watching the television. Without looking at me, he handed me the bottle of beer he was holding. He released the column of locks with a series of clipped, intricate maneuvers. "Sayonara," he said.

"Please."

"What?" He held up his hands.

"Come on, Adam. Give me a break. Don't make this so difficult."

He shrugged, looking over my head. The game show was on again.

"A hunchback, this nineteenth-century French painter immortalized cancan dancers."

Adam murmured, "Toulouse-Lautrec."

"It doesn't have to be this way," I said.

"Who is Toulouse-Lautrec?" said the contestant.

He looked at me without focusing, and after a second the brown of his eyes darkened and he looked down. "Just leave, Cassandra," he said, stepping back. "I'm tired."

The elevator opened on the ground floor. As I left the gloomy lobby, I felt light-headed, as if I might faint. I stood against the side of the building, my back and arms touching the cool brick, and I couldn't help it, I started to cry. I put my hands over my face, hot tears squeezing out between my fingers, my shoulders shaking; and then I cried even harder, angry at myself for crying at all.

After a few minutes I straightened up, wiped my face with my hands, and reached into my bag for a tissue. I took one deep breath and then another, adjusted the bag, and started down the street.

Out in the open, the summer air was warm and solid. As I crossed to the other side I glanced back at the red-brick building, up the four flights to Adam's bedroom window. I could see a light shining inside, probably just the dull glow from the television reflected down the narrow hall.

Her hair was long and black, and her neck was the color of sand on a beach, of wheat bread rising. Her eyes were as dark and bright as a crow's. She wore the newest styles of dresses in colors the rest of us were too well-bred to try—whorehouse vermilion, firetruck red, sunburst gold—and lipstick to match. Nobody else wore lipstick; we were all married and living in the country. We couldn't see what for.

Bryce once said, confidentially, that she'd never really been friends with a woman as attractive and strong as she was before, not one-on-one. She said she thought it was a competition problem. Then she smiled her wide, wine-lipped smile and reached over and squeezed my hand.

"We're alike, you and I," she said. "We've got the same goals."

"How's that?"

She patted her hair, tucking strands into the loose twist on her head, and then she looked me over slowly. "We're not going to sit here for the next fifty years and go crazy, ringing the bell for breakfast and lunch and supper, marking time by what's on the table. We're not cut out for sitting at home while the world goes marching by without us."

"What do you mean, Bryce Davies?" I laughed. "Amory and that little baby are the only parade I want to be a part of."

She was shaking her head even before I got the words out. "For now, maybe, but you'll see. Pretty soon whatever thrill you find in it is going to wear pretty thin. And stuck out here, too far from civilization to even know what the fashions are! It's a crime to do it to a woman, especially a city gal like you."

"But Bryce, I'm the happiest woman in the world," I said.

Our babies, Horace and Taylor, were asleep upstairs, and Bryce and I were on the front porch with a lemonade as the sun settled into midafternoon over distant western trees. It was the end of September. The air was warm and dry. Amory had come back from Baton Rouge a month earlier, and since then it was like I'd never imagined it could be. The house was our cocoon. I'd get up to feed Horace at two o'clock, three o'clock, and Amory would get up too, to throw a blanket over my feet and warm some milk for me on the stove. Then I'd rock Horace back to sleep, and Amory and I would go to bed, and as many times as not he'd kiss me and stroke me, in and out of my dreams. He would get up for work before the sun rose, and before he left he'd lean over and whisper that he loved me. He'd whisper my new name.

"We were that way too for a while," said Bryce. "It gets old fast. Just you wait. He'll get a bee in his bonnet about something, something'll go wrong at work, and then all you're good for is getting the food on his plate when he wants it, and maybe some fun late at night. If you're lucky."

I smiled, thinking of the night before. "That won't happen."

Bryce gave a dry laugh and smoothed the front of her silk dress, lily-pad green. "I said the same thing. Frank was like a honeymooner for a whole year. Then we got the mortgage to pay, and Taylor comes along, and he's working two shifts and dog-tired and yapping at me like I'm to blame."

"I've seen the way he looks at you," I said. "That man loves you to death."

"Maybe." Her expression grew serious. "But love gets coated over, you know? Love and marriage are like water and oil."

Her mouth twisted and she looked down, brushing imaginary crumbs off her dress in jerky motions, and then she put her face in her hands and started to cry. I went over and put my arm across her shoulders and squeezed.

"Lord, Connie, I'm just not meant for this. I didn't know it was going to be this way. How could I? I was a poor farm kid, and he was throwing a lot of money around back then. I thought we'd always be dancing till dawn." She hit the porch rail with the palm of her hand. "Jeez, and now I'm stuck here. I hate this place to death, and everybody"—she choked back a sob—"everybody in it."

"Oh, Bryce, it's not that bad. We have a good time, don't we?"

"Bridge teas," she sniffed.

"You've got friends and family who love you," I said.

She pulled a comb and a mother-of-pearl pin out of her bun and let her black hair fall down around her shoulders, running the comb through it to smooth it. "There's that word again. Love." She made a face like the word tasted bitter. "I tell you, it doesn't mean anything."

"Taylor?"

"Well, of course, but that's different. She can't hurt me. Not yet, anyway." Bryce stood up, bent her head and shook it, then flung her hair back. It was thick and wild. Her eyelashes were dark and shining with tears. "It's quicksand, Connie. We'll never get out. It makes me want to do something crazy." She leaned against the railing, looking out over the hills sloping down from the house. She seemed like a small, isolated ball of fire, burning up with its own heat while everything around it went on as usual. I felt sorry for her, but I didn't really know what to say. I liked my life fine.

"Well, Bryce," I said finally. "The Lord put you here for a reason. All you can do is trust in Him."

"Hmmph," she said.

Horace had started to cry upstairs. I excused myself and went inside, lingering in the dark hallway for a minute. I didn't want to go out again, to face the heat of her frustration in the static warmth of the day. Even then, before my fears had any grounding, she made me uneasy. There was something thrilling in her dissatisfaction, something glamorous about her disdain for the town, and the fact that I was her confidante set me apart. If she said it to me, I wasn't one of them. But at the same time I sensed down deep that if she could feel all those things and say all those things and still smile so sweetly at the farmers market on Wednesdays and hostess bridge with such easy charm, there must be in her something that would always need to undermine and deceive, to erode the base of what seemed solid and good because it didn't have anything to do with her, anything to do with making her happy. I thought, even then, that I would have to be careful not to let her draw me in. If I got too close the fire would blind me and I wouldn't be able to tell when she had had enough, when she started whispering to a newly married young arrival words that bit and chewed and spit me out.

I went upstairs and got Horace and changed his diaper, and then Taylor woke too, so I cleaned her up and brought them down to the front porch, one on each hip. By the set of her shoulders I could tell Bryce was brooding, but when she heard the screen door open she turned toward us with her face arranged in a mama smile and her arms outstretched. She took Taylor from me and cooed at her and undid the buttons of her dress with one hand, lifting her breast for Taylor to suck. There was no one around, so I did the same. We sat on the porch with our babies, not speaking, and Bryce's body softened, finally, the way it always did, around Taylor's tiny form.

This is the story I told Bryce Davies.

"May 17, 1940. Bryce—Without preliminaries I will tell you that I found a letter from you to my husband in his shirt pocket this morning. I do not want explanations or excuses. Its intent was clear. My husband knows I found it and swears to me that he will never see you again. All I have to say is this: I could forgive the fact that you have lied to me, but you have also betrayed me as a friend, and that I cannot forgive. Do not come near me again. But most of all, stay away from my husband. If you cannot do that, I promise with all my heart that I will find a way to keep you away."

But that was only the beginning.

When I got home from Adam's I called my father and told him we'd broken up.

"Good," he said. "Good for you. It's about time."

"And there's something else." I paused. I didn't know how to say it.

"If it's what I think it is, I don't want to hear it."

"What do you mean, Dad?"

"What do *you* mean, Cassie?"

I gritted my teeth. "Well . . . I was thinking of taking that land. You know. Moving down there."

I could hear him sighing all the way from Boston. "That's what I was afraid of."

"Daddy," I said, coaxing.

"I just don't think it's smart. You have no idea what you're getting into."

"Yes, I do," I said. But I was curious. "What are you so worried about?"

"Oh, Cassie, those awful relatives of your mother's, for a start."

"But I wouldn't have to deal with them, would I?"

"Oy vey." He sucked air through his teeth. "Your aunt Elaine called today."

"She *called?* She never calls."

"Well, this is the first time. Come to think of it, this may be the first time in her entire life that she's placed a phone call above the Mason-Dixon line."

"And?"

He went into a singsong. "She told me about the land and the house and how Horace would be willing, bless his heart, to take it off your hands. She said she reckoned it was more of a burden than a blessing and you'd probably just as soon they handle it for you. Of course, I told her she'd better hold on for a while until she heard from you. I had a terrible feeling you might get some cockeyed idea."

"I haven't really been thinking about them," I admitted.

"Well, they're worth some serious thought. I loved your mom, but that family . . ." He sighed again. "They thought I was from another planet."

I tried to recall what I knew about them. Horace was the oldest, Elaine the youngest. My mother was the middle child. I had no idea what either of them looked like. Last I heard, Horace had two boys, and Elaine and her husband had adopted two kids because they couldn't have any of their own.

For ten years or so after my mother died, Elaine dutifully kept my dad up-to-date with Christmas cards—Hanukkah cards when she remembered or could find them. Sometimes she sent the same card two or three years in a row. Several featured a red robin perched on a branch, with musical notes coming out of its beak and snow glitter on its wings. Another favorite was a snowman smoking a pipe, with a wreath around his neck. The accompanying messages were scrawled in a large, looped hand.

"Edgar," one of them said. "We are fine, thank the Lord. Mom and Dad are healthy now. Dad had a herniated disk in September but he's recovered fairly well. Horace and Kathy moved down the road from us into a big house with a pool. Last summer Horace finished building a complex over near Madisonville and named a road Ellen Lane. My Larry's got a church in Soddy Daisy now and an AM radio show and we keep busy. The kids are fine. Take care of that little girl and God Bless. Elaine Burns."

Eventually the notes got shorter, and after a while they stopped coming altogether. I never asked my dad if he had written back.

"Have you told Adam you're leaving?" Dad was asking.

"Yeah, I told him."

"And these new plans of yours have nothing to do with him?"

His knowing tone irritated me. "*No,* Dad. I'm just tired of the city. I'm sick of my job. I've got a chance to try something totally different, maybe even work on my own stuff for a change. What's wrong with that?"

"Nothing's wrong with it."

"I thought you might be proud of me."

"I am proud of you, honey. I just think you should take a good hard look at what you're doing and why you're doing it."

I started to protest, but I stopped myself. The phone call wasn't going the way I'd planned. On the subway home I'd imagined that I'd tell him and he'd gasp with surprise, shout the good news to Susan, offer to help me move.

"Well, I've got to go," I said. "Thanks for the support, Dad."

"Aw, Cassie, come on. Just think about it, is all I'm saying."

"I *have* thought about it."

After taking down Elaine's number I hung up and slouched into a chair. I grabbed a magazine off the floor and flipped through it gloomily before tossing it back on the rug. So maybe he was right. Maybe I was leaving to get away from Adam. So what? Anyway, that was only part of it, not the whole thing; it was much more complicated. I wanted to get away from Adam, yes, and the city, but it was more than that. What had Adam said? *It's just that usually when people pick up and move they're either going toward something or running away.* Yes, I suddenly decided, I was running toward something, something I'd been running from all my life.

I hadn't seen that before but I saw it now, and I was filled with a sense of my own power. I was certain that if I could explain it to my dad that way, he'd hear the strength in my voice and understand. I decided I'd call him again in a few days, when he'd had some time to think it over. When it would be too late for me to change my mind.

* * *

"Dear Mrs. Clyde," the letter began. "You don't know me, but—"

I tore the paper in two and started again.

"Dear Grandmother, I know how surprised you must be to get a letter from me after all these years. To be honest, a month ago I never would have guessed I'd be doing this either."

I sat back in the chair, gnawing the top of my Bic pen. Then I crumpled the letter into a ball and threw it on the floor.

"Dear Grandmother . . . "

I'd been trying to write the letter for an hour. At first I had planned to call, but every time I dialed her number I put the phone down before it started to ring. I didn't know what to say; I didn't know how to say it. I looked up at the clock. Seven-thirty. I was supposed to be at Drew's for dinner at eight.

"I hope that you are doing well! It's been such a long time since I've seen you. You may have already heard from Crystal at the courthouse that I've decided to come to Sweetwater to live in the house on the Ridge Road property. I hope that's all right with you."

I read it over, groaning to myself. I drew a line across the page. The problem was tone. I wanted to sound upbeat, positive, friendly, but the letters kept turning into apologies. What was I apologizing for, for God's sake? It was my land. Why did I feel like such an interloper?

"Dear Grandmother, After much deliberation I've decided that instead of selling the land I would like to come to Sweetwater to live on it for a while."

I crossed out "for a while."

"I plan to quit my job and try to make a go of it as a sculptor."

Reading this sentence over, I laughed aloud. Then I marked through it.

"I will arrive in Sweetwater on August 2. I'm sure you are as surprised about this as I was. Please don't feel that you have to go out of your way to do anything special. I look forward to meeting you, and Aunt Elaine and Uncle Horace and everybody else. Yours sincerely, your granddaughter Cassandra."

I copied the letter over, shoved it in an envelope, and sealed it before I had a chance to think about it again. I stuck a stamp on it and took it down to the mailbox on the corner of Seventh Avenue. Once it was out of my hands I felt a great relief, like I used to feel when I'd finished exams at college. It didn't matter how I'd done; it was over, I could relax for a while.

Continuing down the street, I stopped at a liquor store to buy a bottle of wine, and then turned down Garfield to Sixth. It was a Friday night, and the streets were busy. A radio blared several flights up; I could hear a baby crying somewhere. The air was humid, hazy. Streetlights began to flicker on.

At Drew's building I pressed the button for 3C.

"Yes?"

"It's me."

"What's the average airspeed velocity of an unladen swallow?" he asked, his voice static.

"African or European?"

He buzzed me in.

"You're late," he said accusingly, looking down at me from the third-floor landing as I came up the stairs.

I trudged up the final steps and handed him the wine. "Chardonnay. Will that appease you?"

"Remains to be seen," he said, peering into the bag.

I walked past him into the apartment, which smelled of garlic and basil. "Mmmm. Drew, you are the best."

"Where have you been?" He followed me in and shut the door. "I was begining to get concerned."

I shook my head. "Sorry. Nowhere, really. At home. Writing a letter." I was a little embarrassed. "To my grandmother."

He took down two wineglasses and got out a corkscrew. "You're late because you were writing Lulu?"

"Not Lulu. The Absent Other." These were names Drew came up with in college for my grandmothers. Lulu's name was really Naomi.

"Oh, her," he said. "Did you ask for the money to be delivered in a calfskin suitcase lined with velvet, in crisp hundred-dollar bills like in the movies?"

"Not exactly." He uncorked the bottle and poured two glasses, handing me one. "In fact, I'm not so sure I'm going to sell that land." I took a deep breath. "I mean, I'm definitely not going to sell it. I'm going to keep it."

"Keep it? What does that mean?"

I sat down at the table and looked up at him. "It means I'm going down there to live, Drew. On my land."

"Holy shit," he said. "I've got to check the fish."

"You'll be cruising convenience stores for excitement." We were sitting across from each other at the small kitchen table, a low-burning candle and the empty bottle of wine between us. "You'll meet an auto mechanic named Joe who's a Really Nice Guy." Drew got up to clear the plates. "Is that what you want out of life, Cassie?" he said over his shoulder. "Three squares a day and a home entertainment center?"

"Don't you think you're being a little dramatic? I just want to try something different. I want to have a studio, do my own work for a change."

"You don't have to go a thousand miles to find studio space. There has to be some other reason." He glanced over at me sharply. "You're not pregnant, by any chance?"

I rolled my eyes.

"And this has nothing to do with Adam."

I sighed. "Not really."

"Not really."

"God, Drew, you sound just like my father. What is it with you men? You can't imagine a woman setting off on her own if she hasn't been spurned first?"

"I was just asking," he said, opening the freezer. "And you are a little touchy about it, if you don't mind my saying. I've got Ben and

Jerry's politically-correct-but-very-fattening ice cream or good-for-you dictator-grown grapes."

"What kind of ice cream?"

"Um, Chocolate Fudge Brownie."

"Well, then, I think we should boycott those grapes."

"I admire your conscience," he said. "And you take milk, right?" He poured two mugs of coffee and brought them over to the table. "Look, Cassie, maybe I could understand if it was a villa in Tuscany. I could see the appeal. But we're talking a shack in Tennessee. *Tennessee,* for God's sake."

"It's not a shack. I don't think."

"Let's face facts," he said patiently. "You've never been there. Your relatives haven't bothered to get in touch with you, now or ever. You have no idea what this place looks like except everybody expects you to tear it down. And think of this," he said, sitting down with the ice cream. "Your own mother got out of there as fast as she could."

"I know, I know."

"Well?"

I got up, restless, moved the dishes from the counter to the sink, and turned on the tap. "Haven't you ever wanted to do something just for the hell of it? Just because it's like nothing else you've ever done?"

"Yes, Cassandra. In my youth I had a great need to test boundaries."

I made a face. "Look, my life here is just ordinary, you know that. Go to work, try new restaurants, run around to openings. All I'm doing is filling a little space I've carved out for myself." I poured dishwashing liquid into the sink as it filled with water.

"I hate to be the one to break it to you, darling, but that's the way life is. No matter where you are."

"But nothing I do really *matters* here. When I leave there'll be half a dozen twenty-seven-year-olds with severe haircuts and Danish bags to take my place. Look at Veronica at the gallery. It's as if I never worked there."

"Now we're getting into philosophy," Drew said. "Leave those dishes alone and come sit down. Your ice cream is melting."

I turned around to face him.

"Look, Cassie, it's the same everywhere. It just seems different in small towns because you recognize people on the street and they act like they're happy to see you. Maybe. If someone hasn't been spreading malicious, narrow-minded rumors about you that everybody's heard because the whole place is the size of a parking garage."

"But they know you, at least," I insisted. "That's something."

He sighed. "I just think you have an incredibly romanticized idea of what it's going to be like. Too much *Little House on the Prairie* as a kid or something."

"Well, okay, maybe you're right. Maybe it's a stupid, naive, ridiculous thing to do. Maybe I'm out of my mind. But so what? What do I have to lose?"

He licked his spoon. "Me. I'm what you have to lose."

"Oh, Drew."

"Really," he said. "Not to mention the Met, Central Park, the Staten Island Ferry."

"I've never even been on the Staten Island Ferry."

"But that's just it! You know it's there."

"I'll call you," I said. "I'll write."

"You won't write. You never write. Where are all those friends you had in high school? In college? You never bothered to stay in touch, so you lost them. It's out of sight, out of mind with you, Cassie. I've been there, I know."

"My coffee's cold." I brought the mug to the counter and poured myself another cup. "How many high school friends do you still talk to? We go through life meeting people and exchanging addresses; it's not the same as friendship."

"Thanks for clearing that up for me."

"Oh, stop it, Drew. You're so boring when you're peevish."

"When I'm peevish?" he said. "*Peevish?* Where on earth did that word come from?" We both started laughing.

"Well, you are," I said. "Peevish. You are." I sat down at the table. "My ice cream is soup."

"Forget the ice cream. Let's go out for a drink," he said. "I could use one." I nodded and pushed the ice cream away. He looked at his watch. "I doubt you'd be able to find a bar open in Tennessee at this hour, Cassie. Just one more thing to think about."

"Without you there, Drew, I probably won't need one."

"Rising Sun Gallery."

"Could I speak to Adam, please?"

"May I ask who's calling?"

"Veronica, it's Cassie."

"Oh, hello, Cassie." Her voice was dry and polite. "Hang on, will you?" She put the phone down. After a few minutes she picked it up again. "I'm sorry, I'm afraid he's in meeting right now. Can I have him return your call?"

"Um . . ."

"Oh, just a second," Veronica said.

"Hi," said Adam briskly. "I'm running. I've got an appointment across town five minutes ago."

"I thought you were in a meeting."

"Veronica's started screening my calls. It's amazing how much more I get done."

I laughed. "Start acting like a bureaucrat and maybe you'll turn into one."

"Thanks for the warning. Well? Is there something you need?"

"No," I said. I looked around my apartment stacked with boxes. "I'm just getting ready to leave, is all. I wanted to say goodbye."

"Well. Goodbye."

"How is everything going?"

"Fine," he said. "Great."

"Great. Me too."

"Great. Look, the cab's out front. Give Veronica your address and we'll put you on the mailing list. West Virginia, isn't it?"

I sucked in my breath. "Tennessee."

"And leave a number so she can reach you if she needs to. She's redoing the files."

"Fine. I'll leave a number."

"Have a nice trip."

"Have a nice life." The words were out of my mouth before I even thought about them.

For a long moment there was silence. Then he said, "Is that what you called to say?"

"I guess it is. Isn't that funny? I didn't know it, but I guess that is what I called to say."

"Funny," he said. "Here's Veronica."

"Hello," said Veronica after a bit of shuffling.

"I don't have an address and I don't have a number."

"You can send them when you're settled. No hurry, I've got things pretty well under control. There's not much to it, really. I can't imagine what I'd need to ask."

"Neither can I, Veronica," I said.

They read the will out loud, all of us sitting there in straight chairs in the magistrate's office, and from the moment they spoke her name I knew there would be trouble. Whatever else he was, he was not a frivolous man. Nor was he especially thoughtful. If he'd really cared about the girl he could have contacted her, sent her a letter or some money, but there was nothing before this. He never mentioned her, not once.

And he knew that Horace or Elaine or I would have razed that house the minute we got our hands on it. We would have torn it down and built over and around it so fast that there'd be nothing left of it, nothing to remind us of then except some knickknacks and a few curling photographs of smiling, blue-eyed children with dogs.

I left on a Saturday at the end of July. Earlier in the week I had taken a train to Hoboken to buy a 1979 Chevy wagon with 110,000 miles on it from a man who barely spoke English. Before I paid him I took a test drive around the block. I liked the loose, rangy feel, thick vinyl seats, and solid frame, the power steering and two-tone imitation-wood and metallic-green exterior. Though I knew nothing about transmissions or engines, the car felt strong and sturdy, and instinctively I trusted it. I gave the man seven hundred dollars in cash and drove it back to Brooklyn.

Maneuvering the large, broad car down Brooklyn's streets, I felt like a ship captain navigating through icebergs. The steering wheel, padded with fur, slipped easily through my fingers as I dodged kamikaze taxis and nosed around corners. From this vantage point the city was barely familiar; I scanned street signs as if they were foreign menus. By the time I got back to my apartment on Seventh Avenue I was a nervous wreck.

On Saturday morning, Drew helped me pile the station wagon to the rafters with clothing and books and a small potter's wheel. We tied my futon mattress and a dismantled bookcase to the roof rack with twine, then covered the entire bundle with a piece of tarp.

He stood back when we were finished, his hand under his chin, and surveyed the mass before us. "I can't decide whether it looks more like an undergraduate art project or some very large, pregnant insect with eggs on its back."

“It’s an art student’s rendition of a large, pregnant insect,” I said, tightening a piece of twine.

“Ah, yes, even better.” He looked around. “Is that everything?”

“I think so. Thank you, Drew.”

“Now, don’t be silly and run out of gas or anything. Check the oil, or whatever it is that people who drive are always telling each other to do. Don’t pick up strays or hitchhikers. You’ve got that map AAA sent you?”

“Yeah, did you see it? They planned the whole trip. If I get lost now I deserve to live in New York for the rest of my life.”

I gave him a hug around his middle, kissed him on the cheek, and wedged myself into the driver’s seat.

He leaned through the window and put his hand on mine. “You’re going to go stark raving mad down there. Don’t say I didn’t warn you. Didn’t you hear, we won the war? And for good reason. They’re absolute lunatics.”

“Stop. I’ll be fine.”

“I worry, so kill me.” He kissed me on the forehead. “God protect you. Shalom. I’ll send you the gossip.”

“Tell Adam— ”

“The slides are in the office. Yes, yes. He’ll manage.”

The car smelled of hot vinyl and clean clothes and, faintly, the apple Drew had packed along with a sandwich and Oreos for my lunch. The air was thick and humid. I drove slowly through Brooklyn to the bridge, my hands glued to the steering wheel and my face as close to the windshield as possible. Sweat trickled between my thighs, down my cheeks, into the hollow of my throat. The car rode low to the ground; every time I hit a pothole the bottom scraped against the asphalt.

Stuck in traffic as I crossed the bridge into Manhattan, I looked back at Brooklyn’s humbler, red-brick skyline, the leafy trees lining the Promenade above the East River. During the four years I lived there I was in three different apartments, counting my college roommate’s floor when I first arrived. Brooklyn became my neighborhood, the place I left each morning, walking the five blocks to the F train, and returned to, often by taxi, at night. After a year and a half in my ground-floor apartment on Seventh Avenue I had even gotten to know some of my neighbors: Jai, the Pakistani grocer on the corner; Mrs. Marray, the Irishwoman who ran the dry cleaner's next door.

But much as I wanted it to be my home, Brooklyn was also a place that could never be familiar, never be safe. I learned to live defensively, not to go out alone or ride the subway after a certain hour. I learned that I always had to be guarded, aware, alert. And I found that something in me almost grew comfortable living with danger, with the peculiar challenge of conquering my fear.

Now, as I sat in my car on the bridge, stifled by fumes from the Mack truck in front of me, Brooklyn looked peaceful and clean. People who lived near the Promenade—men in running shorts, women with strollers—were emerging from the side streets to eat lunch by the water. I could see them on benches, spreading napkins, drinking through straws from bottles of fruit juice, laughing in the midday sun. All at once I felt a great relief not to be one of them anymore, not to wear nylons in August, buy salads by the ounce at the deli, fight the crowds in the subway after work.

It was hard to believe leaving could be so easy.

After crossing lower Manhattan in fits and starts—"My grandmother drives better than you, and she's dead," one trucker leaned out of his window to yell into mine—I found myself stuck at the lip of the Holland Tunnel for nearly an hour while they cleared the debris of an accident inside. I edged my car into a tight spot to let police and an ambulance through, and then a tow truck. The ambulance blasted a high, abrupt siren that echoed and was swallowed as it disappeared into the darkness.

The hot smells of tar and exhaust were overpowering. There was no way to turn around; I was too far in. Eventually traffic began to shift, and cars moved like turtles into the dank, metallic light. As I passed the scene of the accident I could see pieces of taillight, shattered glass, slick patches I imagined were blood.

I emerged from the tunnel into New Jersey, weaving past Jersey City, Newark, and Somerville on Route 78, through toxic smells and dense, yellow, low-hanging clouds. Factories clung to the edge of the landscape like faraway nightmarish kingdoms.

Somewhere near Annandale I became aware of a car tailgating me. When the driver realized I'd noticed him he accelerated, pulling just ahead of me in the left lane and then sliding over to the right, forcing me to slam on my brakes. I eased out of my lane to pass him. Out of the corner of my eye I could see him staring at me as he accelerated to match my speed. He was wearing black sunglasses. I was starting to panic. I slowed to forty miles an hour and got in behind him. He slowed further, and I laid on the horn. He got into the passing lane, then slowed and moved behind me again.

I scrawled his plate number on a napkin, my heart racing. After a few minutes the car swung out beside me, and I looked over at him. His hair was ash brown and curly. He had large white teeth.

"I'm calling the police," I shouted.

"C'mon, baby. Loosen up."

"Get the fuck away from me." I held up the napkin with the number on it.

His smile faded, and he said something nasty I couldn't quite hear. Then he zoomed ahead, darting in and out of traffic until I couldn't see him anymore.

I leaned back against the vinyl, catching my breath. With my right hand I pushed the clasp of the glove compartment, and it dropped open, its contents spilling onto the floor. I scrounged for a pack of Marlboro Lights I'd found there when I bought the car, and pulled back the cellophane tab with my teeth.

I thought about the man in Hoboken, who had propositioned me while selling me the car; I thought about the muggers who knocked me down on Seventh Avenue one night. Every time something like this happened I had to readjust, to steel myself, to make myself brave. People had told me they thought I was brave for leaving, brave for striking out on my own, but I didn't see it that way at all. Bravery is something else entirely: a hardening, a defense. It has little to do with choice, with hope. It has little to do with desire.

Near the border of Pennsylvania the landscape began to open and close up again, like a flexing fist. Trees and foliage faded into gravel pits and gutted buildings. Just before Bethlehem I stubbed out a cigarette and stopped for gas. As I got out of the car I was struck by the dullness of the sky, the way color seemed to have drained from people's faces, roadside signs, even stray dogs and cats milling around the station. It was early afternoon, heavy and humid. I still felt a little wobbly, and I was covered with a film of grime and exhaust fumes.

After paying for the gas I set off again. The car smelled like someone had thrown a party in it the night before. Trying to keep my eyes on the road, I reached over to the passenger's side and rolled down the window. In the back seat a stray piece of paper danced on top of a pile of boxes; I could hear a loose end of the tarpaulin flapping against the top of the car. I turned on the radio, but I could barely hear the music through the static; then I remembered that I had pushed in the antenna to make room for the roof rack.

Flipping the radio off, I listened to the sounds of the car: the full-throttle engine, the rustling paper and the slap of the tarp on the roof, the old springs of my seat when I moved around, the dull roar of other cars on the highway, as they passed me, like jets landing.

I drove through the smog of Allentown, past Fogelsville, Lenhartsville, Virginville. I began ticking off the miles to Harrisburg—fifty, nineteen, six—and then started from zero again, counting the miles to Maryland. Slicing through the narrow chunk of West Virginia in less than an hour, I crossed the border into Virginia as the light faded from the sky.

The sun and the low, jagged clouds surrounding it looked like a signal fire raging across the tops of the trees that shaded the highway. A warm breeze, cooled by the speed of the car, brushed my face and lifted my hair softly, like fingertips. I was tired.

Sunday morning I crossed the border into Tennessee, and everything turned blue. Highway 81 cut through lush blue-green valleys, stretching like a runaway Christmas ribbon over wide swaths of gently sloping rises and falls.

The night before, the landscape had been cluttered with small, miserable houses hunched against the highway, dirty convenience stores surrounded by litter and debris, groups of restless teenagers looking for action on a Saturday night. There had been none of this expansiveness, this possibility of hills continuing for hundreds of miles beyond the road, far out of sight. I'd never imagined land so generous, land that yielded up such clear streams, muddied brown rivers, primeval valleys. And all of it—gray and heather and green-brown—blended into something shadowed and somehow blue.

I'd set out early, 6:30 a.m. I had toast and canned juice at a diner in Mint Spring, Virginia, just outside Staunton, where I spent the night. At breakfast I bought a local paper and tried to make sense of the headlines. My search for national news led me to page four, where I discovered tantalizing tidbits, AP releases. I found myself voraciously reading *Parade* magazine and the syndicated humorists just to connect with something I could recognize.

For several hours, as I was driving through Virginia, a dense gray fog had blanketed the lowlands. The air smelled of dew and juniper and fresh grass, with a crispness that melted as the fog slowly began to lift. I drove with the windows down: all I could see out the front still waited to be metamorphosed into the new day. It was an odd sensation; I felt like I was driving into the past.

I thought about the warning Drew had given me before I left.

"You're not going to some fairy kingdom, Cassie," he said. "It's not Oz. There won't be Munchkins. And you'll still be you, with the same paranoias and neuroses you've got now. All that stuff doesn't just go away."

I laughed. "Oh, Drew, I know that. I don't have any illusions."

"Of course you do," he said. "You wouldn't be doing this if you didn't."

As the hours went by, the sun climbed, unseen, in a haze of milky white clouds. Outside Bristol, Tennessee, and again near Fall Branch, I passed churches full of people. The strains of their singing wafted across the highway like music from a muffled radio.

Just beyond Knoxville on Highway 75 the split the road made between ridges had become more extreme, deepening and then rising. The station wagon seemed to be diving and surfacing in and out of the soft Tennessee earth. It rode smoothly, gaining momentum on the sharp falls and coasting halfway up the next rise before the big push to the top.

The afternoon breeze on my face was tepid, like bathwater. I read the billboards, which were garish, almost surreal, framed as they were against the long expanse of sky and the lush countryside: CRAZY ED'S FIREWORKS AND RESTAURANT, AFFORDABLE DENTURES—FULL SET $149—LENOIR CITY. Suddenly my heart leapt and my stomach hollowed: SWEETWATER—16 miles.

Ahead on the side of the road I could make out a small green highway sign framed in white: EXIT 62—SWEETWATER, with an arrow pointing to the right. Switching on the blinker, I ascended the curving exit ramp, turned over a bridge at the top, and found myself in front of the famed Dinner Bell Restaurant I'd been reading about over the last several miles of billboards. The Dinner Bell turned out to be not only a restaurant but also a general store and gas station. A large sign across the top of the building boasted GOOD "OLE TIME" COUNTRY COOKIN. I pulled in, filled the car with gas, and went inside to pay.

As I entered, something seemed odd to me, but I couldn't put my finger on it. It took me a moment to realize what it was: everybody was dressed up. The women were in fancy attire, pearls and pastels; the men were wearing ties. Most of them would have come from church. All at once I felt conspicuous in my old shorts and T-shirt.

The gift shop was crammed with merchandise. Country hams hung from hooks; bumper stickers, hard candy, ceramic figurines, tourist moccasins, and key chains covered the walls and shelves. Rag rugs, also for sale, covered the spongy blue linoleum floor. A fern-topped bar separated the gift shop from the restaurant, but it couldn't contain the smell of fried chicken, which permeated the whole building.

As I paid for my gas I asked the woman behind the register how far it was to Sweetwater.

"How far?" she said, ringing up the receipt. "Honey, you're in it."

"But is there a Main Street somewhere? A downtown?"

"Kinda," she said. She cocked her head. "You looking for somebody in particular?"

I asked her if she knew the Clyde family, and she looked at me with dawning recognition. "You must be the granddaughter!" she said, throwing up her hands. "I should've known! Yankee plates—we don't get those every day. Well, I'll be. Welcome, hon. I'm Lois." She extended a soft, plump hand for me to shake. "Mariflo, come over and meet Clyde's granddaughter. Come down here all the way from up north to live in that old house out past the Ridge Road."

Mariflo stepped out from the other register. "You don't say." She smiled at me. "Well, isn't she pretty."

"Looks like her grandmother."

"Oh, she's got more of Amory's coloring. Remember how he used to be so blond? And kind of wavy, like hers." Mariflo made wave motions down her own gray head. "She's more like Amory than any of his kids."

"May he rest in peace," Lois added.

"Amen," said Mariflo. "Say." She turned to me. "You ever been down here before? I don't recall your face."

Lois nudged her. "Ellen died in '67, remember? It's Ellen's girl."

"Gosh," said Mariflo. "It still makes me sad to think about it. Your mama was a character."

"You knew her?" I asked.

Lois nodded. "My children are the same ages as her and your uncle Horace. They all grew up together." She sighed. "Your mama was the lively one. Kept everybody guessing."

"It was a tragedy, it really was," Mariflo said.

The two women stood silent and a little hunched for a moment at the register. A line was beginning to form behind me. I waited to see if they'd tell me anything else, but they didn't.

"Well," I said.

Lois looked up and seemed to focus again. Mariflo gave me a sympathetic smile and squeezed my hand before going back to her post. Lois gave me directions to my grandmother's house and pressed a peppermint swirl into my hand. As I left, I thanked her and she patted me on the shoulder. She seemed to have something more to say, but then she shook her head with a brisk motion and waved me away.

I got back into the wagon, which now smelled of rotting apples, and pulled off the slope of the station onto 622 East, down a long, twisting road into farmland, past herds of cattle and red-washed barns. It was early afternoon, and sunlight stained the fields with a diffuse yellow light. Wild daisies and Queen Anne's lace lined the roadside in unruly clumps. I zigzagged around hills and ponds, past abandoned, rotting cars, weather-beaten bones of old houses and rusted silos, farm implements left temporarily mid-field.

Eventually the road became littered with the makings of a town. Tony's Pizza sat in one bend, Harry's Used Cars in the next. The American Legion hung their plaque on a white clapboard one-room building off by itself on a stretch of road, with a small American flag on a spindly flagpole out front. A little farther down, I could see white-haired ladies with stiff handbags and old men with slicked-back hair and spit-leather black shoes standing around outside the Gospel Baptist Church and North Sweetwater Baptist Church.

I turned left on Guffey Road, up a steep, winding hill. At the top I bore right onto Fork Creek Lane, which splayed into a network of tributary streets that all looked the same. At the corner of Guffey and Fork Creek, a sign carved in wood rose from a bed of geraniums to announce in large script:

Ridge View Homes
"Welcome to Our Community"
H. W. CLYDE AND SON, DEVELOPERS

The houses were one- and two-story structures with aluminum siding and two-door garages, washed in complementary neutrals. Beige, sandstone, white, gray, shell pink. As I drove down Fork Creek I was amazed at the AstroTurf-like lawns, all the same, house after house, and the almost eerily clean configuration of the development. Marigolds and zinnias, bursts of color, clustered under mailboxes, led up to front doors, closed ranks around streetlamps. Sprinklers, like small geysers, sprouted in military formation across the grass.

Driving slowly down the wide streets, I began to notice the features that made each house minutely individual. A low, broad-slatted white picket fence separated one home from its neighbors on each side; another home sported a gravel walkway lined with gnomish sculptures; at a third, stained glass embellished with hearts and bells had replaced the usual clear glass in the front door. Young trees had been planted along the streets, and tall firs lined the edge of the property behind the houses, but there was barely a rustle. In fact, though I could see people clipping their hedges and washing their cars and walking around the neighborhood in sweat-suits and sneakers, the place was unnervingly quiet.

Following Lois's directions, I turned left onto Cherry Road, descended a sharp hill, and turned right at the bottom onto Webb. The second right was Red Pond Road. I slowed almost to a stop, looking for number 29.

Third from the end on the right, it was powder blue, with large black numbers on the door and daisies and marigolds planted around low bushes on either side of the entrance—almost exactly as I had imagined. When I pulled into the driveway my hands were trembling. I glimpsed a woman with short white hair in the front window, and my breath caught in my throat. Suddenly I couldn't imagine what kind of insanity had led me here, and I sat, paralyzed, gripping the steering wheel. I did not want to get out.

For a long, timeless moment I clung to the car, a no-man's-land between two sandwiching worlds, and contemplated the enormity of what I was doing. Without thinking too much about it, or even understanding why, I had uprooted myself from everything familiar, everything I cared about, exchanging the comfort of a life lived in the present for the fractured uncertainty of a forward journey into the past. I didn't even know what I was searching for.

The front door opened and the woman emerged. She pulled the door shut with one hand and smoothed her hair with the other. I could make out soft folds of skin, glasses with clear plastic frames, pink lipstick, hair like spun tufts of cotton. She was dressed in a polyester outfit, apple-green slacks and a green-and-white floral blouse belted loosely with a ribbon of the same material. On her feet she wore white sneakers and suntan hose, which I could see as she came down the three steps to the path. She moved slowly but without hesitation. Her step was sure and light.

Sitting up straight, I combed through my hair with my hands, brushed off my T-shirt, and ran my tongue over my teeth. By the time I'd grasped the handle and pushed the door open with my elbow, the old woman had already padded down to the end of the drive. She stood five feet from the car, her tiny hands at her sides, craning her neck to see in.

She was smaller than I had imagined and neater, like a package.

She kept a respectable distance and waved. Her eyes were large and wondering behind bifocal lenses. Her smile wasn't sure.

"Welcome," she said. "Well, well, well."

I got out of the car stiff-legged and wary. My body didn't move the way I wanted it to. I thought of New York and its blessing of anonymity; I wanted to sink from this scrutiny, back into the car, back onto the road going north, into the cloak of night. The air smelled of trees and tar.

"Well, well, well," she said. "Cassandra. You take after your father."

I went up to hug her, and it was like hugging a fluffy, small-boned bird.

part two

She's tall like Amory, with long narrow bones and those gray-blue eyes and fine, wavy hair the color of straw. Her nose is freckled and her lips are like a new bruise. Long thin fingers and soft baby nails. She wears baggy shorts that don't show her shape and sleeveless T-shirts layered on top of each other, and she walks like a boy. Until she drove up in that old station wagon with books all piled in the back seat, I didn't quite believe she ever would.

I watched out the kitchen window with a dust rag in my hand. The license plate said "New Jersey, The Garden State." After a minute she looked in here and I ducked behind the curtain. I didn't want her to think I'd been standing there watching and hadn't come out to say hello.

She called from Roanoke last night to tell me she was on her way. This morning I put on some nice clothes and even perfume, and dusted, and made a pound cake and green beans, but it didn't seem possible she'd really come until I saw her with my own eyes, sitting in that beat-up old embarrassment of a car on the road in front of my house.

After getting a couple of bags out of the back I locked the wagon.

"Nobody's going to rob you here," my grandmother said. She sniffed and peered into the car. "It doesn't look like you've got a whole lot anybody'd want, anyway." She turned back toward the house, motioning for me to follow. She made her way to the front door slowly, with her head down, like a cat stepping through clover.

The little entrance hall was bright and sunny and smelled of lemon polish. A brass coatrack next to the door and a small table displaying a vase of daisies were the only furniture. Over the table hung an elaborate gilt mirror.

"Where should I put my bags, Grandmother?"

"You might as well call me Clyde," she said, closing the door behind us. "Everybody else does. Come on in here."

I set the bags in the front hall and followed her into the kitchen. It was spacious and modern. Everything gleamed. The linoleum was spotless; shiny plastic fruit sat in a bowl on the polished pine table. Large silk ferns in copper planters hung in the windows over the sink and counters, facing the street. On the refrigerator, magnets shaped like daisies pinioned coupons, photos, the corner of the letter I had sent detailing my plans.

"What a nice sunny room," I said. I sounded as falsely cheerful as a hospital volunteer.

"It is. Used to be my favorite place."

"Oh?"

She didn't elaborate. I stood there, awkward, like the new kid in school.

"You must be thirsty," she said after what seemed like hours.

"Well, I—"

She opened the refrigerator and took out a bottle of soda. Diet Coke. She took a glass from the cupboard. "All you young people drink this stuff. Alice is addicted to it." She opened the bottle and poured, then handed me the glass. "I can't stand it, myself."

"Thank you. Now, Alice is Elaine's daughter?"

She nodded. "She's about your age. How about some pound cake? I made one fresh this morning."

"Oh, gosh, no thank you," I said. "My stomach feels a little funny from the ride." For some reason I didn't understand, I found myself unable to talk like a normal adult.

All of a sudden a cuckoo clock in the next room exploded into noise. Both of us jumped.

Clyde peered at her watch, as if for confirmation. "Four o'clock," she said. "You've been on the road. You must be tired."

"A little," I admitted.

"Well, come on, I'll show you where you're staying." She led me through the darkened living room, which looked as if it had never been used, like a furniture showroom. The carpet showed vacuum cleaner tracks striped in alternating directions, like a freshly mown lawn. "I've got to do some errands. Everybody's coming over to dinner tonight about seven to meet you." She glanced back at me. "You might want to put on a dress."

I retrieved my bags from the foyer and followed her down a wide hallway. "Is there anything I can do to help?" I asked, tripping behind her into the guest room.

"Oh, no. I've got that pound cake and some green beans, and Elaine's bringing just about everything else."

"Thank you." I paused. "I—I wasn't expecting a party."

"They all want to meet you. They're curious." She turned to leave, then hesitated, standing in the doorway. "We all are."

"I guess I am too," I said.

She looked down, studying the doorknob, and then looked up at me, into my blank face. "What I can't figure out is why in the world you'd even want that old house."

Her directness caught me off guard. "Why I'd want it?"

"It's beyond me," she said. "Why you'd come down here all by yourself to live in a place where you don't know a soul, in a house that's falling apart, in a town that nobody I ever met chose to live in just because they felt like it—it doesn't make any sense." She stood very still, with her head cocked to the side. "What'd you think you were going to find down here?"

Any possible answers had flown out of my head. I wanted to creep away and escape through the window. "I'm not really sure."

"Well." She started out the door. "I just wondered."

"Wait—don't leave," I said, touching her arm. I took a deep breath. "Part of it is that I wanted to get out of the city. I've always lived in cities. I think I came down here looking for something—something I've been missing."

"What do you mean?"

"Like . . . " I shrugged. "Trees, green grass. All the stuff you probably take for granted. And I've always lived in apartments. The idea of having a whole house to yourself is incredible to me."

She didn't say anything, so I forged ahead.

"And I think part of it is that it just seemed strange not to know you, not to know—my mother, and everything. It was so weird to find out my grandfather had died and I didn't even know what he was like."

"Well, if that's it," she said, her voice tart, "I could have told you all you need to know on the phone. He was crotchety and foolish."

Again I was taken aback.

"That surprises you? Why—because I was married to him for so long? You marry somebody, you vow to stay together, and you do it because that's a sacred vow. Till death do you part. Not until you get sick of each other." She rubbed an imaginary speck of dust off the bureau by the door. "You probably wouldn't have liked each other much. He had a hard time with girls who did what they felt like." She looked at me. "You know, don't you, that everybody's wondering what you want from them."

"What?"

"They think they're going to have to take care of you. You'll get nervous out there in that old house and expect them to help."

"Is that what *you* think?"

She shifted her feet and seemed to settle into herself. Her gaze was blank and direct. "Well, I wondered."

After Clyde left I sat on the bed, bouncing up and down on it a little. I ran my fingers over the quilt and lay down, my legs hanging over the edge, my hands over my face. The more I thought about it, the more I thought Clyde was right: I really had no business being there. I wondered if I should just turn around and leave, with all my belongings still in the car. If I left now I could be out of the state by dark.

As I lay on the bed I drifted into a troubled sleep. I was driving in the dark on a road between a tall brick wall and a cliff. If I veered even slightly to the left, the car scraped the wall; to the right, the wheels wobbled over the edge. There was too much traffic behind me to stop. The steering wheel was slippery in my sweaty hands. My teeth were clenched tight.

I woke to a soft, insistent tapping on the door and sat up in a daze, trying to concentrate. The room was still bright with sunlight. "It's six-thirty," Clyde was saying. "Anything you want ironed?"

I couldn't think. "No, thanks." Her footsteps faded back down the hall and I sat forward, rubbing my eyes.

Rummaging through my bag, I found a purple floral cotton sundress with tiny buttons up the front and realized that it did, in fact, need ironing. *Damn.* I went out to the kitchen, which was thick with the smells of baking. Clyde was setting the table and listening to the radio. "I can do this," I said, holding up the dress. "I just need to know where the iron is."

"Give it to me," she said. "You need to get ready."

"You've got things to do."

"They'll get done. Give me the dress."

I went back to my room and stripped out of my clothes. Taking a washcloth from the pile of towels Clyde had left on the bureau, I went into the adjoining bathroom. As I thought about the plans for the evening, a ball of dread formed in my stomach. I flipped on the light, put my hair into a short ponytail, and began to wash my face.

Alice and the baby were the first to arrive. She carried him on one hip and pushed the doorbell with her elbow. The buzz, long and insistent, brought Clyde and me from different sides of the house to answer it.

Alice appeared to be in her late twenties. Her blond hair was cut stylishly short, her freckled nose was long and straight, and she had small white teeth and high cheekbones. She was pretty. She wore berry-colored lipstick, jeans, sandals that revealed berry-colored toenails, and a pink T-shirt. In her free hand she was carrying a foil-covered casserole dish.

"Hello, Clyde," she sang through the screen. She couldn't see me standing in the background. She lifted the casserole and patted the kid's diaper. "Sorry to make you come running. I got my hands full." She moved aside for Clyde to let her in. Once in the foyer, she bent down and kissed Clyde's cheek, tipping the baby forward.

"Mama," he said, pushing his stubby finger into Clyde's chest.

"She's your great-grandmama, you know that," Alice scolded. "I'm your mama." She straightened up.

"Alice, this is Cassandra," Clyde said.

"Well, hello. Did you just get here? You must be beat."

"She's been sleeping all afternoon," said Clyde, taking the casserole from Alice and disappearing into the kitchen. Alice adjusted the kid to her other hip. He was playing with a strand of her hair and talking to himself.

"What's your name?" I asked, holding out a finger. He reached for it tentatively and squeezed it, then let go and hid his face in his mother's hair.

"He's not usually shy," Alice said. "Eric Amory Sommers, be polite and say hello." She jiggled him a little, but his face stayed buried. "Turned three in June." She glanced toward the kitchen and lowered her voice. "And just so it doesn't come up later and embarrass anybody, his daddy and I split up about a year ago. Oh, and Chester too—Horace and Kathy's oldest? He's been divorced twice. Clyde's kind of sensitive about it."

I nodded. "I got that idea. Till death do you part."

"That's it," said Alice. "And at the rate we were going, death probably would've parted us pretty soon. Then we would've broken another rule in the Bible. You can't win." She smiled, and I smiled back. I liked her.

She stood back and surveyed me. "Now, that's a nice dress. You look just like anybody. Horace told so many stories about your parents being radicals I thought you might have a ring through your nose or something."

As we were talking a car had pulled up out front. "That's Elaine and Larry. My mother and daddy," Alice said as a couple got out of the car and started up the walk. "I kinda wish you did have a ring in your nose. It'd give them something new to talk about."

Elaine was soft and bosomy, with frosted hair, a thick waist, and long, thin legs. She was wearing a halter-top pantsuit and high-heeled sandals. Larry, coming up behind her, seized my hand with a practiced grip. His skin was leathery, and his eyes were cautious and alert, like a German Shepherd's. His black, shiny hair was combed back from his forehead.

"She doesn't look a thing like her," said Elaine, pantomiming a hug with me. "Not a thing."

"She looks like her granddaddy," Larry said.

Elaine took Eric from Alice. "You are too cute," she cooed. "Alice Marie, the turkey and everything's in the trunk. I was afraid to even try in these heels, and your daddy's back is hurting again."

"You know I hate it when you call me that, Mother."

"Well, then, *Alice.* My, we're awfully sensitive today. And in front of our guest." She smiled thinly at me.

"Let me have the keys, Dad," Alice said.

I offered to help, and we walked down to the big pink Cadillac with a Mary Kay sticker in the back window. "Mother sells that crap," said Alice. "She's good at it." She opened the trunk and began to load me up with Tupperware and Pyrex dishes. While we were standing there a minivan turned onto Red Pond Road and pulled up behind the Cadillac. "It's really too bad you're so damn presentable," Alice said again, slamming the trunk. "I'd just *love* for you to shake them all up a little bit."

"Hello, cousin." A round-faced, beaming man strode up. He offered an outstretched hand and then, seeing that my hands were full, patted me on the shoulder.

"This is Chester," Alice said.

"Nice to meet you,"

He grinned and wiped his face with a handkerchief. "Hot day, isn't it? Golly, I like to faint out there in the sun this afternoon."

"Chester builds houses with his dad."

"There'll be a quiz later," Chester said, nudging me with his elbow. He took a casserole from me, and we went inside to the kitchen. Elaine was leaning against the stove talking to Clyde, who stood at the sink pouring lemonade powder into a plastic pitcher.

"So I told her that if Daily Defense Complex worked for her and she liked it, she shouldn't take a chance on losing it on the cruise," Elaine was saying. "You never know, a bag might get stolen or something, and then where would you be? Out to sea and no way back, with dry skin. So would you believe she bought all ten tubes I had in stock? Well, hello, Chester!" She turned toward him and held out her arms.

"Elaine." He set the dish on the counter and took her hands, kissing her cheek.

She looked at him closely. "You've lost a little weight."

"No."

"But you've been going to the health club?"

He laughed shortly. "I've been real busy."

"How's your cholesterol?"

"Now, Elaine," he said, an edge to his voice.

"Okay." She pulled back and pretended to lock her lips.

"Clyde," Chester said, crossing to the sink. "As perky as ever."

She flapped her hand at him. "Pshaw. I'm just a wrinkled old woman."

"You're a liar, is what you are."

She flapped at him again and filled the pitcher with water.

Chester turned to Elaine, his face serious all of a sudden. "Troy called this morning. He just couldn't get away."

Elaine looked at him, her mouth a tense line.

"Your cousin Troy is in a band in Atlanta," Chester explained to me. "They're trying to hit the big time, so he doesn't get much leave."

"That's not true and you know it, Chester," Elaine said. "He can come home anytime he wants to."

"Now, Elaine—"

"And why he called you, and not his own . . ." She pursed her lips. "Tell me the truth. He's out there looking for that woman again, isn't he?"

"I don't know what you mean."

"You know good and well what I mean."

"I really don't, Elaine. That's the God's honest truth."

"Listen, Chester—"

"Mother," Alice said, coming into the kitchen loaded up with

dishes. She put them on the counter. "Don't be so paranoid. Leave poor Chester alone."

"I don't think I'm being paranoid," Elaine snapped. "He didn't even call."

"He didn't call me either," Alice said. "There's nothing unusual about that. He knows Chester won't give him a hard time." She held her mother's shoulders. "Don't worry. He's busy, that's all. He'll be back."

Elaine looked around, suddenly seeming to notice me, and gave me a tight smile. I smiled back awkwardly. She excused herself to find Larry.

Chester watched her leave. His ears were crimson. "I hate being in the middle," he said. "I hate it more than anything."

"Oh, Chester, you'll be all right," Alice said.

"Would you call everybody in, Chester?" said Clyde, bustling around the kitchen. "It's about ready. Did your mother and daddy arrive yet?"

He strained to look out the window over the table. "Yep. I can see them on the lawn. They must've just got here." He went out to the steps.

Clyde turned toward Alice, wiping her hands on a towel and adjusting her glasses on her ears. "When are you going to teach your mama to behave in public?"

"You raised her, Clyde," Alice said, munching on a carrot stick, winking at me.

"We are late, late, late!" A small woman waving her hands in the air hurried into the kitchen. Her auburn hair was neatly coiffed, and she was wearing a full denim skirt and a magenta silk blouse cinched by a thick belt. "I hope we haven't held you all up. Horace had to settle some business with a tenant. Leaky pipes." Wide-eyed and smiling, she fixed on me. "And you must be Ellen's little girl. Well, not so little." She reached for my hand. Her fingers were small and cool. "I'm Kathy. It sure is a pleasure to meet you. My, we have a gathering this evening!" She looked at Clyde. "And hello there, Grandmother. What can the tardy one do to help?"

"Why, not a thing except stand here and talk to this old lady while she pots around."

Kathy started rolling up her sleeves. "You let me wash those pans. I need to feel useful."

"Now, don't you get that pretty new outfit dirty," Clyde protested.

"These rags? You've seen me in 'em a dozen times. I haven't been shopping in years."

"Is she telling lies again? I swear I can't leave her alone for a minute without her making up some story." A red-cheeked man in a baseball cap loped up behind Kathy and squeezed her waist. She wriggled away, pretending to be insulted. "Ma," he said, swinging his body across the kitchen and kissing Clyde on the forehead. "Kathy got it in her head to check out a couple of construction sites before dinner. That's why we're so darn late."

"He is just impossible," Kathy said to Clyde. "Why didn't you teach your son to mind?"

"He's your job now," Clyde said.

He came over to me and tipped his cap, which was printed with the words H. W. CLYDE AND SON. "WE MAKE HOMES." "Horace," he said, tilting forward on the balls of his feet. "Pleased to meet you. Bet you didn't expect to come down here and find all your relatives are nuts, did you? Or maybe you did. Hey, you're not doing some kind of study on us or anything, are you?" He laughed and motioned with his thumb toward Kathy. "If you are, I can tell you stuff about her that'll knock your socks off."

"Hush. You behave, now. Cassandra is company," Kathy said.

"Nonsense. The girl's family. Isn't that right, Cassandra?"

I looked around at all the faces. "You can call me Cassie," I said.

Chester came through the kitchen door with Eric under one arm. "Ready to eat!" he said. "Where should I put the turkey?" Eric squealed and squirmed away.

An extra leaf had been added to the table, which was set for eight, with a high chair for Eric. I stood back against the wall as my aunts and cousins argued the merits of placing one uncle next to the other. When the places were finally assigned, I found myself between Alice and Elaine. Clyde hovered at the head of the table, adding trays of relish and butter, setting a large jug of iced tea in the center.

"C'mon, Ma," Horace said, reaching toward her. "Have a seat. Food's getting cold."

"Don't mind me. I filled up cooking." She shooed his hand away. "Now, you all just go on. Let's have the blessing."

Larry, at the foot of the table, bowed his head. One by one the other heads went down. For a moment all I could hear was the hum of the refrigerator and the loud ticking of the cuckoo clock in the next room. I looked at my hands folded in my lap. "For these and all his gifts, God's holy name be praised."

I started to raise my head but looked down again quickly when I realized no one else had moved.

"Lord, thank you on this day for bringing all of us together to break bread in your name. We thank you for our health. Praise God, not one of us is injured or sick. We pray for those who cannot be with us tonight, Troy and Ralph in Atlanta, that they may be safe. We thank you for bringing back to us today a missing piece of the family puzzle."

Out of the corner of my eye I saw Larry look up, a faraway expression on his face.

"You know," he continued, "this kind of reminds me of a story Jesus once told, about a boy who'd gone off far from home and came back a number of years later. Well, his daddy saw him coming down the road, and he said to the servants, 'Quick! Let's kill that fatted calf! Gather up some new shoes and clothes and a ring for his finger, and then we'll all eat, drink, and be merry. For my child was dead and now is living, he was lost and has been found.'

"Well, we haven't got the jewels and the shoes and the new clothes, but we do have a fatted calf—or, well, it looks like a turkey."

Next to me, Elaine tapped her watch with a manicured fingernail, trying to catch Larry's eye.

He saw her and nodded briefly. "So God be praised. Amen. Let's eat."

"What can I pass you?" Alice asked, nudging me with a bowl of coleslaw. "You need to get some meat on those bones."

"Flattery will get you nowhere," I said, smiling.

"Listen, it's not flattery," she said. "I'm going to do everything I can to fatten you up. Now that you're here, you're competition."

Piling my plate with stewed green beans and fresh creamed corn, mashed potatoes and corn bread, I thought about Larry's blessing. I remembered what Clyde had said about all of them worrying that they would have to take care of me, wondering why I came. I thought about how strange it must seem to them that someone would choose to pack up and move to a place, sight unseen, where she knew no one and had no job prospects, a place where schools were shrinking and stores were closing because everyone who lived there was trying to get out.

I looked around the table. Elaine was talking about her blood pressure, which was a little high. Horace was telling Chester about a cement mixer he'd bought on a whim at an auction, which would practically double production. Alice and Kathy were discussing a local school bus driver who was caught driving drunk and got off with a reprimand. Alice said she'd be taking Eric to school herself when he was old enough.

As I sat watching them, I suddenly felt alone and out of place, as if I had fallen there out of the sky on my way to someplace else. Something inside kept me from participating, made me an outsider, an observer. I was reminded of how I had felt when I stepped off the plane in Rome the summer before. I'd been completely disoriented, overwhelmed by the disparity between my idea of what it would be like and the foreign images that confronted me. For several days I had just wandered the streets, taking in the sights and smells and sounds without any capacity to assess or analyze, as if I had no right to pass judgment or to claim it as my own. Even my journal had been little more than a litany of sights seen: the Colosseum, the Vatican, the Spanish Steps. Now, as the conversation swelled up and around me, I was aware of that same numbness, that inability to find my voice, the peculiar sense of being alien in a place that felt strangely familiar.

"How's your blood pressure?" said Elaine, leaning close. "You're young and healthy. You must not have to worry about it."

"I don't even think I know," I said.

"Well, dear, you should have it tested. High blood pressure runs in the family. Now, what about your cholesterol?"

After dinner I helped Alice and Kathy with the dishes while Elaine sat on the front stoop watching Larry teach Eric to throw a baseball. Horace and Chester milled around the backyard with their hands in their pockets, kicking clumps of dirt and talking. Just as we finished cleaning up, Eric hurled the baseball through one of Clyde's basement windows, bringing everyone running to the front yard.

This seemed to signal the end of the evening. Horace inspected the damage and said he'd send someone over first thing in the morning to see to it. Clyde stood on the stoop, and I walked down to the cars to say goodbye.

The sky was a wash of deep blue, and the moon shone faintly in the west, translucent. The light on everyone's faces was soft and gentle.

"You take care, now," Kathy said. "If there's anything we can do, just let us know."

"I'll be over in a day or two to take you out to that house," said Horace.

"I could go out there myself. All I need is the key to the front door."

He shook his head. "Naw, I should go with you. Make sure it's still standing." He rubbed his stomach. "Boy, I sure did eat a lot. Tell that woman over there on the porch to stop cooking such good food."

"I heard that," Clyde said. "It was your sister who did most of it."

"Well, it's lucky for me I got a wife who can't cook to save her life."

"Can you believe him?" Kathy said to me. "Sometimes I wonder why I don't just get a d-i-v-o-r-c-e and find myself a new one."

"Face it, woman, you're in love with me."

Kathy laughed and rolled her eyes. Horace opened the car door for her with one hand and waved goodbye with the other.

As they pulled away, Chester sighed. "Like teenagers. Always have been. I wish I knew their secret."

"You just picked the wrong ones, is all," said Larry, clapping him on the shoulder. "Like I always say, you don't want 'em too independent. Put it this way: if they can get along just as good without you as with you, there's not much point in tying the knot. Isn't that right?" he said, turning to me.

"Oh, for heaven's sakes, be quiet and leave her out of it," Elaine chided. "Don't listen to his foolishness," she said to me. "He's had a few beers."

Clyde leaned forward on the porch, straining to hear. "What's going on down there, a powwow?"

"Nothing, Mother, we're leaving, goodbye," said Elaine.

"Call if you need anything," Alice said, squeezing my arm. "I'll come by in the next couple of days to make sure you're surviving." She scooped Eric up and got into her car.

After everyone left I stood in the road hugging my elbows, looking up at the mountain ridge behind the fir trees that marked the edge of the development. The ridge was long and low and almost black. The warm evening air smelled of fir sap and cut grass.

"You all right out there?" Clyde asked. I turned around. "I'm going inside. I think I'm going to hit the hay."

"I'm fine," I said. "Thank you for dinner—and everything. It was really nice."

"It wasn't anything." She stayed on the porch a minute longer. Then she turned and went inside, closing the door behind her.

I stood in the street for a long time, watching the branches of the tall firs creak and sway in the soft breeze. Then I lay down on my grandmother's front lawn and gazed up at the wide expanse of sky, wider than I could remember ever having seen. Stars began to appear, like silver pins in a blue-black cloth. The moon was filling out, a milky marble. I felt almost light-headed with fatigue and relief that the day was over.

Lying there on the lawn, I fell asleep to the sound of the wind and the crickets. I didn't wake until the first light of the new day roused a mockingbird in a tree near the house.

Amory was the artist, they all said. He was the artist who never lived up to his potential; and I was the one who married him and grounded him, ground him down.

For so long he held me in the vise grip of his passions and I took it as my due, as if I deserved it for trapping him. He might have whispered it to me in my sleep, so willing was I to believe that I had nipped his budding youth and must now expect to pay for it. When he went out of the house with his hat tipped at an angle and his shoulders defiantly braced against my protests, I told myself that I had captured a rare and beautiful bird who must fly free to live, that what I loved most about him was his quest for freedom, his demand that life never be mundane. I convinced myself that by marrying me he had done me a favor.

It took me years to figure out that I was the one who had been trapped: a naive girl pinned like a butterfly to a dance hall wall in the cool insistent darkness of midnight. I hadn't wanted children; I hadn't even wanted marriage. But it was easier for me to live the lie he built to cover his tracks than to face the possibility that I had married a man with wants and needs as basic as a dog's.

Amory had a delicate disposition. Sensitive eyes. Fickle fingers and restless lips. He used to stride around town in a cream-colored suit, white shirt, and spats. He wore a dove-gray hat and tipped it at every opportunity. His blond hair gleamed under the hat, and his eyes shone as blue as the lining of oyster shells. He would take little Horace when he went to do errands in town, just to give women an excuse to come up and talk. "Smile at the ladies," he told his son. "Smile at the ladies and they'll smile right back."

After Bryce Davies there were others: Leonore Greenwood, May Ford, sixteen-year-old Anna Parker. They came into my life like insects through a screen; as soon as I thought I'd gotten rid of one, another appeared to take her place. I saw his imprint on women I didn't even know. He left negatives of himself all over town. Women smiled at me on the street in that way that says, I know what you know. I know what he does. They would smile, and they'd keep walking.

One day Daddy got wind of what was going on, and I never heard precisely what was said, but for a while after that Amory's only mistress was the Sweetwater mill. He threw himself into his work with more ardor, more passion, than he had bestowed on any lover. That was even worse, in a way, because he felt no guilt in his unfaithfulness. He didn't have to choose between us.

As the years passed he established a routine for himself. During the days work consumed him; nights, he gave himself to whiskey; he fit women in the cracks. I was left to fend for myself, to flirt with the pediatrician, the butcher, to while away long afternoons talking to Bible salesmen and Fuller Brush men, anyone who'd listen. We'd sit on the porch in midsummer, Bibles or brushes spread around our feet. I'd serve minted iced tea and fresh, warm pound cake as the mockingbird sang in the bushes and the children played in the yard. Sweating in squeaky black shoes, wiping their faces with limp white handkerchiefs, these men would sit straight and awkward on their chairs, making pathetic small talk that always reverted to the merchandise. I didn't care what we talked about. I was grateful for any conversation at all.

In the end I stopped caring if he cared. I stopped worrying about whether he'd like me in the white dress or the blue, my hair up or down, whether he'd prefer chicken to meat loaf. I stopped staying awake for him at night. At dinner parties I waited dispassionately for him to embarrass me: he'd get drunk, pinch the pretty ones under the table, insult the ones he didn't desire, tell dirty jokes. I expected it. I steeled myself against it. Grasping the slipping center of attention, he'd play out-of-tune pianos, badly, his hands shaking with drink. He'd play songs nobody remembered, including himself; he'd plunk around trying to recall scraps of melodies while people lit cigarettes and whispered under their breath, nodding toward him and rolling their eyes. I would stand back against the wall, sipping Jim Beam and soda, a little more each time, acting like I didn't know him, like it didn't faze me at all. A smile for armor, alcohol as a shield. He almost made a drunk out of me too.

Sometimes he would take me in my sleep and I'd wake to the reek of whiskey, his figure hunched in concentration above me, pawing beneath my nightgown with rough hands, fumbling at the material. But by that time he was masked, emasculated; and I, who had lived a lie of marriage for so many years, felt liberated in my hatred for him. For so long everybody had seen but me; and then I saw it too, though it didn't make any difference; and finally I knew all the stories and there was nothing he could do. In those last twenty-four years he was mine completely, and I didn't want him. I wanted him to know that, the way he made me know for so many years. I wanted him to learn the truth. I wanted him to suffer into it.

I woke in my bed at midmorning to the throbbing growl of a lawn mower outside my window. Sitting up, I fumbled for the shade pull above the bed and raised the shade slowly, letting in a widening slice of bright light. Outside, a shirtless teenage boy with a bandanna over his head was pushing the mower back and forth from the edge of the lawn to the side of the house. He was wearing mirrored sunglasses and a Walkman. After a moment he noticed me and waved. Suddenly modest, I lifted my hand in return and pulled the shade back down.

I got out of bed and made it up in a few short motions, smoothing the covers and fluffing the pillows. I found a wrinkled cotton robe in my suitcase and put it on. The clock beside my bed said ten-thirty. I was ashamed it was so late; Clyde would have been up for hours.

A note on the kitchen table said, "Doing errands. Back around 11. Coffee's made." Except for the distant whir of the mower and the soft hum of the refrigerator, the house was still. The countertop was warm, the room brilliant with sunshine. "Used to be my favorite place," Clyde had said. *Used to be.* I wondered what she meant by that.

I poured myself a cup of coffee and stood at the kitchen sink to drink it, looking out at the street. My car, dented, low to the ground, filled with books and dirtied by the drive, looked as out of place in these pristine surroundings as a rusty old can. Across the street, a gray-haired woman wearing thick gardening gloves and wielding a trowel was planting flowers around a bush in her front yard. I watched a plane overhead leave a disappearing trail of white across the sky.

I tried to remember the last time I had been in Sweetwater: the day of my mother's funeral, twenty-four years earlier. It had been a fine, sunny day, the kind of day you might expect for Easter or a wedding. We all stood on a ridge in a cemetery laid out like a golf course, surrounded by bright, artificial-looking flowers arranged into hearts and horseshoes, staring at a shiny silver box covered with pink carnations under a festive tent. My father and Clyde were crying; I couldn't recall if my grandfather was even there. I wore a blue dress, one I hated, with scratchy lace at the neck. I remembered wanting to dance.

Finishing my coffee, I turned from the window and opened the refrigerator. I found a jug of orange juice and searched the cabinets for a glass, then took my juice and wandered through the house, stopping to look at photos of my cousins in the living room and a large one of my grandparents in the hall. I wondered how recently it had been taken; my grandfather looked old and tired, and his smile was feeble. He was wearing a white shirt and a stiff tie and silver-framed glasses. Clyde sat in front of him in a blue-and-white blouse, hands folded in her lap, her smile opaque. "Grandmother," I whispered, tasting that strange word like metal. "Clyde," I said. *"Clyde."* The hard consonants stuck in my throat.

In her room the bed was so neatly made that I wondered for a moment if she actually slept there. On the mirrored dresser facing the bed sat a hinged frame containing hand-colored pictures of my mother, Horace, and Elaine: high school graduation, I guessed. In her picture Elaine wore black cat's-eye glasses; her teased hair spun away from her head like cotton candy. Horace had a large, square jaw, small, pale eyes, and a football player's crew cut. My mother was slighter than the other two. Her long, dark hair fell behind her shoulders. Her eyes were dark and serious. I searched the face, younger than my own; I picked up the frame and looked closely into her eyes.

"I see you found the juice."

Startled, I set the frame awkwardly on the dresser, and it collapsed. Clyde, standing in the doorway wearing pale blue, looked like a soft white cloud.

"There's leftover ham, and I can fry you up an egg if you like," she said. She turned around and headed down the hall. "Of course, I ate hours ago," she called back, "but you Yankees must be on a different schedule."

I propped up the frame and followed her down the hall to the kitchen, where she was taking a carton of eggs out of the fridge.

"I don't want you to go to any trouble," I said. "I'm not all that hungry."

Clyde paused and straightened. Then she shrugged. "Suit yourself."

"But if you've already started—"

"Are you hungry or not?"

"I'm a little hungry," I admitted.

"Well, all right, then." She set a frying pan on the stove. "You go on and get dressed. This'll be ready in five minutes."

I hesitated. "Clyde . . . there's something I've been wondering about. Yesterday you said this used to be your favorite place, and I . . . I was just wondering why it isn't anymore."

She looked at me as if trying to decide what to tell me. Finally she walked over to the sink. "This is where I found him. Right here." She pointed to the floor. "I had to throw away all the clothes I was wearing that day. Blood all over them."

"Amory?"

She nodded. "I guess if I'd tried I could've gotten the blood out, but who'd have wanted to? I threw away everything, even my underwear."

I looked down at the floor, as if it might yield some clues.

"I asked Horace about putting in a new floor. He said he thought that would be a waste of money, since this one's only four years old. I didn't argue with him, I just cleaned it up real good. But every time I come in here it's like I'm stepping over that body to get to the sink. It's like I'm slipping in that blood."

We stood there in silence for a moment, looking at the linoleum. "You should have a new floor if you want one," I said in a quavery voice. "You shouldn't have to live with that."

"No, Horace is right," Clyde said. "Some things you just got to live with and get over. If he put a new floor in here, it would be like I wanted to pretend it never happened. But it did happen, and a new floor won't make me forget it."

The cuckoo clock shrilled suddenly. Clyde picked a couple of eggs out of the carton and cracked them into a bowl. "Well, you go on and get ready," she said, beating the eggs with a whisk.

"I'm—I'm sorry, Clyde."

She just nodded. She didn't look at me.

I went down the hall to my bedroom. I shut the door and leaned back against it, noticing the stuccoed pattern on the ceiling. I wasn't hungry anymore. I didn't know what to think.

I wondered what she thought of me, what she thought I was thinking. I'd expected that this might be awkward; I had braced myself for indifference or mistrust. But I was unprepared for this stiffly polite standoff between us, the strange assumption of intimacy, the seemingly kind gestures devoid of any warmth.

Hearing the whistle of a kettle, I went into the bathroom to brush my teeth and wash my face. I bent down and threw my hair over my head, brushing it quickly with firm, hard strokes. As I searched through my suitcase I realized that almost every piece of clothing I had was paint-spattered or ink-stained. Nothing seemed to match. I put on a Martha's Vineyard T-shirt and a pair of men's shorts and returned to the kitchen.

Clyde was lifting ham out of the frying pan onto a paper towel, her back to me. Leaning on the counter between the kitchen and the table, I watched her silently. When she turned around I saw that her apron had a cartoon of a gray-haired, smiling woman in a rocking chair above the words WORLD'S BEST GRANDMOTHER.

Clyde set down her spatula and wiped her fingers on the apron. "Hungry yet?" She handed me a plate of ham, eggs, and toast. After getting jam and margarine from the fridge, she followed me to the table. As we sat down, a loud noise suddenly blasted in. I looked out at the boy pushing the mower. He grinned and waved.

"Jimmy Battesin. That boy's headed for trouble," Clyde muttered.

"What do you mean?"

She picked up the salt shaker and poured salt on the table in a little pile, then flattened it out with her finger. "Oh, he's got big dreams. Nothing to hang them on. Never been anywhere in his life but thinks he's something special."

Outside, the mower sputtered and died. Jimmy fiddled with it for a moment and then came up to the window, wiping sweat from his forehead and yanking off his earphones. "The reserve tank's out of gas, Miz Clyde."

"There's more in the shed," she said. She turned to face him. "Jimmy, this is my granddaughter Cassandra from up north."

He smiled at me with renewed interest. "So you're the one," he said. "New Jersey. We seen the plates."

"Hi," I said.

He took his sunglasses off and squinted in at us. "Must seem real quiet down here."

"Not as quiet as I thought it would be. Those crickets are loud."

He laughed. "Gone into town yet? No crickets there. It's *real* quiet."

"Almost done with the mowing?" Clyde asked.

He stepped back from the window and put on his sunglasses. I could see the two of us reflected in them, small. "Almost. Got to get that gas. Nice to meet you," he said, nodding at me. He put the earphones back on and went around the side of the house.

Clyde sighed.

"He doesn't seem so bad," I said.

"If you don't mind paying somebody to do a job and then holding their hand while they do it."

I ate in silence for a while, forcing the food down. When I finished, I got up to clear my plate.

"Don't bother with that," Clyde said. "You run along and get dressed."

"I *am* dressed," I said.

The present was wrapped in tissue paper. I watched as she slowly peeled off each layer, smoothed it, and placed it in a neat, square pile on the table. When she was finished she looked at the bowl, turning it around.

"You didn't have to get me anything," Clyde said. She touched the smooth blue glaze inside. She turned it over and read the bottom. "C. Simon." She looked up. "You made this."

I nodded.

"Is this what you do for a living?"

"No. Not yet," I said, laughing a little. "Maybe someday. I need to work at it."

"Oh."

"That's part of why I came down here."

She ran both hands around the outside. "What is it, a fruit bowl?"

"Sure, it can be. It can be whatever you want."

"Can it go in the dishwasher?"

"I—I don't think so." Carefully, she set the bowl on the table. "It's a little rustic for your taste," I apologized. "You don't have to display it. You could just use it for salads or . . . " I tried to think of other uses.

"I like it." She started to fold up the tissue paper. "Blue was your mother's favorite color, you know."

"I know."

"Mine's yellow, but blue is second." She flattened the paper with her hand. "The couch in the living room is blue."

"I saw that."

"Maybe we can find a place for it in there."

"You could put potpourri in it or something," I said.

She got up and put the tissue paper away in a drawer. "That's what Elaine would do. She's got the stuff all over her house. I tell her it smells like cheap perfume, but she doesn't listen to me."

"Well, you could put cards in it, then."

She crossed her arms and looked at me. "Do I have to put something in it? Why can't I just leave it as it is?"

"You're right," I said. "I don't know why, but I always think I have to fill things up."

"I used to feel that way. Now I guess I like things empty."

"I'd really like to get out and see the house soon." I finished drying the frying pan and put it away. "You could just point me in the right direction."

"I could, but it wouldn't help you any. Horace has the only key."

"Maybe I'll give him a call."

"Well, I don't know," she said. "He's awfully busy. I'd hate to bother him when he's got so much to do."

I felt my face flush. "Then what do you suggest?"

Clyde brushed salt and crumbs off the table into her hand. She wiped the plastic fruit and pushed in the chairs. "He'll call when he's ready. He knows you're here. You just take a day or so to get situated and look around town a little bit. That old place isn't going anywhere."

Taking a deep breath, I turned toward the window. I considered phoning Horace anyway.

"I've got some pictures that might interest you," she said to my back.

I didn't respond.

She started down the hall. "Maybe some other time."

"No, wait," I said, resigned. "Photographs?"

"Back here."

I followed her to her bedroom, and we knelt on the wide space of carpet between the dresser and the bed. Clyde opened the bottom drawer of the dresser. It was full of brown albums stacked on top of each other and a blue box of snapshots. She pulled out the albums and started to shut the drawer.

"What about that box?" I asked.

"Oh, it's just odds and ends."

"If you don't mind, I'd love to see them."

She took out the box too, then handed me the top album. I blew on the cover and wiped the dust off with my hand. I looked at her.

"Go ahead," she said.

The first few pages contained sepia-toned portraits in different sizes, people alone and together, expressionless in stiff clothing. I didn't recognize any of them. I turned the pages, not wanting to ask, and Clyde, sitting beside me, didn't volunteer. On the third page I found her features in the face of a young girl.

"This is you?"

She pointed to the woman holding her. "My mother. Elvira Whitfield. I was five." She tapped another photograph lightly with a ridged yellow fingernail. "My brother Thomas. He was seven years older than me. Died of asthma at the age of twenty-one." She squinted at the picture for a moment. "I had a twin, you know," she said abruptly. "Died at birth."

"I didn't know."

"Apparently they're hereditary. My mother was a twin. I always thought I might have some of my own."

"And none of your children had twins either."

"No, none of my children," she said. "*You* might."

I laughed. "If I ever have children."

"You will," she said, turning the pages of the album. "You're not the type not to."

I nodded. Then, suddenly wanting to know, I asked, "What do you mean?"

She tucked the scalloped edge of a photograph back into its

black, wedge-shaped sleeve. "Some people think, no matter what happens, that the world is a good place and folks are basically decent. If something isn't right, they think they can fix it. You're like that, I can tell."

"You think so?" I said doubtfully.

"Your mother was that way too."

"Are you?"

"No." I watched her fingers bend the thick cardboard corner of a page. "I should never have had children."

I looked down, strangely uneasy. Her breath was loud and uneven.

"Maybe you're wrong about yourself," I said. "Maybe you only started feeling this way after everything that happened."

Clyde studied me for a long time. "I was never what you'd call an optimist," she said. "I never thought I could change the world."

"Where did my mother get it from, then?"

She shut the album. "Not from me," she said. "Not from me and not from Amory. It was something she was born with." She was very still for a moment. Then she hoisted herself to her feet, the album sliding off her lap onto the floor, spilling photographs. "You want all the answers," she blurted. "Well, I don't have any answers. Ask somebody else, because I don't know."

"Clyde—" I started to get up, but she'd already left the room, closing the door behind her. I sank back on my heels. I wanted to go after her, but I didn't have any idea what to say.

Slowly I began picking up the photographs and placing them, like puzzle pieces, back in the album where they belonged. As I found the space for the final picture, the phone rang and I heard her answer it in the kitchen. After a minute, she came back down the hall. "It's for you," she said through the door.

"Thank you, Clyde." I reached over to the nightstand and picked up.

"Cassie, this is Alice. How's it going?"

"Fine." I tried to sound cheerful.

"Uh-huh. How's Clyde?"

"Fine. Just fine."

"You got in an argument," Alice said matter-of-factly.

I sighed. "Not exactly an argument. A disagreement. No, not even that. I'm not sure what it was. All I know is something I said upset her and she left the room." I got up from the floor and sat on the bed.

Alice laughed. "Well, don't take it personally. It happens to the best of us. Look, I'm calling because I'm packing Eric off for a few days with his daddy and I am as free as a kite. I'm going into town this afternoon, and I thought you might like to come along. There's not much to see, but it beats sitting around looking at the marigolds and trying not to start a disagreement."

"I'd love that," I said gratefully.

"I'll pick you up around two. Don't do anything desperate before I get there."

Hanging up the phone, I sat back against the headboard. I looked around the room at things I hadn't noticed earlier: the beige walls, needlepointed pictures of dogs and flowers, a hooked rug covering part of the green shag carpet. In the mirror above the dresser I saw a pale, freckled girl in baggy shorts and a faded T-shirt, dirty-blond hair pulled back in a ponytail, sitting against pink pillow shams on a floral bedspread with a matching ruffled bedskirt.

I could hear the tinny hum of the television in the living room. I reached down for the box of photos Clyde said were odds and ends. The pictures were jumbled together in no apparent order: old black-and-whites with scalloped borders, orange-tinted Polaroids, glossy color prints with the dates in small digital numbers on the front. I thumbed through them slowly, a collection of outtakes from funerals and birthday parties and especially weddings: Horace and Kathy's, Elaine and Larry's, a young, pink-faced Chester standing proudly in a maroon tuxedo beside his redheaded, flower-bedecked bride. A few photos later, I found an older, balder Chester in a gray suit, another bride on his arm. I stumbled across a picture from my parents' wedding—my father, handsome and beardless, clowning beside my mother, elegant and slender in a simple white satin dress. ("Before the revolution," Dad said of that clean-cut couple from long ago.)

I searched hungrily for snapshots of my mother. Growing up, I had pored over my dad's few photographs of her until they were dog-eared and tattered. Now, sifting through the box, I found her everywhere: sitting on the hood of a car with Horace, as a bridesmaid in Elaine's wedding, as a young girl in a crisp white blouse on the steps of a church. I separated her pictures from the rest and put them in order. There was one of her at three or four, in Clyde's young, firm arms; one at about ten, in a studio portrait of the family. I saw her laughing, dancing, musing, frowning. Here she wore pigtails, there pearls. And through all those years of posing for photographs—with Horace, Elaine, her parents, even my father—my mother was often the only one looking straight into the camera.

Near the end of the pile I found a color photo of my mother, my father, and me. Her hair was short, pixieish, above her ears; my dad's was long and uneven. The two of them were thin, almost gaunt. She was wearing that same lime-green dress. His arm was around her waist; she held me between them. They stood in front of a white Volkswagen bus on a crowded urban street. I must have been about two.

Holding the picture up to the light, I studied the faces. I was pale, my mother was dark; we looked nothing alike. But there was something about the tilt of the chin, mouths parted as if to ask a question, something behind the eyes—a level, inquisitive stare—that linked us unmistakably. The snapshot blurred before my eyes, and our faces ran together. I felt my hands shaking, as if of their own volition. I sat watching them as they shook, as the photo slipped from my fingers, as my fingers moved up to touch my face.

Sitting there on Clyde's bed, pictures scattered all around me, I heard a light rapping at the door. I shook my head to clear it, gathered up the pictures, and tossed them back into the box. "Come in."

Clyde opened the door a crack.

"Come in, it's fine," I said, rising. "It's your room. I was only . . . sitting here."

She stood wedged in the doorway, her hand on the knob. "What did Alice want?"

"Oh, she's going to show me the downtown this afternoon."

"I see," she said. She started to shut the door, then hesitated. "You all right?"

"I'm all right." I smiled. "Thanks for asking."

The years have turned me irritable, and all she can see is that stretching between us—the irritableness of the years. I was young once, I want to say, I was young once and I know how you feel. But I don't say anything, and when I get up I'm stiff from sitting, and my stiffness enrages me.

She came all the way from New York City looking for something she says she's been missing all her life, something she says we take for granted. She came down here all sophisticated but wanting what we have instead, and it's hard to figure out. Wanting it both ways. I think she can't quite believe this is the stock she's from.

I want to tell her about her grandfather, about how people came from all around to see him play the piano when he was young. People used to say his fingers had wings. I want to tell her about when Ellen won the county spelling bee and her name was in the paper along with the word—"effluvium." I want to ask her what she likes to read, what she's thinking about when she looks off in the distance, but there's too much space between us.

She talks to me like I'm old. Who can blame her? I act old. But her careful pity irritates me. It's not her fault. She doesn't know anything. But if she's here she's going to figure it out. How many pieces do you need to put the puzzle together? I want to ask her. How can you sit there looking at me with that blank smile and not know anything? My old face is a cage and my feelings are roaming around inside it, waiting. Waiting for her to get too close.

So I hold back. I don't want to hurt her. What's she ever done to me? I keep my mouth shut, and the silence between us confuses her, makes her want to leave. I was young once; I had those feelings. I want to tell her, but if I tell her I'll have to tell her everything.

I'm afraid I'll die with all of it inside me and lost forever. But there are so many ways to tell this story. I wouldn't know how to begin.

Alice drove recklessly over the serpentine back roads of Sweetwater. She talked as fast as she drove, and as the jeep squealed around corners, I held on tight to the strap above the door, my head bobbing in response.

"Mother is about to drive me up a wall. You know about Troy and me being adopted, right? Well, you know that little tantrum she threw with Chester last night? She's got it in her head that Troy's off looking for his real mother and that's why he won't come home. Troy told her about some family reunion he'd seen on *Oprah* a few months back—you know, where the kid sees the mother for the first time in thirty years and everybody's bawling—just to rattle her, I'm sure. He loves to do that. Anyway, now she's just obsessed about it. Absolutely *obsessed.*"

"Do you think he *is* looking for his mother?"

"Lord, no. When all's said and done, both of us know we were pretty damn lucky to land where we did. Let's face it, our real mothers are probably white-trash illiterates living up in the hills." She shook her head. "Still, Mother can be a handful. One time Horace told me this story about when she was little and somebody gave her a bunch of newborn chicks to take care of. Well, she started hugging those chicks so hard she strangled 'em. All of 'em. Literally loved them to death. Sometimes, I hate to say it, but I know just what those chickens must've felt like."

We were behind a slow-moving cement truck. Alice kept acceleraling and trying to pass, only to duck back into the lane to avoid oncoming cars.

"I swear, I am going to move away from this place as soon as I get up the money. Have you been to Atlanta? I take Eric down there every now and then to see Troy and Ralph, and we have a good old time. Now, that's a city! Mother doesn't like it. She thinks it's a bad influence on Eric, and she thinks Ralph's a bad influence for sure, but lordy, I tell you, at least in Atlanta a girl can go out and have fun without everybody in the universe calling up the papers to report it!"

"Ralph is Horace and Kathy's other kid, right?"

"Right."

"How's he a bad influence?"

Alice sighed. "Ralph came out of the closet last year, and some people around here are having a little trouble with it. Not that it wasn't perfectly obvious before, but you know how folks are. They believe what they want to believe until the truth hits them in the face." She flashed her brights and honked at the truck driver until he pulled onto the gravel shoulder to let her by.

"So anyway, Saturday I had a date, got all dolled up, hired a baby-sitter, the whole nine yards. This one was special—a banker from Knoxville I met when I was up there this summer. So we're just out having a nice time, a few drinks, dancing, get back to my house around one—not early, maybe, but no all-nighter either. We send the baby-sitter home, and then—well, you know how it is, late and all. I don't want to turn him out in the middle of the night, so he leaves Sunday morning around five. Eric doesn't have the slightest idea he's been there.

"Wouldn't you know it, who should call at seven a.m. but my dear mother, sniffing at the trail before it's barely even light out. How she pieced it all together I don't know, but I'll tell you one thing: this town's too damn small. How old am I, fourteen? Twenty-nine, for Jesus' sake! I said, 'Mother, my business is my business, and I'd appreciate you leaving it alone,' and she goes off on this tirade about how 'your father has built a loyal congregation through years of righteous living and sacrifices, and I'll be durned if you're going to jeopardize that by acting like a tramp.' A *tramp.* I said, 'Mother, give me a *break.* It's a free country and I am an adult, and furthermore *nothing* happened.' Which it didn't, that's what's so aggravating about the whole thing. And she says, 'It doesn't matter if you two stayed up all night eating cookies and playing Scrabble, I could care less. What matters is what it looks like.' And it's true, that's what matters to all her so-called friends, so that's what matters to her."

We came to a screeching halt behind a line of cars stopped at a train crossing. Alice slapped the dashboard in exasperation.

"Are we in a hurry?" I asked.

She looked over at me. "I suppose not," she said. "I just don't like waiting. It makes me feel like I'm dead or something."

We watched the train go by, the rhythm of its passage humming against our feet. It was a cargo train, black and old, chugging northward so slowly I could see the motion of the wheels as they turned. A person hiding in one of those cars, I was thinking, could jump off and roll without fear of being injured, like in the movies. They could roll off and wander into town, dust-covered and anonymous, and if anyone asked what they were doing there, they could say they were just passing through.

"You should thank your lucky stars you don't have a mother around to meddle in your business," Alice resumed. "I mean—oh lordy, what am I saying?" She clapped her hand to her forehead. "I'm sorry, Cassie, forgive me."

"Oh, it's okay," I said.

She smiled, then reached over and patted my knee. "Sometimes I'm as sensitive as a hard-boiled egg. But honestly, think of all the headaches you avoided. No matter how strict or irritable a daddy can be, he won't drive you up a wall, because men aren't nosy like that. And you can always tell him he has no idea what it's like to be female. That gets them every time."

The last car of the train rumbled past, and Alice beeped at the driver ahead of us to get moving. When we were back on the road she asked, "What does your daddy do?"

"He owns a restaurant outside Boston. Grasshopper's."

"That's a funny name. What's it like?"

"Oh, salads and pastas and whole-grain bread, that kind of place."

"Is your dad remarried?"

"No, but he might as well be. He's been living with somebody for years—Susan. They're about to have a baby."

"So if you don't mind my asking, why don't they just tie the knot?"

I looked out at the retail stores and garages we were passing as we approached town. "I asked him the same thing once. He was kind of evasive. He gave me all that stuff about marriage being a legal technicality that doesn't mean much to them, but I don't know. Before Susan came along, when I was little, he told me he'd never marry again."

"Because of your mother?"

I shrugged. "I think it's taken him a long time to get over her. I don't even know if he's over her yet. He's not very good at expressing his feelings."

"Have you ever met a man who was?" Alice laughed. "Well, don't tell Mother about them living together. It'll just confirm her worst suspicions."

At a four-way stop we turned left on Main Street, which took us straight into town: a three-block strip of buildings and a small public park, virtually deserted. A faded flag on a pole in the park fluttered limply in the breeze. The windows of the tallest buildings, three or four stories high, were dark and empty; half the storefronts were boarded up, handwritten FOR LEASE signs taped against dusty windows.

"This used to be a real nice place to shop, but there's not much left of it," Alice said, laboriously parallel-parking in front of the hardware store.

"Alice, there are spaces open all down the street," I said.

"I know. I just don't like to see cars all straggled out. Three in a row looks like a crowd." She turned off the engine and opened her door. "The mall finished it off down here. Let's face it, when you can choose from fourteen restaurants in the Food Court, not many folks are going to come downtown to eat at the Eagle." She slammed the door behind her. "People think, why go to the post office when you can get stamps at the checkout counter?"

"Why do you still come?"

"I don't know." She sighed. "Even Mother gave it up. You can't ever get what you need, you have to run all over the place to find stuff. And the crazies have taken over the park."

"The crazies?"

"From the mental home down the road. Out on furlough or whatever. It seems like there are more of them every day. I have to admit it makes me nervous having that place so close by, with Eric and all. Granddaddy used to call it the contagious hospital. Like being crazy was a sickness you could catch."

I looked at her. "That's William Carlos Williams."

"What?"

"He's a poet. My mother's favorite poet. 'Contagious hospital' is from one of his poems."

"Oh, well, *that* just figures," Alice said. "Bless his heart, I don't think Granddaddy ever had an original idea in his life."

As we walked along Main Street, Alice pointed out the park, the post office straight ahead, the spire of City Hall one block over. We went into a small dry-cleaning shop, and she picked up two blouses. "I guess I still come down here because nobody else does," she said, bending over the counter to write out a check. "You know what I mean. Like you moving into that old house nobody else wanted." She straightened up, putting the cap back on the pen.

Alice needed toothpaste, so we stepped into a drugstore on the corner and then went into a used-book store in the middle of the next block. As we left, a short, round, gray-haired woman was coming in.

"Alice Burns!" she said.

"Good morning, Mrs. Ford," said Alice. "This is my cousin Cassandra."

Mrs. Ford grasped my hand between hers and peered at me. "Spitting image of Amory. Very pleased to meet you."

"Cassie's a sculptor. She's moving down here from New York."

"You don't say. Where will you be living, dear?"

"Out in the family house off Briarcliff," Alice answered.

"Clyde's house?"

"Clyde's on Red Pond Road now, Mrs. Ford. Has been for years."

"I know that, but . . . well, never mind. I thought they were going to sell that house, is all."

Alice smiled, all teeth. "I can't imagine where you heard that," she said. "I'm afraid you'll have to excuse us. We're running late."

"Heavens, don't let me keep you! But tell me, how's Clyde feeling these days? She hasn't been to services lately, and I've been a bit concerned."

"Well, you should give her a call and find out," Alice said tartly. "As far as I know, she's just fine."

"I'll do that. I'll give her a call." She turned to me. "Nice to meet you—tell me your name again?"

"Cassie. Cassie Simon."

She raised her eyebrows. "Oh, yes," she said. "Ellen's girl."

Alice suggested that we get a cup of coffee across the street at the Eagle, the shabby diner she'd pointed out to me earlier, but the place looked closed. We walked over anyway, and as we got closer I could see a woman in a pink uniform playing solitaire on the lunch counter inside. We sat at a booth in front, facing the street, and the waitress brought menus.

"That May Ford is the biggest gossip in town," Alice said as soon as the waitress left.

"She seems harmless enough."

Alice shook her head. "That's just an act. She's lethal. From what I've heard, after your mother died, May Ford and all the other 'harmless' ladies in town turned their backs on Clyde. It hurt her a whole lot."

"Why would they do that?"

"I don't know," she said. "I really don't know."

"There's so much about Clyde I can't figure out. She's so weird about Amory, and about . . . a lot of things, really. She seems almost angry."

"She *is* angry," Alice said, nodding her head. "She's been like that for years. I remember one time when I was little I was over at their house—the house you're moving into—playing in the yard. I had to go to the bathroom or something, so I went inside and found her and Granddaddy in the kitchen, fighting. It wasn't like I'd never seen an argument before—Mother and Daddy used to fight all the time—but there was something about the way she was grabbing hold of him, digging her fingernails into his arms, that just freaked me out. It was awful. Her face was all twisted and red, and she was spitting at him, and there was blood running down his arms from where her nails had broken the skin. He didn't even move, he just stood there with this strange, glazed expression I'll never forget, like he hated her and felt sorry for her at the same time, like . . . like . . . I don't know—now that I think about it, he'd probably been drinking.

"They didn't see me standing there, so I just crept away, went out and peed behind the barn. After a while Clyde came out on the porch and called me in for lunch, and it was like everything was fine again, except Granddaddy wasn't there. But the whole time we were at the table she was singing some tune under her breath. I asked her what it was, and she told me it was the song he was playing the night they met."

"What song?"

She shivered. "I didn't ask. I've never told anybody about that. I don't like to think about it."

The waitress came by to take our orders. "So," Alice said abruptly, "what do you think of your newfound relations? Starting with Chester."

"Really sweet. There seems to be something kind of sad about him, though," I said cautiously.

"Well, he's got worse luck in the love department than I do. See, he's in love with his mama, the perfect little homemaker, and nobody else can measure up. But I don't feel too sorry for him. In a few years, when he inherits Horace's business, there'll be gold diggers lining up around the block."

The waitress brought two coffees. I added cream to mine and stirred it. "I didn't really talk to Kathy. What makes her so perfect?"

"Well, she's as sweet as can be, and she just dotes on her 'boys,' Horace and Chester and Ralph." Alice shook her head. "The whole situation with Ralph has been hard on her, though. Horace isn't exactly thrilled at the idea of his son being gay, but I think he'll come around one of these days.

"They're all nice people," she continued. "We've been lumped together for so many Thanksgivings and Christmases that we have a lot to talk about, and having a lot to talk about makes us feel like we've got something in common. Even if we don't." She ripped open two packets of Sweet'n Low and a packet of creamer and added them to her coffee.

"Do Ralph and your brother ever come home?"

"Ralph doesn't much anymore. I mean, would you, if you were him? Troy used to, but Mother's always clawing at him to stay, and he can't stand that." She was staring out the plate-glass window. I followed her gaze to the flag in the park, wilting against the pole in the still heat of afternoon. "Soon as I can get up the money I'm going to Atlanta to join them," she said. "I really, really am. I'm tired of this one-horse town."

When we got back to Clyde's, Alice stopped at the curb with the motor running. "About what I told you. About Clyde." She leaned forward as if she thought we might be overheard. "I'd appreciate it if you wouldn't repeat that story to anyone."

"I won't."

"Well, I know. I'm just making sure. Things have a way of slipping out sometimes, at least they do with me." She shifted in her seat.

"Clyde is just about the proudest person I know. She'd *really* be upset if she thought we were talking about her."

"I'll be careful," I said. "I'd hate to see her *really* upset."

Alice grinned. "Boy, watch out!" We started to giggle. "Hey," she said, "sometime soon maybe we can go swimming or something. Mother and Daddy belong to a club." She grimaced. "I guess that means I have to get back on her good side."

"That won't be too hard, will it?"

"Not if I kiss her manicured toenails and beg forgiveness."

"One minute of groveling for a whole afternoon in the pool. That sounds reasonable."

"Sure, why not?"

As I walked toward the house I saw Clyde in the kitchen window, staring out at us. She looked small and frail, with her thin white hair and thick glasses. She's just a little old lady, I was thinking, just a sad, lonely little person. I smiled and caught her eye, and she ducked out of sight.

After dinner I called my dad from an extension in the bedroom. He wanted to know why I hadn't seen the house yet.

"Clyde's holding me hostage," I whispered.

"What's the ransom? Do I have to pay?"

"No. I think the ransom is the house."

He laughed. "I never say I told you so, so I'm not going to start now."

"Oh, go ahead. It'll make you feel better."

"Told you so. So how do you like your relatives?"

"I like them," I said. "Alice is great."

"She's Elaine's daughter, right?"

"Yeah, don't hold it against her."

"This is purely academic information for me, Cassie. I'm not planning on coming down there anytime soon. I'll let you conduct the field study."

I twirled the phone cord between my fingers. "You know, Dad, I'm kidding, but I'm serious. There's something strange about all of this. I get the feeling Clyde really doesn't want me to move in."

"Well, that's understandable," he said. "She did live in that house for almost forty years. Giving it up to you will be like giving up a big part of her life. I'm sure she's incredibly ambivalent."

"I can understand that," I said, chewing my lip, "but for some reason I get the feeling there's more to it. It just constantly seems like I'm overstepping some invisible line."

He sighed. "Don't make it more than it is, Cassie. She's a difficult woman, always has been, and she's not getting any younger."

"Okay. You're probably right." I remembered my first encounter with her. "Clyde says they all think I want something from them."

"Well, that doesn't surprise me. They're not the most generous-minded bunch you'll ever meet. And to be fair, you can hardly blame them for being suspicious. Look, you're a complete stranger. They don't know you, so how can they possibly know why you went down there? I'm still not sure myself. Give them time, Cassie."

"Maybe this was all a big mistake."

"Maybe, but consider it grist for your artistic mill. Someday they'll call it your blue period."

"Oh, Dad."

"I'm always here if you need me, honey," he said. "If you want to come home, you know you always can."

I thought about Susan and the baby in the small apartment above the restaurant. The place had been crowded when Dad and I lived there alone. "Thanks," I said, "but I think I'll tough it out here for a while. Anyway, Horace is coming by tomorrow to take me out to the house."

"The great escape, huh?"

"I plan to be armed and dangerous."

Drew picked up the phone, breathless, on the second ring. "Cassie, I'm running out the door, can I call you back?"

"Where are you going?"

"To a party at Mara's."

"Oh?"

"It's her boyfriend's birthday."

"Her boyfriend?"

"You know, the chain-smoking Israeli," he said, impatient. "Look, I really have to go. How is everything?"

"Oh, Drew, I'm not even going to talk to you now. Call me later."

"You're mad."

"No, I just don't understand what the big rush is."

"Oh, for God's sake, Cassie, it's New York, that's what the big rush is. Joel's waiting for me downstairs in a taxi."

"Joel, huh?"

"Yes, Joel."

"So you're seeing Joel now."

"Don't start with me, I'm warning you."

"Will you tell me everything later?"

"Maybe."

"Drew . . . "

"What? What?"

"You've forgotten me already," I said petulantly. "And now Joel is moving in on my territory."

"Honey, if I'm lucky Joel's going to be on territory you've never even *imagined*."

"I don't want to know."

He laughed. "I'll call you later in the week."

"No, I'll call you. You don't have my number."

"Oh, yeah."

"And Drew? I know deep down that you're sad I left. You're drowning your sorrows in parties and men, and I understand."

"Is that what I'm doing? How long does this mourning period last? A while longer, I hope."

"Have fun tonight."

"I will. Give my best to the Absent Other. *Goodbye!*"

When Ellen went north and stayed I felt like everything I had lived for was meaningless. Amory didn't approve of what she was doing, taking up with a troublemaker who didn't have any money, harboring draft dodgers and inciting the blacks to riot. He said society had certain rules and you had to live by them. But in my secret heart of hearts I was a little proud of her, standing up for what she believed in that way. Amory never stood up for anything in his life except to give a lady his seat. He said that the country had its big problems and we had our small ones and neither should meddle in the other's affairs. But Ellen said it wasn't like that at all: we had a responsibility to meddle. If we murdered and raped and pillaged we were accountable for it in the courts of the land, and if our country killed innocent people, sanctioned and encouraged discrimination, it should be held accountable too. Amory would shake his head and say, "Whose side are you on?"

"I'm on your side, Dad," she'd say. "The side of the people."

"The people are idiots," he'd answer.

She cut her beautiful hair short like a boy's, and her husband grew his long. From the back it looked like she was the husband and he was the wife. The last time she and Ed visited together, she was wearing a skimpy dress in a sickly green color and he had on a shirt with big bright flowers all over it. It was kind of embarrassing. They drove a white Volkswagen bus with giant cheerful butterfly stickers on the doors, little Cassandra in a car seat in the back.

Ellen was the first of the neighborhood children to get political, and it made a big splash. Horace and Elaine were mortified. Larry was trying to get started on his preaching career, and Elaine didn't want anything to sully his reputation. "You know how people talk, Mama," she said. "Why can't Ellen just behave herself and act normal?" Taking Edgar aside one evening, Horace told him that he suspected him of brainwashing Ellen and was considering turning him over to the police, and furthermore, it was about time Edgar stopped acting like a freak and started taking responsibility for himself. It was time to act like the husband and father he was and make some money.

But I knew it wasn't Edgar's fault. Ellen had always been different. Horace was captain of the high school football team, Elaine was crowned Sweetwater Sweetheart, but Ellen hung around with another crowd. I found cigarettes in her pockets when I did the laundry. She'd buy New York magazines and try to imitate the fashions she saw. Elaine told me that people were laughing behind her back, but Ellen didn't seem to care. In fact, she was almost proud of it. She scrawled poetry on napkins, left paperbacks all over the house: Kerouac, Ferlinghetti, Ginsberg, names I saw for the first time and then read some of myself, trying to understand the person she wanted so desperately to become. Funny, but she was more like the Amory I had fallen in love with than either of the others were. She was high-strung, nervous as a racehorse. She wanted to live the kind of life Jack Kerouac talked about, to burn like a fabulous Roman candle.

Ellen wasn't the only one to leave, but she was the only one to stay away. She got a big scholarship, which she'd applied for without even telling us. One day I returned from doing errands to find her standing in the kitchen by the sink, clutching a letter in one hand and sobbing. I threw down my packages and rushed over to her, thinking maybe she was pregnant or expelled from school. I grabbed the letter out of her hand and read: "The Admissions Committee of Wellesley College is pleased to offer you a place in its Freshman Class of 1958." I looked at her in astonishment. "I'm finally getting the hell out of here," she said, tears streaming down her face.

Horace had left for UT Knoxville two years before, but it never really felt like he was gone. On Saturdays Jeb Gregory and I would take the girls to see him play football (Amory wasn't really interested), and on Sundays Horace came home for church and dinner. Sunday afternoons he'd sit at the dining room table concentrating on his books as long as he could—fifteen minutes or so at a stretch—until one of the Clifford boys from over the hill came by to toss a few. Horace flunked his second semester, but he met Kathy at a Memorial Day barbecue at his fraternity and she convinced him to take summer classes, so he stuck it out. They were married a year later. We saw them every weekend.

The summer before Ellen left she spent a lot of time in her room with the door shut. I'd go up and stand in the hall, straining to hear. I was worried about her. She was smoking openly now, quarreling with Amory all the time. She wanted to learn how to drive and he said she was too young. "You taught Horace at my age," she'd yell, and Amory would say, "Horace didn't smoke cigarettes. Horace respected my rules." This made her even madder, and she started going out at night with reckless boys in fast cars. They'd drive up to the house, wheels screeching, and honk the horn for her to come out. The screen door banging shut behind her echoed in the stillness like a dirty word.

The day she left for college was a scorcher. There was no wind at all; the air smelled of rhododendron, so thick and humid that it was like walking though a hot loaf of bread. Amory took off from work to drive her to the bus in Atlanta, and they almost didn't make it. She was up in her bedroom getting ready while he stood at the bottom of the stairs, fuming with impatience, hollering, "What in the name of God are you doing up there?" She hollered back, "Nothing in the name of God, Daddy," and came out half an hour later with hair the color of copper and bright red nails, wearing black skintight pants and a black sleeveless cardigan. Amory almost refused to take her.

As she left she took my shoulders and brushed my cheek with her own, imitating a kiss she must have seen in a movie. "Don't let them get to you, Mama," she whispered. "Leaving isn't so hard." I held her hand and tried to smile, but my mouth was trembling. She had a distracted look in her eyes, as if she were already gone. Each time she came home after that—Christmases, summer vacations—that look became more and more familiar. After a while it wasn't like she was coming home anymore; it was like she was just passing through.

Horace came to Clyde's around eight o'clock on Tuesday morning to pick me up. He wore a gray suit that was a little tight through the waist, a pink tie, Reebok sneakers, and a red baseball cap. His neck was burnt. He kept playing with his cap, taking it off and putting it on again, stepping back in a restless dance when he removed it, as if he were about to bow with a flourish. When he arrived Clyde and I were at the kitchen table reading the paper.

"Get yourself some grits and a biscuit, son, they're on the stove," she said.

"Thank you, Mother, I think I will." He banged around for a minutes, then came over and sat down. "Fred Conroy's leaving town," he said. "I'm putting his house on the market today."

"Well, I'll be." Clyde was scanning the color ads. "Where're they going?"

He spread his napkin on his lap. "Kansas. Wife's got folks out there." He started to eat, reaching for the salt. "Sad story, really. That restaurant never had a chance. Tried to tell him, but he wouldn't listen."

Clyde got up. She went over to the counter, took out a pair of scissors, and settled back into her chair to clip coupons. "It couldn't decide what it was," she said. "Too expensive for a burger place but not somewhere you'd want to go special. It scared people off."

He nodded. "Now I hear Harold and June Watkins want to buy it, expand their barbecue business."

"Doesn't surprise me." She cut out another coupon. "They're greedy people. Can't be contented with what they've got."

Horace shook his head energetically, his mouth full of grits. "You can't say that, Ma! That's what's so darn special about this country. If I told my kids once I told them a hundred times, what you want is here for the asking. You just got to work a little, that's all."

"Well, those people are vultures, if you ask me. Waiting until a man's down and going after all he's got."

"They probably saved him from bankruptcy."

"It's not Christian."

Horace stood up. He took his cap off and put it back on. "They just want to make a living like everybody else. God bless 'em if they do a better job of it."

"I'll never eat there," she muttered.

"Well, Cassandra, you ready to see that old barn up there on the hill? I got about an hour to show you the place." Horace looked at his watch. "Just under an hour. We better get moving."

"I'll be out when you get back," Clyde said without looking up. She shuffled the coupons into a neat pile. "I'll leave the garage open."

I followed him to his car, a green Buick Le Sabre, and he opened the passenger door for me. The plush gray interior smelled of musk. When Horace got in he leaned over confidentially and said, "We all wear seat belts in this neck of the woods." He sat back and buckled up, and I did too. "Lots of kids around here get their license and start drinking at the same time. They say there's not much else to do. Next thing you know, they've gone and got themselves killed, and probably killed somebody else in the process." He pulled out of the driveway, looking over his shoulder. His suit jacket hung open awkwardly, stretched tight at the armpit.

"Same in New York, except with semiautomatics," I said.

"So I heard." He was driving with his left hand, his right arm dangling across the top of the seat. "How do you like it down here so far? About what you expected?"

I thought for a moment. "I didn't know what to expect. I was surprised when I saw supermarkets—I guess I thought there'd be a general store with barrels of sugar candy and bolts of cotton behind the cash register."

He grinned. "Wait till you see the Fair Oaks Mall. They've got escalators and everything."

"I passed it yesterday with Alice. Eighty-nine stores."

"And a Food Court." He slowed for a red light, looked both ways, and glided through it. "What about Clyde? You getting along okay with her? She giving you a hard time?"

"We're getting along fine."

"Well, that's good," he said. "'Cause, *whoo-ee,* she can be tough to deal with."

Out my side window, fields were flashing by: rich red dirt, lush green crops, the occasional scarecrow in the distance. I could see farmers riding tractors, testing the soil. Clusters of cows dotted the sloping hills in the distance like flocks of birds. Though it was early, the sun was hot.

"She wasn't always like this," Horace was saying. "Must be her age or something turned her cranky. She used to have the sweetest disposition you ever saw." He flipped the sun visor down and up again, then reached over my legs to the glove compartment and retrieved a pair of sunglasses. "You know, she loved your mama like nobody else. I think she would've given her own life if she could've saved Ellen's."

"Really?"

"I don't think she ever got over it."

We sat in silence for a few miles.

"Yesterday we were looking at old photos and she got kind of upset," I said. "I was asking some questions, and she—she acted like I was attacking her or something."

"Pictures of your mama?"

"Yes."

He shook his head. "Ellen's death just tore her up. I think for her it's as fresh as if it happened yesterday."

We pulled off the road onto a dirt drive marked by a wooden stake. Horace told me that the turnoff was exactly four and a half miles past the intersection of 622 and Briarcliff Road, on Briarcliff going south. "You'll know when you're close because of that big old sign for the Cooperative Tire Center we just passed on the left," he explained.

The drive was overgrown with grass and lined with orange and yellow wildflowers. A gully ran alongside it, and beyond was a stand of trees. After about five hundred yards the trees thinned out, and we wound up an incline to the left. As we reached the top I could see a large white house sitting alone on the next rise, with the deep-rutted drive leading up to it.

"Well, there it is," he said, pointing as if he wasn't sure I'd seen it.

From a distance the two-story structure looked solid and imposing, even grand, as if still inhabited by a prosperous family. As we got closer, though, I could see the results of years of neglect: the screen door hanging against the frame, one-hinged; broken windows on either side; peeling paint. Tall dry grasses, wild and yellow-green, poked up through banister spokes and porch slats.

"What's wrong with that dang door?" Horace said, peering out the windshield. "I swear, every time I come out here there's something new to fix."

He stopped the car and we got out. Beer bottles and crumpled cigarette packages littered the ground near the front steps. Horace told me that local kids had been coming up here to get into trouble late at night. They weren't bad kids, just mischievous, but he'd see to it that this kind of activity stopped right away. We made our way to the porch, Horace kicking at bottles with the side of his shoe. He had assumed a resigned air, as if he was showing me the place against his will.

"Nobody says you got to live here, you know. And I, for one, won't blame you a bit if you decide to let me get rid of the place for you and put some money in your pocket. I'm sure we could sell it in a handshake. This is prime land."

He tested the steps one by one, holding out his arm to keep me back until he was sure they were safe. Making his way across the porch, he jumped on each slat first with his right foot, then with his left, like he was tap-dancing in slow motion. When he got to the screen door he moved it aside cautiously and tilted it so it leaned against the house. Waving me over, he took out his keys.

"Got to put new panes in these," he said, nodding his head toward the windows, "but otherwise, so far so good. The inside should be just as Clyde left it."

The door swung inward, and we were in a dim hallway. To the right I could see the kitchen, to the left a large room with furniture piled up in it. Straight ahead the hall narrowed and a staircase led to the second floor. I wandered slowly into the kitchen, with Horace following. It was narrow and bare except for an old white refrigerator with rounded corners, a gas stove, and a porcelain sink set into a built-in counter that ran the length of the wall. The wallpaper, curling at the edges and faded from the sun, was pale yellow. A window above the sink faced the drive. The room smelled faintly of pine.

Horace examined the refrigerator and told me he thought it should work fine. He pointed to electrical outlets and tried the water faucets and the stove, which needed to be hooked up. He opened all the cupboards and drawers and, crouching down, ran a finger along the baseboard. "You like cats? Might want to get one," he said. "There's a nest of mice in here somewhere."

The ground floor was designed so that each room led into the next: kitchen, dining room, living room, hall. I followed Horace through the large dining room, where he pointed out a dusty gold and-crystal chandelier and a large cherrywood sideboard. In the adjoining living room he showed me the carved mahogany fireplace Amory had found at an abandoned plantation near Knoxville. With no shades or curtains, the rooms were brilliant with sunlight.

Back in the kitchen again, Horace opened the door to the basement. We went downstairs and he explained the fuse box, the water heater, how to check for gas leaks.

At the landing on the way to the second floor I stumbled over a stuffed animal, badly worn and missing an eye. I picked it up.

"That was Ralph's. Must've been left in the moving." Horace took it from me and rubbed its ear between his fingers. "He used to carry this thing everywhere." He dropped it and continued up the stairs.

"What's Ralph doing now?" I asked.

"He says he's an actor, but as far as I can tell he's just waiting tables." His voice was clipped. "He's sharing an apartment in Atlanta with another cousin of yours."

"I know—Troy."

"Yeah. They both have what you might call abnormal life-styles. I guess Troy's in some kind of band."

"Have you ever been down there to visit?"

"No." Horace looked at his watch. "I'm about out of time. Let's get a move on."

We glanced around the second floor, one bathroom and three bedrooms filled with box springs and mattresses and bureaus. I asked Horace to show me the room that had been my mother's, and he led me into a bedroom in the southwest corner, with windows on both sides. "Twin beds," he said, pointing to two walls. "Ellen and Elaine had to share. I got my own room, of course, being the only boy." He motioned toward a dark walnut bedframe with a carved headboard leaning against the wall. "I believe Elaine took her bed for Alice. That must be your mother's."

I went over and ran my hand slowly along one of the uprights. It was covered with dust, but the wood was smooth.

"If you want to use it, all you need is a mattress." He grinned. "Of course, that'd be assuming you weren't expecting visitors. A single bed is awful small."

On the way downstairs Horace said he'd send somebody over to fix the screen door. He measured the broken windows for glass and jumped up and down on a few more boards. He told me who to call for plumbing and gas and electricity.

As we stood on the front porch I thanked him for showing me around. "I know it must be strange for you," I said. "I mean, it's your house. You grew up here."

"I never liked it much. It was too small for the five of us."

"But still. All the memories you must have—"

"Ma hated this place. She felt trapped out here in the country with nobody around except us kids. They fought about it all the time." He laughed a little, removing and replacing his cap. "As for the memories, I'd just as soon forget."

"There must've been *some* good times," I insisted.

"Well, sure. Christmases were generally pretty nice, as I recall. I used to like to hunt out there in those woods." He leaned against the porch railing. "To be honest, though, I try not to think about the past too much. There's no sense in dwelling on things you can't change."

I nodded, running my toe along a crack between the wooden slats.

"What's done is done."

I heard an edge in his voice and looked up.

"Cassandra—I don't know how to say this. It's just . . . well . . . "

"What?"

"I'd hate to see you looking for something that isn't here."

"Like what?"

"Like I don't know. Whatever it is you packed up and came down here looking for."

"But—"

"You got to understand, we don't talk about Ellen," he said. "We don't talk about what happened. Your being here—well, you stir up memories folks are still trying to forget. It's not your fault—that's just the way it is. So what I'm saying is, what's over is over. Ellen's dead. That's all there is to it."

"So what you're saying is, don't ask any questions. Leave well enough alone."

Horace shrugged, looking down into the yard, his hands in his pockets. After a moment he wheeled around and started down the steps to the car. "You could say that. Come on, I'll drop you back home."

part three

It is somewhere in that house. He buried it somewhere the same week we buried Ellen. I tried to find it but it was all he had left and he wouldn't give it up. He wanted Cassandra to find it. I'm sure he thought that if she found it she would forgive him, though what difference that makes now is beyond me. In the years of silence and then of waiting I searched when he wasn't looking, under floorboards, behind furniture, tapping the walls for hollow spaces, scanning for new nails. Sometimes I wondered if he took the pages one by one and burned them, until nothing was left but ash; sometimes I speculated that he threw the box into the reservoir, the pages inside bloating like dead skin, ink seeping into the water like blood from a wound. But I knew him too well, and I knew he couldn't die with what he knew. He hated keeping secrets.

And maybe he really loved that woman; I don't know. Maybe he would have left me for her if he'd had any backbone at all. She might have gone the way of all the rest if he had been more careful or if she had been someone else. But he was terrible at keeping secrets, and he had a fatal habit of forgetting that some things aren't meant to be found out, not ever. He went and destroyed our child and then he was destroyed himself, and both of us had to live with all those lies and truths until the end. I had been the one, always, to suffer for his sins, but now things were different. He learned what it meant to feel pain. He learned what it meant, but he'd never had to build up a resistance to it, so it broke him.

I moved into the old house the day after Horace took me to see it. When I left Clyde's she was quiet, as closed and expressionless as a cat. She acted as if we might never see each other again and it didn't particularly matter. She waved me off quickly and went back inside.

"She's never been much for goodbyes," Horace said, shrugging. "She's just that way."

He started his car, and I got into the station wagon to follow him. I didn't look back to see if she was at the kitchen sink, but I imagined her standing there. I thought I could feel her eyes on me. But I didn't feel bad. I don't like goodbyes either.

I spent the first few days cleaning and scrubbing, the smell of ammonia constantly in my nose. The wooden staircase and banister were coated with a sticky film; the wallpaper was faded and dirty. Scouring the kitchen linoleum on my hands and knees, I discovered that the floral pattern was blue and red, not the blue-green and pink it originally appeared to be. The bathrooms—one upstairs, one down—were fairly clean, but the pipes were rusted and none of the plumbing worked. Until the plumber came on the third day I had to haul water from an old pump two hundred yards from the house and go outside to pee.

By the second day the telephone and answering machine I'd brought from New York were hooked up and ready to use. The phone sat on the floor of the living room like a turtle in its shell. I couldn't bring myself to call anyone. I knew I could never convince people that I liked it here and things were fine, because even as I mouthed the words to myself they sounded hollow. I *was* fine, but I was lonely, and it was the kind of loneliness that crept through phone lines, permeated the pages of a letter. It was what everyone expected, what they were looking for. So I kept my distance.

I guess if I'd tried I could have told them about the view from the dining room windows, down a slope covered with tiger lilies and the odd mountain ash to a tiny pond in front of a stand of trees. I might have described how in the mornings as I lay in bed the slope outside my window would be covered with a sheet of dew, glistening in the sunlight, glinting through the rain. I might have attempted to convey what I felt when sometimes, late at night, I thought I could see shadows of people from long ago and hear voices echoing in the darkness. And how, in the morning it seemed like everything had been swept clean.

But I just wasn't ready to tell anyone any of these things. So I held onto my loneliness, almost as a shield, and the phone stayed silent.

By the evening of the third day I was ready for contact. "Do you want to hear about the ants?" I asked my dad, flopping down on the bed.

I thought I'd never get rid of them. Three hours after I scrubbed the kitchen with disinfectant and sprayed with insecticide they'd be back, a few at a time, and before long the place would be swarming again. Finally, in desperation, I called an exterminator, who discovered an enormous and well-established colony under the floorboards behind the refrigerator. Two hours and forty-five dollars later, the ants were gone.

"If I have to," he said.

I kicked off my sneakers and adjusted the phone on my shoulder.

"Well, Horace warned me about the mice, but they were easy. I put flour on the floor and traced them to the dining room, and then all I had to do was sprinkle poison against the baseboard."

"Brilliant detective work."

"I thought so, but it's kind of disgusting. I have to wear sneakers all the time to avoid the dead ones. I've been finding them all over the place with white dust on their noses, like little coke addicts."

"Charming."

"Then I found these incredible birds' nests hanging from the rafters on the front porch. Great big circles of droppings underneath. And it's so sad, sometimes the little baby birdies, birdlings, whatever they're called—"

"Chicks."

"Right. Anyway, they fall out before they can fly, and they land on the porch—"

"I get the idea."

"Yeah. So I took down the nests. But I put up a birdhouse I found in the basement, and they seem to like that."

"So-o-o—what about the ants?"

"I was just getting to them," I said. When I paused I could hear his patience hanging on the line between us. "You're not bored, are you, Dad?"

"Oh, no, Cassie. No, no, no."

I sighed. "This is important, Dad. I'm taking control here. This is a new thing for me."

"Didn't you have cockroaches in Brooklyn?"

"Oh, sure, but those were rented. These pests I own."

"I see," he said. "The ants. Tell me about the ants."

"There's all this old furniture here," I told Drew . "An old couch, a couple of musty beds, a few tables and chairs."

"Don't worry about it. Just throw it all out and go to Ikea."

"No, no, you don't understand," I said. "This is great stuff. Ikea is pretend furniture, particleboard. This is *real* wood."

"Oh, *real* wood," he said.

"Yes, it's amazing, Drew, really amazing. All this stuff I've never paid any attention to before, like furniture. I've even been getting up at the crack of dawn to go to yard sales."

"Yard sales."

"You wouldn't believe the things people throw out. Yesterday I bought this great old chest of drawers with about ten layers of paint on it for ten dollars. I'm going to strip it. I got the turpentine and paint thinner and everything. I want to refinish all the furniture in the house."

He clicked his tongue.

"What?"

"This is only the first step, Cassie. Next you'll be making your own bread. Then you'll start wearing bonnets."

"Funny you should mention that. I bought some yeast yesterday," I said. "Good night, John-Boy."

"Good night, Mary Ellen."

Truth. You want the truth? The truth is I was born on October 14, 1917, in a house with huge white columns and a ten-foot-high front door, on a wide, tree-lined street in Chattanooga, Tennessee. They didn't tell me until my wedding day that I'd had an identical twin who died at birth. She and Ellen float around me like shadows. The truth is I married not for love but to get away from my father, whose raging possessiveness almost destroyed me. The truth is that when Ellen died my world exploded into a thousand jagged pieces; and I let Cassandra and her father crawl on their own bloodied knees back to the North, leaving us to lick our wounds and snarl at each other.

Nothing I've ever thought I had or cared for has really been my own, even when it seemed that the love I had to give must be enough to claim it. And I know that covetousness is a sin, but there are worse sins I can think of: betrayal, for one, lying, theft. Time after time, in a pattern that became sickeningly familiar, the illusions I had were shattered. It took me years to recognize that the truth can be as brittle, as deceptive, as colored glass.

When my mother was in labor with me the birthing was so difficult, the story goes, that the midwife wouldn't tell my daddy anything except to get out of the house for the afternoon and come back when it was over. In a state of nervous agitation Daddy roamed the streets of Chattanooga, drinking from a whiskey flask and smoking one cigar after another, wandering in and out of boutiques scattered down Market Street. Somewhere along the way he went into a china shop and bought a figurine, a tiny deer, and then, in the excitement of returning home to a healthy newborn baby (even if it was a girl), promptly forgot all about it. Not until days later, going through the pockets of his coat in search of something else, did he find the object, still wrapped in tissue. He put it on the mantelpiece above the fireplace in my room, and every year after that on my birthday he brought home another glass animal to add to my collection. In the end I had seventeen figurines in all.

When I was growing up in Chattanooga the town was bustling with the railroad and industry, and people walked with a sense of purpose. Now it's gutted and blank, like the burned-out center of a piece of paper when you hold a match too close: jagged, curling edges, that charred smell that goes up into your nose and gets behind your eyes. But then, when I walked along the street with Daddy, the air was crisp even on the hottest days and all the men smiled and tipped their hats and looked me right in the eye and said, "Hello, Miss Constance. It's a fine day," and I smiled shyly and swayed behind Daddy's big gray-suited form. He tipped his hat to them in return and squeezed my hand as if he was proud of me for being pretty and inspiring comment.

And the only place I wanted to be then was with my daddy, walking down those hot friendly streets on his lunch hour, stopping every so often to talk to someone of importance who wanted a minute of his time. They all seemed to want a minute of his time. And I, who had his time and his heart whenever I wanted them, grew up knowing that he would give me wholly and unconditionally what others begged for piece by piece, getting a little or none at all, depending on Daddy's whims.

But eventually Daddy's whims came to claim me. I found out what it was like to be ignored on the street, or worse, simply acknowledged. As I grew, shedding plain frocks for full skirts and blouses, he changed too, as if he didn't know how to treat me. As if I were a stranger inhabiting his house. He started hitting me: one time he slapped my face for staying out past nine; another time he left a welt on my neck for sharing a soda with a boy he didn't think was good enough.

Once when I was high school he came home from work at six o'clock and demanded to know where I was. "She's gone for a walk with some friends," my mother told him, and when he pressed her—"What friends? What friends?"—my mother said, "Nice boys, Charles. She'll be home safe and sound, don't you worry." He sat in his study waiting for me for four hours, refusing food or company, waiting with his hands clenched on the leather blotter on his mahogany desk while the weak white southwestern light drained from the windows into dusk into darkness.

When I got home my mother met me in the hallway, white-lipped, and dug into my arm with her long, bony fingers, whispering, "Your father is in the study," looking into my eyes like she was the one in trouble, like she wanted me to save her from what was coming. She was a wickless candle to me, dripping the thinnest kind of wax. She could no more stand up for herself or anyone else than she could spark a flame. I felt such contempt for her meekness that I almost welcomed my father's brutality. At least it was something I could feel.

When I opened the door to the study I could sense the heat of my father across the room in the darkness, a solid black bulk amid the dim outlines of furniture. I saw or imagined that I could see the whiteness of his knuckles, like teeth in a skull, sitting on the desk. When he spoke it was as if the desk spoke; the voice was deep and level, and seemed too large to have come from a man, even a man as substantial as my father.

"Where have you been, Constance Whitfield?" he asked, but it wasn't really a question or even—the usual tone—an accusation. This time the words seemed merely the wrapping for his rage. He spoke my name like he'd never heard it before, like a judge, enunciating the syllables clearly and decisively, as if they spelled out my crime.

What could I tell him? I had been down by the tracks with Willy Hughes and Sam Allen, who was Jewish and whose banker father Daddy hated with a passion. We had been sitting by the tracks, that's all, mashing pennies under trains when they came by, and not thinking about the time, and telling jokes. To tell the truth, I had known in the back of my brain somewhere that I should leave, and I watched the sun drop, pale and tired, behind Lookout Mountain with a sinking feeling of my own. But the air was fresh, and Willy and Sam made me laugh, and the longer I stayed out the more invincible I felt, so that by the time we all picked up to go I thought that maybe Daddy would be able to see the fresh air on my cheeks and the sparkle in my eyes and he would understand.

He didn't see a thing except that I was late and disheveled, and there was something about me that didn't seem to care. I don't think he was worried, even; I don't think he had ever thought about the possibility of danger, the way Mama might have done. For him the only danger was that I was out with a boy in the darkness, and not even a boy who hurt me: his greatest suspicion and creeping fear was that I was out with a boy who touched me and I liked it.

"Where have you been, Constance Whitfield?" he asked again, and then he leapt at me across the desk, sending papers and pens and his gilt-edged blotter and a paperweight in the shape of a Confederate soldier flying to the floor. When the blow came, the back of his hand across my cheek, it didn't surprise me. I had been expecting it. He stood there, shaken and trembling, and asked me again where I'd been, and still I didn't answer, and he hit me again and again, the flat of his open hand on my other cheek and across my nose. A thin trickle of blood ran from my nose into my mouth, and the taste was thick and metallic-sweet. I bent forward and let the blood drip onto my cotton dress, staining it with scarlet streaks; I shook my head a little to further the blotchy proof of his abuse. I didn't say anything and I wasn't crying, and before I left the room I told him that I had received notification that day from the Chattanooga Teachers College and that I would matriculate in the fall and live in the dormitory with the other young ladies in the program.

He stood with his shoulders hunched forward and his hands on the desktop like a bear on its hind legs, his great head swaying back and forth, and it was crazy but even as my face stung and blood spattered my dress I wanted to reach out to him because it seemed as if he was the one who was hurt. I was beyond him now, and he knew it; he could hit me, but it wouldn't stop me from growing up, and it wouldn't stop me from leaving. But I didn't reach out to him, and when I left the room he was still standing there, motionless.

Mama was waiting and met me with a gasp, her hand over her mouth, and then hurried me into the kitchen, where she sat me down at the table and sponged the drying blood off my face and neck. We heard the door to Daddy's study open and close and then the front door open and close and neither of us said a word. There didn't seem to be anything to say.

Later that night, it must have been two or three, I was woken by the slam of the front door and sat bolt upright in my bed, my heart pumping faster than the train. The sound of Daddy's drunken jagged steps and labored breathing as he made his way upstairs, crashing into the banister and cursing to himself, scared me in a way that his anger never had. I heard my doorknob rattle and then the door was flung open, banging against a dresser, and Daddy staggered in. In the light from the hallway I could see sweat beading on his forehead and mustache, and I could almost see the bourbon thick around him like a glow.

"Constance, your name is a blasphemy," he said. "It's a lie. A joke." He laughed and wiped his face with his forearm, stepping back and steadying himself. "You used to be a good girl. You'd come to the office and everyone would say that Charles Whitfield's daughter was a beauty—do you remember?—and she adored him, everybody said."

He was talking to himself now, pacing my room in the darkness, running his hand aimlessly along the wall until he settled on my collection of colored-glass figurines on the mantelpiece, picking them up one by one and squinting at them against the feeble hall light. "And now they're all talking behind my back, you know. They're all saying that he can't control his own daughter, that she's as wild as a cat in the woods, and they're all laughing. At me." He spit the words out and swayed drunkenly against the mantelpiece, into my figurines, sweeping them over the edge in a horrifying, cascading crash.

They shattered on top of one another, delicate hind legs of deer and horses' necks severed in a terrible tinkling. I cried out, but it happened so fast that my cry only echoed the crash. At first he stood stunned, and then, groaning, covered his face with his hands. He bent slowly to examine the glass remains. After a moment he got up and careened out of the room, slamming the door so hard that the drawers of my dresser rattled and the pile of glass shifted and caved in.

I wonder sometimes why I never screamed or tried to hit him, why I just took it silently while my own rage accumulated like sand in an hourglass. I sat in my bed on that hot night with the covers pulled up around my shoulders, my teeth chattering, trying to keep warm. Early the next morning I swept up the pretty glass and found a single figure intact: the one I'd received on my eighth birthday, a brown dancing bear with sturdy neck and haunches. Reindeer and horses near the front of the mantel must have broken its fall. Holding it up to the strong morning sun, I watched how the light brought out different colors.

I set the lone figure back on the mantel and stroked its head with the tip of my finger and slowly pushed it to the edge and over. It was larger and heavier than the other pieces, so when it broke, shards flew across the room, under the bed, between cracks in the floor.

For months afterward I was reminded of that night each time I encountered a fragment of the bear, each time my foot grazed a piece of it.

"Let's face it," Horace said. "These old houses might look romantic, but what they are is one big pain in the behind."

It was Saturday. Dropping by with some brushes and rollers, Horace had found me in the kitchen cooking on a hot plate because a gas leak discovered two days before still hadn't been traced.

"I'll tell you what," he said in a confidential tone. He took off his baseball cap. "Why don't you cut your losses and let me rent you a real nice place over at Forest Lakes Village, dirt cheap?"

"I'm fine," I said, stirring canned soup with a plastic spoon. "Really. As soon as the gas is hooked up I'll be all set."

He nodded absently and then shook his head, scrutinizing the sink. "Looks like it's sprung a leak. We'll have to get somebody over here to fix it soon as—"

"Horace, *I'm* going to fix it. I bought some caulking stuff today." With the bottom of my T-shirt I wiped dust out of a mug and poured soup into it. "I can't believe you haven't noticed how much work I've done. I've been at it for three days! Can't you see a difference?"

"All I see is an old firetrap of a house and a girl with more brains than sense."

"Is that a compliment? Look, you can stop worrying about me. I really like it here. I like the trouble. That's what I came down here for."

He sighed and assumed a pained expression. "Well, frankly, Cassandra, it's not that simple. Elaine is worried to death. She says, and rightly so, 'What if she falls down the stairs and hits her head or breaks her leg and nobody finds her for a week?' She feels responsible. Hell, we all do."

I put my hand on his arm. "You are sweet, Horace. But I'm not your responsibility. I lived by myself for years in New York, which is a lot more treacherous than this place, I can tell you." I leaned back against the counter, blowing into my soup. "And anyway, I'm getting a dog. I saw an ad in the paper for black Lab puppies. I'll train it to run to Elaine if anything happens to me."

Horace put his cap on backward and headed for the door. "I'll never understand why some people need to make life harder for themselves than it has to be," he muttered under his breath.

The eight-week-old pups were being sold for fifteen dollars each. The moment I laid eyes on them I knew which one I wanted. Most of them were asleep, nestled together in a heap in the pen, but one, wide-eyed, was staring at me through the wire, pushing his dark, wet nose up to my outstretched hand and wagging the tip of his tail. His coat was so black it was iridescent, like the body of a fly: so black it was blue.

Once I had him home I sat cross-legged in my spartan living room, surrounded by boxes, watching him explore. I'd carefully cleaned up the poison and disinfectants; the floor was so shiny that the bare light bulb in the ceiling socket was almost perfectly reflected.

The dog pawed at the spot of light until I flicked off the switch. "Come here, Blue," I said. I patted the floor and he came trotting over. I leaned my head forward and he sniffed, licking my nose, my eyelashes, my lips. I closed my eyes, the puppy's muzzle next to my chin, his hot breath on my face. I had never owned a dog before. In fact, now that I thought about it, I'd never really owned anything. I opened my eyes and looked at him. So far it seemed pretty easy.

* * *

Late Sunday morning I was upstairs in the bedroom when I heard a knock on the screen door. "Who is it?" I yelled, balancing my paint roller on the edge of the tray. I went out into the hall and leaned over the banister.

"It's just me," Alice called. "I brought over some stuff I thought you might could use." She surveyed the dark hallway, the scattered drop cloths and paint cans. "Decorating, I see."

"Starting to," I said. "Come on in."

With her arms full of bags, she pulled open the screen door. "When I was married to Chet he wanted all the walls in the house to be white—eggshell, to be precise. So as soon as he left I went through and painted every room a different color. I loved those little sample squares. Avocado, honeysuckle, seafoam." She laughed. "Some worked and some didn't, but anything was better than white." She disappeared into the kitchen and set her bags on the table. "Hey, nice color in here! Tangerine! Really livens the place up."

"I was thinking about robin's-egg blue for the bathroom," I said, coming down the stairs. "I bought a pint to see what it's like."

Alice started unpacking jars of food and putting them on the counter. "I tried that one. It's darker than you'd think, and brighter. Kind of what it looks like on cloudless afternoons. Good bathroom color." She held up a mason jar of green beans. "Where d'you want these?"

"You didn't have to do that."

"I didn't do anything. All this is from Clyde. She told me to tell you she would've called but she doesn't have the number. In other words," she said dryly, "she wants to know why you haven't been in touch since you left."

"Oh, I've been meaning to. I've been so busy."

"I know. That's what I told her." She took out a bag of apples. "But all it takes is a simple gesture. I'm not telling you what to do, just suggesting."

"To be honest, Alice, I didn't really think she'd care."

She shined an apple on her T-shirt. "You never know with her, do you? She's a tough old bird. Lord, it's no surprise Mother turned out as neurotic as she did. My policy is to give her a call every now and then, just to be on the safe side." She bit into the apple. "The banker called me again," she said abruptly, grinning. "Hal. He's taking me out tonight to the fanciest restaurant in Knoxville. I think he's in love." She peered into a bag. "You want a pear?"

"Sure." I took one from her. "So what about you?"

"What do you mean?"

"Are you in love?"

She wrinkled her nose. "Who knows? There's not a hell of a lot to choose from around here. You can only go bowling with Billy Bob McCallahee so many times before you start getting a scary picture of yourself in curlers watching soaps, four screaming kids clinging to you while you pack ham sandwiches and cheese curls into a row of lunch boxes." She sighed. "Besides, it's been a long time. Would you believe I haven't been with anybody since I split up with Chet? Everybody talks about saving yourself for the right one. Hah! All I'm saving myself for is middle age." She took another bite of apple and waved her hand. "But enough talk about me. How are *you* doing? This place looks great."

I led her through the dining room to the living room, asking her advice about colors and light fixtures. We stood talking for a while in a patch of sunlight in the middle of the floor.

"It's so different from when Clyde and Granddaddy lived here," she mused, looking around. "It was always so dark." She went to a window and leaned out over the sill, then pulled back in surprise. "Holy bejeesus! Is that dog yours?"

"Blue. I got him yesterday." I came up behind her and looked over her shoulder. Lying in the shade under the window, the puppy gazed up at us and wagged his tail. "He doesn't bark yet. I think he's shy."

"What a cutie." Alice made kissing noises out the window. "You should keep him in here with you, though. Dogs are like men. They want lots of loving, they just don't know how to ask." She turned and inspected the room. "You need some furniture. Mother's bound to have some old chairs somewhere she's decided are out of style. And what about a dining room set? Maybe Kathy's got something you could use."

"Actually, I bought a few pieces I'm starting to refinish. They're out back. But I'm keeping the dining room bare, for a studio. I want to take advantage of all this light. I figure as long as I have the space— "

"Sure, you might as well use it." She twirled around slowly, holding her arms out. "It's hard to believe a family of five used to live here."

I leaned against the wall and slid down it to the floor. "What I can't understand is why they'd just let this house sit here all this times. When did they move out—ten years ago?"

"More like fifteen."

"There are still beds here. Even my mother's."

"When they left, they just left," Alice said. "Clyde didn't keep anything. What she couldn't give away she threw out or just abandoned."

"And it's been empty ever since? Why in the world didn't they sell it?"

She sat down cross-legged on the floor. "From what I heard, she wanted to, but Granddaddy wouldn't do it. He said somebody in the family might want it, which seemed a little strange, seeing how he never offered it to anybody. Of course, now it all makes sense. He was saving it for you."

I shook my head. "I can't understand why."

"Well, we all have our own ideas. Guilt about your mama being at the top of the list. Getting back at everybody else maybe somewhere in there too. After the accident he felt like everybody blamed him for it—Clyde mostly, but all of us. And he was right, we did. There's no question he was drunk and had no right to be." She leaned back on her elbows and stared at the ceiling. "But nobody really knows what he was thinking. He pretty much closed up after it happened."

"Do you think he really thought I'd come down here?"

"Well, he must've. What point would there be if you didn't?"

"But even *I* didn't know. For a while I was all ready to sell it."

"Look at it this way. What did he have to lose?" She rolled over onto her stomach. "I don't think it ever occurred to him that you wouldn't come. That's just how he was."

"He never even contacted me. Not once."

Alice reached over and squeezed my foot. "I think it would've been easier for him to give you a million dollars than to face you after what happened." She looked at me for a long moment. Then she pulled back and sat up, brushing her hand along the floor, absently tracing patterns. "Can I ask you something? Don't you get lonely out here?"

"I get a little scared sometimes at night." I smiled. "But now I've got an attack dog."

"Hah! That dog couldn't frighten a rabbit."

"So he needs a little training." I paused. "Sure, I get lonely sometimes, but I think it's a good thing. This is the first time I've ever been alone like this."

"Isn't it weird for you, being in this house? Your mother growing up here and all?"

I nodded. "You know, it's funny. Sometimes it feels like there are all these people here and I'm not alone at all."

Alice shivered. "Ugh. You've got to admit it's a little creepy when you think about everything that happened here." She winked mischievously. "Like that both our mothers were conceived right up there, for example." She jabbed her finger at the ceiling.

"Now, how do we know that for sure? It could have happened right here where we're sitting. Or maybe even at a drive-in."

"Oh, come on—look at Clyde." Alice giggled. "Does she strike you as the drive-in type?"

"Who's to say? I saw some pictures of her when she was young, and she had this kind of gleam in her eye. And she was very pretty."

"Really?" Alice said doubtfully.

"Haven't you seen them?"

"Oh, I don't like looking at old things. The past just seems so sad to me."

"Does it? I always think of the past as happier."

"Well, not for Clyde, at least from what I've heard. I don't think she was ever very happy with Granddaddy."

"Why not?"

"Well, for one thing, they used to call him 'lunch-hour Romeo' down at the mill. Remember that old gossip we ran into downtown, May Ford? I guess she was one of his Juliets."

I sat up. "Who'd told you that?"

"Oh, nobody ever told me directly. If you live in one place long enough you get wind of everything." She stretched out her legs. "Anyway, they say after your mother was killed he never so much as looked at another woman. Of course, he didn't look at Clyde either, but at least he wasn't catting around anymore."

"How terrible for her."

"Yeah, well." Alice shrugged. "Who's to say she didn't drive him to it?"

"Oh, come on." Suddenly, inexplicably, I felt protective toward Clyde.

"Look, everybody knows they had to get married because she was pregnant with Horace. So what if Granddaddy just got stuck with some woman he didn't even love who nagged him and nagged him and drove him to drink and everything else?"

I frowned. "Alice, no one can 'drive' anybody to do anything."

"Now, how do you know that? Have you ever tried it? My ex-husband used to say I drove him up a wall." She looked at her watch. "Jiminy! Hal's coming by in three hours. I've got to get my nails done and pick Eric up at the pool." She stood. I stayed where I was on the floor. "Hey, are you all right?" she said, touching my shoulder. "I didn't mean to upset you."

I tapped the wooden floorboards with my fingers. "I just didn't know about all this."

"All what?"

"Amory. The affairs and everything."

"Well, it doesn't matter now."

"It does matter."

"I shouldn't have said anything."

"No, I'm glad you did. Now I know what he was really like."

Alice crossed her arms. "Well, I'm sorry I told you, because now that's all you know."

"What else is there?"

She hesitated. "You'll never believe this now," she said finally, "but I think he was a kind person."

I contemplated the floor.

"Look," she said. "All you know about him is that he drank too much and he fooled around—and he was responsible for your mama's death. But there was more to him than that. That accident—it was a shame, Cassie, it really was, but it was an *accident*. He was the one who had to live with it. He did his time."

"Oh, for Christ's sake! She was my mother, Alice. I'm the one who had to live with it, not him."

"He had to live with the guilt, with Clyde, with it never being over. You and your daddy could go home and start again."

I looked up at her. "I can't believe you're saying that. You have no idea what it was like."

She leaned against the doorframe and shut her eyes. "You're right. I don't have any idea. It's just that it was so terrible for so long, and Clyde was so awful to him, that in the end all I could feel was pity. And on top of that, knowing he left you this house as some kind of apology— "

"Did you want this house, Alice?"

She opened her eyes and blinked. "I don't know," she said. "It sure would've made things easier for me and Eric."

Her honesty surprised me. I didn't know how to respond.

After a moment she smiled wryly. "Anyway, it wouldn't have worked out. He'd have left it to my mother, not me, and she'd have blackmailed me for it somehow."

"But Alice, if I had known—"

"No," she said firmly. "I don't want the house, Cassie."

I climbed to my feet, brushing off the seat of my shorts. "But—"

"Now, let's just drop it, all right? Period, the end." She poked at a large splinter of wood on the doorframe. "Besides, the place is falling apart."

"It's true," I said. "Just making it livable is costing me a fortune."

"I was wondering about that. If you don't mind my asking, how can you afford it?"

"I had a little money saved, but it's running out pretty fast, a lot faster than I thought it would. I guess I didn't add it all up. I've dealt with more plumbers and electricians and exterminators this week than I've seen in my whole life."

"You could sell off some of the land."

"I know, but I don't want to do that. Not yet. I want to hang on to it for a while."

"So what are you going to do?"

"Well, maybe I'll look for a part-time job, fifteen or twenty hours a week."

"Doing what?"

"It doesn't matter. I haven't thought about it much. Just something to make a little money."

"Hmm." Alice put a finger to her chin. "Have you ever waitressed?"

"Not really."

"Well, that's okay. You don't have to be a rocket scientist to serve drinks." She snapped her fingers. "I know just the place. Nice folks, not too smarmy, good tips. You mind working at night?"

"No."

"The Blue Moon. I heard one of their waitresses left her husband and ran off to California." She grinned. "With a woman."

We went out to the front porch. The puppy came bounding around the corner, and Alice reached down and picked him up. "Little boy Blue," she said, holding him like a baby. He sniffed her face and started to lick it. "He's got this lonely look in his eyes."

I took him from her and held him against my chest. "Are you blue, Blue?"

Alice walked down the front steps to her car. "Wish me luck tonight. I'm trying to decide whether to wear black or white—whaddaya think?"

"You're pretty tan. I'd say white."

"Yeah, that's what I was thinking."

"If you need somebody to take care of Eric—"

She flapped her hand. "He's got a regular baby-sitter. Thanks anyway. Of course, if it turns out Mother's paying her to spy on me, I might have to give you a call." She got in the car and started it. "Call your grandmother one of these days," she yelled above the noise. She waved goodbye, turned the car around, and disappeared down the long drive to the road.

On the slab of wood in front of me I shaped a human form out of red clay. The form was about a foot high, with arms the size of legs and legs slender, joints like elbows. The head rested in the belly. Long toes extended from the feet like fingers. The face was long and thin, and as I worked I kept checking the mirror propped in front of me: the face I was shaping was my own. I narrowed the nose with my index fingers, carving a cheekbone into the curve of a hip.

Out the dining room window I saw the field stretching in front of me like a child's game, a coated cardboard landscape. I imagined it bedecked with life-size plastic shapes: black cows, a tall green tree with foliage like pom-poms, a yellow stile, a brick-red barn. Wiping my hands on a rag, I pulled out a pad and a piece of charcoal to sketch the slant of the hills, the jagged line where trees met sky, a black dip of pond, stooped lone trees scattered in the foreground. I imagined the clay figure in front of me five times the size it was now, sitting out there in the field. Drawing it to scale, I placed it in the lap of a hill and put X's where other forms would go.

I thought of the sculpture park I'd seen last summer at the Villa Orsini, the Stravinsky Fountain near the Pompidou Center in Paris, Niki de Saint-Phalle's Tarot Garden in Tuscany, all filled with huge, fantastic creations. At the time the pieces had seemed unreasonably large, even grotesque, more strange than inspiring. But now, thinking back, I was struck by their claim to the land they populated and their hold on my imagination.

With a hunk of clay I started on a head, as large as my head. I touched the bones in my face—the jaw, the hollow of a cheek, the line of my brow—smearing my face with red clay, like war paint. I traced the curve of my lips in the mirror and then repeated the motion on the soft, formless clay. I sat on the stool in the waning light of afternoon, working with my hands until it was too dark to see.

She was my oldest girl, my charm. The other two were his; I don't know where they came from, but they never had much to do with me. I named her Ellen Iris because irises were in bloom when she was born and he brought me some in the hospital—the last time, I believe, he ever brought me flowers. She was sickly and they didn't know if she'd make it, but I knew. I knew.

I had her to myself for fifteen months before Elaine came along. By then Ellen was walking and talking. She had thick dark hair and narrow fingers. She could always tell when I was feeling bad; she'd come and pat me on the face when I was upset, and when Elaine was crying she'd waddle over to her crib and stroke her hand through the slats.

Elaine has been good to me over the years, she and Horace both. They're good children. They didn't move too far away; they invite me to dinner often enough so I don't feel neglected; they call me, sometimes twice a day. And they never ask questions I might not want to answer. But they know, as they always knew, that to get Ellen back I would have done anything. I would have given up the both of them.

Sitting at a round wooden table at a midsize bar on the outskirts of town, I filled in my social security number on a job application. The place was dark and virtually deserted and smelled faintly of ammonia. Chairs were piled up around me with their legs in the air, like a little forest. Behind the bar, a man with large forearms and a well-trimmed mustache was polishing glasses and hanging them up on a rack. He was wearing a T-shirt that said BETTER WET and whistling a country-western tune I was startled to find I recognized.

Experience. I thought I should put something down, so I listed Grasshopper's. Dad had never let me work there—"This is your home," he always said. "I don't want my kid to feel she's got nowhere to go just to live"—but I had certainly seen the business firsthand. Besides, I reasoned, checking out-of-state references probably wasn't a priority at the Blue Moon.

"Where you from?" said the bartender.

I looked up. For a moment I didn't know what to say. "Just outside of town."

"Related to the Clyde family, by any chance?"

I nodded. I was getting used to being recognized; in Sweetwater, my face was my ID.

"But you're not from around here," he said matter-of-factly.

"No. New York."

"That's what I'd've guessed." He started putting away a case of beer steins.

"Why?"

"Your accent, for one thing," he said. "Weird shoes. No makeup. Expensive haircut, no perm."

"You're very observant."

He held a stein up to the light. "Cracked." He tossed it in the trash. "You know, it's a funny thing—you kind of look like your cousin."

"Which one?"

"Well, that's what's funny about it, 'cause from what I understand, he's adopted."

"Oh, you mean Troy Burns? I haven't met him."

"How long you been here?"

"Almost a week."

"Well, that explains it," he said. "Do you know Alice?"

"Yeah, she's the one who told me about this place. She heard you might need a waitress."

"Maybe." He was putting steins on pegs behind his head. "You know, Troy used to have a band that played here all the time. They were real good, so they went off to Atlanta. He's living down there with some other relative of yours—"

"Ralph."

"Yeah, that's him. I got to say Troy's braver than I am, living with a guy who's queer as a three-dollar bill. Braver or dumber, I don't know which. People here don't take too kindly to the swishy types. If he wasn't Troy's cousin I'm sure someone would've kicked the shit out of him a long time ago. He's better off in the city."

While we were talking a tall, slim black woman came in. She was wearing a green sarong and a tank top, her thick hair pulled back with a green ribbon. "Ryan, why are you always so willing to act like a redneck at the slightest provocation?" she said, hands on hips, and turned to me. "Hi. Elizabeth Gibbons."

"It's Troy's cousin, Liz," Ryan said. "She wants a job."

"Cassie Simon," I said, getting up.

She put out her hand to stop me. "No need to rise. I'm not the Queen of England."

"I'm looking for something part-time," I said, sinking back into the chair. "I wondered if you might have any openings."

"Maybe for a new bartender." She glared at Ryan, who flipped a towel at her. She laughed. "Sometimes I think about firing him, but he makes a damn good drink. Where you from?"

"New Yawk," Ryan said.

"Boston, originally. I moved to New York a few years ago."

"I used to live in Boston. My ex still does. Where'd you live?"

I described my father's restaurant on the crowded street in Brookline, and she said she thought she'd eaten there. She took a chair off one of the tables and sat down with me, and after a while Ryan brought over two beers and a bowl of pretzels. We stayed there talking until another bartender arrived and the staff started getting ready for happy hour.

"Why don't you just give it a try tonight and see how things work around here?" she said as they set up the tables around us. "Saturday nights can get pretty rowdy. You might as well know what you're in for."

By the end of the evening I was weaving through the crowd like a pro, dodging drunks and memorizing orders for tables of twelve. Smoke hung in the air like a fog, glasses clinked, eyes glittered in the dark. Laughter rose and evaporated and rose again, mixing with the smells of beer and sweat and tobacco and perfume. Up in front, people danced on a packed floor to the thumping rhythm of the band.

In the course of my shift I settled a quarrel between a jealous man and someone trying to pick up his girlfriend, I was propositioned by a guy wearing a wedding ring who told me I looked like Rosanna Arquette, and I made seventy-eight dollars in tips. By two in the morning, when the bar closed its door, I was exhausted. I sat at a long table with Liz, Ryan, two other bartenders, and three waitresses, drinking beer and swapping stories. The smoke in the room had settled low, like mist hugging a riverbank.

"Congratulations," said Liz. "I think you passed Waitressing in a Hick Bar 101 with flying colors."

"Happy graduation," Ryan said, raising his glass. "Not a bad place, for a redneck town, is it?"

"Not a bad place at all," I said.

On the way home that night, driving through the darkness, I suddenly thought about my grandfather. I saw him driving reckless and fast, my mother beside him, over a narrow back road like the one I was on. I took my foot off the accelerator and slowed down. I could imagine my mother's white knuckles, the look of terror on her face, the stink of whiskey on his breath. I pulled to the side of the road, turned off the engine, and sat there with my eyes closed, leaning back against the seat.

Once, in college, up to my elbows in potter's clay, working a revolving wheel with one kicking foot, I found myself sculpting my mother's face in a simple earthenware bowl. In confusion, I formed the clay into a funneled mask that collapsed under its own weight, spilling like memory over the edges of the spinning surface.

I used to believe that my memories of her were abstract and benign, distant, cool, indistinct as a city at dawn seen from a neighboring hill. I used to think that I couldn't miss what I'd never known—that I couldn't mourn what I didn't remember. But now, when I listened closely, I could hear my mother's voice in the wind in the grasses, the patter of rain on soggy ground. When I concentrated I could smell her skin in the rich wet clay turned to mud, the sweet forsythia in the meadow. She was everywhere. All I had to do was let her in.

In the morning, rising sore and late after my first night at the bar, I searched for the small electric potter's wheel I'd brought from New

York. I found it in a cardboard box along with clay-flaked wooden modeling tools, a needle, a fettling knife, and several trimming tools wrapped in plastic like artifacts. I washed them in the kitchen sink, remembering the size and shape and purpose of each instrument as I scrubbed it clean. Later, forgetting that stores would be closed on a Sunday, I went out to buy clay. Driving back to the house past banks of rich red Tennessee earth, I decided to look for it on my property. I went down to the pond and scooped mud into buckets. I filled the buckets with water and carried them back to the house, Blue trotting along beside me. When the mud had melted into soup I poured it through an old window screen twice, to sift out rocks and pebbles, and set it out to dry.

On Monday I tested a slab of clay in the oven to see what temperature it fired to. I put the rest, a lump the size of a small TV, in a garbage bag. I called a professional potter named Elise, someone Liz had told me about, who said she'd be willing to let me use her kiln and recommended a clay company where I could get twenty-five-pound bags for eight dollars. She also gave me a tip about a used kickwheel, the kind with a seat and a foot pump, on sale for two hundred dollars.

"It's a great deal," she said. "They usually cost at least five hundred. The guy who owns it bought it as a surprise for his wife—right before she left him and moved to California. Needless to say, he wants to get rid of it."

"This woman didn't by any chance work at the Blue Moon, did she?"

"As a matter of fact, she did. Do you know her?"

"No, but I think I might have been hired to fill her spot."

"Ohhh," she said. "What a coincidence. You must have some kind of karmic connection. That settles it, you've got to have this wheel."

In the afternoon I took off on a long run with Blue down the dirt drive, exploring old roads and paths cut into the meadows and woods around the house. We ran through the stiff, slanting grass, past gnarled and distorted tree trunks, up sloping hills, around rough edges of exposed earth where the land had slid out from under itself. Standing at the top of the highest ridge, I could see only one other house in the distance.

With Blue at my side, I stretched out on my back in the grass, watching clouds in a panoramic sky bleaching into each other, filling gaps of blue, mottling and fading in and out of form. Lying there, I realized why I was no longer interested in spending weeks on a single shape, perfecting nuance, seeking understatement. I would have to be bold to compete with the broad curves of this landscape.

The most difficult thing to explain is that the little things take over. Life keeps going along at the same pace, minute following minute like soldiers in a parade. When the phone rang and it was Horace in the hospital in Athens—I don't know why they called him first; some nurse must have known him—I didn't suspect anything. In the split second after he told me, I could hear a laugh track on TV. I hung up the phone and ran a finger along the mantelpiece in the living room and looked at my finger and saw dust, and then I ran my hand flat along the mantel and wiped it on my blouse. I looked at the sofa and the pillows were misshapen, so I plumped them up, punching each one lightly and then patting it down. I went around the room straightening pictures on the wall, moving the throw rugs with my feet. Horace was on his way to get me, since I didn't know how to drive. All I had to do was wait. I went into the bathroom and got the Comet and a sponge from under the sink and poured the blue lumpy powder over everything: the faucet, the taps, the toilet bowl, making the water like a swimming pool. I ran a little water and scrubbed the sink with the sponge until the powder became a paste that I smeared all over the basin and the fixtures. I got down on my knees and scrubbed the inside of the tub in diminishing circles until the porcelain had a toothpaste-blue design. I rubbed the chrome spout until it shone. Then I ran water in the sink and splashed it all over, cutting through the Comet, wiping the grit down the drain. When I had finished I caught a glimpse of myself in the mirror above the sink, but I didn't look at my face; I concentrated on the streaks on the mirror.

When Horace came he found me down on the bathroom floor, scouring the tile with a toothbrush. His eyes were wild and he looked stricken. His wiry hair was coiled in uncombed clumps.

"Ma! What are you doing?" He took my elbow and hauled me up to my feet.

I didn't want to go with him. All I wanted to do was clean. I wanted to tear the house apart and put it back together; I had an urge to wax the floor under the piano and polish every bit of silver. The last thing in the world I wanted to do was get in that car and drive fifteen miles to the hospital to see the broken corpse of my daughter and the helpless terror on Amory's face. I just didn't want to see it.

"You've got to come, Ma," said Horace. "Kathy and Elaine and Larry are all over there already." He wiped a smudge of powder off my face.

"But there's nothing I can do," I said.

"Daddy needs you."

"No, he doesn't."

Horace just stood there for a moment, stumped. I remember thinking at the time that if I was raising him again there were a lot of things I'd do differently.

"We're all in shock, Ma," he said finally. "It's natural."

"None of this is natural," I snapped.

He bundled me into the car, and I was silent. I could see that his heart was torn up, probably as much if not more for his daddy as for his sister, whom he'd never quite understood.

I was thinking then that evil breeds evil, that you tell yourself you can get away with a little indiscretion and then another and you're in control of what you're doing, and then you find yourself lying a little bit, changing the hours here and there, playing with time. But time keeps marching along, and you can't mess with it, and after a while you start to trip up because the pace never slows and you've pretended that it did, or that it sped up when really it was tick-tick-tick, the same full hour at the same time it was yesterday. And so you lie and you lie and you get out of sync and pretty soon you're marching to your own beat, which has no connection to anyone else's, and then all those people you were trying to convince they were crazy come to realize that you're the crazy one, you're off beat. And you can't get back in line in time. It keeps on going, and it crushes you.

I wanted to explain all this to Horace, but he was gripping the steering wheel like he thought it might try to escape, and his bottom lip was white where he was chewing it. There was a spot of blood on the corner where he had bitten through.

"Just forget about the house," he was saying. "Nobody's going to notice the damn house. There's a lot more important things to think about."

In truth I had already forgotten about it. Now I was noticing that the inside of Horace's truck was a pigsty, and if he was going to be driving people around, it could use a good vacuuming. But I kept my mouth shut. I didn't want to push him too far.

Standing naked after a shower in the robin's-egg blue bathroom, at the old mirrored cabinet that had been painted with the wall so many times it had become the wall, I inspected the lines on my face.

I'm growing old, I thought, and there's no one around to see it.

Aside from running errands, I hadn't been out since I left the bar five nights before. Now it was Thursday, and I was getting ready for work. It was strange to be so alone.

Living on my own in that big old house, I was starting to feel trapped in a world within myself I couldn't share with anyone. Some days I sang or hummed just to hear the sound of a human voice. Blue barked. But mostly I'd begun listening to voices that came from somewhere inside, voices I heard in New York only in the dead of night, voices that whispered, *What are you doing? Where are you going? Why are you here?*

My routines and expectations had already adjusted to the new pace of my life. Time, which seemed so elusive in New York, now presented itself to me in great stretches. I was aimless; I dawdled; I slept late. I finished *Jane Eyre,* took baths, started a journal in a spiral notebook. I read the local paper, which was delivered to the box at the end of the drive, and I was even beginning to recognize names. I no longer felt compelled to know what was going on in the rest of the world; current events seemed entirely abstract, as removed from my life as if they were happening on Mars.

In the mornings I worked around the house, painting, stripping furniture, cutting the grass with the hand mower I'd found in the basement. By early afternoon I'd usually be in the dining room with all the windows open, working into the evening. The loneliest time, I found, was around five o'clock, when silvery shadows fell across chairs, the potter's wheel, the glass-fronted cabinet. I was haunted by the shadows; they seemed restless, expectant. They seemed to me like ghosts.

Standing at the mirror in the bathroom, I found a crease beneath my left eye—not a wrinkle, a crease. I grimaced and the crease rose; I pulled the skin taut over my cheekbone and it disappeared. Around my mouth I spied another and traced it with my finger. One on my forehead, narrow and straight across, I could only see in a certain light.

In some ways I liked how I was aging: how bones were becoming visible on my upper chest, like an excavation, how my fingers and wrists had thinned, how my collarbone joined an uneven ridge of shoulders, the serious line under my eye. I turned around and looked back into the mirror. I arched and hugged myself, stroking my waist as if my hands were someone else's. My palms glided up my sides and touched a weighty curve of breast, spread fingers over erect nipples. Sunlight hit my shoulder, and I turned again and touched my collarbone, running a fingernail down to the hollow between my breasts, down to my abdomen and up again, over my chin, into my mouth, startling myself.

After the last exam before winter break in my junior year of college, I had found myself drinking gin and tonic—mostly gin—in the attic apartment of a friend from class. The gin helped me see everything with incredible clarity: a narrow slice of lime clinging to ice cubes in my glass; orange light hanging in ridges in an opaque cold gray sky outside the window, like a Japanese lantern; the footprints my shoes made when I came in out of the snow, slowly disappearing on the rug by the door.

We'd first met because people told us we looked so much alike. But before that night I had never even imagined kissing her, or feeling her soft stomach beneath her sweater, or unbuckling the belt of her jeans. We touched each other like mirror images, and it was breathtakingly easy. "This is so normal it's weird," she whispered, stroking my face.

As I studied my reflection I thought about her hands, about the familiarity of her touch, the sureness of her fingers. Sometimes, living by myself, I felt like two people—one acting, the other responding. Sometimes I felt connected to the land and the passing of time the way I felt connected to my friend that night: hills into valleys, shapeless nights into formless days.

I dried off and took my floral cotton robe from the hook behind the bathroom door. I'd have to hurry; it was getting late. Bending over, I towel-dried my hair, combing my fingers through it, shaking out the tangles. When I rose, my face in the mirror was flushed and clean. At a distance it was hard to see any lines at all.

I parked the station wagon on the road in front of her house. When I pushed the doorbell I could hear it ringing inside as if the house were a hollow cave. I rang three times before she answered.

"Hello, Clyde," I said, summoning a smile as she opened the screen. I held out a loaf of bread, still warm. "I brought you this."

"Hello, Cassandra." Her voice was soft. She took the bread from me and squeezed it lightly. "Fresh, how nice. You made it?" She turned to go inside, and I held the door, hesitating. "Come in, come in," she said.

"Thank you." I followed her into the kitchen. "I'm sorry I haven't called, I've been so busy trying to get the house put together—and I haven't even thanked you for all the stuff you sent over with Alice, all those beans and tomatoes, they're gorgeous. But anyway, I was thinking about you and I wondered—well, I just wanted to check in and find out how you're doing."

"Oh, same as always, just fine." She set the bread on the counter. "I canned those vegetables last month."

"You know, I'd love to learn how to can," I said.

She raised her eyebrows. "My goodness, Cassandra, you're turning into quite a country girl, aren't you?"

I laughed awkwardly. "Um, did I tell you I've started working a few nights a week? It's a place Alice told me about, the Blue Moon."

She shrugged. "I've never heard of it."

"It's a restaurant." I found myself nervous, skittish, flailing against her reticence like a moth trapped in a jar. "Well, actually, it's—it's a bar. Terrific people. And pretty good money. Not great, but reasonable."

"Well. That's good, I guess." She clasped her hands. "Can I get you anything? Soda? Some lemonade?"

"Oh, no, I—I don't want to interrupt whatever you're doing."

She took a jar of lemonade out of the refrigerator and poured me a glass.

"Well, okay, I'll have some lemonade. That'd be nice," I said as she handed it to me. "Clyde, is there—I was wondering, I'm on my way into town, is there anything I can do for you while I'm there?"

"I don't believe so."

"You're—you've got everything you need?"

"Yes. Cassandra, listen—"

I gulped the lemonade and put the glass on the table.

"I'm glad you stopped by. I was meaning to call you."

She moved to the sink. The counter stood between us like a wall. She looked at the linoleum for a moment, and then she said, "How are you doing in that house?"

"I like it very much, it's—" I had to restrain myself from gushing. "It must have been a good house to raise a family in."

Her mouth formed a brittle smile. "I suppose it needs a deal of work."

"Not much, not really," I said. "It's such a sturdy old house. Solid."

"Yes." Shadows of words paced around me, advancing, retreating. She stood very still. I watched her hands as they worried over objects on the counter. "That bread smells nice, Cassandra," she said finally. "You really made it?"

I nodded.

"That's very industrious of you. You must have a lot of time on your hands."

"I guess I do," I said, drawing a deep breath. "Are you sure you don't need anything from town?"

"No, I'm just fine. I've got some time on my hands myself."

"Really? Well, I was wondering if you might want to come over and visit one of these days. I'd love to repay you for—"

"You don't need to repay me."

"I didn't mean that. What I meant was that I'd like to have you over—if you'd like to come."

"Oh." She seemed unsettled. "That's very kind of you, Cassandra, but I don't think so. No, I don't think so," she repeated, shaking her head.

When I left the house I felt like I was leaving worlds untouched. There was a weight of unsaid words between us. As I got in my car and drove away, I had the peculiar sense of being trapped in someone else's story, a story I didn't understand and could participate in only as a bystander, a passerby.

So he left her the house and he left her the land and he knew exactly what he was doing. He hid that box and didn't say a word about it for twenty-four years, not a word to anyone. He knew that if he said anything all of it would come out: that he'd been messing around with Bryce all that time, that while the men he employed were toiling away in the mill he was meeting their wives for car rides, for picnics, for romance in his office with the blinds shut. They would not have been pleased to hear it. But he knew that there's not much you can do to punish a dead man, so he hid the box and waited.

And now she's living down there on that land that used to be mine. I raised three children in the rooms I've heard she fills with junk from garage sales, I sliced and pared and baked in the room she covers with newspaper and knickknacks. Ellen was conceived and born in the bed Cassandra calls her own. She was born crying a tinny cry, six pounds two ounces, red and wrinkled and dark-haired like an Oriental. There were complications, and we had to rush to the hospital. The bloodstains on the mattress never came out. I nursed her and bathed her and changed her in that bedroom with the drafty windows on two sides and the soft pine floors.

Nobody's lived in that house for years, and with good reason. It always had too many windows, and now half of them are broken, screens rusted and torn. The floor creaks, the plumbing drips. I guess she thinks it's romantic, I don't know. Young people think they want to hold on to the past, but the past they're holding on to is nothing like the life we lived. The house was always needing work, and the land was wild. In winter the chill came in through the windows and under the doors, and the children got sick. The yard was mud when it wasn't ice, and I worried that the gas stove in the kitchen would kill us all in our sleep, by fumes or explosion.

I have no romantic notions of the past. If I could have lived then the way I do now, I'd have done it in a minute. It wasn't the past to us, it was just the best life we knew how to make.

But now she comes down here digging in the past like it holds some kind of answer, playing the part he gambled she'd take. She's there by herself in the house on the hill, exploring the attic and the cellar, shoveling up the earth to plant flowers, searching under the porch for where her dog took her shoe, replacing rotten floorboards.

In her own sweet time she's getting closer and closer. In her own sweet time she's going to find it.

The bar was smoky and hot and it was only nine-thirty, but I was already off duty. I sat in a back booth with a drawing pad, drinking tequila and smoking a cigarette. I hadn't smoked since I was a junior in college, and then it was more of a statement than a need. But tonight my mouth was watering for a cigarette—something I'd never imagined possible—and I bummed one from Patsy, another waitress, and then just one more. I kept telling myself to stop, but almost without realizing it I'd be lighting up again.

It was a quiet night, unusual for a Friday. The band hadn't started playing yet, so people were talking in quiet groups or drinking alone at the bar. I was sketching ideas for the large clay pieces, three in all. Since coming up with the project I'd been moving quickly, working late into the night, rising early to watch the light on the field, trying to catch where the shade fell and when. I wanted to know how shadows would fall on faces and hands when I positioned the pieces. Now I was working on a reclining female form resting on an elbow. I sketched alternatives for hands: tree roots, clocks, vines.

Liz and Ryan were out of town for the weekend, and Cal, the new assistant manager, was in charge. Until they left together, I hadn't even realized something was going on between them; they seemed to trade the same easy banter with each other as with everyone else. Ryan told me they were going camping at Great Smoky National Park, and I still didn't get it. "You mean *together?*" I said finally, and he laughed: "I promise we'll keep one foot on the floor."

Cal told the staff that a few of us could quit early, and I jumped at the chance. I'd been preoccupied all evening, thinking about my project and pushing down a now familiar and general panic at having set myself adrift in foreign waters. So I was getting slowly drunk and working my way through Patsy's Salems, holding a pencil and a cigarette in one hand like chopsticks and drawing the other: long fingers with scalloped folds of flesh over the knuckles, uneven nails.

The music, when it erupted from the stage in front, startled me. I looked up. The band was called Tidewater; they played here a lot, pretty standard Southern country rock. The four boys in the band were local, and they harmonized with the careful facility of self-taught novices. I tried to return to my sketchbook, but the music was distracting, and I found myself tapping my feet under the table to an acoustic-guitar and drum version of "Blue Suede Shoes." I sat up straight, stretched, and flipped the notebook shut, shoving the pencil through the holes of the wire binder at the top. I propped the notebook against the wall and went over to the bar, sliding onto the vinyl-covered seat of a tall wooden stool.

"How about another tequila, Cal? And a pack of cigarettes."

"I thought you didn't smoke."

"I don't."

He tossed me a pack of Winstons and poured a generous jigger of gold liquid into a whiskey glass. "You want a lime?"

"Sure."

He put four wedges of lime on a plate and got out a shaker of salt. I poured some into the web between my left thumb and forefinger, licked it, tossed back the drink, and sucked on a lime. The tequila sat in my stomach like a burning coal and then sizzled up to my head. The band was playing "Blue Moon."

"Does every band that comes through here think they're obligated to play that song?"

"It's in the contract," he said.

I slid my glass across the bar. "I think I'll have another one."

"I think you've had enough." He was counting change in the cash register.

"What?"

"You heard me."

"Excuse me, are you my father?"

"No, I'm your boss."

"Cal, I'm *off duty*."

He shut the drawer with a click. "I just don't want you getting into any trouble. You sit there and cool your heels a little while."

"I want to dance."

"So dance."

"I don't know anybody but you, Cal."

"I'm working. Just ask somebody. Somebody single, okay? No rings." He put a glass of ice water in front of me and wiggled his ringless fingers.

I sighed. A hand appeared on the bar. "I'm single," said a low, soft voice. "Want to dance?"

I stared at the hand for a moment. It was wide but thin, with veins visible through the skin like a raised map. The index finger was callused. I looked up the bare, tan arm to the rolled sleeve of a work shirt, and then into eyes that were pale chips of blue.

He seemed about my age, maybe younger. His fair hair was short and wavy, and he had sandy stubble on his sunburned chin. These were the first things I noticed.

"Sure," I said.

I slid off the stool, and we threaded our way to the dance floor through the clusters of people sitting around it. I knew he was watching me walk, but the alcohol felt good inside me and I didn't care. When we reached the front he touched my waist, and I turned to face him. He pulled me toward him, his hand on the small of my back, and my hand rose automatically to his shoulder. He held his other hand out for me to clasp, and then we were dancing.

Our closeness made me feel drunker than I was. He led easily, his steps small and graceful. He was about four inches taller than me; my breasts grazed his ribs, and I could feel his thighs through his jeans. As I looked into his face I imagined drawing the simple curves and clean lines of his nose and brow and jaw. It was a strong face, but with something delicate about it, something refined, though it was clear this was a part of himself he tried to keep under wraps.

The song was still "Blue Moon," but now that I was dancing with my body against someone else's, someone I wanted to dance with a little while longer, I didn't want it to end. The singer was holding the microphone close, slurring the words. My partner put his mouth to my ear and said, "I've been watching you over there, sitting all alone, getting drunk by yourself."

"I'm not drunk."

He took his hand off my back and I lost my balance, staggering a little. "You're not?"

"That wasn't fair."

"I don't care if you're drunk," he said. "I like your voice this way. Maybe it's always this way. I hope so."

I leaned my head on his shoulder, and he drew me closer. He ran his hand up my side. For the first time in a long time I felt the warmth of desire, a low, dull heat moving through my veins. I touched his stomach through his shirt, and he stroked my waist with one finger, his lips in my hair.

The song ended, and I pulled away uncertainly. He steadied me with his hand on my arm. The band began a fast song, and we stood still for a moment in the motion around us.

"Let's get some air," he said, and I told him to wait while I got the cigarettes I'd left at the bar.

Cal looked over at him and said to me in a quiet voice, "You know what you're doing?"

"I can handle myself, boss," I said, smiling.

I made my way back across the floor, and we went outside to sit on the wide wooden steps extending from the front porch. He sat on the step above me, leaning back against the rail.

I took out a cigarette. He searched his pockets for a lighter, but I was faster with a match.

"What do you need me for?" he said.

I blew smoke out into the cool dark air. The place was lit haphazardly by a string of bulbs on the roof. I could see the outline of the first row of cars in the parking lot. I laughed, bold and drunk. "I don't know yet."

We sat in silence for a while. People trickled in and out of the bar, and we overheard bits of conversation: "She didn't look half bad from the back." "The sitter's going to have a fit." "Why didn't you tell me you could see right through this dress?" The occasional car coming or going crunched on the gravel in a sweep of headlights.

"Slow night," he said. "Is it always like this?"

"What makes you think I'd know?"

"You work here, don't you?"

I looked at him curiously. "How do you know that?"

"The way you were talking to the bartender—unless he's your boyfriend or something."

A car screeched out of the parking lot, blaring its horn. Someone swore loudly.

"So you're not from around here," I said.

"Grew up here. I'm just back for a visit."

"Why?"

"See some friends. See if things are still the same."

"Are they?"

"Yeah. But you're here—that's different."

"You know everybody?"

"Used to."

I stubbed out my cigarette on my step. My mouth felt dry and sooty. "I want another drink."

"I've got some tequila at my place."

"I can get it here for free."

"You don't want to go back in there," he said.

I leaned back lazily, looking up at him. "Why not? And anyway, why should I go with you?"

"Why shouldn't you?"

I considered. "I'm sure there are about a million reasons, but I can't think of any of them right now."

"Sweetwater isn't New York, you know."

This sounded logical, though I couldn't remember telling him where I was from. "You don't even know my name."

"Cassie. I heard the bartender say it."

"Well, now that that's taken care of. . . "

"Mine's Bernie."

He got up and pulled me up gently with him, moving down onto my step and touching me under the chin. I could feel his breath on my eyelashes. I tilted my head, and he kissed my upper lip softly, like a feather stroke, and then my lower one. I pressed him to me, my fingers in his belt loops, and kissed him back, running my tongue over his teeth.

We took his jeep, leaving my old station wagon in the parking lot. The jeep was black with red seats. Cassettes were lined up under the dashboard and scattered all over the floor: Lyle Lovett, Dwight Yoakum, k.d. lang, and some others I'd never heard of. When he turned on the ignition, Patsy Cline was singing "Crazy."

We drove through the darkness over winding wooded roads. The high beams made it look as if the trees were parting to let us pass. I asked him if he minded if I smoked.

"Not if I can watch."

"You'd better watch where you're going," I said. I smiled and lit a cigarette and looked out the windshield at the road coming up to meet us. He was driving slowly; cars skittered past us like brightly colored beetles.

His "place" was a room in a one-story motel on the other side of town. A red-and-green blinking neon sign advertised MOUNTAIN VIEW INN—VACANCY; several of the letters were burned out. He pulled up in front of his room and asked me to wait in the jeep for a moment, then hopped out and came around to open my door.

I told him he was a gentleman, and he said he just wanted another excuse to touch my hand. I slid down beside him, and we stood against the open door of the jeep. He kissed my jawbone and stroked my neck, combing his fingers through my hair, and I pushed my knee between his legs, parting them. We managed to get to his door, and he fumbled for the key while I ran my hand down the hard ridge of his spine, and then the door was open and shut behind us and we were inside the darkness, my back against the wall. He tugged on the soft cotton of my shirt, pulling it up and placing his hand on my belly. I unbuttoned his shirt slowly, starting from the top. Out of the corner of my eye I could see red and green letters flashing on the opposite wall, above the bed, as he crouched down and gathered me in.

The next afternoon I went to work in a red silk shirt tucked into faded jeans tucked into cowboy boots I'd bought at a yard sale. I had made a ritual of getting dressed, laying clothes out on the bed, then taking a bath and wrapping myself in a towel to paint my toenails. Standing in my bra in front of the bathroom mirror, I anointed the hollow of my neck, my temples, the insides of my elbows and thighs with French perfume I'd found still packed in a box from New York. I couldn't remember the last time I'd lavished such attention on my body. I slipped on a peach camisole trimmed with antique lace and rummaged through my makeup bag until I found a lipstick to match my shirt. When I left the house I felt invincible.

Cal whistled when I walked into the Blue Moon. "*Whoo-ee,* it's somebody's lucky night."

"I hear you've been up to no good," said Liz. She was sitting at the bar with a Perrier, reading the paper.

"You're back," I said brightly. "How was it?"

"It was scenic. I got restless."

"How's Ryan?"

"He got poison ivy. Turns out that rugged outdoorsy shtick that reeled me in is just an act."

I smiled and started taking chairs down from the tables.

"But at least *you* had a good time," Liz said.

"Cal's got a big mouth."

"I didn't hear it from Cal. I heard it from your cousin."

I slammed down the chair I was holding. "Alice has no business—"

Liz let out a laugh, throaty and deep. "Look, I already know what happened, so you can stop playing dumb. It's no big deal—you're not even technically related to him, right? Of course, it's still a little weird. I mean, some people might think it's weird. I don't give a damn."

"I don't know what you're talking about."

She gave me an incredulous look. "Come on."

"What are you saying, Liz?" I asked in a small, flat voice.

Her eyes dropped to the paper. "Oh, Jesus Christ. You don't know, do you? That little bastard."

Fragments of conversation and observation from the night before flashed through my head: the cadence of his voice, the lines of his face, familiar. "I grew up around here, but I only come back to visit." He said he was a musician. He said I reminded him of someone he knew a long time ago.

"He said his name was Bernie."

"It is. . . . Well, that's what the band calls him. But his real name is Troy. Troy Burns."

I felt sick. I couldn't think straight. The dull hangover I'd woken up with in his bed that morning was burrowing its way through the aspirin I'd cloaked it in. "When did you see him?"

"About an hour ago, maybe less. He said he'd be back this evening."

"I have to go."

Liz nodded reluctantly. "It's going to be busy tonight, but I guess I can't blame you. I'll call Patsy, see what she's doing."

I looked over at Cal, who was wiping down the bar. "Why didn't you tell me?"

"Honest to God, Cassie, I didn't know who he was. You know I started working here just before you did. I'd never seen him before in my life."

"I've been watching you," he had said, and later, "I believe we've got a lot more in common than you think."

"Like what?" We were lying in bed in the darkened motel room just before dawn.

"We both like tequila. We both like to dance. And you like taking chances as much as I do." He reached for me again. "Don't go," he said. "I think you're a part of me I'm missing."

Now, in the bar, I couldn't believe I'd overlooked all the signs and signals, every last one of them. I was filled with a vague dread and a spreading shame. It was worse, too, that I'd had to hear it from Liz. Other people must know. It was a small town. I looked down and felt exposed by my eager red shirt, my perfume. Suddenly all I wanted to do was leave Sweetwater for good and get back to the city, where the rules of conduct were steadfast, where you screened dates like prospective employees, where a situation like this was inconceivable, absurd. In New York I'd never have let it happen.

The moon was faintly visible in a violet sky, and the sun hung low over the hills. Driving west toward home, I watched it drop to the horizon like an egg yolk sliding down a bowl. I began thinking about what I'd need to do to leave, how crazy it would be to stay. I remembered what my dad had said about grist for the mill. My relatives didn't want me here; they thought I was a burden. I'd never fit in; I didn't *want* to fit in. And now the only person I'd really opened up to, the only one I'd trusted, had made a game out of humiliating me.

By the time I reached the long drive leading to the house, mortification had hardened into anger. I was outraged at his seduction of me, at the self-conscious deception. I imagined him plotting it out, long before he even saw me, planning to stick it to his cousin from up north who was lucky enough to inherit land she had no right to and stupid enough to claim it. I wondered if Alice knew all along, if they had planned it together. She did have an odd sense of humor. She could push things too far. She must have told him that I worked at the Blue Moon—otherwise how would he have known?

As I coasted over the slope, my stomach flipped over. Parked in front of the porch was the black jeep, the one I had ridden in the night before with my feet up on the dash.

He was sitting on the bottom step playing a guitar, wearing a cowboy hat and black jeans.

I got out of my car and slammed the door. "Get off my property."

He laughed uneasily and looked down, his fingers still softly plucking the strings, and then he looked up into my face. "I wrote a song for you, Cassandra," he said.

Later, after he'd left, I tried to remember why it was I didn't stop him from explaining, why, even in my anger, I wanted to know. I was sure he wouldn't have any answers that made it all make sense; there was nothing he could say to justify himself, and even if there was, it didn't matter. Plain and simple. But nothing's plain and simple. So I walked up to the porch, trembling, furious, and he put down the guitar and squinted at me, holding up his hand to shade the last rays of sun.

"Cassandra—"

"What the hell are you doing here?"

"I came by to see you."

"You *bastard.*"

"I meant to tell you—I meant to tell you as soon as I knew for sure. When I came up to you at the bar, when we started dancing, I just . . . One thing led to another, and then—"

"What the hell were you *thinking?* That it was some kind of *game?*" I spit out the words. "Some kind of joke?"

"No, Cassie—" He reached toward me.

"Don't touch me," I said, recoiling.

"Let me explain. Please." He waited a moment, watching my face. "It wasn't like I planned it or anything. At first I just wanted to see you, I wasn't even going to introduce myself. I didn't tell anybody I was coming home except Liz. I talked to her a few days ago and she told me she hired you, so I thought . . . well, maybe I'd see what you were like."

"So Liz is in on this."

"No, not at all."

"Oh, she isn't? Then why didn't she at least tell me you were coming?"

He shifted his feet. "I asked her not to. I wasn't sure I wanted to meet you. I wanted it to be my decision. I didn't want it to be . . . forced."

"Oh, you didn't want it to be *forced,*" I said fiercely.

"Right. And then when I saw you, it seemed like you might be who I thought you were, but I wasn't positive—does that make sense?"

"No."

"So I didn't want to make a fool of myself—and I figured that if I asked you to dance I'd find out for sure."

"I thought you heard Cal say my name."

"You mean the bartender? No, he never said it, not that I heard. I was just making a wild guess."

"You lied to me."

"I wasn't lying."

"You deliberately misled me."

He let out a long breath, as if he'd been holding it in for some time. "Look. I knew that if you knew who I was, none of that would've happened."

"You're damn right," I said. I started past him up the steps.

He put a hand on my arm. "You're not giving me an inch, are you?"

"Why the hell should I?"

"Cassie, please. I know what you're thinking, but—I wasn't playing games."

"What would you call it, then?"

For a moment he was silent. Then he looked up at me and said, "Do you believe in love at first sight?"

I shook my head slowly. "You are unbelievable." I turned to leave.

"Wait." He rose and softly touched my chin. I didn't move. He touched it again, his fingers tentative, guiding my face toward his own. "I'm sorry."

"That doesn't help."

"It's all I can say. I am really sorry."

"You had no right."

"I know."

"You're my cousin."

"Technically."

"Technically or not, now it's weird and awkward and we have this between us. Now things can never be normal."

"I don't want things to be normal."

"Well, I do."

"No, you don't, Cassie."

"You don't know what I want."

"I know this. I know you felt the same way I did this morning."

I stood there, mute, barricading myself against the tenderness in his voice.

He looked into my eyes, working against my resistance. "It's like—it's like we're the same person. Last night I'd look at you and know things about myself—"

I pulled away. "You sound like a bad movie."

"I don't care how I sound." His blue eyes held mine. "Do you want me to leave?" he asked evenly.

I lowered my head. "I think you should, yes."

"But do you want me to?"

When I didn't reply, he picked up his guitar, and then he was gone.

I watched the taillights of his jeep bump down the long drive and disappear over the ridge, clouds of dust swirling in his wake. I could hear Blue barking inside the house. I opened the front door and he came bounding out, sniffing across the yard, yapping into the distance. After a while he trotted back over and lay down beside me, his chin on my leg. We sat on the porch watching day fade into night.

Later what I remembered most was the sky, the way yellow and violet overlapped like layers of frosting on a slice of birthday cake, the way the sun slipped behind and in front of clouds, gold-tipping them like illuminated manuscripts as the violet turned to purple and the yellow deepened. By the time I went inside, the sky resembled a ripe bruise, the blood beneath it drawn up close to the surface.

part four

While Ellen was packing to go off to college, Elaine was downstairs in the living room at the sewing machine, working on her cheerleading uniform. She'd been elected captain of the squad. I kept pacing back and forth between the kitchen and the living room, fussing with the pillows on the couch, straightening pictures, dusting. Amory was reading a newspaper, rustling it impatiently, muttering under his breath. I went out to the hall and looked upstairs, as if I could will Ellen to hurry up and come down.

When I went back to the living room I didn't know what to do. I stood in the middle of the floor, clasping and unclasping my hands. Amory looked at me over the top of his newspaper and threw it down. He stalked out into the hall and shouted, "What in the name of God are you doing up there?"

"Nothing in the name of God, Daddy," she shot back.

Amory came back and sat down, cursing, mopping his brow in the heat. "Stop standing there like a moron," he barked at me.

I looked over at Elaine, sitting at the sewing machine, facing the window. I went and stood behind her, watching her quick, nimble fingers stitch the outfit together. "You're doing a nice job, Elaine," I said.

She stopped sewing and sat up straight. "Thank you."

"Real nice."

"Thank you," she said again.

"That's a complicated piece of work."

She sat very still, running the fabric between her fingers. "Mother," she said finally, "don't just talk to me for something to do." She turned around, gripping the uniform with both hands in her lap. Her eyes were red; she had been crying.

"Elaine—" I reached out to her.

"No!" She shrank away. I could hear Amory throw down the paper again. "Can't you just stop thinking about her, Mama?" she said, her voice rising. "Ellen's gone! She's already gone." She was crying again and trying not to. "She doesn't want to be here, and she sure doesn't care how you feel. It just kills me to see you—to see you care so much."

"But, Elaine. . . " I didn't know what to say. "I care about all of you."

"No," she said, shaking her head. "Not like this. She's the only one. And it just—it just kills me!" She got up and ran out to the porch. I ran after her. "I hate her," she yelled, sobbing, her hands over her face.

"Hush, she'll hear you," I said.

"I don't care. I hate her. I hate her!"

When Ellen left that day I felt a tug on my heart as if it was tied to her. I stood on the porch waving goodbye in the suffocating heat, waving goodbye to keep from having to speak. "Leaving isn't so hard," she whispered as she went.

Afterward I turned to go inside, and I could see Elaine watching me through the window. She wasn't crying now. She watched me like a deer or a rabbit watches a hunter, to see what I would do. I put my hand out carefully, as if she might bolt at any second.

She came out to the porch. "Look, Mama," she said, holding up the uniform. "I'm almost finished now."

"That'll look real pretty on you, Elaine," I said.

"You really think so?"

I smiled the biggest smile I could muster. "I really do."

She turned it around and inspected it. "It will," she said softly. "I know it will," she said again, and went inside.

I lay in the old double bed and stared at the hanging lamp swaying above my head in the breeze brought by the rain. Blue was sleeping at my feet. Drops fell hard on the slanting roof and drummed against the upper windowpanes, and the gauzy curtains danced and twisted against the wall. Through the open window I could see the shining fields. Rain trampled the high grasses, stirred dirt into mud, made the trees quiver as the thin gray light of early morning washed over the floor, the sheets, the pale walls. Blue scratched himself, jingling his collar. I could just make out the photos I'd put up around the room: my father, Drew, my mother with my father and me.

In that moment I felt I might live my whole life in that falling-down house with its creaky porch and rusted screens, never being allowed to forget the history of it, always wanting and not wanting to forget. When I closed my eyes I felt as solid and substantial as a rain-smoothed stone.

I was up to my elbows in clay when the phone rang, so I let the machine get it.

"Cassie? It's Adam. Are you there?"

I didn't move.

"I'm going to wait here until you pick up."

He waited and I waited, sitting in a chair in the dining room, watching the clay dry on my caked hands, looking at the clock. After about six minutes I heard the click of his receiver and considered calling him back, saying I'd just come in. But I didn't want to call him back, so I erased the message.

The next day the phone rang and I answered, regretting it as soon as I heard his voice.

"I miss you, Cass," he said, and it took me a moment to realize he was serious. "What are you doing down there, anyway? Come on back, just for a little while. I'll throw you a party. I'll help with the plane fare. Oh, hell, all of it—we can write it off as a company expense. I want to see the stuff you're doing. Maybe we could find out about getting you a show or something. You know I know a lot of people. Maybe we can interest Julian or Dmitri in taking a look.

"And I need your advice on a couple of things. To be honest, I'm not sure how I'm going to set up this next show, and Veronica's lacking something, I'm not sure what it is, but she just doesn't have that critical eye. I mean, she's fine once everything's on the walls, but I just can't trust her judgment, you know? At least not yet. It could be freelance or something. I could pay you as a consultant. And I mean it when I say I miss you, Cassie. I know it sounds trite, but I really do—"

No, a voice was saying in my head, *no, Adam, no,* and then the voice got louder and escaped through my mouth. "No, Adam. Can't you see I'm trying to leave you and all of it? I don't want to come back. I can't come back. I have to find out what's happening here, what happened in this family, what happened with Troy, what's happening to me. I can't expect you to understand, I'm not asking you to. I just need some time to figure it out for myself."

I don't know how much of it I actually spoke out loud, but before I had finished he was saying, "Troy? Who's Troy?" in a thin, high voice. I could see him sitting in the office, cupping the receiver between his left shoulder and his ear, twisting the phone cord with his right index finger the way he always did when he was making a difficult call.

"Nobody," I said. "Nothing. And anyway, that's not the point."

I imagined him looking at a crack in the wall above the computer as he said, "Fine," with an edge now, "fine," and then lashed out—it was so familiar, I could see it coming—"*Jesus Christ,* all I said is that I miss you. Can't you listen to somebody else for a change? Must you always be totally selfish? You left me with this place, and now you just want to pretend it's evaporated into thin air, and me with it."

While he was talking I felt panic swelling within me. I thought of my dad, of Drew; I thought of all I'd left behind and seemed unable to connect with this new life I was living. All I wanted was to be left alone for a while, to have some time to sort things out without needing to explain or analyze or defend the experience to anyone else before I was ready.

"I can't stand this, Adam," I said. "I have to go. I'm not thinking clearly, this is hard for me."

"Hard for *you*?"

"Yes. I have to go." I hung up, his voice ringing in my ears.

I went out to the porch, down the steps into the yard, fleeing the words that followed—Hard for *you*? Hard for *you*?—until finally they were swallowed up in the grass, tangled in spiderwebs and wildflower pollen.

In the afternoon I went to see Liz's friend Elise, who had bought the kickwheel from the jilted husband and was holding it for me. After I paid her she offered her truck, helped me load the large contraption into the back, and drove through the rain to the house. I followed in the station wagon. We carefully carried the wheel inside and maneuvered it into the dining room.

That evening, with Blue at my feet, I sat at the kickwheel, its whirring the only sound in the room. The rain had stopped and the sun was setting and the air smelled of pine and red dirt. The clay felt almost alive under my fingers, a breathing thing, coaxing my hands to unravel the skein of my imagination.

Elaine was talking into my answering machine, explaining something about a party.

"Hello?" I said, picking up. "I just walked in."

"Hello? Hello? I can never get used to those things," she said. "Hello, Cassandra. You can call me back if this isn't a good time."

"No, it's fine." I dragged the phone out to the porch. I'd bought an extra-long cord just for that purpose.

"I hear you stopped in to see Clyde the other day. That was nice of you."

"Well, I hadn't seen her since I moved in. She'd sent some food over with Alice." Blue came and lay against my leg, his tail thumping on the porch. He was getting bigger, I noticed; the sound of tail against wood was solid and strong. His soft puppy fuzz was turning into stiff, short adult fur, his high-pitched yap becoming a deeper bark. I scratched his stomach.

"Alice told me she'd been by. You're painting."

"I've finished now. She gave me some good advice about the bathroom."

"Really? I'm surprised. Alice's taste is—let's just say our tastes are different." She laughed dryly.

I broke off a stalk of grass and chewed it. "Well, the bathroom looks good."

"I'm relieved to hear it. Anyhow, the reason I'm calling is first, because I just looked at the calendar and realized how long it's been, and second, because I'm having a 'ladies' night' for the Clyde girls Thursday evening and I wondered if you might like to come."

"The Clyde girls?"

"Sure, you know—me, Kathy, Alice, Clyde. Nothing fancy. We just laugh a lot and play some games. It's a hoot."

"Of course, I'd love to come."

"Great. About six-thirty."

"Should I bring anything?"

"Just your sense of humor," she said.

The rain had stopped for good. By the end of the week the hot August sun was drying leaves on the trees, reducing streams to creeks, and turning dirt into dust. I had started rising early to take advantage of the morning coolness, going into town to read the paper and have coffee at the Eagle before buying groceries or doing errands. There were seldom more than a few people in the Eagle at a time, but the coffee was cheap and good, so I'd made it part of my routine. I sat in the same booth I'd shared the first time with Alice, facing the street. I liked to watch the goings-on outside, though there generally wasn't much to see.

It was nine-fifteen Thursday morning, and I was later than usual. I slid into the booth and ordered a cup of coffee. I was wearing shorts, and the cracked vinyl scratched against my thighs. As I stirred my coffee I watched the regulars at the counter, two old men and a tired-looking middle-aged woman who acted like she wanted nothing to do with them.

I sipped the coffee and started a list on a napkin: flowers for Elaine tonight, two bags of clay from the supply company, take Blue to the vet. I wanted to find out about shots and make sure I was feeding him right. He seemed sturdy, but I wanted to be certain. I didn't want to take a chance on losing him.

I looked at the list and added "stationery/pens." I needed to touch base with Drew, but I was afraid to call him after what had happened with Adam. I didn't trust myself not to tell him about Troy, and I wasn't prepared to deal with his reaction, which was bound to be scathing. And though I hadn't seen Troy since Saturday, I'd found that try as I might, I couldn't stop thinking about him. I reasoned that writing Drew would be the safest bet. I'd begun a letter with a pencil stub on a scrap of paper, but I couldn't find the right tone; it started chatty and ended banal. Maybe if I had the proper tools the writing would come easier.

I scanned the front page of the newspaper. An electrical fire, no one injured; a car accident, one person killed; rumblings of a strike at the textile mill. Siamese twins born to an Oklahoma mother of four on page two; a presidential press conference on the economy, page three. Turning to the weekly Weddings section, I studied the young, eager faces and read the information about each couple. I was fascinated by the way people met—through church groups a lot of the time, or in high school—and what they planned to do. Most of them were Sweetwater natives, but one or the other might be from Chattanooga or Knoxville, sometimes Atlanta. Some were in the military, stationed in Texas, Florida, Germany. The majority planned to settle and begin jobs somewhere else. There were quite a few accountants, some secretaries, and many recent high school graduates, about half employed in nearby factories and mills.

I had imagined that going into town might help me meet people my age, but I didn't notice many around. The ones I did see were working service jobs—like my waitress at the Eagle, who played solitaire on the lunch counter to pass the time. Of course, during the week many of them would have been at work, but even on weekends the downtown was quiet. Judging by the paper, a lot of them married young and moved into trailer parks if they didn't move away.

"Refill?" the waitress asked, standing over me with a pot of coffee.

"Sure." I leaned back against the booth as she filled the cup and tossed two creamers on the Formica. "Slow morning," I offered.

"It was full up at seven."

"Who's winning?"

"What?"

"The card game." I smiled.

She seemed puzzled. "It's solitaire."

"I know. Sorry, it was a bad joke."

She looked at me. "You want anything else?"

"No, this is fine, thanks."

The waitress started to walk away, but she turned back. "You can't lose," she said. "I guess that's what I like about it."

I watched her walk leisurely back to the counter, then turned to look out at the square across the street, at the people from the mental home sitting on benches under the fluttering flag. The fountain in the center was dry. I finished my coffee, tucked the napkin with the list into my bag, and folded the newspaper, leaving it on the table with a dollar bill.

Out on the street, a small breeze battled the heat. I went into the drugstore on the corner for stationery, then walked another block to the tiny florist shop, lingering over cut flowers arranged in buckets on the floor of the narrow room.

"Anything I can help you with?" the clerk asked, looking up from a magazine spread open on the counter.

"Mind if I just pick and choose?"

She shrugged and went back to reading.

"Those irises are mighty pretty," said a floury-soft voice behind me. I turned around. "May Ford," the short, gray-haired woman said, holding out a hand. "I met you one time when you were down here with Alice."

"Oh, yes." I shook the plump white hand. It felt strangely boneless.

"It's the state flower, you know."

"What?"

"The iris," she said. "If you care about such things. And those tulips over there are nice too. It's cheating a little, but the tulip poplar is the state tree, so I'm always partial to irises and tulips both." She went over to the bucket of tulips and bent down, peering into it. "These don't look altogether healthy, though. Course, they're imported from somewhere—who ever heard of tulips and irises in August?" She straightened. "Are you buying these for somebody? A boyfriend?"

"No," I said a little hastily. "They're for my aunt."

"Which one?"

I hesitated. "Elaine."

"Elaine, hmm." She canvassed the shop, scratching her chin. "She prefers roses, I believe. Yellow ones, if I recall correctly. Yes, I think that's right." She threaded her way through the buckets. "And look here, they're on special! Six for five dollars." She clapped her hands. "Isn't it a lucky coincidence we ran into each other!" She beamed and picked out six yellow roses, holding them up one by one for my inspection.

As the clerk wrapped the flowers I said, "I appreciate your help, Mrs. Ford."

"No trouble at all. Now, do you have more errands to do?"

"I'm finished down here."

"Where's your car parked at?"

"Up that way." I gestured to the left.

"Another coincidence! I'm heading that way myself."

Main Street was virtually deserted. A sunburned farmer leaned against a truck, talking to a young woman with a baby in one arm and a toddler pulling at her dress. Several blocks down, three men were loading furniture into a van.

"Simon," she mused as we walked along. "Isn't that your last name, Cassandra?"

"I'm surprised you remember."

"Oh, well, it's a little hobby of mine to remember things like that. I have all kinds of tricks. Not many Simons around here—that's a Jewish name, isn't it?—so I just think of Simon Says. 'Simon Says—jump three times.'" She paused in front of the bank and hopped lightly in place. "Whew!" she said, her hand on her chest. "Hold on a minute."

"Actually we're almost to my car, Mrs. Ford, so I guess I'll say goodbye here." I pointed across the street at the station wagon.

She grabbed my arm. "Please, just come sit with me a second while I catch my breath."

I glanced at my watch.

"I won't keep you long."

Reluctantly, I followed her to the small park across from the Eagle, where we sat on a bench next to the idle fountain.

"That's much better." She looked around. "I remember when this park was first built, in 1967. Beautification project of the Ladies' Guild, which we all belonged to in those days. Back then they'd never have thought of turning off the water." She leaned closer and whispered, "Of course, it was meant for respectable folks, and look what it's turned into." We watched a grizzled old man on the other side of the fountain fingering a soiled brown bag. "Sad, sad, sad," she said, shaking her head. After a moment she added, "Nineteen sixty-seven. That's the year your mother died, isn't it?"

I nodded slowly.

"How old were you, dear?"

"I was three."

She put her hand on my knee. "It was a terrible tragedy, just terrible. We were all just sick about it. Ellen was so—lively, the liveliest one. It didn't seem possible." She shook her head again, clucking at the memory. "Two funerals in two weeks," she said. "Terrible."

"Two funerals?"

"Well, first Bryce and then Ellen."

"Bryce?"

"Bryce Davies." She looked at me closely. "You've never heard that name before?"

"No."

She drew back. "Well, I certainly should not be the one to tell you. I guess I thought you knew."

The old man across from us tossed his bag into the fountain, shattering the bottle inside, then got up and walked away.

"She was a friend of yours?" I asked levelly.

"I shouldn't—" She fussed with her pocketbook. I could tell the temptation was getting to be too much for her. "Oh, well, what harm can it do?" She sighed. "We were both in the Guild. We had lunch together now and then. Doesn't mean I *knew* her, really. When you get right down to it, who knows anybody? But sure, I guess you could say we were friends."

"So what happened?"

She squirmed. "Lordy, it's hot," she said, fanning herself with her hand.

"What happened?" I persisted.

She stared intently at her lap, then shot me a quick glance."Well, if I tell you that, I might as well tell you the whole story." She exhaled loudly. "Bryce Davies was not the nicest lady in the world," she said, choosing her words. "Oh, she was nice on the outside—friendly, generous to a fault. And beautiful. Lordy, she dressed up this town. But there was something about her, you could just tell she was NTBT."

"She was what?"

"NTBT. That's what we used to say—Not To Be Trusted. I knew it from the day she moved to town. But Clyde—well, Clyde wasn't what you'd call real savvy. She trusted too much. She didn't want to know. And your granddaddy called the shots. If he said jump, then even if she had three kids clinging to her and lead weights around her ankles, she'd jump just as high as she could. But I thought it was strange from the beginning. Everyone did. Here's this shy little mousy type, best friends with the hottest ticket in town."

"They were best friends?"

"I think Clyde thought they were. They raised their kids together. But you know, I bet deep down your grandmother suspected something. She had to have some idea of what was going on."

"What do you mean?"

"Heavens, dear, *you* know."

"With Amory?"

"I didn't say it," she said. "You figured it out for yourself. We all felt so sorry for her, but what could we do? Your granddaddy and Bryce were like two peas in a pod. They didn't care a straw about anybody but themselves. Some people said they were truly in love. I don't know about that. I do know they were mad for each other, though—you could see it on their faces.

"I heard it rumored Clyde got the goods on him once, a long time ago, when she and your granddaddy were first married. There was a big to-do about it, and then she thought it was over. So you just have to wonder what it was like to find out twenty years later that your husband and your best friend—your best friend!—were having an affair the entire time! I can't imagine," she said, pursing her lips. "But then, my husband never went out sniffing up trees on other folks' property like some foolish dog."

"Bryce was married too?"

"Oh, yes."

"Did her husband know about Amory?"

She shrugged. "He must've had his suspicions. It's not like Bryce was the most discreet person you ever met. But you know, we all see what we want to. He didn't want to see it."

My mind was racing. "How did Bryce die, Mrs. Ford?"

"It's all in the papers." She paused dramatically. "You should probably just go look it up yourself." She watched my face, but I didn't respond. "Well," she said, "Bryce drowned at the swimming hole down behind the old house. The house you're living in."

"I didn't know there was a swimming hole."

"They've closed it off now, there's a barbed-wire fence around it. Nobody swims there anymore. It's dangerous—there's a whirlpool in it. That's what happened to Bryce, I guess—she got caught in that whirlpool. Or so they say. Your grandmother was the only witness."

I took a deep breath.

"And then, less than two weeks later, your mother was dead too, bless her soul. As a matter of fact, they're buried right next to each other, up on the ridge at Pine Crest Cemetery. It was all anybody could talk about at the time. But after a while it died down, as these things do, and everybody went on with their lives. Nothing ever happened about it. I mean, there was never an investigation or anything. There wasn't any evidence of wrongdoing, of course"—she sounded like she'd been listening to a lot of detective shows on TV—"and nobody went looking for any. I think folks just wanted to forget it fast as they could. But your grandmother and granddaddy were never the same. And to be honest, none of us could look at them the same either. Each of them responsible for the death of a living, breathing human being, even if they were both accidents—and maybe they were."

I stiffened against the bench and said nothing. My silence flustered her.

"Oh, dear, I didn't *want* to bring this up, you *made* me tell you. And now you're upset."

"So the story is that Clyde drowned Bryce because she was having an affair with Amory," I said stonily, "and then Amory got drunk and smashed up the car and my mother to get back at Clyde. Is that right?"

"I'm not saying that's what I think."

"But that's the gossip you've been spreading around."

She sat up indignantly. "Look, Cassandra, I just thought you might appreciate knowing what everybody's been saying about your family all these years. I thought it might help you to understand some things."

"Oh really."

"Come on, now," she said. "You can't tell me you haven't noticed there's something wrong with that family. A blind person could see it. They're all eaten up. If you'd stop hiding in that big old house and start paying attention to the people around you, dear, maybe you'd learn something. Ask Clyde about it." She rose to leave. "Ask Clyde about Bryce Davies."

I watched her make her way out of the park to the sidewalk, her head held high. Pulling my knees up to my chest, I pressed my back into the hard bench and looked up at the pale expanse of sky. I closed my eyes and saw orange shapes, felt the heat of the sun on my eyelids. For a moment I imagined I was on a beach, bathed in sunlight on a big towel, making a mold of myself in the golden sand. When I opened my eyes I had to shut them again; the world was too bright, it was overexposed.

When he died it was not so much sorrow I felt as relief. The door had closed between us long ago, so long that sometimes I forgot what I hated him for, though the hatred was as real and as strong as when it happened. Under my raging cold eye he first was broken and then hardened and finally a drunk again, as if that was the only identity he could hold on to.

The last time I saw him alive he was standing at the front door in a white Hanes T-shirt, his trousers bagging around his narrow hips and his suspenders hanging down around his knees like swinging bridges. Lazy and disheveled and a little anxious. Bald pink head. "Clyde, where're you going?"

"Don't you worry, I'll be back in an hour," I hollered from the driveway.

"What?"

"Got to get some curtains."

"Why?"

"Who cares why?" I was irritated. He was like a big baby, for God's sake. "It's springtime and I need some curtains for the den. The ones we have are too heavy." I opened the car door.

I watched him out the windshield, standing there in the doorway like he was lost. Then he turned around with a shrug and went back inside the house.

I didn't have any premonitions as I nosed down the driveway and steered our green Oldsmobile through the development, past all the houses that outsiders say look exactly the same. I was thinking how *much I liked it here, how it was so sensible and friendly and clean. How all the wallpaper matched perfectly at the corners. How all the closet doors shut flush with their frames. Paved driveways sloped up toward built-in garages with doors that opened like magic. The shower units were all of a piece. You knew you'd see your neighbor every day when you went to collect the mail, and you knew your neighbor was counting on seeing you too.*

I didn't think about him at all on the bypass. I opened all the windows with the button on my armrest, and the wind whipped through my thin white hair and cooled my neck. I thought of the curtains I would buy—blue or floral?—and wondered whether Kathy was bringing dessert when she and Horace came for dinner that evening; she had mentioned something about fresh peaches going bad on her kitchen counter, but I wasn't sure what that meant.

They had changed around the floor plan in Sears, and I wandered the aisles noticing merchandise I'd never seen before. You become accustomed to things; you make routines for yourself, and after a while they're habit. I bought some kitchen towels in Housewares and contemplated a crock pot, and then, moving through Furnishings, I calculated what it would cost to reupholster the couch in the living room. I bought throw pillows as a compromise. The store was almost empty and smelled like the inside of my refrigerator, and the salesladies were indifferent and hard to locate, but I didn't much mind. I settled on blue curtains—they shade you better from the sun—and eventually made my way out the automatic doors to the parking lot, which was like a huge baking tray.

When I pulled into the drive the house was quiet. I was humming "Three Times a Lady"; it must have been playing in the mall. When I think back I don't know why I didn't suspect something: it was so still, so silent. But I went in the door humming and pushed it shut with my hip, juggling my packages.

"Amory!" I called. I wandered back to the bedroom, looked into the darkened living room—I keep the shades drawn so the couch won't fade more than it already has—and then went into the kitchen.

He was sprawled out on the floor behind the counter. I guess I knew right away. He was on his back, his face turned from me, and I ran over and knelt beside him, pulling at his shoulders. It was a sight I would never forget: his mouth was open, blood running out of it, and his neck was practically black; his eyes were wide and glassy. One hand was gripping the pullout coupon section from the Sweetwater Gazette, *and the other a pencil. Later on, when I was cleaning up, I looked at the glossy sheet and saw he'd circled the ones he wanted to save: Pillsbury Poppin' Fresh Biscuits, Minute Maid Orange Juice, Wonder Bread English Muffins. He knew I made biscuits from scratch; why did he want store-bought? That's nagged at me ever since.*

There wasn't anything to do but call an ambulance. I sat on the floor next to him, unclenching his hands and smoothing them out, wiping the blood from his chin. I looked into his face and saw lines I hadn't noticed. He had even less hair than I thought. I closed his eyes with two fingers of one hand, the way you see them do it in the movies. I didn't cry. The top of his white T-shirt was damp, the color of raspberry juice and darkening. The cuckoo clock Elaine and Larry had given us struck three, and the silence of the house absorbed the sound like a sponge.

In those moments I think I felt closer to my husband than I had in twenty-four years. I think in that quiet space I almost forgave him. After the shock of seeing his face pale and distorted and helpless, I studied it with something verging on sadness, and I saw age spots and small white hairs growing out of his nose. His face in death was kind. I thought of how he had looked a few hours before, standing at the front door, wanting me to stay, and I wondered if he had somehow known and hadn't wanted to face it by himself.

I learned a long time ago that you can't bring back what's gone, but the problem is that everything happens when you're not looking, when you're at Sears thinking of curtains and there's no chance to say, You are not alone, and maybe I forgive you. Amory and I had moved with and against each other, mostly against, for over fifty years. We had acted roles so long they had become part of who and what we were together. In the end we had become brittle, statues, stuck in poses we'd long forgotten the meanings of.

The smiling man at the cemetery gate looked up the names and pointed me toward a ridge off to the right, section E7. "If you get lost just follow the main road," he said, making a circular motion with his finger. "It's a loop. Either way will bring you right back to the front."

"Is everybody who died in the same year buried in the same section?"

"Well, that all depends." He wiped his neck. The sun was hot, directly overhead. "We try to keep families together, but sometimes it just ain't possible. Lot of times a husband and wife will buy a plot and ask us to save the spaces around them for the kids, but we just can't do that without money down. What happens if a kid decides to get buried someplace else, next to his wife's family or something? Then we're left with one open space in G, and we got to let it go for a special price." He shook his head. "Folks don't understand what all goes into it. Accidents, family tragedies, you never know what's going to happen. That's why it pays to plan ahead."

"Yeah," I said. "Well, thanks."

"No problem at all. Enjoy your visit with us, hear?"

Driving on the white gravel road through the grounds, I passed new graves mounded with dirt, straggling mourners in high heels carrying flowers, a man on a riding mower cutting a swath across the hillside. The place was peaceful and quiet and clean and smelled of grass. High on a slope, people were gathered for a service. I drove slowly, reading names on tombstones. Neat white rows of them, like baby teeth, stretched out in the distance as far as I could see.

Halfway up a broad, flat-topped hill I came upon a green wooden marker with a large white *E* painted on it. I parked the car on the side of the road and got out. I wandered through E1, up to E3 and over to E6, and then I saw E7. For a moment I stared at the marker, unsure whether I wanted to keep going. Maybe it was enough, I thought, to know where the grave was, to know that it was there.

I had looked for my mother in a lot of places, but never in a place where she might actually be. The prospect of finding her was terrifying. The name and the dates etched in stone, the narrow plot of land with grass or gravel over it, tombstones on either side, all of them alike. Having never seen the grave, I had been free to nurture the small, secret fantasy that she might still be alive, that she might even come back one day.

"How do you know for sure she's dead?" I'd asked my dad once, when I was ten and questioning everything. "Did you see the body? Maybe there was a cover-up. Maybe she just ran away."

"I wish she had run away," he said. "Then we could try to get her back."

"Do you believe in God?" I asked suddenly.

He gazed at me for a long time with vacant eyes, as if he were looking through me. He touched my hair, my cheek. He put his hand on my shoulder until I squirmed away, uncomfortable. "Sometimes. When it helps," he finally said.

Standing on the hillside, I saw the other tombstone first.

Bryce Lee Davies
December 18, 1918–May 2, 1967
Loving Wife, Beloved Mother

I felt dizzy. This much, at least, was true. I looked over at the adjacent stone, and there she was.

Ellen Clyde Simon
March 17, 1940–May 13, 1967
"Memory believes before knowing remembers."

"Believes longer than recollects, longer than knowing even wonders. Knows, remembers, believes," I whispered to myself. I knew it by heart; it was one of my father's favorite passages. He taught it to me long before I had any idea who Faulkner was or what he might have meant by it. I used to lie in bed saying the words aloud, turning the shapes of them over in my mouth like lozenges.

"Knows remembers believes." I felt light-headed, delirious, short of breath. I looked back and forth at the tombstones. Bryce Lee Davies. Ellen Clyde Simon.

Each of them responsible for the death of a living, breathing human being.

May 2 to May 13, eleven days.

If you'd start paying attention to the people around you, maybe you'd learn something.

I stepped back, stumbling over an arrangement of plastic flowers, banging my knee on the sharp edge of a tombstone, words jumbled in my head: *Believes longer than recollects. A blind person could see it.* I made my way to the car and fumbled for the door handle, wrenching it open, and sat in the sweltering heat of the driver's seat. *A blind person could see it.* People walking by glanced in at me, curiosity on their faces. I wrapped my arms around myself and closed my eyes. *Believes longer than recollects, longer than knowing even wonders.* I sat in the car until the voices subsided. Then I turned the key in the ignition and headed for home.

At the funeral my evangelist son-in-law did the honors. Elaine and Horace sat on either side of me in the front left pew of the funeral home chapel, holding my hands. Elaine kept dabbing my face with a Kleenex whether I needed it or not. The grandchildren sat sniffling in the pews behind us. Behind them were our friends and Amory's business colleagues, and then neighbors and employees and a few people I'd never seen before—but I expected that. Probably children he didn't know he had.

"Amory Clyde was a good man, Lord," said Larry, warming up. "He was a family man."

People said "Umm-hmm" and "Yes, Lord" and "Amen," but I wanted to hear Larry back that up before I opened my mouth.

"He was a good husband."

I wondered what gave Larry the authority to say this. Out of the corner of my eye I could see people looking at me, nodding their heads. I think they expected me to be crying, but I couldn't seem to get started.

"A good father."

Horace and Elaine both squeezed my hands, tears streaming down their faces.

"A loving grandfather, and a kind and generous great-grandfather." He looked at Alice holding Eric in her lap. "You see, Amory Clyde lived to a ripe old age," he went on.

"A ripe old age," someone echoed in the back. It sounded to me like Jeb Gregory, the handyman from the old place, who'd never had much

use for Amory as far as I could tell. We hadn't seen Jeb in years. Why had he felt compelled not only to attend Amory's funeral but to take an active part in it? I wanted to turn around and find out if it was him, but good manners forced me to keep my eyes forward.

"And in his full and active lifetime, he touched many of us with his warmth and generosity. His gentle spirit. Yes, Amory Clyde was an industrious and upstanding pillar of our community." Larry put the emphasis on "industrious." I thought he was really going overboard; but then, I suppose evangelists aren't known for their restraint. And so far nobody had stood up and screamed that it was blasphemy, though I wouldn't have been at all surprised if someone did. Death does interesting things to people.

"How many of us have benefited from the presence in this community of the Whitfield Mill?" asked Larry in a quiet voice. There was silence in the room. Even the most vociferous were stumped by this question. "How many of us can say, 'My life has been enriched and enlivened by the people I have met and the business the mill has brought to our little town'?" Some woman finally emitted a halfhearted, "Praise the Lord," enabling him to continue.

He tried a different approach. "Amory Clyde was a good man. He gave and gave to this community, and he never gave up." Larry smiled, evidently pleased with this neat turn of phrase, and I wondered for a moment if he expected applause. "He always strove to be fair and just in his business and personal dealings. In many ways, he was a role model for the people of this town."

"God love him," somebody cried.

"He experienced personal tragedy, Lord, and it made him stronger. He weathered the strike at the mill, staged by a vicious and corrupt union, and it made him stronger. He lived in this town for over fifty years, through thick and through thin, a whole lot of good times and some bad times too, and it only made him stronger!

"Yes, my friends, Amory Clyde was a good man." Larry stopped and wiped his brow. Then he paused meaningfully, looking out over the audience as if he were about to divulge a tremendous secret.

"My friends, let's be frank here for a moment. Amory Clyde was not known for being a man of God. He didn't go to church a whole lot, and he did not freely discuss the role of Jesus Christ our Savior in his life." Larry's eyes roamed the room as if he were awaiting a sign from heaven. "But let me tell you, people, that Amory Clyde was a man of God."

"That's right," "Yes, Lord," "Umm hmm," came from the pews in a dislocated chorus.

"He was a man of God, my friends. Jesus said, 'By their fruits ye shall know them.' He said, 'Let my actions speak louder than my words.' Amory Clyde was a simple man, and a good man. He lived a life of faith without even trying."

By this time my ears were ringing. Amory had been by no means a simple man, and certainly not a good one. He had abandoned the Baptist church and started worshiping more tangible gods long before we were married. Over the course of his life the trinity of women, work, and whiskey provided him with far more inspiration than the church ever had.

Beside me, Elaine was sobbing, overcome by the power of her husband's oratory. Horace was still holding my dry hand in his clammy one. I had had enough.

"I want to leave," I whispered fiercely to Elaine.

She clasped my hand. "I know this is hard for you, Mama," she soothed. "Please try to hold yourself together just a few minutes more. Larry's got a grand finale planned."

Dry-eyed and defeated, I sat listening to the grand finale. It was filled with clichés like "God helps those who help themselves," which, I had to agree, described Amory to a 'T.' By the end, more than half the congregation was audibly in tears, which must have been a satisfaction to Larry and Elaine.

When the service was over, I received people's condolences and heartfelt embraces with the appropriate air of a bereaved widow, and allowed myself to be helped into the limousine that would lead the parade to the cemetery. As I sat there in the dim plushness, squeezed again between Horace and Elaine, I thought of Ellen, and of her funeral, which had been so different from the one today. The bright sun, the shock, the horror of it. Her death had been like the amputation of a healthy limb; Amory's was like finally giving up a part of you that is serviceable but diseased. I was relieved that the pain was gone.

On our way to the cemetery, drivers in both directions pulled respectfully to the side of the road to let us pass. I had forgotten this custom, and it made me feel like a queen. But I would not be like Queen Victoria mourning Albert; I would not, as I read somewhere that she had, let my husband's death consume my life. I thought it was about time, finally, to live for myself. And though I couldn't tell anybody, I was looking forward to doing it alone.

"Yellow roses!" Elaine exclaimed.. "I was *hoping* these would be for me. My friend Bernadette saw you walking down Main Street this morning with that old busybody May Ford—I hope she didn't talk your ear off—and Bernadette said you were carrying yellow roses and I just started anticipating. I guess May told you these are my favorite, favorite things in the whole wide world." Cradling the bouquet as if it were a baby, she brought it up to her face. She closed her eyes and breathed deeply. "Ummm. Perfection." She held the flowers out in front of her and headed down the hall, motioning for me to follow. "Everybody else is already here. They're out on the deck."

"I'm late," I said. "I'm sorry."

"Just a little. Don't worry, we wouldn't have started without you."

In the kitchen Elaine found a vase and filled it halfway with water. She opened the little foil packet of preservative that came with the flowers and poured it in. Then she unrolled the paper wrapping, separated the roses from the greenery, and began arranging them in the vase.

"They look a little tired," I said. "They sat in my car for a while in the sun."

"They'll perk right back up, you wait and see," Elaine said, concentrating on the arrangement.

I looked around the spacious kitchen. It was as neat and folksy as Clyde's. A collection of bright copper objects covered one wall; a pine sideboard against another wall was filled with cheery plates standing on their rims. Above the breakfast nook hung a cuckoo clock identical to the one Clyde had in her living room.

The house was a two-story gray-shingled split-level in one of Horace's developments, Whispering Pines. It was only a few miles from Ridge View. The houses were larger and more distinctive here than in Clyde's neighborhood; it had taken me a while to figure out, as I drove along the broad, quiet streets, that each house was a variation on three or four standard models. Some had shutters, some large oak doors, some shingles, some siding. "You won't believe it, but every house in the neighborhood is less than five years old," Elaine had said as she gave me directions over the phone. "Horace has quite a flair. Who knows, maybe that's where you get it from."

"This place is lovely," I said.

"Why, thank you." She set the vase of roses in the middle of the round kitchen table. "I try my best." She wrapped the extra greenery in the paper and deposited it in the trash bag under the sink. "So," she said casually, "what did May Ford want with you this morning?"

"Oh, I don't know."

"What'd you all talk about?"

"Nothing important. She just wanted to gossip, I think."

"About what?" She propped her elbows on the counter between us.

"Um, not much. I don't really remember."

She looked at me closely. "I have a little piece of advice for you. I suggest you stay away from that old woman. She's mean and spiteful, and she's a liar." She stood up straight. "People in this town gossip a lot because that's all there is to do. Most of it's outright lies. So you come to me if you hear something that doesn't sound right, okay?"

"Okay." I fidgeted under her sharp gaze.

"Is there anything you want to ask me about?"

"I can't think of anything."

"Well," she said, looking troubled. After a moment her expression changed to a tight smile. "Then let's join the others on the deck, shall we?"

I followed her out of the kitchen into a wide, sunny room at the back of the house, with a cathedral ceiling and a slate floor covered with dhurrie rugs. A couple of overstuffed couches, a large-screen TV, and a spotlessly clean fireplace dominated the room. The entire rear wall was glass; through it I could see Alice, Kathy, and the back of Clyde's white head. They were sitting in lawn chairs on a red-stained deck, bowls of tortilla chips and salsa on one folding table, and a blender half-full of a slushy green drink on another. Behind them stretched a well-kept yard, penned in on three sides by neighbors' fences.

"Look who's here!" Kathy said, jumping up as I came out on the deck. "My goodness, it must be nearly three weeks since you moved into that house, and I haven't even had you over. I said to Horace this morning, 'She must think we're the snootiest people she ever met.' I did come by once last week—did you get the pie?"

"Thank you, yes, it was beautiful. I found it on the porch railing when I got home from work. I've been meaning to call and thank you for it." I glanced around at the group. "I'd like to have all of you over one of these days, as soon as I get a few more chairs."

"We can *bring* chairs," Alice said. She gave a little wave. "Hi! I'm not getting up, I'm too comfortable."

Clyde looked at me over her shoulder. "Hello, Cassandra."

"Hello, hello, hello," I said.

"Over here," said Elaine, patting the seat next to Alice. "Now, let me find one more." She disappeared inside the house.

I sat down. "Well."

"Well," Alice said.

"Well!" said Kathy. "And what have you been up to lately?" Everybody looked at me expectantly. "All moved in and everything?"

"Just about," I said. "I got a dog."

"Well, that's good. I don't know how you can stand it out there all by yourself." She reached for the chips. "I get nervous when Horace is gone overnight on a business trip, and we've got neighbors."

"She's an artist," Alice said. "They like to be alone."

"Want a chip?" Kathy offered the basket around.

"What have you been doing with yourself?" I asked Alice.

"This and that." She craned her neck toward the house. "Well, okay—quick, before Mother gets back—Hal and I are in love. *Truly.* He invited me and Eric to Knoxville for a few days last week, and we just packed up and went. Stayed in a great hotel, room service, the whole bit." She grinned. "I'm thinking maybe it's time to move. We'll see how it goes."

Clyde frowned. "Your mother doesn't know about this?"

"No, and don't you say a single word, either," Alice said. "I'll tell her when I'm good and ready."

"Well, it's nice to be loved by somebody," Kathy said diplomatically.

"Don't I know it. I have never been treated this way before, not by Chet, not by anybody. I didn't have any idea how wonderful it could—"

"What are we all gabbing about out here?" Elaine returned, lugging a chair behind her.

There was a short, awkward silence.

"We're still talking about chairs," Alice said. "Cassie needs some chairs. Do you have any extra ones in the garage or somewhere?"

"We maybe could rustle some up. I don't have enough lawn furniture myself, as you can see. Will you remind me to order more from Penney's, Alice Marie?"

"*Don't* call me that, Mother."

"Touchy, touchy. My Lord, I can't say a single thing." Elaine smiled apologetically at the group. "Mother-daughter tiffs. I thought it was just a stage."

Alice got up. "I'm going to check on Eric."

"I just did. He's fast asleep," Elaine said.

"I think I'll check on my own child myself, if you don't mind," Alice said, and went inside.

"Well, what will it be tonight? Monopoly or bridge?" Kathy looked around at everyone brightly.

"It's been bridge the past four times," Clyde said.

"Monopoly, then. Okay with you, Elaine? Cassie?"

"Fine," said Elaine shortly.

"Sure, whatever," I said.

Kathy began setting up the board. "You think it'll be all right with Alice?"

"Who knows what's all right with Alice. I don't. Anybody wants to go in and find out, be my guest." Elaine waved vaguely toward the sliding glass door.

"I'll go," I said.

I found Alice at the kitchen table, flipping through a magazine.

"They sent you in here to get me, huh?"

"I volunteered." I sat down. "What are you reading?"

"Some trash."

"How's Eric?"

"He's breathing. As predicted." She looked at me quizzically. "Is something up with you? You seem a little jumpy."

"I could ask you the same thing."

"She drives me nuts. What's your excuse?"

I reached for the magazine. It was *Good Housekeeping*. "'A Hundred and One Holiday Gift Ideas for You and Your Family,'" I read aloud.

"Yeah, she saves the old ones. This is a woman who gets ready for Easter at Thanksgiving and goes Christmas shopping in the middle of July."

I turned the page. "Twenty-seven kinds of Christmas cookies. Yikes."

"Do you celebrate Christmas?"

"Jews for Jesus? No."

"Hmm," Alice said. "But your mother wasn't Jewish."

"My dad is, though. It's all he knows, so I was raised that way." I thought for a moment. "Sort of. By the time I came along he wasn't much of anything. We lit the menorah. I got presents for eight days. Most of my friends did too, so it wasn't really a big deal."

"You know, I think you're the first Jewish person I've ever met."

"Really?"

She nodded. "And I have to say it's been a pleasure," she said. "But you never answered my question."

I shut the magazine and fiddled with the cover, bending and unbending a corner. "What do you know about Bryce Davies?"

"Bryce Davies?" Her eyes widened. "Who've you been talking to?"

"Nobody, really. I went to my mother's grave today, and I saw the marker, and I just—I just wondered what the story was."

"That was a long time ago."

"So you've heard of her."

"Did your dad just tell you about this or something?"

"No. I don't think he knows."

"Have you been talking to May Ford?"

"May Ford? " I tried to sound surprised.

"Cassie, I think you should be aware of something," she said, lowering her voice. "People talk a lot in this town. Rumors are like brush fires. They get started with a little spark, and pretty soon if you're not watching they get out of control. And they can burn for years. I told you this before. May Ford—"

"That's why I'm asking you."

She sighed. "What'd she tell you?"

"Not much." The corner of the magazine came off in my hand. "She said something about how she died. Drowned or something."

Alice leaned back, crossing her arms.

"And Clyde was there when it happened. I guess they were friends."

"What else?"

"That's all. That's all she said."

Alice plucked a napkin from a holder on the table and tore it into narrow strips. "It was a terrible accident. Can you imagine having to witness something like that?"

I shook my head.

"That's part of—that's what I didn't want to drag you into before. She's never really gotten over it."

I nodded. Questions were lining up behind my teeth. I pushed them back.

"Anyway, I think Bryce Davies' husband married somebody else pretty soon after and moved away to Virginia or somewhere. There aren't any Davieses left around here." She bunched up the shredded napkin and rolled it into a ball between her hands. "It's probably just as well. The memories and everything."

"Um-hm."

"So—anything else you want to know?"

"I don't think so." I forced a smile.

She tossed the ball at me. "Well, we'd better get out there. They'll be wondering what happened to us. Maybe if I get drunk on margaritas I can sit through a whole game of bridge."

"Monopoly. We voted after you left."

She groaned. "Monopoly! That's three hours."

"There's a lot of tequila," I said. "I checked."

"Mother, you're a bandit," Alice said, sitting back in her chair. "You win. I'm out."

Elaine counted her money, dividing it up into piles of green, blue, yellow, and pink. "Now, Alice M—Alice M, can I call you that, at least?"

"No."

She shrugged. "You're just a poor loser, is all."

"I'm out too," I said. "Bankrupted by a member of my own family."

"Stop that," said Elaine. "You'll only encourage her."

Kathy looked at her watch. "Goodness! The time has flown! Horace will be wondering where I am."

"He knows exactly where you are," Clyde said. "But it *is* getting late."

"Don't tell me y'all are leaving right when I'm about to win," Elaine protested.

"Those fajitas or whatever you call 'em were just great," Kathy said, collecting glasses and napkins on a tray. "And those brownies." She patted her stomach. "I spend all week taking off a pound, then I come over here and put it right back on."

Elaine looked around in exasperation. "You'll stay, Mother, won't you?"

Clyde shook her head and yawned.

"Well, holy smokes!" Elaine tossed the money on the board.

"Elaine, you should've gone into real estate," Kathy said. "Eight hotels. And the best I can do is a couple of railroads and a utility." She wrinkled her nose.

"Give me a call sometime this week," Alice said to me. "Let's go out for lunch."

I started sorting red and green plastic houses into Ziploc baggies. "Should we make a time now? How about Saturday?"

"Um . . . no. I think I'm going away this weekend. Camping."

"Who with, Alice Marie?"

"Mother—"

Elaine clamped her hand over her mouth. "Alice! Sorry, I forgot. It just slipped out."

"Anyway"—Alice gave me a tense smile—"maybe next week sometime."

I got up. "What can I bring inside?"

"You're all terrible sports," Elaine said. "Alice is so bad she won't even answer my question."

"What question?" Alice dumped the melted margarita mix over the side of the deck.

"I asked you who you're going camping with. Is that so hard to answer?"

"Yes, it is."

"Tell me," Elaine said, turning to Clyde. "How could I have raised a daughter like that?"

"You spoiled her rotten, what do you expect?" Clyde said. "Kathy, which way are you headed?"

Kathy folded up the Monopoly board and put it in the box. "Horace is over watching a football scrimmage at East High practice fields, so I thought I might stop by there."

"Oh."

"But I'd be happy to drop you home if you need a ride," she added quickly.

"It's out of the way."

"Don't be silly. Five minutes."

"I should've taken the car, but driving at night makes me nervous."

"I'll take you," I said. "I go right past your street."

"Well—"

"Are you ready to leave?"

"I don't want you to go to any trouble."

"It's no trouble."

"It's an inconvenience," she murmured.

"Not at all. Of course, you do know I charge by the mile."

Clyde looked at me.

"I was just teasing," I said.

"Don't even bother," said Alice. "This family has the sense of humor of a barn door."

"Alice Marie!" Elaine said.

Alice smiled sweetly. "See what I mean?"

There's something I want to ask you about.

It took a while to locate the passenger seat belt, which was buried in the seat. Clyde wouldn't get in the station wagon until I found it.

"Just let me take you, Mother," Elaine said, standing in the street jingling her car keys.

"We're all decided now, Elaine," I said, buckling in.

There's something I want to ask . . .

I drove slowly through the development with both hands on the wheel. Clyde was clutching the door handle and staring out the side window. She looked small and frail in the big seat. My hands were damp with sweat.

There's something . . .

We stopped at the curb in front of her house. It was twilight; the trees were silhouetted gray against the sky. A dog yapped, canned laughter from a TV floated across the yard. On the lawn next door a sprinkler moved slowly back and forth, a perfect fan of water.

"Clyde—"

"I appreciate you giving me a ride home." She opened the door.

"Wait." I put out my hand. "Wait. Just a second. There's something I want to ask you about."

She sat frozen in the act of getting out.

I took a deep breath. "I went to the cemetery today to see my mother's grave."

She didn't move.

"There was this woman buried beside her—Bryce Davies, I think her name was." I swallowed hard. "I believe they died right around the same time."

I watched her hand as she gripped the door handle, veins and muscle visible under the thin skin.

"So I was just wondering who she was, if you knew her," I said, trying to keep my voice neutral.

"I knew her," Clyde said.

"Did you know her pretty well?"

She looked out her window at the house.

"She died young," I said.

"Not so young."

"Forty-eight. That's pretty young."

She didn't answer.

"What did she die of?"

Suddenly her head snapped toward me as if she'd been slapped. "Where is it?"

"What?"

"Just tell me." Her voice was clear and steely. "It's mine. It wasn't his to give."

I gaped at her. "What are you talking about?"

"Don't play stupid," she said contemptuously.

"Look, I really don't understand."

"I know it's in that house somewhere. I'll find it, don't worry." She gave the door a violent push and got out.

"Wait—" But she was already hurrying up the walk toward the house. I went after her, catching up just as she got to the door. "Clyde—" I reached for her arm.

She wheeled around. "Don't you touch me! Leave me alone!"

I stepped back, palms up. "I don't have anything, Clyde. I don't have anything. I don't know what you're talking about."

She was breathing heavily. For a short while we stood together in silence, two shadowy shapes in the waning light.

"You can look for the answer, but there isn't one," she said finally. "Whatever you think you know, you're better off to forget."

"I don't understand."

"That's right. You don't understand. You can't. Don't ask to. It's none of your business."

"It *is* my business," I said, emotion rising as I spoke. "I need to know what happened, what happened to my mother, what was going on with you and Amory. . . . I can see why you want to forget it, I know it was a long time ago. But I can't even . . . I don't even . . . I don't know how I can know her, or anything about her, if—"

"Her dying has nothing to do with her life."

"For me it does. It has everything to do with it."

"No," she said. "It has to do with my life. *My* life." She pounded a fist on her chest. "And you don't know anything about it." She grabbed the doorknob, then paused and turned around, head up. "I'm not going to beg you. I'll only ask one more time. Where is the box?"

I was trembling. "What box? What are you talking about?"

"Don't lie to me."

"I'm not lying to you."

She clenched her jaw, gave the knob a twist, and slammed the door in my face.

When I got home there was a message on the machine from Alice.

"Well, you survived one evening of Chinese water torture. Now you're officially a Clyde girl, like it or not. Listen, I didn't get a chance to tell you before, but my brother was here last weekend, hiding out in some motel room. He wouldn't even tell *me* where he was staying. Anyway, he said he'd be back this weekend, and I thought you might want to meet him, so maybe we can set something up. Don't tell anybody. If Mother finds out she'll have a fit. Oh, and by the way—that stuff about Bryce Davies? I know you wouldn't, but don't mention it to Clyde." There was a pause, and I could hear her breathing. "Actually, I just think it'd be better to leave it alone in general, okay?"

The second message was from Drew.

"Cassie, are you there? If you're screening me I'll never speak to you again. I just ran into Adam at a party, and he said there's some new man in your life. Now tell me the truth—is this for real, or are you just making it up to get Adam off your back? Enquiring minds want to know. Call me."

I sat on the floor by the phone and replayed both messages. Then I put on some old pajamas and crawled into bed, but I was wide awake. Hours later I called my father. I dialed the number without thinking, automatically, like an animal finding its way home in the dark.

"Hi, Dad. I just wanted to hear your voice."

"I'm afraid it's pretty groggy," he said. "What time is it?"

I twisted the cord in my hand. "I don't know." I could hear him telling Susan to go back to sleep.

"It's two o'clock in the morning. Are you all right? Is something the matter?"

I bit my bottom lip to keep from crying.

"Hey, Cass." His voice was suddenly gentle. "Tell me."

I choked back a sob.

"Are you okay? . . . Are the ants back? . . . The dog? The dog's okay?"

"Dad," I said, wiping my nose with my hand. "Dad, did you ever hear of somebody named Bryce Davies?"

"Bryce Davies?"

"She—she was a friend of Clyde's."

"Oh, yes. Yes. She drowned, I think, right?"

"Right. Just before Mom was killed."

"Right." He waited.

"Well, I just found out."

"Found out?"

"About . . . you know. That she . . . drowned."

"I see."

I took a deep breath and let it out in a long sigh. All at once I had an urge to hang up. I wished I hadn't called. He didn't know anything, as I'd guessed at the start, and now the prospect of explaining seemed overwhelming.

"Did somebody tell you all this?" he was saying.

"Yes. Well, no. I . . . I saw her gravestone next to Mom's. Then I asked . . . I asked Clyde about it."

"And she told you?"

"Sort of."

"Hmm." After a moment he said, "You seem awfully upset about this, Cass."

"I . . . I know. I guess I am. I guess . . . it was a shock. To find out some whole new thing . . . "

"I'm not sure I understand. Is there something I'm missing?"

"Dad." I tried to laugh. "I'm sorry. I'm overreacting. It just seemed so weird that somebody else died too."

"Right." He sounded puzzled.

"I'm being silly. I shouldn't have called you. Sometimes this old house makes me obsess about things."

"Are you sure you're all right down there, Cass?"

"Oh, yes, fine. Really, Dad. Things are fine."

"Because you can always—"

"I know, Dad. Thanks. But really. Really, I'm fine."

"Well," he said.

"Well. Sorry to wake you up."

"Hey, anytime. I mean it."

"I love you," I said.

I hung up the phone and sat very still against the headboard. I thought I might cry. I thought I might cry, but I didn't.

When we buried him I thought that long awful stretch of my life was over, that the years I had left would be quiet and peaceful and only how I wanted them, not anybody else. It would be back to one way of remembering, not two competing memories whispering at each other in the night. Time was, he would wake with a cry and I'd put my hand on his arm and he'd shrink toward the wall, and I'd know he was thinking about it, though which part he was thinking about he wouldn't say and I wouldn't ask. Our words were bars keeping each other out, both of us locked inside a place nobody else could get to. We never talked about it, any of it, after that one time; we just lived together in a terrible illusion of intimacy, terrible in its rigor and exactness. He would kiss me on the cheek in front of the children, open the car door for me and take my hand to help me out. Reach for me sometimes in the obscurity of darkness, in the space between nightmares, and touch me tenderly and coldly, like a butcher preparing a chicken for sale—coldly, that is, and tenderly.

I try to think the simpler thing; it's easier that way. But then life complicates it, two minds living and thinking in the same small space. You think you've placed a thought or a memory so you can live with it, and then that other mind comes crowding in and knocks it down.

After he died I anticipated long, quiet nights like black velvet. I thought I would wrap myself in them. Only me, only my dreams as I chose them and not as they were willed to me. The whole bed would be mine. I should have known that death doesn't end anything, no, not even when you want it to. And memory is funny; it doesn't do what you tell it. So now the bed is all mine, but in the night I think of him—and her. And her. I think of them and my head aches. My heart aches.

It was Friday, a little after ten, and the bar was packed. I didn't see him come in, didn't even realize he was there until I was at the booth and saw his sandy hair under a dark felt hat. He'd been watching me as I approached. I felt my mouth go dry.

He ordered Dickel's straight up and introduced me to his friends, playing it straight. "This is my cousin Cassandra. She's from up north. Tom, Billy, Ed," he said, pointing at each with a trigger finger.

They all half rose. "Pleased to meet you." They tipped their hats and shook my hand.

"She's an artist," Troy said. "Not much money to be made in art these days. Got to supplement your income."

"Don't you know it's true," Tom said agreeably.

"You paint pictures?" Billy ventured.

"Sculpture, mostly. Clay." I glanced toward the bar. Liz and Ryan were watching me like mothers.

The guys laughed politely. Tom excused himself to play a video game.

"Well, you came to the right place if you're looking for clay," said Billy. "Hell, take some home with you when you go! You'll be doing us a favor."

As we were talking, I could feel those pale-blue eyes searching the bland mask I was wearing to hide the fact that I was caving in. He didn't try to speak to me alone, didn't say anything about anything, even when Ed and Billy went over to watch Tom rack up points on the screen. When I brushed his hand by mistake it was like touching an electric fence. I was sure he felt it too.

Saturday morning I was reading the newspaper in my booth at the Eagle when I heard a rap on the window. I looked up to see Troy in a white T-shirt and a frayed jean jacket, his hands cupping his eyes against the glass. I was startled to see his face so close. He bounced back on his heels, motioned toward the door, and pantomimed drinking coffee. I realized that I'd never seen him in the cold light of morning, except that one time, and mornings after don't count. They might as well be the night before.

As he came toward me now his hair was wet and his face was clean and pale, as if it had been recently scrubbed. The waitress looked up from her card game and watched him. He smiled at her.

"Hey," he said to me, tapping two fingers on the Formica tentatively. "Mind if I sit down?"

"How'd you know I was here?"

"Pure coincidence. You never know who you might run into."

I just looked at him.

"Okay, Alice told me. She said you come here every day."

"How does she know that?"

He shrugged. "Better be careful, Cassie. Life gets predictable around here pretty fast."

I laughed nervously. "So she sent you over here, huh?"

"That's right." He bent forward, holding out his hand with exaggerated formality. "And you must be Cassandra. I'm your cousin Troy. Nice to meet you."

"Nice to meet you, Troy," I said, shaking his hand.

"May I join you?"

I gestured to the seat across from me.

He slid in, and the waitress brought over a menu. When she left he said, "So you're from the Big City, I understand."

"Most recently. Boston before that."

"Boston," he said. "I believe I've heard of it. Something about a tea party. Some guy on a horse with a feather in his hat trying to get someplace by midnight."

"Fourth-grade social studies?"

"Fifth. We're a little backward down here, you know."

"And you live in Atlanta," I said.

"Indeed."

"Something about a big fire, Rhett and Scarlett, the Peachtree Hotel?"

"That's it. You ever been there?"

I shook my head.

"Well, we'll see what we can do about that." He scanned the menu. "This place has fantastic grits. You like grits?"

"I don't know."

"You don't know?"

"I've never tried them."

"Oh, well, then you have to."

"I think I'll stick with toast."

"Come on, now. Expand your horizons."

"I think I've expanded my horizons enough lately, thanks."

We sat in silence for a moment. Behind the lunch counter the juice machine made gurgling sounds. The large clock ticked loudly on the wall above it. When the waitress returned he ordered coffee, black, and she brought it right over. I watched him tear open three sugar packets and pour them in, one after another. Looking at the top of his blond head, I thought of how I had stood by the door inside his motel room as he sat on the bed pulling on his boots, head bent, tongue stuck out in concentration. When he glanced up and saw me watching, he had blown me a kiss.

He stirred the coffee and then settled back against the corner of the booth, one leg propped on the seat, his arm dangling over his knee. He took a sip of coffee and watched me over the rim of the cup.

"You're even lovelier in daylight."

"Have you told anybody?" I asked.

"I'm sure they can see it for themselves."

"You know what I'm talking about."

"What are you talking about?"

"Don't play games, Troy."

Outside, a teenager in a large aqua convertible was trying to parallel park in front of the diner. The first time, his back wheels jumped up on the sidewalk; the next time, he couldn't get closer than three feet from the curb. He kept hitting the front bumper of the car behind him. We watched him out the window until he gave up and left.

"I came back this weekend because of you," Troy said. He seemed to be studying my features. "I went to the bar last night because I knew you'd be there."

"Don't."

"What?"

"Don't say that."

"Why not?"

"Troy, we can't—" I sighed. "We can't even hold hands in public without creating a scandal."

He reached for my hand across the table and grasped it firmly before I could draw back. "I don't see anybody screaming."

"You know what I mean."

He looked around. "I don't see anybody calling the police."

The waitress came toward us with the coffeepot, and I pulled my hand away.

"D'ja see that kid out there trying to park?" she said. "Didn't look old enough to drive."

"Probably isn't," Troy said.

"Nice car, though," said the waitress.

"Fifty-seven Cadillac. I wouldn't mind one of those myself. They're hard to come by."

"Just wait a month or two." She laughed. "Check the junk lots. It might even be salvageable." She filled our cups and went back to the counter, whistling.

"Does your mother know you're here this time?" I asked.

"No."

"What'll she say if she finds out?"

He shifted in his seat, casting around for an answer. "Look, who the hell cares?" he said finally. "I have my own life. I can't go around worrying what other people think all the time."

"But she's your mother. And she's hurt that you haven't been in touch."

He shrugged. "To tell you the truth, I don't even want to be around her. I always feel like she's trying to swallow me up."

"What do you mean?"

"The only way she can get people to stick around is to control their lives, make them dependent on her. Look at my dad—she does everything for him but deliver his sermons. I know she writes them. And look at Clyde." He shook his head. "It's pathetic."

"What about Clyde?"

"My mother treats her like a child. She can't make a decision on her own without Mother butting in. Why do you think she lives in that development five minutes away? Mother didn't want her too far out of sight."

"She *is* getting older, Troy."

"It doesn't have anything to do with age. And it doesn't have anything to do with Clyde's well-being."

I stirred my coffee. "Well, whatever the reasons, I feel uncomfortable being seen with you when you haven't told your mother you're here. What would she say if she walked in right now?"

"Alice told me you were here. We're cousins. What can she say?"

"Oh, yes, that's right," I said. "We're starting from the beginning. Nice, normal, friendly."

He leaned forward. "Look, Cassandra. I can be your friend. I can be the best friend you ever had. But I'm not going to pretend that night didn't happen."

I thought of that night: of how when he kissed me I smelled the tequila on his breath, of the way he cradled my arms and head beneath him, his fingers laced through my hair.

He reached over and touched the line of my cheekbone with two fingers, and I watched his face, feeling a flush rise in my own. After a moment I lowered my eyes, and he let his hand drop to the table. We sat that way, listening to the loud ticking of the clock and the gurgling juice machine, until the waitress came by with the check.

He glanced at it. “I suppose I should be going.”

I nodded and waved my hand as if to say he was free to leave. He pulled a dollar out of his back pocket and put it on the table. The bill sat between us like a truce.

He stood up. “See you soon,” he said, and softly touched my hand, running a finger down my wrist to my thumb.

Through the glass I watched him walk down the street, his shoulders hunched forward a little, as if he were heading into a strong wind. I put some change on top of the dollar, and the waitress came over to clear the table.

“That your brother?”

“No.”

“Y’all look an awful lot alike.” She picked up the change and put it in her apron pocket.

I folded up the newspaper. “Well, we’re cousins.”

“You don’t say,” she said, with sudden interest. “Hey, listen, I was thinking that maybe if I found out if that car might be for sale I could call him and let him know. You got a number for him, just in case?”

“No, I’m sorry. He’s staying at some motel on the other side of town.”

“And what motel would that be?”

I looked at her steadily. “I really don’t know,” I said, getting up. “If I see him I’ll tell him you’re looking for him.” I put the paper under one arm and gathered my bags in the other.

“See you tomorrow,” the waitress said. “And bring your cousin.” She smiled, and I noticed she had lipstick on her teeth.

He stood in the doorway fingering his felt hat. Through the screen he could see me sitting on a stool in the dining room, my hands molding a figure, clay streaking my face and sweat trickling down my blouse, straw-colored wisps of hair falling out of a blue bandanna. It was early afternoon. Birds were quiet, keeping cool. Bugs sang in the hot grass. From where I was sitting I could see into each room on the ground floor and out a kaleidoscope of windows. When I heard the muffled rumbling of a jeep coming up the long grassy drive, I knew it was him and my heart started beating faster. Now it was racing and my sweat had turned cool and my hands were unsteady, though he couldn't see that.

"Hey," he said, leaning against the screen, his right arm over his head as he squinted in at me. "Mind if I come in?"

I shook my head, and he opened the door. The spring was loose, and the door slapped back against the side of the house. He put his hat on the table in the kitchen and came over to me. I looked at his jean jacket, wondering how he could stand to wear it on such a hot day.

"What brings you to this part of town?"

"I wanted to see you, Cassandra." He said my name slowly, enunciating each syllable as if it were a word he'd never said before, and then he lifted my chin and kissed me softly, lightly. He leaned back for a second and looked into my eyes, one at a time, and said, "Why don't we just forget all the bullshit for now."

"Okay," I whispered. *Okay.* I was willing to forget everything in that moment, and he kissed me again, his tongue in my mouth, then around the rim of my ear. He pulled off the bandanna, and I lifted his T-shirt with clay-covered hands and drew chalky lines across his chest with my fingers, feeling his skin, like fine-grained wood, the muscles of his stomach, the narrow feather of hair. I touched his nipples, making them hard; he slowly unbuttoned my blouse. He bent down, cupping my breasts with his hands and taking one and then the other into his mouth as my nipples rose and tightened in response to his hot breath, the cooling wetness of his kisses.

His hands moved up my spine, and he slipped the shirt off my shoulders as I sat on the stool in the center of the room. I ran my fingers through his soft hair, all matted down by the hat. I felt like a sun he was orbiting; he touched my hair, the small of my back, my breasts, my stomach, my face, and then I slid off the stool and we knelt together, bare chests touching. I licked the salt off his neck while he undid my shorts, pushing them down, pushing me down, running his tongue between my breasts as I lay back on the pine floor, running his tongue down my ribs and flicking it over my stomach. My hands were in his hair, on the curve of his neck, gripping his shoulders as his tongue moved down to the hollow between my hips, leaving a trail like a snail. He kissed each hipbone and moved down one leg, brushing my thigh with his lips, stopping to bite a knee before coming up the other side.

"Cassandra," he whispered without looking up, "I wrote you a song."

I had never felt so exposed or cared so little as I lay there in the thick heat and brightness of midday in that house with twenty-eight windows, all of them open. Gently his tongue probed, and soon I didn't care at all. His hands touched inside me, rubbed my breasts, clutched me from behind; his tongue was steady, insistent, and I was on a roller coaster, panting, twisting, and the ride got faster and suddenly I was soaring through the air, off the track. He held my thighs and kept licking, and I sailed higher and again, resisting and panting and saying his name, and then the feeling melted inside me like ice cream.

I put my hands over my face and he came up, kissing my belly button and my freckled breasts and my collarbone, and then, moving my fingers aside, he kissed me on the mouth. After a while I stopped trembling and we lay side by side, facing each other, my hands curled against his chest, one of his arms under my neck and the other in the dip between my hipbone and rib cage.

Later, in the dusky heat of early evening, he went around the room looking at clay pieces that were drying on plastic squares all over the floor. He ran his hand along the rounded side of one, as if feeling the flank of a horse. He tapped it. "Hollow."

"They all are," I said. I was scraping clay off the bat of my potter's wheel and lumping it into a pile.

He looked over at me. "That piece is ruined."

I picked up the clay, weighing it in one hand and then the other, molding it into a ball. "I didn't stop you."

"But still—I'm sorry."

"I didn't like the way it was turning out anyway." I smiled.

He held up a small piece and examined it carefully. "How do you do this?" he asked. "How do you know what to do?"

"You don't, really—I don't. You start with a basic idea and then just keep trying until something works, until it all comes together somehow. Or doesn't."

"Like writing songs."

"Maybe. I don't know what to compare it to. It's the only thing I've done that feels this way."

He contemplated one of the glazed pieces. "Aha," he said. "This is a head."

"Um-hm."

"And this is a leg." He picked up a long, broad piece next to it. "Are all these parts going to fit together?"

"Well, there'll be three figures." I covered the ball of clay with a damp cloth and went over to him. "See, this fits here." I placed the head at an angle on a larger torso. "The different parts rest on top of each other like a rock pyramid. The ones at the top are smaller than the ones at the bottom."

"So the feet must be huge."

"Yeah. I haven't done them yet. I'm a little afraid of feet."

"I can model for you. My feet are really weird."

"Are they thirty inches long?"

He laughed. "How tall will these things be?"

"About six feet."

He ran his fingertips down the front of the torso with the head on it. "This one's female."

"How'd you figure that out, Sherlock?"

He grabbed the waistband of my shorts and kissed me. "Nothing gets by me." He held my face in his hands. "I can't believe you do this stuff. I love it."

"Why?"

"Why? Because it's completely foreign to me. It's a part of you I can't touch."

"I don't know, it might be the part you can touch most easily."

"No," he said, shaking his head. "You can use what you are—even what we do—and turn it into something else. So maybe I could be in it, or a part of it, but I'll never get close enough to touch it or find out for myself how it works. That's what I love about it," he said. "The mystery. The transformation."

"You've thought about this."

He shrugged. "It's the same with music. If you can take what you are, what you know, and use it to express what you feel, not what you think—and not in some obvious way, but in a way that's yours alone—then you have something. Something real."

"But the thinking is a part of it too." I went into the kitchen. "It can't just stop. Otherwise you'd end up with sentimental garbage, whether you wanted to or not." I opened the refrigerator. "You want a beer?"

"Sure." After a moment he said, "But the thinking has to come later."

"You can't say that so absolutely." Coming back into the room, I handed him a beer and kept one for myself. "You can't separate thinking and feeling into distinct categories. They're always connected."

"So you knew exactly what you wanted when you did this." He gestured toward the torso.

"I knew I wanted to do three women. Generations."

"And the shape and the size and the texture—all of that you already knew?"

I moved some rags off a windowsill and sat down. "I had an idea."

"And when your hands started working . . . "

"But I'm talking about before."

"Unh-unh. We're talking about the whole process."

I tossed a rag at him. "When my hands started working, it's true, I didn't think much anymore."

He sipped his beer and looked around the room. "Who *are* these people, Cassandra?"

"Don't you know you're not supposed to ask that? Or I'm not supposed to answer."

"So who are they?"

"I don't know," I said. "Maybe they're ghosts."

"How close were you to Amory?" I asked. We had gone out on the porch to watch the sun set.

"Not very. I don't think anybody was." He took another sip of beer. "He was waiting to die for a long time."

"What do you mean?"

"You could see it in his eyes. They were dull-looking, glazed over. Like he didn't care about anything."

"Always?"

"When I knew him. I guess he was different before."

"Before . . . "

"You know—the accident."

Blue came racing around the side of the house, wagging his tail. "Have you ever heard of"—I patted the porch, and Blue came and sat beside me—"a woman named Bryce Davies?"

"Yeah," he said. "How do you know about that?"

"I don't know much. She was a friend of Clyde's."

He nodded.

"They went swimming, and she drowned."

He set his beer on the step.

"She was . . . she was having an affair with Amory—"

"Wait, hold on. Where'd you hear that from?"

"I just heard it, Troy," I said. "What does it matter where?"

"It matters. People say things—"

"Well, if you must know, I heard it from May Ford."

"Hmm." He ran his hands through his hair. "Listen, Cassie, May Ford is notorious—"

"I know, I know. I didn't believe her at all, at first. But then I asked Clyde about it, and she acted really strange, like I'd found out some big secret she's been trying to keep. She thought I'd gotten hold of some box that has something to do with it."

"A box?"

"She said, 'I know it's in that house somewhere.'" I stroked Blue absently, remembering. "'It wasn't his to give.'"

"His?" Troy said. "Who's he?"

"I don't know."

"Amory?"

"Who else could it be?" Blue rubbed his shoulder against me and fell against my leg. I burrowed my fingers into his fur.

"Wait," Troy said softly. "Wait, wait, wait."

"What?"

"I don't know. I just remembered something."

"Tell me."

"I . . . I don't know. This might be crazy."

I put my hand on his knee. "Tell me."

He looked at me for a moment, a long gaze. "This is what everybody was afraid of, you know."

I felt the skin on the back of my neck prickle. "What do you mean?"

"That you might start poking around."

"And find what?"

"Cassie, there's a lot of stuff . . . there's a lot of stuff you don't understand." He sighed. "I'm not sure that it does much good to go digging around in the past."

"But I didn't go digging around. All this just bubbled up."

"Okay. But maybe now it'd be best to let it go."

"Aren't you interested in finding out what happened? Isn't anybody interested?"

He stood up and tucked in his shirt.

"What are you all hiding?"

He averted his eyes. "I've got to leave." I listened as he went inside to get his jacket, his shoes. The air was soft and dark. He came back to the porch.

"What if she did drown that woman like everybody thinks? What if he did smash up the car on purpose? It's not going to bring your mother back, Cassie. It's over. There's nothing you can do to change it."

From where I sat I could see into the darkened dining room. The clay pieces on the floor looked like a gathering of grotesques and misfits. One of the heads, its face tilted toward the kitchen, seemed to be watching me.

Suddenly I felt almost unbearably sad. I imagined myself shrouded like the old women I had seen in Greece, dressed in mourning for the rest of their lives, wearing black like armor.

"It's not over," I said quietly. He came and drew me up and put his arms around me, and I leaned into him, gathering warmth from his embrace. "It's not over for me."

As soon as he left I began searching for the box. I started downstairs, in the hall closet, tapping behind coat hangers, then I got down on my hands and knees and cleared away the tools and umbrellas on the floor. Crawling around inside the closet, rapping on the wood with my knuckles, I felt like a third-rate detective in a B movie: I didn't really know what I was looking for, I didn't know where to look, and I wasn't even sure what a hollow sound sounded like.

I moved on to the living room and peered up the fireplace, tapped around the baseboard, then navigated around the heads and limbs on the dining room floor. After checking the kitchen cabinets, I went upstairs to look in the bedrooms. I was in my mother's room when I heard the bump and clatter of Troy's jeep up the drive.

He got out, slamming the door behind him, and knocked on the screen. Blue started barking from the landing.

"Shush, Blue. Come in," I yelled down.

He followed my voice upstairs and came into the bedroom. "I've been thinking," he said. "This is probably stupid, but . . . " He rubbed his chin with his hand. "I know about this hiding place. Granddaddy showed it to me when I was little. He said he made it when he built the house, so he'd have a place that was private, that was all his own."

"I wonder why he told you."

He shrugged. "Beats me. Maybe he just wanted somebody to know. Maybe he was tired of keeping it secret."

"Where is it?"

"I've never told anybody. He asked me not to."

I just stood there.

"To hell with it," he said. "Let's find that box."

The basement was dark and cool and dusty. Troy turned on the light, and the single bulb swayed back and forth over our heads, rattling against the chain. We groped around in the dimness, finding an old wooden crate. He climbed up on it and began moving his hands along the low ceiling.

Our breathing and the rapping of his knuckles were the only sounds in the stillness. Blue sat at the top of the stairs, watching us quietly, thumping his tail whenever I looked in his direction. As Troy finished with each section he got down and moved the crate. "I don't know," he muttered, "maybe I'm crazy. Maybe I dreamed this."

As he tapped across the ceiling, I stood on the cool, hard-packed floor in my bare feet, holding my arms against my chest.

"I can't find it," he said.

"Are you sure it was in the basement?"

"I'm going to try again." He started in the far corner, above a row of shelves. He moved slowly, knocking and scratching and listening for hollow spaces. He got down and put the crate in the far left corner and climbed up on it again. Blue whined and pawed the floor. I could just make out Troy's face, his eyes narrowed and his mouth open in concentration.

All at once he stopped tapping. His fingers pushed at the ceiling, his nails scrabbling at rough wood. He shoved hard with the heel of his hand, and a board gave way, leaving a hole about two feet long and six inches wide. I went over to him as he reached inside and felt the space, and after a few seconds I saw his body tense. "There's something here."

He pulled out a pile of rags and handed it down to me. I sifted through the mildewed pieces—a skirt, a blouse, and a bra—and bundled them under one arm. When I looked up again he was standing on tiptoe, reaching as far as he could into the hole. I could hear something solid scrape against the inside of the ceiling as he drew his arm out.

The box was long and narrow. It was heavy, made of dark, smooth wood. I held it to my chest, wiping the dust off. Blue was whining again.

As Troy replaced the board, I turned and went up the stairs, stroking the dog on the head to calm him when I got to the top.

I set the box and the bundle of clothing on the table in the kitchen, flipped on the overhead light, and sat in one of the folding chairs I'd bought at a church sale. Inspecting the box, I found that it was scratched and moldy, the latch mangled and the lock broken.

Troy came up and went to the sink to wash his hands. "So," he said, shaking the water off and wiping his palms on his jeans. "What've you found?"

"I haven't looked yet. Thanks a lot for helping me with this. I mean it."

He waited.

"Troy . . . I think I need to do this alone." There was an awkward silence. "Sorry. I just—"

"It's okay." He disappeared into the dining room and came back, putting on his jacket. "Let me know what you find."

"I will," I said. "I'll let you know."

"I'll be at the motel."

I nodded. "Don't . . . just don't tell anybody else, okay? This is our secret."

"Okay."

He came to the table and took my hand, looking into my eyes. "Are you sure it's worth it, Cassie? Are you sure you want to know?"

Memory believes before knowing remembers.

"I have to," I said. "I have to know."

part five

It was late spring or early spring; at any rate, it was springtime. I'm not one to remember dates. The air was warm and smelled of growing things: honeysuckle, daffodils, the first harvest of strawberries. Some afternoons it was already so warm that there wasn't much to do but sit on the porch swing or take a rest with the shades drawn upstairs. The kids were grown and out of the house, and Amory's days were long. His hours were unpredictable; I had to take chances with dinner, keep it hot on the stove or sometimes whip it up in a hurry when I heard his truck at the end of the long drive. I usually ate alone.

Afternoons tossed the sun across the sky like a slow-moving ball. I swept and dusted, taught myself tunes on the piano, read stories in magazines and books from the library, sometimes several at once. I needlepointed, worked in the garden with Jeb Gregory or his daughter Lattie. I still hadn't learned to drive—Amory said he didn't want me to, that one of us driving was enough, that it made him nervous to think what kind of trouble I could get myself into with a car. Back then, when I listened to him and paid real close attention, I could almost always convince myself that he was right. So I didn't drive, and I didn't go anywhere unless Jeb took me into town for a few hours or I got a ride from one of my friends from the book circle or the other clubs I'd joined to keep from dying of boredom.

Forty-nine seemed old then, but I was so young. If I'd listened to my body instead of my husband, maybe I wouldn't have been stuck all those years in that house I hated on its island of land. I had never been anywhere on my own, not by car or by bus or by train. I had never flown. So I sat in that house year after year and resented him for leaving when he left in the morning and hated him more when he returned home at night—for thinking of home as a place you return to when you feel like it and not one you never leave.

It got so that when I saw him coming up the walk I'd know which vice he'd indulged in, and sometimes which were in the works. By the time I had hold of his suit jacket I knew by the smell where he'd been, where he'd be going back to when he told me he had business after dinner or an out-of-town company guest to entertain. I couldn't complain about the business, could I? What was it that put food on our table, clothes on our backs? What was it that put the rabbit-fur coat in the closet in the hall? If you want to move up in this world you got to make sacrifices, honey, he'd say if I complained. You got to go that extra mile.

I wanted to believe him, I really did. I wanted nothing more than to look into his eyes and have him look into mine when he told me where he'd been. Instead, he'd start to act annoyed and talk to me as if I were an unreasonable child. His speeches were perfectly patient and perfectly timed, so that if I was still objecting by the time he was ready to leave, he'd don his hat and stand in the door and say, "I have tried to be a reasonable man and a good provider, and I don't know what more could possibly be expected of me." And then he'd be gone.

I could live with the drinking; and a little poker, as vices go, was pretty tame. Nobody around here was willing to bet enough to get him in real trouble. The woody smell of tobacco was almost a comfort, since it meant he'd been in the company of men; he himself had an aversion to cigars. But there were other smells, perfume the least of them, that tied my stomach into knots. I can't even remember feeling jealous, though I'm certain there was a time when I did. But every time he lied he strangled one more part of my love for him, and after a while it wasn't that I didn't want them to have him; in fact, it would have been a whole lot easier if one of them had taken him off my hands for good. What made me so furious was the thought of him slid-

ing his hand up some woman's leg and unbuckling a garter while I nursed Ellen through scarlet fever, or the thought of him in some pay-by-the-hour motel room, unclasping a brassiere while I picked his laundry off the floor.

I never sent a letter to Bryce, or to any of the others I found out about. I wrote them all and kept the letters locked up in a box. At first I didn't send them because I almost couldn't believe it. These were my dearest friends. They had children the ages of my own, husbands who kissed my cheek at company barbecues. We'd gather for bridge and talk about fabrics and recipes and where we'd go if we ever got the chance: Paris, Morocco, New York. What would they want with my husband? And then, as time went on, I didn't send the letters for a hundred reasons: because I knew that if I stopped one affair he'd just start another; because I came to the miserable conclusion that it was a small town and I needed all the friends I could get; because I was a coward. There's a way people have of living with lies when the truth is too painful to confront.

So I put my best face forward, smiling and gracious on the outside, the hatred locked up in a box. And I would probably have continued that way indefinitely if I hadn't discovered in his breast pocket, long after I'd stopped looking, a single hairpin, its head made of mother-of-pearl.

I sat on the bed with the small volume in my hands. The binding was cracked, the red cover faded. The tiny lock on the leather flap had rusted; gilded page corners were two decades smooth. The key was lost or missing. "Diary" was scrawled across the cover in gold script.

Since Troy left I'd been going through the contents of the box, folded newspaper clippings and letters mostly, a few photographs. I hadn't read anything yet. I was taking my time. I came across a black-and-white photograph of my parents, smooth-faced and smiling, leaning together awkwardly on a couch, holding a baby wrapped in a blanket between them—me. I studied the picture. When my mother died she was exactly my age. She had married, given birth; she left a legacy. What did I have to show for my years? Who would be left to remember?

As I held a sharp pair of scissors in one hand and the diary in the other, I imagined my mother holding it, anticipating what to say, how to make sense of her life. The act of cutting the flap felt momentous; scissors sliced through leather with a decisive snap. When I opened the book the musty pages stood up in stiff sections. On the frontispiece "Diary" was printed again, in black script, with "1959" in wide-spaced, tiny block numerals at the bottom. In watery blue ink my mother had written, "Ellen Iris Clyde, 1959–1962." And in another, darker ink: "Ellen Clyde Simon, 1962–."

I started at the beginning.

9/10/59. Went into Boston with Cynthia Blackwell and bought this book—we've decided to record our fascinating lives. Let's see how long this resolution lasts.

Trees turning already—I can't get used to it. All settled into Merton with three *very* nice girls for roommates, Nancy Dew the only one with any life in her. Taking Eng Lit 1820–1914, art history, bio, political science with Connelly ("Let us consider, ladies, the Negro question"). The sophomoric cattle roundups have begun—mixer tonight at 8. Mary and Helen are all aquiver. Not me—never again.

Turning the pages, I found that the handwriting changed from year to year. The early entries were large and loopy; later the script darkened, condensed. As time went by—'60, '62, '63—my mother confided in her diary only periodically. On June 20, 1962, she had written:

What kind of people go to Boston—or, worse, stay in Boston—for their honeymoon? A poor graduate student with a thesis to finish and an art teacher with evening classes to lead. Ed promises that someday we'll do it right, but I assure him this is fine with me. We're booked into a bed-and-breakfast with a private bath for a three-day weekend; no students can drop by, no parents can call—it's heaven.

Flipping ahead to the year I was born, I found this entry.

3/18/64. I'm convinced that Cassandra is trying to talk to us, the way dolphins do. Ed's skeptical—but I'm certain she's a genius. She's also vain—*loves* to look at herself in the mirror.

I read somewhere that babies can't see colors in the early months, so I've been making black-and-white collages and putting them up on the walls around her crib. I want to do everything right. I want her life to be perfect. Wouldn't it be amazing if we pulled it off?

I turned to the final entry. The writing was cramped. I had to look twice to believe it: it was dated the day she died.

13 May 67. Ed, *where are you?* Mother and Daddy are fighting and everything's awful. I was in the kitchen a while ago kneading bread, and I could hear them upstairs—I've never heard him cry—he sounded hysterical, practically incoherent, shouting "You killed her—you knew, so you killed her—" and she wasn't saying a word. Afterwards I heard a door slam and his footsteps on the stairs. He came into the kitchen with his hat on, wiping his face with his hand, saying that his car had a flat and could he borrow the bus? What could I say? I said, "Do you really think you should be driving right now?" and he gave me this look—angry, desperate, I don't know how to describe it, more naked than you'd want to see—and he said, "Ellen, don't make me explain." I asked him what I could do and he said there was nothing anybody could do. So I said he could take the bus, but then I remembered the Vietnam meeting I want to go to later tonight, so I went running out to catch him. He doesn't like that stuff, so I didn't tell him the specifics; I just asked him to be back by 8:00 to give me a ride. He didn't even turn around, just put his hand up and left.

She's still up there, and I'm down here writing this, and it's strange, I feel like every thought in my head is magnified a thousand times. I can hear her pacing around. She must know that I heard. This tension is unbearable.

Since I've been here it's been just terrible between them, the worst I've ever seen. Now he's blaming her for what happened to Mrs. Davies—it has to be her, who else could it be? But why? What's wrong with him? What *happened?*

I put the diary down and sat very still for a minute. My heart was thumping against my chest. I reached into the box, pulling out and unfolding a yellowed clipping: "FATAL CRASH ON ROUTE 6," with a fuzzy photograph of the mangled bus turned over on its side.

A 27-year-old woman was killed instantly last night when the van she was a passenger in skidded out of control on a rain-slicked stretch of Route 6. Ellen C. Simon was pronounced dead on arrival at 6:07 a.m. at St. Joseph's Hospital in Athens. The driver of the van, Amory Clyde, the victim's father, was treated for minor injuries and released. Clyde is President of the Whitfield Mill in Sweetwater.

Mrs. Simon, a graduate of East Sweetwater High School and Wellesley College, worked part-time as an art instructor at Boston University. She leaves behind a husband, Edgar, and a daughter, Cassandra, 3. She is also survived by her father, her mother Constance Clyde, her brother Horace Clyde and sister Elaine Burns.

Funeral services will be held at Cease Funeral Home on May 16 at 2 p.m.

I picked up another clipping, "LOCAL WOMAN DROWNS AT SWIMMING HOLE," which was brief and vague, and then I leafed through the letters my grandmother had saved, all written by her, each one a carefully worded accusation of treachery and betrayal. One, I saw, was addressed to May Ford.

I don't know if anything is going on between you and Amory, but it's perfectly obvious that you'd like there to be. Don't pretend to be my friend, and don't for a minute think you're being discreet. One thing I'm certain of, May, is that you'll never find what you want. You'll never be happy. And I feel pity for you, but I'm not sorry.

At the bottom of the pile I found a note on rose-tinted stationery, dated May 1940, written in a different hand. "Dearest Amory," it read:

> Until last week I'd given up hope of ever being happy. Now all I think about is you. I hear the whistle blow at the mill and wonder who you're with, what you're doing when we're not together. I get crazy jealous. When Frank comes home from work I endure hearing the details of his day just to get word of you. I think of your fingers on the keys of my piano, "Mood Indigo"—your soft voice making those sad words poetry.
>
> You've told me this is all I can expect, and I accept it. But I want you to know that I'd leave all I have—all of it—in a second, to be with you. If only we had met three years ago!
>
> I am—and always will be—thinking of you. Bryce.

I folded the note, thinking about what Clyde had said: *You can look for the answer, but there isn't one. Whatever you think you know, you're better off to forget.* I remembered Horace telling me, *We don't talk about what happened.* I picked up the newspaper clipping about Bryce's death: "The accident took place on the property of Mrs. Constance Clyde, Mrs. Davies' swimming companion."

I went through all the letters again, but Bryce's was the only one addressed to Amory. As I started to put them away I noticed a long silver pin in the bottom of the box. Holding it up to the light, I twirled it around slowly. The head, large and distinctive, gleamed gray-pink and silvery, mother-of-pearl. I studied it for a moment and then put it back, replacing the letters and tattered clippings as I found them.

Moving the box aside, I sat back against the wall. Now that there was room for him, Blue jumped up on the bed and started licking my face. I pushed him away, then pulled him close, stroking his head.

I thought of my mother downstairs in the kitchen, twenty-seven years old, rolling up her sleeves to knead dough on a floured board, counting one, two, three, four. She is standing very still, cocking her head to listen—*You killed her, you knew, so you killed her*—and then she hears the crying, the feet thudding on the steps. When her father comes in to ask for the keys, his eyes are red and watery, his hands shaky, his body bowed in the doorway.

I imagined them hours later, alone in that bus on a narrow back road. The night is dark and cool and rainy; the pavement is slick. The car weaves back and forth across the road, scraping tree branches; wet leaves slap across the windshield. Gripping the passenger's seat, she asks him, *Daddy,* she begs, *Daddy, please stop and let me drive.*

Ellen, he says, *don't make me explain.*

I picked through the bundle of clothing Troy had found in the basement. A short yellow skirt, a torn long-sleeved patterned blouse, a milk-colored bra. I stripped out of my clothes and tried the pieces one by one, flimsy fragments of fabric that smelled faintly of mold. The bra was too small; it didn't fit around my back. I could get the skirt over my hips and zip it almost all the way, and the blouse, with its jagged rip down the side, buttoned easily. In the mirror above my dresser I looked awkward and gangly, my washed-out features overwhelmed by the faded geometric pattern of the blouse.

My glance fell on a small, curled color photo propped against the mirror. My dad, young and scruffy, was standing behind my mother with an intense look on his face, his wiry arms draped over her thin shoulders. My mother wore that familiar lime-green dress and a detached, ironic smile. Her pose was cool, and her eyes were bright and clear. I watched my reflection rub the wispy blouse, smooth the textured skirt, touch the rents and the rust-colored streaks splashed across the material. Bloodstains, I realized suddenly. These were my mother's clothes. These were the clothes she died in.

In the car my grandfather is muttering to himself, cursing, his hands unsteady on the steering wheel as my mother pleads with him: *Daddy, let's go back, these roads are dangerous at night,* her eyes open wide in alarm. All at once, the back right tire thumps into a ditch, slamming her head against the seat, knocking her knuckles against the side window. He turns the wheel sharply to the left, straight toward a tree, then violently to the right. She is screaming, or maybe she's too scared to move or cry out, her hands up in front of her face. I can see him hunched forward, his chest pressed against the wheel, choking out something she strains to hear. *You killed her—you knew, so you killed her*—and all she can say is *No—*

When I think about it now it's funny that Amory acted like he was so worried about my driving but didn't even pretend to be concerned about the reservoir a half mile from the house on our property where I spent so many afternoons alone. The kids had used it as a swimming hole for years; when they were little I'd pack picnic lunches and lead them, single file and barefoot, down a path Jeb had cut through tall grass and a short stretch of woods. I'd sit on a large rock and sew or read magazines while they splashed around. Sometimes I'd stick my toes in. I had never learned to swim, but for some reason we didn't worry about that, and nothing ever happened to any of them. But when Horace got old enough he got it in his head to teach me.

I was afraid of the water, the cold blank surface of it giving no clue as to its depth, but nothing I could say would dissuade him. So I went to Carole's Fashions and purchased a swimming costume—blue-striped with yellow flowers—and a matching robe, and very gently, very slowly, he coaxed me in and taught me to float. I'd lie on my back in three feet of water looking up at the heavy green leaves hanging over us, the blue sky with veins of white running through it, and Horace would say, "Relax, Ma, stretch into it, keep your chin up, weightless, weightless." When I mastered that, he taught me the breast stroke and the crawl, and then it hardly seemed possible that I could have spent so many years stranded on the rocks.

For a long time Horace wouldn't let me swim by myself. He showed me where to steer clear of jagged outcroppings and made me promise to keep away from the whirlpool by the boulder. "One hundred feet deep right here," Horace told me, standing on top of the boulder and pointing down. "If you get caught in the slide of that funnel it'll be near impossible to get back out." He showed me how to watch for mud-colored moccasins, which swim with the current and surface in the sun. He bought me a whistle to wear around my neck, to alert Jeb or Lattie up at the house if I was out too deep and got tired, or got bitten. I told him it was a silly idea: who'd have the presence of mind to blow a whistle when they were drowning, and what chance would they have of being heard anyway? But he said it would make him feel better, so I wore it.

As long as Horace was living at home he went to the reservoir with me or made sure someone else did. But after he left for college and Ellen went north and Elaine got married, I was free to do as I pleased. Some days I'd take my lunch and go down to the rocks and never even step in. I'd just sit and watch the way the leaves twirled on the glassy surface like hurricane patterns on the weather report, the way the wind ruffled the water like a shirred dress.

I was there by myself on the day JFK was shot. It was near the end of November, too cold to swim, but I was sitting on a blanket in a chiffon scarf and a sweater, writing a letter to Ellen. The whistle blasted at the mill and it wasn't lunchtime, so I knew something was wrong. I jumped up, scared to death. All I could think as I hurried along the narrow path was that Amory was hurt and I needed to reach him as quickly as I could. When I got home I insisted that Jeb drive me to the mill to see for myself.

I arrived to find the workers listening to the radio, wiping tears from their eyes, and I knew the whistle had nothing to do with Amory. My husband was not hurt; in fact, he was nowhere to be found. Martha, his lazy, well-fed secretary, said he'd left a few hours ago for an appointment and probably wouldn't be back. There was nothing in his appointment book, but that didn't mean much, she said. And of course it was fine with her; she got to sit at her desk and read magazines until quitting time.

"Where is he, Martha?" I demanded. "The President of the United States has died and I need to know where my husband is."

"I can't tell you that, Mrs. Clyde. I honestly have no idea."

"You're lying."

Twitching her nose like a fat little rabbit, she sat forward and stared at me. "If I knew I would tell you, but I don't, so I can't," she said. Her voice was testy, but there was no malice in it, and I thought I could detect a note of pity. Amory had chosen wisely; she'd be loyal to the last.

There were plenty of these times when I'd run up against the obvious. It was almost as though people were daring me to say it: "He's with another woman, isn't he? He's not at a meeting at all. He's in bed at some hideaway on the other side of town." When Horace cut his first teeth; when the telegram arrived from my mother—"Your father is dead. Come at once"; when the brains of the President of our country fell into the lap of his wife. When, on a warm and sunny day in 1967, Bryce Davies dived off a flat-topped boulder into the whirling depths of the reservoir on his property and never made it up for air.

I cannot recall a time, in all those years, when Bryce and I weren't friends. When I found that first letter in my husband's pocket, I did indeed confront him about it, but he took me by the shoulders and very kindly and patiently told me that it's a hard reality of life, but sooner or later the wife of a successful man has to face the fact that a lot of women out there are going to find him attractive and are going to make up all kinds of malicious lies to try to get their way. He said he purposely left that letter there as an indication of the lengths some gals would go.

"Now, I'm not judging her," he said. "Only God can do that. But I can surely understand if you choose not to be friends with her anymore."

"But she's the best friend I've got," I said.

"Evidently not," he pointed out. "And besides, there are other fish in the sea. I wouldn't trust her as far as I could throw her."

That made me suspicious. I may not have known much about the world, but I had learned that there's often a big gap between what people say and what they believe. When he said she was a ruthless backstabber who only befriended me in a futile attempt to get closer to him, I was willing to concede that some of that might be true. But I also knew that my friendship with Bryce made Amory uneasy; he was afraid one would tell the other too much and he'd be caught in the middle with nowhere to turn. It would be much more convenient for him to keep us separate.

So Bryce and I stayed friends. I wrote her that letter to help me calm down, and then I took her letter and mine and sealed them in my box, and that was the end of it. We watched our children grow up together, sitting on the porch or over on her veranda, making up games for them to play, sewing costumes for school. And some afternoons I wouldn't see her and I'd imagine that she was with him, sneaking down a back road, his arm around her waist, the wind in her long black hair.

Oh, it was terrible; it was intolerable. But I had learned to live with it the way I'd learned to live with other things, like the fact that I'd probably never be a teacher again, or that Amory would never really know how to show me he loved me, or that I'd probably never have the guts to find a man who could. After a while it got so that when I knew and she knew he was off with someone else I almost felt sorry for her, as if she was the one he was being unfaithful to. Without either of us saying a word, I could tell she'd grown to care for him almost as much as I did. I loved him for what we'd had together long ago, for what we'd been through over the years, for the day-to-day intimacies we shared as husband and wife. She loved him, I'm sure, because he was powerful, her husband's boss, because he made her feel young and daring and free, because he thought she was exotic and told her so.

But all that was years before. By 1967 we had weathered Taylor's pregnancy at age sixteen and her elopement with a local garage mechanic, Ellen's move up north and marriage to a Jewish graduate student, a plant closing, a strike, the births of six grandchildren. I thought it was long over between them. I thought we were old. So when I found that hairpin in his breast pocket—a Thursday morning, rain falling as soft as cats' paws outside the bedroom window onto the roof—I felt a pain in my chest as if she'd stuck it in me. I held the pin to the light and looked at it closely: it was fairly ordinary, as hairpins go, except for the luminous quality of the head. I have never seen another one like it. I thought of her taking her hair down while we were talking, placing the pin between her lips while she made a chignon, and then carelessly, gracelessly, inserting the pin again to hold it together. There was no question that it was hers; I'd seen her wearing it hundreds of times. Did he take it as a keepsake? Did she put it there for him to find? It didn't much matter. What mattered to me was that I thought it was over and it wasn't, and the wounds I thought had healed were as raw, as painful, as the first time I suspected.

I locked the pin in my box of letters. I thought about how much time had passed. In some objective part of my brain I respected Amory for sticking with her instead of some bottle-blond twenty-year-old who laughed like a hyena and snapped her gum, though Lord knows he'd gone through plenty of those in his prime and probably still did. I thought about Bryce's breasts: they were larger than mine, but they sagged more. I wondered where she kissed him and how.

I was alone in the house that day, and Amory called from the office to tell me he had a board of directors banquet in Chattanooga. I knew he was with her. When he came in, singing, around one in the morning, I pretended to be asleep. But I wasn't asleep; I was lying there thinking about the two of them together. Thinking about the two of them together and me in that house by myself.

When I woke up the next morning he was gone. Around ten-thirty Bryce called. She was hot and bored, she said, and wanted to go swimming.

"I'm kind of busy today, Bryce," I said. "Maybe another time."

"What can you be doing that's so dang important you can't take out an hour to be with a friend?"

"I'm in the middle of spring cleaning."

"Spring cleaning! Well, that can wait. I'm packing us a lunch, and I'll be over in an hour."

When Bryce pulled up in the little blue convertible Frank bought for her birthday, waving her hand gaily, a scarf around her head and black sunglasses sliding down her nose, it was all I could do not to lunge.

"Gosh, Clyde, darling," she said, getting out of the car and reaching in back for the basket. "You look a little peaked this morning. 'Pee-kid'—is that how you pronounce it? I'm trying to learn a new word a week. You're never too old!" She wagged a finger at me. "Now, I brought hard-boiled eggs and potato salad and cheese sandwiches and iced tea. I vote we take it down to the water and have us a picnic on the rocks. I've got my suit on underneath, so I'm all set. How about you?"

I told her I was feeling a bit under the weather and that I didn't think swimming would help. "But I'll go down there to keep you company," I said. "I'll sit on the rocks and stick my toes in."

She seemed slightly irritated at this, but it was better than nothing, so I got my whistle and we made our way through the field behind the house to the narrow path that went down to the water. With a towel slung over one arm and the basket of food in the other, Bryce led the way. Walking close behind her, I could see single strands of white in the black of her hair. Her step was as sure and light as a ballerina's. In the nearly thirty years I'd known her she had hardly gained a pound.

"Isn't this fun?" she said, turning around suddenly. "Aren't you glad you came? Now that we've got the kids out of our hair we should do this every day." She closed her eyes and breathed deep. "There's nothing finer than the smell of tree moss in the sun. Nothing," she said, and turned forward again.

As soon as we reached the clearing Bryce began unbuttoning her blouse. She spread the towel on a large, flat rock and set the basket on it. I watched her as she let the blouse fall from her shoulders and stepped out of her skirt. I thought about Amory seeing the same thing and comparing her body to mine. Her skin was smooth and honey-colored, and her breasts were perky and firm in the pointy push-up bra of her black bathing suit. The only real signs of decay that I could detect were a few spidery veins on the backs of her legs.

We sat on the rock and ate the picnic she'd prepared, she in her suit, I in my plaid shift, as the sun beat down on us from directly overhead and the trees around the reservoir reflected patterns on the water. Lying back against the warm rock with her eyes closed and her arms spread wide, she whispered, "Glorious!"

After a few minutes she sat up. "I don't know if I can hold off any longer." She edged over to the side of the rock, stuck her toe in, and quickly pulled it out. Again she dipped her toe in, more cautiously this time, and then up to her ankle, up to her calf. "I'm going to do it," she announced. She looked up to the left and shaded her eyes. "Off the top of that big boulder over there, all at once. It's better just to get it over with." She stood up and stretched her arms over her head, her fingers interlaced. "Wish me luck!"

"Good luck," I said.

I might have tried to stop her, to remind her about the whirlpool she knew herself was there, to convince her that the water was colder and deeper than it looked, to insist that she come back and wade in from the shore, where it was safe, but I did not. I didn't say anything as she hopped from rock to rock in her shimmery black suit to get to the boulder, holding her arms out like a tightrope walker. I imagined I was Amory, admiring her strong, tanned arms, her long, perfect nose, the supple curve of her waist. When she smiled at me and crossed her fingers, standing on the slant of the big rock, I imagined Amory smiling and crossing his fingers back. When she dove in I heard the splash and then nothing, and I sat very still. I thought of Amory wanting her; I thought of him holding her in his arms. I sat there and gazed out over the water.

After a while I took off my watch and waded in. The water was cold at first, but I clenched my teeth and submerged my chest up to my neck before dipping under to wet my hair. I waded back to shore and blew my whistle, three sharp blasts and one long one, and then climbed up to the boulder in my dripping dress, up the same path Bryce had taken, and stood at the top peering into the swirling depths below.

Jeb arrived faster than I'd expected, with Lattie right behind him. I had worked myself into a panic, and my teeth were chattering; I was freezing in that wet clammy dress. Jeb kicked off his shoes as he ran, and kept on going straight into the water.

"Where she at, Miz Clyde?" Lattie screamed.

I pointed down, speechless.

"The whirlpool!" Lattie shrieked. "She must've gone under at the whirlpool, y'all know that's dangerous."

"I tried to tell her," I said, creeping down off the rock.

"I know you did, Miz Clyde. And you shouldn't have jumped in there yourself." She spied the towel laid flat on the rock beneath the remains of our picnic and bent to pick it up. "I was always afraid something like this would happen, but nobody'd listen," she muttered. "This is not a place for ladies to come by theirselves, Miz Clyde. I knew it would happen someday, I just knew it."

I stood in front of her, shaking all over, while she dried me off with the towel. "Find anything?" she shouted as Jeb surfaced.

"No sign," he called. "I'm going back under."

A number of minutes passed. Jeb came up again. "I can't see a thing right now, Miz Clyde." He got out and sat on a rock, wrapping his arms around his stomach. Goose bumps stood up on his flesh. "Too murky to see a thing."

The three of us sat silently, our eyes fixed on the water. The ripples from the wind looked like fish scales in the sunlight. The tree trunks reflected on the surface looked like bars.

"Well, there's not a whole lot to do right now but get you home and dry," Lattie said. "God bless that poor woman's soul, her husband will be beside himself. But we done what we could. And you are lucky, Miz Clyde, real lucky that you weren't swept away with her. You must be stronger than we all thought."

Much stronger, I was thinking. Stronger than I thought myself. But I was glad Jeb hadn't found the body, pale and bloated, while we waited on the rocks. Lattie walked behind me all the way up to the house, and Jeb walked behind her. We didn't speak; none of us had much to say. For a moment I wondered if she might be at the house, waiting for us on the step, and my heartbeat quickened. But as we rounded the corner I could see her car sitting empty in the drive, and the house was still.

Late in the night I watched him sleeping. His breath was shallow, like a child's. One narrow, almost invisible line ran across the middle of his forehead; deeper lines had started at the edges of his eyes, like tracks of a rake through sand. "Oh, Cassie" he'd said quietly when I called. His voice had calmed me. Now I looked at his strong cheekbones and full lips. I outlined my lips with a finger, and then his; I touched the curve of his nose, so like my own.

He opened his eyes and stared at me blankly, then focused with a start. "What are you doing?"

"Just watching."

He turned toward the wall, wrapping the sheet around himself, tugging it off me. "No wonder I'm dreaming about you."

I put my hand on his shoulder, and he leaned back into me. When I kissed him he slid under me. Through the cotton sheet between us I could feel the tension in his legs. My hair fell across his face like straw, and he threaded his fingers through it, pushing it back over my ears.

"God, you're lovely." With the back of his hand he traced my cheek, down my chin. He kissed me and I kissed him back. He rolled over on top of me, reaching down to touch my hip inside the oversize T-shirt I wore. He slipped his finger under the elastic band of my panties. "Where'd these come from?"

"I don't know you very well, Mr. Burns. I'm shy."

"You weren't too shy an hour ago."

I stroked the light stubble on his face. "When I was in the fourth grade my best friend's mother told us that we should always wear underwear to bed, in case there was a fire."

"A fire?"

"You know—so when we jumped out the window into the trampoline none of the firemen would see." I kissed his neck. "That sounds pretty funny now, doesn't it? But I've always slept in my underwear. I never really thought about it, but I guess that's why."

"It's time to break some old habits," he murmured. "To hell with the firemen."

His hand moved up inside my shirt to my breast, and I shifted to make room between us. He kissed my parted lips, biting the bottom one, nuzzling my ear. I ran my hand down the slope of his back, the ridges of muscle rising like hills on either side, to a small hollow at the base of his spine. I pulled him to me, running my hands along the entire length of him. We lay facing each other, side by side.

"We could have known each other all these years," I said softly. "You were here all the time in this little town, and I didn't even know."

"We'd have grown up cousins."

"That probably would've been better."

"Probably, but it wouldn't have been as much fun."

Sighing, I put my hand on the center of his chest.

After a moment he drew back and looked at me. "What are you thinking?"

"Nothing."

"That's an awfully big sigh over nothing."

I put my head on his shoulder. "I just can't understand why my mother went to that meeting. She must've known he was drunk when she got in the van."

He circled me in his arms. "He was her father, Cassie. Fathers aren't supposed to run their cars off the road."

"I guess." I closed my eyes. "You know, I've always thought of her as my mother. But she was just a girl." I could feel tears welling up. "It seems so monumentally unfair."

"It is. It was."

"What was he trying to do? Was he trying to kill her? Or kill himself? Or was it that he just didn't care?"

He stroked my hair. "Maybe it really was an accident. Maybe that drowning was too. We'll probably never get the whole story."

"Amory believed that Clyde killed Bryce Davies," I said.

"I think a lot of people did."

I sat up, sniffling. "Do you?"

"No."

"Why not?"

He leaned back against the headboard. "I just don't think she did it. I don't think she was capable of it." He paused. "You know, it's funny. Because everything was so indirect and no charges were ever brought, Clyde never had a chance to tell her side of the story. She could never be cleared. And my mother . . . "

"What?"

He rubbed his face. "She just perpetuated it. She made it into a big family secret that none of us were allowed to talk about. But not talking about it didn't make it go away, it just made it all the more shameful."

"Why wouldn't your mother want everything to be out in the open?"

"I don't know," he said. "I think it gave her a weird kind of control over Clyde."

"It just all seems so unnecessary."

He shook his head. "My mother was so jealous of your mother, Cassie, it was ridiculous."

"Jealous? Why?"

"She always thought your mother was Clyde's favorite—and she was, from what I've heard. When the accident happened she wasn't exactly jumping for joy, but I don't think she was heartbroken either. She finally had Clyde all to herself."

"That's awfully cynical."

"I lived with her for a long time."

"It seems so ironic. Here I am, trying to find my mother, and you're trying to escape yours."

He looked down. "I do love her. I don't want you to think I don't. It's just that I don't like her very much sometimes."

"I want to ask you something," I said quietly. "How much did your mother have to do with that first night I met you at the bar?"

"What do you mean?"

"You were getting back at her a little bit, weren't you? You knew that getting involved with me would be her worst nightmare."

For a moment he didn't respond. Then he said, "I don't know. I hadn't thought about it. But maybe—at first—there was a little of that. Everything changed so fast, though. If that was a factor at the beginning, it certainly wasn't by the end of the night."

I drew a deep breath.

"I really never thought about it before. I'm just trying to be honest."

I sank into my pillow and covered my eyes with the heels of my hands. "This family is so fucked."

"All families are fucked," he said. "You think this one is different because it's yours."

"Murder and betrayal and revenge." I looked up at him. "I call that pretty majorly fucked."

"Yeah," he agreed, "and now incest."

"Oh, God." I covered my eyes again.

He pulled my hands aside and kissed my nose, and then he lay down beside me. "I think I love you, Cassie."

"Troy—"

"Shhh," he said, putting his hand to my lips. "Don't say anything. Not yet."

Sometimes at night I think about the commandments.

Thou shalt not steal.

That woman was a blackbird, hair black, eyes black. She took what she wanted with long, grasping talons; she made herself at home in other nests. In the night she was invisible: the ruffling of her feathers was the wind across the water; her eyes, glinting in the moonlight, might have been reflections of my own.

Thou shalt not commit adultery.

For years I smiled and pretended, hid what I felt, put up with what I put up with because I didn't know that I deserved better. I didn't know that I could ask.

Honor thy father and thy mother.

When I was seventeen I went to college to escape my father's impotent rage and my mother's infinite capacity for forgiveness. When I left that white-columned house on its wide Chattanooga street I thought I was leaving it for good. But instead of escaping my past I merely circled back to it: I went out and married a man as thwarted and confused as my father, and I became everything about my mother I used to loathe.

Thou shalt not kill.

She jumped from the boulder and the water was so cold it cut her breath. She thought a thousand thoughts, or nothing. She thought of him. In the stillness of the afternoon a lowly pigeon finally took flight—

waiting, watching, beating my wings as her lungs filled up with deep, sweet water.

Thou shalt not bear false witness.

From the day it happened I wanted him to believe the worst. I wanted him to know what I had discovered and put one and one together. I knew he would assume the obvious; his brain was lazy. He had learned enough to dazzle early on, to charm local girls like me; and that was enough for him. Enough for him to repeat the pattern over and over again until I put a stop to it. I had had enough of repeating patterns. They were making me dizzy, like a kaleidoscope.

By the time I'd found out what the worst can do it was too late to take anything back.

It was midmorning. As we sat on the porch eating bread and cheese and oranges and reading the paper, we heard the telephone ring inside.

"Are you going to answer that?"

I shrugged.

It rang twice, three times, before the machine kicked in. We waited until we heard a voice.

"Cassie, you're off my A list and teetering around C. Pretty soon you're going to be off it entirely unless you get your act together and call me. So *what's going on?* Have you run off to Cancún with this mystery man? I swear, it's always the same with you, Cassandra. The minute a new toy comes along you drop off the face of the earth.

"Now look, I'm thinking of coming down for a visit, but maybe we should meet in Atlanta. I require running water and cable, and it sounds like both are luxuries in your neck of the woods. So call me. Soon."

"Who's that?"

"Oh, Drew." I laughed, embarrassed. "He's my best friend." I got up, tugging my T-shirt down, went inside the house, and returned with an ashtray and a pack of cigarettes. I tapped one out and lit it.

Troy picked up an orange, an amused expression on his face. "So you've been telling people about me."

I shook my head. "I didn't tell him anything. I was talking to someone earlier in the week—oh, this is too complicated."

"No, go ahead."

"Well, there's this guy, Adam." I took a long drag on my cigarette. "We were talking, and somehow your name came up."

"So . . . this is an old boyfriend or something?"

"Or something."

"And you mentioned me because—"

"Because he was hassling me about coming back. I don't even remember what I said."

He reached over and flicked the cigarette, knocking off the accumulated ash. "You're not used to this, are you?"

"Used to what?" I said, bridling.

He laughed. "Smoking."

"Oh." I looked at the cigarette.

"You don't have to deal with anyone you don't want to. You don't have to tell anybody anything."

"You don't know Drew." I ground the cigarette out in the ashtray.

"I do know one thing," he said, tossing the orange back and forth from hand to hand. "Whatever this is between us, Cassie, it's very simple. It's you and me. And they can talk about it if they want to, but it doesn't matter. What they say—what anyone says—doesn't have anything to do with us. "

"We live in the world, Troy. Maybe if we were on a desert island somewhere—"

"Cancún"

"—but we're not. Your family, my dad—"

"It doesn't matter."

"Troy—"

"It doesn't matter."

I searched his face. "I wish I could believe that."

"Come to the city with me," he said suddenly, tossing me the orange.

I missed and it rolled off the porch. "What?"

"Come to Atlanta."

"You're crazy."

"Ralph and I have a big place, you can live with us. We can find you a studio. You can get a job if you want, or we can get by on what I'm making for a while—"

"Troy, please."

"What?"

"Don't you think this is a little soon? We don't even *know* each other."

"How can we get to know each other if we're always hiding out?"

"But—"

"None of this bullshit means anything there, Cassie. Come with me."

"You know I can't do that."

"Give me one good reason why not."

"This house," I said. "I came here for this house. That's why I'm here."

"The house is that important to you?"

I looked out over the railing. Blue was sniffing around in the grass. "I'd feel like I was running away."

"From what?"

I closed my eyes.

"Running away from what?" His voice was quiet, insistent. After a moment I turned to face him. "I came down here to figure things out. And with everything that's happened—finding that box, learning about Bryce Davies—I need some time to sort it all through."

"How long do you think you'll need?"

"I don't know. How can you know these things?"

He rubbed his forehead with the fingers of one hand. "Well, do you have any idea how you feel about me?"

My silence stretched between us. "I—I don't know yet," I said at last.

He looked out toward the line of trees beyond the drive. "All right, then, I guess," he said. "Okay."

Standing on the front porch with Blue, I hugged my elbows. Troy sat in the jeep toying with the steering wheel, then he turned the key and revved the engine. I went down the steps to say goodbye. *I think you're a part of me I'm missing.*

He put the jeep in reverse, watching me. "Take care," he said softly. "You know where to find me."

After he left, I put on jeans and sneakers and went walking with Blue through the field behind the house, to the wooded area below. The trees and bushes were thick and brambled, and I tried in vain to find a clear pathway through them. Finally I stopped and stood very still, obeying my Girl Scout instincts, and heard what I was listening for: the dull roar of water.

We made our way down a slope through the woods, toward the sound. As the trees thinned at the bottom we were suddenly confronted with a ten-foot chain-link fence. Old rusty signs—KEEP OUT, NO TRESPASSING—were posted at intervals along the way. We followed the fence for some distance, eventually coming upon a gate bolted with a large, heavy lock.

I threaded my fingers through the holes and pressed my face to the fence. There was no water in sight. For a moment I considered climbing over, but then, sagging against the fence, I realized that I didn't need to see the water—it was enough to know that it was there. I turned around and started back through the trees, Blue trotting behind.

When I reached the field in back of the house, I stood in the grass listening to the crickets, the singing birds, somebody mowing in the distance, the hum of a small plane overhead. Blue barked and scrabbled after some animal. I stretched my arms over my head and looked up at the blue, blue sky and the tiny plane carving a path through it.

Once Bryce was gone I thought he might be mine again, that it might be like it was in the beginning when he was only mine. But he pushed me away more than ever; he wouldn't talk, he wouldn't listen. I'd find him hunched over, crying in the bathroom, and I'd try to comfort him, and he'd tell me to go away and leave him alone. He'd sit on the porch for hours just staring off at the sky, and when I'd come over beside him he'd act like I wasn't there. And then that night, that awful night, I'd had enough, I just couldn't take any more, and I grabbed his arms and said, "Tell me! What can I do to make you love me again?" and he stood there in the bedroom staring at me with dull eyes and said, "I loved her so much I don't care if I die."

I reeled back as if I'd been hit. And then I struck him across the face as hard as I could and told him to get out of the house, to get out and never come back. He looked at me with tears running down his face and said, "You did it on purpose, didn't you? You knew and you did it on purpose." He sank down on the bed sobbing, and it was terrible, a noise like a donkey braying, and he was shouting, "You killed her! You knew, so you killed her!" and I just stood like a statue in the middle of the floor. After an eternity I said, "And what if I did, Amory? What if I did?"

He gave me a look verging on pure hatred and got up and left the room. I heard him ask Ellen for the keys, and then I heard him drive off in the bus. I knew he was going to get drunk; it was the only logical thing for him to do. As soon as he left I started shaking, and I couldn't stop. I knew that Ellen must have heard everything, and I couldn't bear to face her. So on the last night of her life, with the two of us in the house alone, I never saw her, never left my room until I heard Amory drive up and honk, yelling that he'd take her where she needed to go. I heard the door slam and then the bump of tires, careless and fast, down that long grassy drive.

After that there was the sorting, the notifying, the clearing out. Her belongings were a ghost town, left behind to rot. I burned most everything; I couldn't stand to have her stuff in the house knowing she'd never be back to get it. But when I found her diary I locked it in the box with the letters, the newspaper clippings of the drowning, the obituaries, the photo in the paper of the bus smashed to pieces. The diary seemed like a piece of her soul.

I hid the key, as I always did, on a little ledge underneath the bed frame, and I put the box in our closet. It stayed there for months on the top shelf, all my secrets gathering dust. But one evening I was up in the bedroom by myself, and I was thinking of Ellen and crying a little, and I remembered the diary and wanted to read it again. I located the key and then reached for the box. It was gone. It simply wasn't there. I searched the closet, under the bed, inside the armoire where he hung his suits.

Amory was sitting out on the porch reading the paper, so I crept down the stairs very quietly and scoured the kitchen cupboards, the closet in the hall, behind the couch and chairs and a chest of drawers in the living room. I went down to the cellar and pawed around behind jars of preserves and pickled tomatoes. I couldn't find it anywhere. Standing there with the single dim bulb swaying over my head, its pull-chain rattling, I felt as naked and exposed as it was. I suddenly became deathly afraid of going upstairs. I wondered how long I might be able to stay down here, living off canned beans and peaches.

I heard the screen door slam shut and Amory trudge into the kitchen. His footsteps paused at the open cellar door.

"Hello?" he called. "Clyde, you down there?"

I didn't say anything.

"Hello?" He waited a moment and then clicked off the light.

I groped for the chain in the dark and turned it on again.

"Something wrong with you?" he said.

I looked at the swaying bulb and reached up to stop the motion, burning the tips of my fingers. "Where is it?"

"What?" He started down the stairs.

"Where is that box?"

He paused, and our eyes locked. "I can't tell you that," he said.

"It's mine."

"You will never know."

Both of us were silent for a moment. I could hear him breathing, hard and slow. I looked into his face, and for the first time I saw pain etched across it as clearly as the path of a scalpel across flesh. Then he turned and went back upstairs, his shoulders slumped forward like an old man's.

I stood in the cellar until there was no reason to stand there anymore. When I came up he was already in bed. I went out and sat on the porch in the early summer heat, watching the fireflies flicker above the velvety soft darkness of the grass.

It was Thursday afternoon and I was out in the field behind the house, digging holes for cement-block foundations. For several days, ever since Troy left, I'd been putting together the large hollow figures that would populate the field. One of them was almost fully assembled; she stood like a sentry in the dining room, guarding the smaller pieces still scattered on plastic squares. I'd been cutting little indentations in the separate pieces so that they'd fit together smoothly and could be taken apart without much trouble. But before I could move any of them outside, I needed to finish the foundations and let them settle.

As I knelt in the grass, fortifying the inside of a shallow hole with packed dirt, I heard Alice's car coming over the ridge. So few people came to visit that I could recognize the hum and clatter of each vehicle. I stood up, brushing dirt off my knees. "Back here, Alice!" I called. A moment later she appeared, with an amused expression on her face and Elaine right behind her, teetering on high heels and clutching a piece of paper. Blue circled them, wagging his tail and panting.

"She insisted on me coming—," Alice began.

"Young lady!" shrieked Elaine, shaking the paper in the air and walking toward me as fast as she could. She tripped on a small rock and her knee buckled, but she struggled to keep her balance. "I would never have believed it! Never! First it was May Ford tried to tell me she saw the two of you together, and I said, 'May, darlin', I think you must be mistaken, that's impossible, he's been living in Atlanta since June and hasn't even been back to visit.'"

Alice smiled at me. "Her friend Bernadette saw you and Troy getting cozy downtown the other day and was so kind as to drop Mother a note about it," she explained.

"May Ford is one thing," Elaine went on. "*Nobody* believes her. But to hear it *in writing* from Bernadette—" She brandished the paper in my face. "Can you even begin to *imagine* my embarrassment? What greater humiliation than to be informed by a neighbor that my own son is not only back in town, but he's sneaking around with—with—" She lifted her arm and pointed at me. "Oh! I can't even think of a word to describe you! And to think I was willing to give you the benefit of the doubt. When they said, 'Don't trust her, she'll take what she can get,' I just replied, 'Judge not, that ye shall not be judged.'

"I fed you in my house. I brought you a casserole—and even a pie! You ungrateful little—" She bunched her fists and jammed them down at her sides, as if she were afraid she might strike. "And all that time you were"—red splotches showed through her impeccable makeup and down her neck, and her mouth was contorted with rage—"*whoring!* That's what you were! There, I said it." She put her hands over her face and started to cry.

Alice shrugged and rolled her eyes. "Oh, Mother, they aren't hurting anybody. And besides, there's nobody around here who should be throwing stones."

"Well, it just makes sense that you would say that, Alice Marie," Elaine sobbed, her voice rising shrilly. "Running all over east Tennessee with some sex-starved Knoxville banker when it's as plain as the nose on my face that he's nothing but a big dead end." With the back of her index finger she dabbed at the rivulets of mascara streaming down her face. "At least *you're* not breaking God's laws."

"Mother," Alice sighed. "They aren't breaking any laws, God's or otherwise. They're not even related. Don't you think we should calm down and be rational about this?"

"DON'T TELL ME TO CALM DOWN! I AM CALM!" Elaine screeched.

"Just *wait* until Mother hears about this. It will break her heart."

"Oh, lordy, you're not going to tell Clyde," Alice groaned.

"And do you think I have a choice? At the very least she should know what kind of—" She slowly wiped her nose with her hand and tottered over to me. "You know," she said, standing very close, "your mother had a wild streak in her too. And then she went up there and married that hippie. That—that—Jewish hippie. Now that I think about it, I guess I'm not surprised at all."

"You're not surprised at what?" I asked.

"At how you turned out."

I stuck my trowel in the ground. "Look, Elaine," I said. "What do you want?"

"I want to know why you really came down here."

"What are you talking about?"

"From the moment I laid eyes on you, I knew you'd be trouble. Running all over the place digging up dirt anywhere you could find it, playing people against each other, upsetting Clyde—"

"Did she tell you that?"

"Do you deny it?"

I took a deep breath. "Elaine—"

"I know why you came down here, Cassandra Simon," she said in a quiet voice. "You came down here to destroy this family."

Alice was shaking her head, a hand over her mouth.

"I didn't have to come down here to do that," I said. "You were doing just fine without me." I stepped around her and headed for the back door, Blue at my heels.

Once inside, I stood trembling in the middle of the kitchen floor. After a moment I could hear Alice speaking in low tones to Elaine, and then the crunch of gravel and the slamming of car doors and the roar of the engine, and finally the muffled vibration of tires down the drive.

I stroked Blue's head and scratched his ears. "You ain't never been blue," I whispered, "till you've had that mood indigo." I held his muzzle and looked into his liquid black eyes. Then I went upstairs to get ready for work.

The night was dark and quiet and clouded over. Every now and then I could see a sliver of moon. I knew she wasn't home, because Elaine had told me she worked Thursdays at that low-life bar that clings to the edge of town like a tick on a dog.

Before I left the house I put on black pants and one of Horace's old sweatshirts and the big-heeled sneakers Elaine bought when she was trying to convince me to get some exercise. Looking at myself in the mirror, I felt like some batty contestant in the Senior Olympics they show on TV. I waited until nine o'clock, when most of the neighbors would have settled down for the night. From the front window I could see that the street was calm and empty. I let a few more minutes pass to be sure. I didn't want to take any chances. The neighbors all knew that I was usually in bed by nine-thirty at the latest, so they'd suspect something was up if they saw me leaving the house at that hour.

From a drawer in the kitchen I got my big red flashlight, the one Horace had given me in case of blackouts, and then I went out to the garage and started the car. All of a sudden I felt a strange tingling mix of excitement and fear. I'd had so much time to search, to imagine; I had dug through my memory like I was mining for gold. I'd decided it was best to be systematic: I would start in the cellar and work my way up, room by room. I figured it wouldn't take me long to find where she'd hidden it. I know that old house as well as I know my own mind.

I coasted down Red Pond Road with the lights off until I reached the corner of Webb, where I figured I was safe. My hands were shaking. I hadn't had my license all that long, and I still wasn't comfortable driving at night. I'd never driven to the old house myself; I hadn't even seen it since we moved out all those years ago. The road felt unfamiliar—I couldn't remember where to slow down for curves, where to accelerate for hills. I crept along cautiously, as if on tiptoe.

And yet I recognized the old drive right away. As I made my way up over the ridge, the house appeared in a dim arc of moonlight, and my heart leapt. It looked small and still, shabbier even than I remembered. When I got closer I could see wild grass growing where planted flowers used to be. The porch sagged; paint was peeling from the eaves. Seeing it this way sent a pain through me. I stopped the car by the side of the porch, cut the engine, and retied my shoelaces while I tried to gather my thoughts. I left the keys in the ignition and started to get out.

All of a sudden out of nowhere came this black dog, barking and leaping against my door, scaring me to death. I yanked the door shut, my heart racing. After what seemed like hours the dog sat down, cocked its ears at me, and began to wag its tail, and I could see that it was still a puppy. I rolled down the window a bit and said, "Good dog." I opened the door. "Nice dog," I said, but it jumped up and I pulled the door shut again. It sat down again. Mustering my courage, I cracked the door and stuck out the top of one sneakered foot. It sniffed the new leather and looked up at me. I got out gradually, one leg at a time, and it came toward me, sticking its wet nose in my lap. I patted it on the head. "Good doggy. Quiet doggy." It followed me up the creaking front steps to the door, which was unlocked, and then inside.

The house was a different place than I remembered. It smelled like the yard, like mud and wood and old dying leaves. Standing in the front hall—my hall—I shined the flashlight into the living room on one side, then the kitchen on the other. Every window seemed to be open; cheap muslin curtains flapped inward like ghosts dancing toward me in the dark. The living room looked bare. The dog was wagging its tail and kept brushing against my knees.

Since Amory had been so strange with me in the cellar that night, I decided to try there first. I passed through the kitchen, banging my hip against a table that was never there before and didn't fit. I pointed the flashlight at the far wall. Strange, weedy things were hanging from the curtain rod above the sink; old green mason jars of dried beans and spaghetti cluttered the counter. The place was a mess. A newspaper was scattered half on the floor, half on the table, where a paperback cookbook lay open, facedown and broken-spined, next to a crumpled cigarette package and a book of matches. I was surprised, but I shouldn't have been. Ellen smoked too.

The cellar door was stuck. After some tugging it suddenly gave, slamming me in the shoulder. Gingerly, rubbing my shoulder, I went down the stairs, shining the light in front of me like a ship's beacon. At the bottom I swept the light around the walls, making giant shadows. An inch of dust had settled over everything: a battered toolbox, jars of rancid fruit, a bicycle Horace used in high school, cans of paint. Picking my way around the floor, I knocked on the walls behind the shelves for hollow spaces. I looked inside crumbling boxes, an old chest of drawers, under a mildewed mess of rags.

Nothing. The dog started whimpering and yapping and pawing the top stair. "Hush!" *I told it, but then I took one last look around and scurried upstairs. I don't know what I was afraid of; nobody around there could hear, and if they could they wouldn't think much of it. Raccoons, rats, snakes—a dog barking for a reason in the country is like Peter crying wolf.*

I moved across the hall into the living room, stumbling over a few chairs in the dark. With all the windows open the place was a little cold, and I pulled down the sleeves of my sweatshirt. I got down on my knees and went around the room, tapping on the floorboards. There wasn't much furniture to speak of: a beat-up old couch that I think we might've left; an end table; a standing lamp. In the far corner I found a hand-painted cupboard she must've rescued from a trash pile. Groping around inside it, I knocked over a glass, which smashed on the floor, sending the dog skidding backward in surprise like an ice skater.

The dining room looked like a junkyard. There was no furniture except a wooden contraption with a seat on it in the middle of the room. All over the floor large, strange-shaped objects squatted on heavy plastic and canvas spattered with paint. They were like the rocks I'd seen in pictures of the moon. Training my flashlight on each one, I could see that some were faces, some hands. Some were giant feet. When she said she was a sculptor I had imagined earthenware bowls like the one she gave me, candlestick holders, uneven pots. I thought of her sitting out here making teapots and mugs to sell at the Dinner Bell or maybe at a gift shop at the mall. But these pieces were ugly, nothing anybody I knew would ever want to buy. I touched one of them with my foot and pushed it over. I rapped on it with my knuckles, and the sound it made was hollow. I tried another, and another. All of them sounded the same. They reminded me of the piñatas we hung at Christmas in church. On Christmas Eve the kids all stood in a circle while one of them, blindfolded, beat the donkey with a stick until it burst. Candy flew from its insides like guts, and the children scrambled around on the floor trying to get as much as they could. I tapped one of the pieces again. Why were they hollow? Why were they so big?

All at once it came to me. I picked one of the faces up—it was fairly light, like a gourd—and felt for an opening, but there wasn't one. I realized what she must have done, and my heart started beating like the dog's tail, thump thump thump, and my head felt fuzzy. I shook the face and held it to my ear, listening for a swishing sound, the sound of paper. I looked around the room. There were at least a dozen pieces scattered on the floor—a dozen possibilities, a dozen hiding places. Now it all made sense: she found the box—she knew I knew she'd found it—and thought I might come after it. She made these ugly pieces to hide my letters in.

Cradling the face in one arm, I shined the flashlight at it. It was a flat face, a woman's face, and it looked strangely familiar. It had a funny expression, not frowning, but not smiling either. I put down the flashlight and tossed the face in the air like a beach ball. When it landed back in my hands the weight of it drew me forward. I shook it again and heard a rustling sound. Then I closed my eyes, gritted my teeth, lifted it above my head, and let it drop.

There was a loud, dull crash, and I jumped. The dog yipped, trotting around in a skittish circle. "Get out," I said, raising my hand. "Out. Out!" It slunk back into a corner, looking at me. I could see its pupils shining in the dark. I grabbed the flashlight and pointed it at the floor. There was an eye staring blankly up at me, a broken mouth, an ear, part of a nose. I moved some of the fragments with my toe. A cloud of dust rose up. There were no letters.

The dog was whimpering now, circling the room, sniffing at the broken pieces. When it came close to me I hit it on the nose, and it shut up for a moment. Putting down the flashlight, I picked up a hollow, pillow-shaped piece with two mounds on the front and let it drop. It shattered.

Nothing.

The dog was really barking now. My heart felt like a marching band in my chest, THUMP THUMP THUMP. I kicked at the shards on the floor, then at the dog, but it jumped out of the way. I lifted another piece, bigger and heavier than the others, and hurled it down with all my strength, stamping on one section until it cracked in half. I seized a longer, thinner one, an arm or a leg, and swung it against the seat in the middle of the floor. My breath was coming hard now; I was covered with clay dust; my glasses were foggy. My whole body was trembling. I started coughing, choking on the dust. The dog ran after each piece as it broke across the floor. I stumbled around the room, not even thinking now, looking for those letters in the rubble.

By the time they were all smashed, I was so weak I could hardly stand. I leaned against the wall, mopping my brow, fanning myself with the bottom of my sweatshirt, trying to catch my breath. The dog sat down right in front of me, intent, quiet.

My eyes had adjusted to the darkness and I could see everything. The room was a shambles. There was silence like the silence after a rainstorm. All at once I began to feel a spreading shame, a shame so deep it paralyzed me. There were no letters hidden here. This was her project.

"Oh my Lord." The dog pricked up its ears. "Oh my Lord," I gasped, hugging myself, crying, shaking. I turned toward the wall for a long

moment to steady myself, then stepped around a broken face and picked up the flashlight. I went through the kitchen to the hall. Gripping the banister, I started up the stairs toward the bedrooms, away from the dust and destruction.

I found the box in the closet in my bedroom, on the shelf where I'd left it, as if it had never been moved. When I saw it there I thought I might faint. Standing on my toes, I could barely reach, but I did, dragging the box toward me with my fingertips, with all the strength I had left. It was heavy, larger than I remembered. It fell into my arms with a thunk.

I carried it to the bed. For several minutes I just looked at it, running my fingers down the sides, clutching the corners like I was afraid somebody would take it from me. Then I opened it and beamed the light inside. The papers were jumbled, but it looked like everything was there.

The dog had followed me into the room and was lying by the bed with its front paws crossed. "Shoo, dog, you dumb dog." I flapped my hand at it. I clapped, but it just lay there, watching me. I went through the papers in the box and lifted out Ellen's diary. The leather flap had been cut. I remembered reading what she had written all those years ago. Amory must have read it too. The thought made me feel old and sad.

Replacing the letters and the diary, I gathered everything in my arms. I had to get back to my car and out of here before she came home. I hurried down the stairs, dropping the flashlight and almost tripping over it, recovering and then almost tripping over the dog, pausing for a second at the bottom to collect myself.

All at once the dog whined and raced to the screen door, wagging furiously. I followed, standing very still behind it, listening, barely breathing. Before I heard anything I could see the small bright headlights of a car way down below, coming fitfully up the long drive. The dog was scratching at the door. Almost without thinking, I rushed into the kitchen, grabbed the matchbook from the table, and slipped past the dog onto the porch. I shot down the steps and ran for the back.

When I rounded the corner I could hear the unmistakable asthmatic wheeze of her car as it crested the ridge halfway to the house.

In the backyard I set the box down and opened it, crumpling some of the papers on top, fumbling with the matches as I tore them off and tried to strike them, dropping each one I managed to light into the box. At first the points of flame burned like votive candles, one for each match. Before long, though, the dry papers were on fire, roaring and crackling, giving off heat. I could hear the dog barking its head off inside the house. Watching the blaze as it ebbed and then strengthened, turning the letters to ashes, I heard the car come to a stop in front. She called to the dog and then she called my name. The car door slammed, then the screen door, and then the backyard was bathed in weak yellow light. Smoke was getting in my eyes and nose and I was starting to feel light-headed when I looked up and saw her face in the dining room window.

When I got home that night the first thing I noticed was my grandmother's car. I recognized it immediately: the mint-green siding, the white roof, the tires that looked like they'd never been used. The house was dark. I called for Blue. I was sure I'd heard him barking.

It had been another slow night at the Blue Moon, and they'd let me go a little early. I had been happy to leave. One of the clay figures was finished, and the next day I planned to assemble it outside. On the drive home I thought about how the pieces would look: a triangle of women, with faces and hands of clocks and trees and flowers, feet poised, skirts blowing, arms outstretched, as if dancing together in the field. I imagined the movement between them as continuous, each one reaching toward the others, their backs to the rest of the world.

As I got out of the car my mood of preoccupation vanished. "Blue?" I yelled. *"Clyde?"* I ran up the steps to the porch and opened the front door. Blue came barreling out, barking and leaping. I stroked his back to calm him and hurried inside, flipping the light switch in the hall. The door to the basement was wide open. I turned left into the living room and switched on a lamp. In the darkened far corner, pieces of broken glass sparkled like jewels. The night's clouds had dissipated; moonlight gave surfaces a bluish sheen.

"Clyde?" As I headed to the back of the room, my voice seemed to echo in the empty house. I went to the cabinet and looked down at the broken glass, then glanced to the right.

What I saw made me gasp. The dining room looked like a slaughtering army had been through it. The floor was covered with a terrible carnage of hands and eyes and feet. I surveyed the mess in horror, my hand over my mouth to keep from screaming. I took a few dazed steps and picked up a curved piece of clay, the outer side smooth, the inside rough—part of what had been the back of a head. Scrabbling through the rubble, my frantic fingers searched for a piece that might be whole, but found only jagged lips, a flared nostril, the curve of a shoulder. I rose shakily, rubbing soft, silky clay dust between my fingers.

Suddenly, through the window, I smelled smoke. I looked outside and saw the hunched figure of my grandmother. Her face, twisted toward me, was feverish and stricken in the warm light of a small fire.

I turned and ran to the kitchen and out the back door, Blue at my heels. "Clyde! What are you *doing?*" I shouted.

"Stay away from me!" she rasped. She coughed, bending double. In a dark, oversize sweatshirt and bright sneakers, she looked like a wizened child in the feeble glow from the fire.

"Do you realize what you've done? You've destroyed my sculptures! You've destroyed *everything!*" She shrank from me, but I grabbed her arm. "What were you *thinking?*"

"Let go!"

I dropped her arm. *"Are you totally insane?"* I screamed.

Her eyes met mine. "You're a liar," she said. "I knew you had it. If you hadn't lied to me in the first place, I wouldn't have had to come looking for it."

I looked down at the smoldering mess. Gray smoke was rising from it in a steady stream. It took me a moment to realize that it was the box. "Oh, *Jesus.*" I took the waitress apron from around my waist and threw it over the top, then crouched down, squelching the fire. "I *didn't* have it. I didn't start looking until you told me about it! You're the one who gave me the idea."

"No!" she said. *"No!"* She reached for the box, but I pushed her away, guarding it fiercely.

Lifting the apron, I poked through the charred, smoking papers and singed my fingers on the metal lock of the diary. I turned the book over quickly; the leather cover was scorched, but the fire hadn't burned through.

"Give that to me!"

I ignored her.

"Give that to me!"

I stood up slowly. "I've already read it, Clyde."

"It's none of your business!"

"Of course it is. It's my mother's diary, for God's sake!"

She snatched the diary from my hands and pressed it to her chest, looking at me steadily. "You can't prove anything. Just because Ellen said what she did doesn't make it the truth. There are things you can't understand, things that happened a long time ago—"

"You were afraid I was going to find out what really happened, weren't you?"

She stepped back. "I . . . I don't know what you mean."

"That you killed Bryce Davies—"

"Shut your mouth."

"And then Amory found out and he ran off the road in revenge. Is that what happened?"

"Shut your mouth," she said. "That's not what happened!"

"What happened, then?"

She looked around desperately. "It was an accident. She dove in and—and the whirlpool sucked her down, and there was nothing I could do. I couldn't do anything!" she said, her eyes filling with tears. "He jumped to conclusions. It was what he wanted to believe. And I was so mad about everything that happened before, I didn't want to try to make him think different, and then—and then that night . . . Just leave me *alone!*" she sobbed. "I don't have to tell you *anything!*" She turned, hugging the diary, and stumbled away from me, out into the field.

"Stop, Clyde!" I shouted. "Don't go—"

She screamed, and then I heard a sickening thud. I ran to where she was lying sprawled over a shallow pit, groaning and holding her side.

"Are you all right? Can you move?" I knelt beside her. She tried to get up but cried out in pain. "Are you okay? I'm calling an ambulance."

"No," she whimpered.

"I'll be right back. Don't move."

"No, no!" She winced. "Don't leave."

"Clyde—"

"No." Her voice was barely audible.

I hesitated. Blue had followed me and was pawing at the edge of the hole. I noticed a glint and saw that her glasses had fallen off. I cleaned them and put them back on her face as gently as I could.

"Look," I said. "I'm not going to tell anybody any of this."

"No, no, no," she moaned, grasping my wrist.

"Clyde, I have to get help."

She dug her fingers into my flesh. Her hand was cold.

I looked at her soft, frail form, her halo of snowy hair, her clenched hand. "Just tell me one thing," I said. "Why did you destroy my sculptures?"

"I thought . . . I thought you'd hidden the diary in there."

"Why didn't you just ask me?"

"I didn't think you'd tell me the truth."

I shook my head slowly. "Oh, Clyde. Whatever happened, that diary doesn't prove anything."

She tightened her grip, and I felt a shudder run through her body.

"And for what it's worth, I don't think you did anything."

"But I did," she said. "I did."

I pried her fingers loose and clasped them.

"I was so upset, all I wanted was for him to hurt like I did—and then Ellen—"

"That wasn't your fault."

"Yes, it was. Don't you see? I let him think I did it. I *wanted* him to think it. And—oh, God—then—"

I sat very still.

"My words killed your mother, Cassandra. If I'd kept quiet he wouldn't have gotten drunk that night, he wouldn't have been driving that car. And just to see that look on his face when he thought I was capable of it—I was so glad." She was sobbing again, her body quivering, her mouth twisted in a grimace. "I was so, so glad."

I looked up into the sky. The moon was large and pale, and pinprick stars were beginning to appear. I looked all around us—at the grasses swaying in the light wind, at the fields stretching out to the edges of darkness, at the sturdy white house and the single light inside.

When I turned back to Clyde, she had stopped crying. For a moment the only sound was her breathing, heavy and labored. She clutched my hand tightly. "Oh, Cassandra," she said. "There are so many stories I could tell you—"

"I'm here," I said softly. "I'm listening."

In the hospital waiting room I called Horace from a pay phone. He didn't ask any questions; he just said gruffly that he'd be right there and would call the others.

I picked up a magazine reflexively and found a seat, looking around at the drawn faces of the few other visitors, yellow-gray under the humming fluorescent lights. I glanced at the clock; it was one in the morning. The hospital smelled of anything but human beings: new carpeting, old venetian blinds, liquid cleanser. Over by the nurses' station two orderlies were joking and leafing through baby pictures. Their laughter evaporated quickly in the antiseptic air.

Elaine blew through the emergency room entrance first, with

Larry right behind her. "Where is she?" she demanded, walking straight toward me.

I dropped the magazine. "They won't let me in yet," I said, standing up.

"What happened?"

"She fell."

"Where?"

"At my house." I flinched slightly at her incredulity. "Well, actually, behind the house, in the field."

"In the *field?*"

"Yes, Elaine." I looked at Larry. "Hi."

"H'lo, Cassandra." His face was expressionless.

Without makeup, Elaine looked surprisingly old. She was wearing a floral scarf around her hair and a faded pink sweatsuit. There was a greasy spot of cold cream on her neck.

"In the field?" she repeated impatiently.

"Yes. In the field."

"Well. Are you going to tell me what she was doing there, or am I going to have to guess?"

"I think Clyde might want to tell you herself."

"But Clyde's not here now, is she?" she said, with exaggerated politeness. "And I need to find out what happened. So why don't you fill me in."

As we were talking, Horace and Kathy arrived with Chester in tow, his hair sticking up unevenly and his shirt on inside out.

"Cassie!" Kathy squealed. "You poor thing!" She hugged me and then pulled back, pinning my arms to my sides. "We came as fast as humanly possible. I am so relieved to see you're not here all alone."

"Hello, Kathy," Elaine said curtly. She acknowledged Horace and Chester with a nod. "Cassandra was just about to do us the favor of explaining what happened tonight."

"Hey, y'all," Alice said, coming in with Eric on her hip. "Is Clyde okay?"

"Oh, for goodness' sake, Alice Marie." Elaine rolled her eyes. "I cannot believe you brought that child to the hospital."

Alice frowned. "What'd you expect me to do, Mother, leave him by himself?"

"Well, I thought perhaps your banker friend—"

"My banker friend is no longer in the picture." Her face colored, and she cleared her throat. "You might as well all know, since I'm sure good old Bernadette will soon be spreading the joyous news far and wide. My banker friend is married." She shifted Eric to the other hip. "Are you satisfied now, Mother?"

"Oh, Alice Marie, what a thing to say."

Horace, who had left the group and gone to the front desk, came back and said, "We'll be allowed to see her in a minute. A doctor's coming out to tell us what's going on."

Elaine looked out me expectantly. I looked at the floor.

"I do not want to get into what we discussed this afternoon. This is not the time or the place. But I expect that when I ask you a simple question you will treat me with respect enough to answer it." She stared at the top of my head until I looked up again. "Now, what *happened* to my mother?"

"She fell," I said evenly. "It was dark outside, and she didn't see the hole. I came home from work a little early, and I guess I startled her."

"What hole? What was she doing out there at night in the first place?" Horace asked.

I looked at him, at his anxious, wrinkled brow; I looked into Kathy's kind, sympathetic eyes and Larry's unreadable ones. Elaine's arms were crossed, and her lips were a thin waxen line. Alice raised her eyebrows at me and smiled. "She was looking for a . . . keepsake."

Elaine leaned closer. "What do you mean?"

"Something she lost a long time ago," I said. "She thought it might be in the house. I guess when she heard me coming she panicked and—"

"Was it there?" Elaine interrupted. "In the house?"

"Yes, it was."

"Well, what the hell was it?" Horace said.

"I don't—"

"What was it?" said Elaine.

I hesitated. "It was a box. Full of letters. We . . . I . . . found it in the basement. I think Clyde knew it was in the house and she just wanted to get it back."

"Do you know what the letters were about?" Kathy asked.

"They were . . . personal."

Elaine squinted at me. "I don't know," she said after a moment. "Something just doesn't seem right about this, Cassandra. Something doesn't add up. This kind of thing didn't happen before you came down here."

"Now, Elaine—," Larry said.

"No, let me finish. Mother is not the type to go running around in the dark looking for old letters. She just *isn't.* I think there must be something you're not telling us."

"Come on, Elaine," Horace said. He smiled at me apologetically. "It's been a little bit of a shock. We're all kind of worked up."

"No!" Elaine said fiercely. A rash was spreading across her neck. "What kind of game are you playing, Cassandra?"

Everyone stepped back.

"I think you know," I said.

She looked shocked. "What—"

"You've been living with that secret all these years too. And so have you," I said, turning to Horace. "The problem is, it's not really a secret. And it's probably not even true."

"What in the *world* are you talking about?" Elaine said.

"Clyde has lived half her life in the past. And *you*—you act like you're helping her, protecting her, when all you're doing is keeping her from dealing with it." I turned to the rest of them. "When is it going to end? When it's too late? When she's dead? Everybody goes around whispering behind each other's backs—"

"You're a fine one to talk about going behind people's backs!" Elaine broke in bitterly. "Slutting around town with my son—your own *cousin.*" She spit the word out. "The very thought makes me ill."

"What's all this about?" Larry said, looking back and forth between us, his eyes narrowing to flinty chips.

"I didn't think it was my place to tell you," I said quietly to Elaine. "It was his. Why he didn't tell you, I don't know. But I think it's got something to do with all of this, everybody keeping secrets from everybody else, afraid of—I don't know what. And the secrets just get worse the longer they're kept."

Elaine was fuming. "You may find this difficult to believe, Cassandra, but things were just fine before you got here. *Just fine.*"

"Not for Clyde they weren't."

"Don't you say another word about her! You don't know anything about what she's been through!"

"I know that she's been in a lot of pain for more than twenty years about what happened to my mother—and that you haven't been much help."

"Cassandra, I think that's enough." Horace cleared his throat and signaled to the white-coated man coming toward us with a clipboard under one arm. "Doctor," he said, "I'm Horace Clyde. I believe you've got my mother in there."

The doctor transferred his clipboard to the other side and shook Horace's hand. He nodded at the group. "Mrs. Clyde is doing just fine," he told Horace with a hearty smile. "You all can come on into her room, if you like. She should be waking up shortly."

Horace headed down the corridor with the doctor, bombarding him with questions.

"I don't think this is between you and me, Elaine," I said as we followed along.

She stared straight ahead.

I watched her profile. "I don't want to be your enemy."

She stiffened but kept walking. "You're just exactly like Ellen," she said. "You think you have the God-given right to pass judgment on anything and anybody you choose, no matter who you hurt."

I felt my face flush. "What did my mother ever do to you?"

"She hurt Clyde. She hurt her a lot."

"But what did she do to you?"

For a moment she was silent. Then she said, "That's all in the past."

"I don't think it is. I don't think you can let go of it."

She stopped abruptly and turned to face me. "Aren't you a piece of work," she whispered. "You're the one living in the past."

"At least I'm facing it."

"Maybe it isn't yours to face."

I looked at her for a long moment. "You never really liked my mother, did you, Elaine?"

"No," she said. "No, Cassandra, I never did."

When I woke up, everybody was standing around my bed. Horace and Kathy were white-faced and solemn. Chester looked half awake, his hair sticking up in clumps where he'd slept on it. Alice was bouncing Eric on her hip. He was wearing pajamas and sucking his thumb.

"All this fussing over me," I said.

Elaine had a sorrowful expression on her face, like she thought I was already dead.

"Don't furrow your brow, Elaine. Fastest way to wrinkles."

"Oh, Mother," she said, trying to smile. "I'm the one who told you that."

"How are you feeling, dear?" said Chester, coming over and tugging on my hands. "You look as perky as ever."

"Pshaw," I said. "Just a wrinkled old woman."

"You're a liar, is what you are," he said, but there was no force in it.

"Don't cry, Chester," I said. "I might not believe you."

He touched me on the shoulder and turned away.

Over to the right I saw Cassandra, leaning against the wall, watching. "Hey."

"Hey," she said.

I kept looking at her. Out of the corner of my eye I could see Elaine looking from her to me. "Cassandra," I said, "I'm sorry. I'm sorry about what I did."

She came to the bed. "I know."

"There's so much I want to tell you—"

"There's so much I want to hear."

"I broke all the pieces, didn't I?"

"Not all," she said. "I think there was one you missed completely. And the rest of them were mainly just practice. Now I can start on the real ones." She smiled, but I could tell she was sick about it.

"That's right," said Elaine. "Clay pots can be mended. Who's the one with the broken hip?"

"Leave her alone, Elaine," I said. I beckoned Cassie closer and whispered, "Troy's my favorite too." I reached for her hand and squeezed it.

"Mother, you rest now," Elaine said, fussing with my blankets.

"I'm all right, Elaine. You look like you could use some rest yourself."

"Shush now. Close your eyes and sleep." I felt her long, moisturized fingers on my face. Her voice was strict. I closed my eyes.

At five o'clock in the morning, the trees by the roadside were gray-green, the ones behind them black silhouettes against a grainy sky. The few cars I passed had their lights on. I wondered about them: where they'd come from, whether they had been driving all night. I passed fields of sleeping cattle, the black and white of them distinct in the cool gray air. Small, warm, yellow buds, millworkers' windows, shone like fireflies down in the valley.

My eyes were tired, so tired that they stung and the sockets felt raw. When I left the hospital Clyde was under sedation, breathing loudly, tubes coming out of her arms. A broken hip, painful but mendable. The doctor looked at his clipboard, read the vital signs to the relatives, and explained about old women and childbirth and calcium deficiency. Hip fractures in women are common, he said, the baby in the womb needing so much calcium to grow that it robs from its cradle to get it. Most women never fully make up the loss. But her break wasn't bad, as breaks went. She'd be up and about in no time.

I didn't say it, but it looked to me like Clyde was going to die.

Staring at the road, I thought of her, quiet in the bed, surrounded by family. When I had held her, waiting for the ambulance, she was as soft and solid as a sack of flour in my arms. I was calm as the attendants questioned me, calm as I called Horace, waited at the hospital, dealt with Elaine. But now, by myself, I thought of the cold yellow tint of her skin, her blue lips and red-rimmed eyes, the raised bones of her chest, visible through the flimsy hospital gown. I thought of her frail hands covered with age spots. I thought of my mother, in her lime-green dress, and I started to weep. My voice rose out of me like an animal sound, and I didn't even try to contain it.

When I got home I would strip out of my clothes and take a long bath. I would lie back, staring at nothing, considering only the strange paths by the cracks in the wall. And when I was ready I would call Troy and tell him that maybe I'd had all the time I needed to figure things out on my own. There were no more secrets here; the house had given me everything I'd asked of it. In that last long space of lightening darkness I had come to the conclusion that maybe I did know how I felt about him. Maybe I'd known all along.

For all those years the thought of that box festered in my mind like an open wound. I was certain that when I found it the wound would heal and I could finally forget. What I couldn't see is that sometimes the healing is not in the forgetting but in the letting go. Sometimes the answer you need is to a question you don't know how to ask.

There are so many ways to tell this story.

She climbed up that boulder and stood on top with her hands on her hips, staring out across the water.

"Sure is beautiful, Connie," she said.

"Sure is," I agreed.

From the flat rock where I was sitting she looked like a beauty contestant in that blue-black swimsuit, her hair as dark and shining as it had been when we first met.

She walked to the edge and leaned over, looking down into the water. "I don't believe what they say about that whirlpool. It looks perfectly normal to me." She stood up. "I think it's a lie to keep us from having fun. Like Amory not letting you drive."

"I don't know," I said. "You'd think there'd be a reason for them to say it."

She peered over the edge again and shook her head. "Old wives' tales. I'll be damned if I'm going to stop doing what I want because of some old wife." She laughed, and her laugh was deep and scornful. I felt like she had spit in my face. I turned away from her and started cleaning up the picnic.

"Come here, Connie," she said suddenly. "Let's jump off together."

"No, thank you."

"Oh, come on. It'll be fun. Don't be such a spoilsport," she teased.

"Bryce, I'm not even wearing a suit."

"What do you need a suit for? It's only you and me out here."

I looked up at her standing there. She was looking down at me. I have never hated anyone more than I hated her right then.

"I'll watch," I said.

I saw something flash across her face—doubt, maybe, or fear. Whenever I think of that day I think of how she looked for that one moment: eyes cloudy, shoulders uncertain, slightly quivering lips. It lasted less than a second. Then she seemed to brace herself. She stood very straight and gazed over the water again, then crossed two fingers at me and smiled. I smiled back at her.

"Wish me luck," she said.

"Good luck," I said.

I watched her, poised on the rock, her knees bending slightly as she gathered her strength, the tips of her fingers rising, rising, over her head. As she arched her body forward I felt a lift in my own shoulders, something like the pull a bird must feel in its wings just before it takes flight.

About the author

2 Meet Christina Baker Kline

About the book

3 Reading Group Guide

Read on

4 *Desire Lines*

8 *The Way Life Should Be*

11 *Bird in Hand*

15 *Orphan Train*

Insights,
Interviews
& More . . .

Meet Christina Baker Kline

CHRISTINA BAKER KLINE is the author of five novels. Born in England and raised there as well as in the American South and Maine, she studied at Yale, Cambridge, and the University of Virginia, where she was a Hoyns Fellow in Fiction.

In addition to the #1 *New York Times* bestseller *Orphan Train*, Kline's novels include *Bird in Hand*, *The Way Life Should Be*, *Desire Lines*, and *Sweet Water*. She is coeditor, with Anne Burt, of *About Face: Women Write about What They See When They Look in the Mirror*. She commissioned and edited two widely praised connections of original essays, *Child of Mine and Room to Grow*. She is coauthor, with her mother, Christina Looper Baker, of a book on feminist mothers and daughters, *The Conversation Begins*. She has taught creative writing and literature at Yale, New York University and Fordham, among other places. Her essays, articles and reviews have appeared in the *San Francisco Chronicle*, *Psychology Today*, *More Coastal Living*, *the Literarian*, and others. Kline is currently at work on a literature anthology for Facing History and Ourselves and a novel based on the iconic painting *Christina's World* by Andrew Wyeth. She lives in an old house in Montclair, New Jersey with her husband and three sons, and spends as much time as possible on the coast of Maine.

Reading Group Guide

1. Why do you think the author chose to tell the story from two different perspectives? What impact does this have on the narrative?

2. Adam tells Cassie, "It's just that usually when people pick up and move they're either going toward something or running away." Which do you think Cassie is doing?

3. Why do you think Clyde is so unwelcoming to Cassie at first? What does Cassie represent to her?

4. When Cassie gifts her grandmother a bowl she mentions that she's always felt the need to fill things up. Her grandmother says, "I used to feel that way. Now I guess I like things empty." If we read this statement as a metaphor, what do you think it means in the context of Clyde's story?

5. The author does an incredible job of evoking a sense of place. Which do you think is most successful in painting this picture: the cast of characters, the author's use of imagery, or the stories that Clyde tells?

6. Troy tells Cassie that it doesn't do much good to go digging around in the past. Many members of the Clyde family seem to feel this way. Do you think it's better to leave the past behind, or better to face your demons?

7. Why do you think it was so important to Elaine to preserve her mother's secrets? What good did she think she was doing?

8. Do you think that Cassie will stay in Sweetwater? Or will she go back to New York City? What do you think will happen between her and Troy?

9. Family secrets lie at the center of this novel. How might the story have been different if all of the members of Cassie's family had been honest with one another?

Read on

On the night of her high school graduation, Kathryn Campbell sits around a bonfire with her four closest friends, including the beautiful but erratic Jennifer. "I'll be fine," Jennifer says, as she walks away from the dying embers and towards the darkness of the woods. She never comes back.

Ten years later, Kathryn returns to the Maine town where she grew up, determined to answer one simple question: What happened to Jennifer Pelletier?

Desire Lines

All traces of the Pelletiers are gone, save the faint outlines of pictures and mirrors on faded wallpaper. The house seems less grand than Kathryn remembers, though she knows from her mother's real estate training course that unfurnished rooms always appear smaller. She walks through the living room, with its dark wood floors and bay window, to the olive-green dining room to the blindingly white kitchen. This is the one room that Linda Pelletier designed from top to bottom, and her vision is evident in each gleaming detail: the gold drawer pulls, the shiny linoleum, the starburst crystal light fixture hanging over a phantom table. Kathryn runs her hand along the Formica countertop, remembering how obsessive Linda had been about keeping it clean. She was constantly brushing off crumbs, spraying Fantastik and rubbing it in circles, scolding the twins to put their dishes in the dishwasher. "I think she'd be happy if we didn't eat here at all," Will had groused to Kathryn one time as his mother wiped around him.

Walking up the stairs to the second floor, looking out the long windows at the patchy grass and unruly hedges in the broad expanse of yard, Kathryn thinks about how many times she's done this—let herself into the house and then made her way unnoticed up to Jennifer's room. At the door, though, Kathryn always knocked. Jennifer was very private, and anyway she usually locked her door.

Kathryn had always loved hanging out at the Pelletiers'. She and the twins played cards and Monopoly and Scrabble and watched *Little House on the Prairie* on the small red black-and-white in Jennifer's room, or sat on the back porch doing the crossword and the anagram and reading the funnies out loud to each other. They made batches of brownies and ate all the batter. It was in the Pelletiers' attic that Kathryn smoked her first cigarette, and then her first joint.

With Will and Jennifer, Kathryn had often felt like the single friend of a sophisticated married couple who keep her around to amuse them. Part of it was that they were both so striking: white-blond hair as fine as corn silk, light-blue eyes, small regular features. In the summer their skin was smoothly tan, like wet white sand. Kathryn, who was freckled and pale and had hair the color of a murky puddle, somehow felt enhanced by association—which was strange, she realized; usually around such attractive people she felt diminished. But Will and Jennifer seemed to care so little about their appearance. Like old money, their looks were just a given.

The twins were smart and subversive and cool, with a ready wit and a mischievous glint in their eyes. When Kathryn was with them, she felt sharper and stronger, emboldened by their glamorous insouciance. With the two of them she did things she wouldn't have dreamed of doing alone: sneaking out of the house when she was supposed to be asleep, convincing a gullible bouncer at the Bounty that she'd left her ID at home, skipping a day of school with a transparent excuse and going to Bar Harbor.

In high school the twins had been effortlessly popular. Will was humble and friendly but also sure of himself, and, through some combination of confidence and obliviousness, unconcerned with what people thought. Though less outgoing than her brother, Jennifer could be equally charming. She mocked her imagined awkwardness, cultivating a sense of herself that was so much at odds with who she was that it was impossible to take seriously, but had the effect, intentional or not, of evaporating envy.

Although they looked alike, the twins were in many ways opposites. They seemed to share different halves of the same personality. Will liked to be with people, and Jennifer, shy by comparison and somewhat melancholy, preferred to spend long stretches of time alone. Kathryn guessed it was this character trait that made her closer to Jennifer: They spent long, quiet afternoons together talking; they found comfort in their shared solitude. They told each other intimate secrets—not about the facts of their ▶

lives, Kathryn realized later, but about how they felt about them. Kathryn knew, for example, how hurt Jennifer was that her mother seemed to favor Will; Jennifer knew all about Kathryn's father's betrayal. Even at the time, these moments together seemed rare and special; the intimacy felt to Kathryn like a gift. It seemed that these secrets they shared with each other were the most important ones they had.

But sometime during senior year, Jennifer began holding back. There was never any discussion about it; Kathryn just felt her withdrawing by degrees. It was so subtle that for a while Kathryn told herself she must be imagining it. Jennifer wasn't becoming more diffident or remote; Kathryn was just clinging to this friendship out of a fear of the unknown—of graduating from high school, leaving home, going away to college. She didn't want to admit to herself that Jennifer might be pulling away, so she pretended it wasn't happening. Later she recognized this as a self-protective impulse; she'd learned from painful experience during her parents' divorce that knowing too much could be worse than not knowing anything. So she was willfully ignorant, and this ignorance haunted her when Jennifer disappeared and no one seemed to have the slightest idea why.

Now, stepping into Jennifer's room, Kathryn looks around at the peeling pink wallpaper with its faint floral pattern, the grungy hot-pink carpeting, the row of skeletal coat hangers in the otherwise empty closet. The last time Kathryn had been in this house was a week before she left for college. She remembers it well: Will pale and tense, with dark hollows under his eyes, his mother chain-smoking on the front porch, clutching cigarette after cigarette with nervous fingers. For over two months Will had been in charge of the volunteers who were trying to find Jennifer, and they'd turned up exactly nothing. Kathryn fumbled through a good-bye, but she didn't know what to say, and he, distracted, barely noticed. It had gotten so that whenever she tried to talk to him, she felt false, and she hated herself. It wasn't that she had stopped caring—it was that her caring felt so inadequate. It couldn't bring Jennifer back, and it couldn't dull Will's pain. So after the shock, the disbelief, the heart-clamping two and a half months of waiting to hear, Kathryn went away to a new life, relieved to be leaving. Will stayed behind, organizing search parties, tacking up posters, writing legislators, and congresspeople, asking for something, anything, in the way of help.

When she telephoned from college, Will's voice was tired and defeated. He rarely called her; he said it always seemed as if he was interrupting something. And it got harder and harder for her to call him. She'd sit on her bed in her sterile dorm room, listening to his listless voice as she watched her roommate get ready to go out to a party, the sounds of guys playing hackeysack drifting up from the courtyard below. It felt as if her life had been split in two. After a while she stopped calling and began sending postcards instead, and then, eventually, she stopped writing, too, not knowing what effect it had on him, feeling only the monumental numbness that had crept in like a fog and settled over all of them when Jennifer disappeared.

"I think that's enough," Kathryn's mother calls up the stairs. "There's a cross-breeze. Where are you?"

"I'm in here," she says. "Just a moment." She starts to cry, and then she stops herself. Jennifer is gone. Words can't express the enormity of the loss. No story can contain it. Her absence is a presence, ghostly and haunting, touching all who knew her. It is impossible that she disappeared, inconceivable that she will never return. She is at once nowhere and everywhere, a constant shadow, elusory and insubstantial, her life an unkept promise, a half-remembered dream.

The Way Life Should Be

Angela is single in New York City, stuck in a life that seems to have, somehow, just happened. On a hope and a chance, she decides to pack it all up and move to Maine, finding the nudge she needs in the dating profile of a handsome sailor who loves dogs and Italian food. Far from everything familiar, Angela begins to discover the pleasures and secrets of her new small-town community and, in the process, realizes there's really no such thing as the way life *should* be.

I CLICK ON A PHOTO, and the profile is revealed. Chuck, thirty-four, is an actuary who knows how to have a good time. He has been burned before but remains confident that the woman of his dreams is out there. Robert, thirty-one, wants a mutually satisfying relationship with a fellow bodybuilding enthusiast from the tristate area. Colin, a thirty-nine-year-old firefighter, is looking for a red-haired beauty who is ready to start a family and would be happy living on Staten Island. It doesn't take much reading between the lines to spot the guys who live in the same house with or next door to their parents.

As I consider these options, my gaze strays from the computer screen to the bulletin board on my wall. Tacked to the gray synthetic fabric is a photo, torn from a magazine, of a weathered elfin cottage on the Maine coast. Several times a day my glance strays to this photo; the image has become totemic, as unreal a place as Middle Earth. Just looking at it soothes me, the way sound machines of waves or rain can calm your nerves. I have never been to Maine, but in my imagination life there isn't so complicated. I picture a lump of dough rising under a tea towel on a kitchen counter; pansies spilling from a window box; seagulls the size of small dogs, circling in slow motion overhead.

Impulsively—perhaps recklessly—I widen my search, inching up the East Coast. Near Boston I find fewer Italians and bankers, more Irish Catholics and lawyers. Curiously, my qualms about serial rapists and ax murderers diminish the farther north I go, as if all the miscreants and deviants in the northeastern U.S. have confined themselves to the New York area, and the rest is safe.

Moving up the coastline, the pickings get slimmer. Maybe there's a dating website specifically for Mainers, or perhaps Internet dating hasn't really caught on there yet. There is a grand total of six profiles. Most of the head shots feature guys wearing baseball hats with obscure local slogans. Then, all at once—hey! I am gazing into the ice blue eyes of a thirty-five-year old with the screen name "MaineCatch." His opening teaser is "Sail away with me . . ." No baseball cap, a nice tan, a full head of slightly tousled blond hair, navy blue tennis shirt. I sit up straight in my desk chair and click on his picture.

". . . in the night, and all day, too," the teaser ends. As I read the profile I have to remind myself to breathe. It turns out that Rich, thirty-five, runs a sailing school in a coastal town on Mount Desert Island (*Where?* I must Google it immediately). Five eleven and 180 pounds, he has never been married, is a nonpracticing Protestant, loves Italian food and shellfish. Besides sailing, his interests include curling up with a good book, "my dog Sam (short for Samantha)," hiking, and . . . cooking.

My heart thumps.

I click a button that says "Register for free!" I can post my profile and picture, and receive and respond to inquires, but if I want to contact someone, I'll have to pay the monthly charge of $29. There's a feature called "tagging" that allows you to comment on someone's profile without joining by using one of ten canned lines they provide ("You're hot! Check me out—maybe we can start a fire together").

I fill in the blanks:

Name: Angela (no last name).

Age? Am tempted to lie, then realize that it might lead to a potentially unpleasant spurning scenario. 33.

Religion: Nonpracticing Catholic.

Profession: Event Planner.

Hometown: New York City.

Vital statistics: Hmm. Tempted to ignore or minimize, but realize that this is risky. How is it that most people on this web-site describe themselves as "slim" when most Americans are overweight? I check "medium height, medium build." Then, reconsidering, change it to "slim."

Hobbies /activities: Watching old *Lifetime* movies in bed, drinking vodka tonics, going out with friends, reading the Styles section, trolling the Chelsea flea market, eating out. Going to the gym every four or five days and trotting on the treadmill for the duration of *Access Hollywood*.

My fingers hover over the keyboard.

Had I the kind of lifestyle wherein one might actually cultivate interesting hobbies, what would they be? Not that I have ever actually done it, but if I did exercise in a nongym way, I think I might enjoy hiking.

So—"Hiking."

The one time I went sailing, with friends at a time share in the Hamptons, I threw up over the side of the boat, but I'm sure I could grow to love it. I like everything except the water part. The beautiful wooden vessels, the salt-crisp nautical wear, picnics on deck with a glass of wine. The shiny, curving wood in the cabin and the rounded windows belowdecks.

"Sailing."

When I was little I wanted a dog. I begged for years, and finally got a mutt named Rusty. He didn't take well to house-training and tended to snap, and ▶

when he was almost a year old he met an unfortunate end after ingesting rat poison left in the garage by my dad. But I have no doubt that I could grow to love someone else's adored dog, particularly a Lab named Sam.

"Dogs."

And then there's cooking. For this one I don't have to lie or fudge. I write, "Enjoys cooking Italian food and shellfish with friends, al fresco dining under a clear, star-filled sky." The lyrics of that oldies song about piña coladas and getting caught in the rain waft through my head.

So call it coincidence, call it kismet, call it what you will, but my interests dovetail quite nicely with those of MaineCatch.

Several months ago the publications director of the museum took a picture of me for the annual report. It's like a yearbook photo—stiff smile, white blouse—but it's all I've got. I fish it out of a drawer and hurry down the hall to the industrial-strength printer/scanner, scanning it through before I have time to second-guess myself. On the computer screen, I am cheered to see, I look a little better than in real life.

I finish filling out my profile and hesitate over the screen name. It should convey cool nonchalance as opposed to sluttish desperation. What would appeal to Mr. Catch? I try out a few. "Ready2Sail"? Too obvious. "NewYorkCatch"? Erk. I flash through a few possibilities—SpicyGirl, LemonLover (like my grandfather, I do love lemons, but—no)—before trying out NewYorkGirl.

NewYork . . . Girl. I think about it for a moment. It's a stretch, but anyone can see my age on the form. It's breezy. I'm going with it.

Since I am disinclined to pay for this, I scroll through the short list of generic options and fix on the one that seems most neutral: "I'm intrigued! Check me out."

I send my profile and the canned tagline to MaineCatch and get a confirmation notice from the website. I feel a flash of regret, and then a tingle of hope. It's the same feeling I had when I was ten and stuffed a message in a bottle and tossed it off a pier into the ocean. Now that I remember it, the bottle kept washing up onshore with the tide and I finally gave up—but still. My message is out there, and now all I can do is wait and see.

Bird in Hand

IT HAD BEEN A RAINY MORNING, and all through the afternoon the sky remained opaque, bleached and unreadable. Alison wasn't sure until the last minute whether she would even go to Claire's book party in the city. The kids were whiny and bored, and she was feeling guilty that her latest freelance assignment, "Sparking the Flame of Your Child's Creativity," which involved extra interviews and rewrites, had made her distracted and short-tempered with them. She'd asked the babysitter to stay late twice that week already, and had shut herself away in her tiny study—mudroom, really—trying to finish the piece. "Dolores, would you mind distracting him, please?" she'd called with a shrill edge of panic when three-year-old Noah pounded his small fists on the door.

"Maybe we shouldn't go," she said when Charlie called from work to find out when she was leaving. "The kids are needy. I'm tired."

"But you've been looking forward to this," he said.

"I don't know," she said. "Dolores seems out of sorts. I can hear her out there snapping at the kids."

"Look," he said. "I'll come home. I have a lot of work to do tonight anyway. I'll take over for Dolores, and then you won't have to worry."

"But I want you there," she said obstinately. "I don't want to go alone. I probably won't even know anybody."

"You know Claire," Charlie said. "Isn't that what matters? It'll be good to show your support."

"It's not like she's gone out of her way to get in touch with me."

"She did send you an invitation."

"Well, her publicist."

"So Claire put your name on the list. Come on, Alison—I'm not going to debate this with you. Clearly you want to go, or you wouldn't be agonizing over it."

He was right. She didn't answer. Sometime back in the fall, Claire's feelings had gotten ▶

On the drive home from a rare evening out, Alison collides with another car running a stop sign, and—just like that—her life turns upside down. Exquisitely written, powerful, and thrilling, *Bird in Hand* is a novel about love and friendship and betrayal, and about the secrets we tell ourselves and each other.

hurt—something about an article she'd submitted to the magazine Alison worked for that wasn't right, that Alison's boss had brusquely criticized and then rejected, leaving her to do the work of explaining. It was Alison's first major assignment as a freelance editor, and she hadn't wanted to screw it up. So she'd let her boss's displeasure (which, after all, had eked out as annoyance at her, too: "I do wonder, Alison, if you defined the assignment well enough in the first place . . .") color her response. She'd hinted that Claire might be taking on too many things at once, and that the piece wasn't up to the magazine's usual standards. She was harsher than she should have been. And yet—the article was sloppy; it appeared to have been hastily written. There were typos and transition problems. Claire seemed to have misunderstood the assignment. Frankly, Alison was annoyed at her for turning in the piece as she did—she should have taken more time with it, been more particular. It pointed to something larger in their friendship, Alison thought, a kind of carelessness on Claire's part, a taking for granted. It had been that way since they were young. Claire was the impetuous, brilliant one, and Alison was the compass that kept her on course.

Now Claire had finished her novel, a slim, thinly disguised roman à clef called *Blue Martinis*, about a girl's coming-of-age in the South. Alison couldn't bear to read it; the little she'd gleaned from the blurb by a bestselling writer on the postcard invitation Claire's publicist had sent—"Every woman who has ever been a girl will relate to this searingly honest, heartbreakingly funny novel about a girl's sexual awakening in a repressive southern town"—made her stomach twist into a knot. Claire's story was, after all, Alison's story, too; she hadn't been asked or even consulted, but she had little doubt that her own past was now on view. And Claire hadn't let her see the manuscript in advance; she'd told Alison that she didn't want to feel inhibited by what people from Bluestone might think. Anyway, Claire insisted, it was a novel. Despite this disclaimer, from what Alison could gather, she was "Jill," the main character's introverted if strong-willed sidekick.

"Ben will be there, won't he?" Charlie said.

"Probably. Yes."

"So hang out with him. You'll be fine."

Alison nodded into the phone. Ben, Claire's husband, was effortlessly sociable—wry and intimate and inclusive. Alison had a mental picture of him from countless cocktail parties, standing in the middle of a group with a drink in one hand, stooping his tall frame slightly to accommodate.

"Tell them I'm sorry I can't be there," Charlie said. "And let Dolores know I'll be home around seven. And remember—this is part of your job, to schmooze and make contacts. You'll be glad you went."

"Yeah, okay," she said, thinking, oh right, my *job*, mentally adding up how much she'd earned over the past year: two $50 checks for whimsical personal essays on smart-mommy Web sites, $500 for a parenting magazine "service" piece called "50 Ways for New Moms to Relieve Stress," a $1,000 kill fee for a big feature on sibling rivalry that the competition scooped just before Alison's story went to press. The freelance editing assignment with Claire had never panned out.

"The party's on East End Avenue, right?" he said. "You should probably take the bridge. The tunnel might be backed up, with this rain. Drive slow; the roads'll be wet."

They talked about logistics for a few minutes—how much to pay Dolores, what Charlie might find to eat in the fridge. As they were talking, Alison slipped out of her study, shutting the door quietly behind her. She could hear the kids in the living room with Dolores, and she made her way upstairs quietly, avoiding the creaky steps so they wouldn't be alerted to her presence. In the master bedroom she riffled through the hangers on her side of the closet and pulled out one shirt and then another for inspection. She yanked off the jeans she'd been wearing for three days and tried on a pair of black wool pants she hadn't worn in months, then stood back and inspected herself in the full-length mirror on the back of the closet door. The pants zipped easily enough, but the top button was tight. She put a hand over her tummy, unzipped the pants, and callipered a little fat roll with her fingers. She sighed.

"What?"

"Oh, nothing," she said. "Listen, Dolores will feed the kids, you just have to give them a bath. And honey, try not to look at your BlackBerry until you get them in bed. They see so little of you as it is." She yanked down her pants and, back in the closet, found a more forgiving pair.

When Alison was finally dressed she felt awkward and unnatural, like a child pretending to be a grown-up, or a character in a play. In her mommy role she wore flat, comfortable shoes, small gold hoops, soft T-shirts, jeans or khakis. Now it felt as if she were wearing a costume: black high-heeled boots, a jangling bracelet, earrings that pulled on her lobes, bright (too bright?) lipstick she'd been pressed into buying at the Bobbi Brown counter by a salesgirl half her age. She went downstairs and greeted the children stiffly, motioning to Dolores to keep them away so she could maintain the illusion that she always dressed like this.

She went out to the garage, got into the car, remembered her cell phone, clattered back into the house, returned to the car, remembered her umbrella, made it back to the house in time to answer the ringing phone in the kitchen. It was her mother in North Carolina.

"Hi, Mom, look, I'll have to call you later. I'm running out the door."

"You sound tense," her mother said. "Where are you going?"

"To a party for Claire's book."

"In the city?"

"Yes. And I'm late."

"I read her book," her mother said. "Have you?"

"Not yet."

"Well. You might want to."

"I will, one of these days," Alison said, consciously ignoring her mother's ▸

insinuating tone. Then the children were on her. Six-year-old Annie dissolved in tears, and Dolores had to peel Noah off Alison's legs like starfish from a rock. Alison made it out to the car again, calling, "I'll be home soon!" and madly blowing kisses, and realized when she turned on the engine that she didn't have a bottle of water, which was annoying, because you never knew how long it would take to get into the city, but fuck it. There was no way she could go inside again. Halfway down the driveway she saw Annie and Noah in the front window, frantically waving at her and jumping up and down. Alison pressed the button to roll down her window and waved back. As she pulled the car into the street she could see Noah's cheek mashed up against the glass, his hand outstretched, his small form resigned and motionless as he watched her drive away.

Orphan Train

STANDING BEFORE the large walnut door, with its oversized brass knocker, Molly hesitates. She turns to look at Jack, who is already back in his car, headphones in his ears, flipping through what she knows is a dog-eared collection of Junot Díaz stories he keeps in the glove compartment. She stands straight, shoulders back, tucks her hair behind her ears, fiddles with the collar of her blouse (When's the last time she wore a collar? A dog collar, maybe), and raps the knocker. No answer. She raps again, a little louder. Then she notices a buzzer to the left of the door and pushes it. Chimes gong loudly in the house, and within seconds she can see Jack's mom, Terry, barreling toward her with a worried expression. It's always startling to see Jack's big brown eyes in his mother's wide, soft-featured face.

Though Jack has assured Molly that his mother is on board—"That damn attic project has been hanging over her head for so long, you have no idea"—Molly knows the reality is more complicated. Terry adores her only son, and would do just about anything to make him happy. However much Jack wants to believe that Terry's fine and dandy with this plan, Molly knows that he steamrollered her into it.

When Terry opens the door, she gives Molly a once-over. "Well, you clean up nice."

"Thanks. I guess," Molly mutters. She can't tell if Terry's outfit is a uniform or if it's just so boring that it looks like one: black pants, clunky black shoes with rubber soles, a matronly peach-colored T-shirt.

Molly follows her down a long hallway lined with oil paintings and etchings in gold frames, the Oriental runner beneath their feet muting their footsteps. At the end of the hall is a closed door.

Terry leans with her ear against it for a moment and knocks softly. "Vivian?" She opens the door a crack. "The girl is here. Molly Ayer. Yep, okay."

She opens the door wide onto a large, sunny living room with views of the water, filled ▶

The #1 *New York Times* bestseller that has captured the hearts of readers everywhere. . . . Between 1854 and 1929, so-called orphan trains ran regularly from the cities of the East Coast to the farmlands of the Midwest, carrying thousands of abandoned children whose fates would be determined by luck or chance. When seventeen-year-old Molly Ayer is tasked with helping an elderly widow clean out her attic, she uncovers not only a little-known part of American history, but also an unexpected friendship.

with floor-to-ceiling bookcases and antique furniture. An old lady, wearing a black cashmere crewneck sweater, is sitting beside the bay window in a faded red wingback chair, her veiny hands folded in her lap, a wool tartan blanket draped over her knees.

When they are standing in front of her, Terry says, "Molly, this is Mrs. Daly."

"Hello," Molly says, holding out her hand as her father taught her to do.

"Hello." The old woman's hand, when Molly grasps it, is dry and cool. She is a sprightly, spidery woman, with a narrow nose and piercing hazel eyes as bright and sharp as a bird's. Her skin is thin, almost translucent, and her wavy silver hair is gathered at the nape of her neck in a bun. Light freckles—or are they age spots?—are sprinkled across her face. A topographical map of veins runs up her hands and over her wrists, and she has dozens of tiny creases around her eyes. She reminds Molly of the nuns at the Catholic school she attended briefly in Augusta (a quick stopover with an ill-suited foster family), who seemed ancient in some ways and preternaturally young in others. Like the nuns, this woman has a slightly imperious air, as if she is used to getting her way. And why wouldn't she? Molly thinks. She *is* used to getting her way.

"All right, then. I'll be in the kitchen if you need me," Terry says, and disappears through another door.

The old woman leans toward Molly, a slight frown on her face. "How on earth do you achieve that effect? The skunk stripe," she says, reaching up and brushing her own temple.

"Umm . . ." Molly is surprised; no one has ever asked her this before. "It's a combination of bleach and dye."

"How did you learn to do it?"

"I saw a video on YouTube."

"YouTube?"

"On the Internet."

"Ah." She lifts her chin. "The computer. I'm too old to take up such fads."

"I don't think you can call it a fad if it's changed the way we live," Molly says, then smiles contritely, aware that she's already gotten herself into a disagreement with her potential boss.

"Not the way *I* live," the old woman says. "It must be quite time-consuming."

"What?"

"Doing that to your hair."

"Oh. It's not so bad. I've been doing it for a while now."

"What's your natural color, if you don't mind my asking?"

"I don't mind," Molly says. "It's dark brown."

"Well, my natural color is red." It takes Molly a moment to realize she's making a little joke about being gray.

"I like what you've done with it," she parries. "It suits you."

The old woman nods and settles back in her chair. She seems to approve. Molly feels some of the tension leave her shoulders. "Excuse my rudeness, but at my age there's no point in beating around the bush. Your appearance is quite stylized. Are you one of those—what are they called, gothics?"

Molly can't help smiling. "Sort of."

"You borrowed that blouse, I presume."

"Uh . . ."

"You needn't have bothered. It doesn't suit you." She gestures for Molly to sit across from her. "You may call me Vivian. I never liked being called Mrs. Daly. My husband is no longer alive, you know."

"I'm sorry."

"No need to be sorry. He died eight years ago. Anyway, I am ninety-one years old. Not many people I once knew are still alive."

Molly isn't sure how to respond—isn't it polite to tell people they don't look as old as they are? She wouldn't have guessed that this woman is ninety-one, but she doesn't have much basis for comparison. Her father's parents died when he was young; her mother's parents never married, and she never met her grandfather. The one grandparent Molly remembers, her mother's mother, died of cancer when she was three.

"Terry tells me you're in foster care," Vivian says. "Are you an orphan?"

"My mother's alive, but—yes, I consider myself an orphan."

"Technically you're not, though."

"I think if you don't have parents who look after you, then you can call yourself whatever you want."

Vivian gives her a long look, as if she's considering this idea. "Fair enough," she says. "Tell me about yourself, then."

Molly has lived in Maine her entire life. She's never even crossed the state line. She remembers bits and pieces of her childhood on Indian Island before she went into foster care: the gray-sided trailer she lived in with her parents, the community center with pickups parked all around, Sockalexis Bingo Palace, and St. Anne's Church. She remembers an Indian corn-husk doll with black hair and a traditional native costume that she kept on a shelf in her room—though she preferred the Barbies donated by charities and doled out at the community center at Christmas. They were never the popular ones, of course—never Cinderella or Beauty Queen Barbie, but instead one-off oddities that bargain hunters could find on clearance: Hot Rod Barbie, Jungle Barbie. It didn't matter. However peculiar Barbie's costume, her features were always reliably the same: the freakish stiletto-ready feet, the oversized rack and ribless midsection, the ski-slope nose and shiny plastic hair . . .

But that's not what Vivian wants to hear. Where to start? What to reveal? This is the problem. It's not a happy story, and Molly has learned through experience that people either recoil or don't believe her or, worse, pity her. So she's learned to tell an abridged version. "Well," she says, "I'm a Penobscot Indian on my father's side. When I was young, we lived on a reservation near Old Town."

"Ah. Hence the black hair and tribal makeup."

Molly is startled. She's never thought to make that connection—is it true? ▶

Orphan Train ***(continued)***

Sometime in the eighth grade, during a particularly rough year—angry, screaming foster parents; jealous foster siblings; a pack of mean girls at school—she got a box of L'Oreal ten-minute hair color and Cover Girl ebony eyeliner and transformed herself in the family bathroom. A friend who worked at Claire's at the mall did her piercings the following weekend—a string of holes in each ear, up through the cartilage, a stud in her nose, and a ring in her eyebrow (though that one didn't last; it soon got infected and had to be taken out, the remaining scar a spiderweb tracing). The piercings were the straw that got her thrown out of that foster home. Mission accomplished.

Molly continues her story—how her father died and her mother couldn't take care of her, how she ended up with Ralph and Dina.

"So Terry tells me you were assigned some kind of community service project. And she came up with the brilliant idea for you to help me clean my attic," Vivian says. "Seems like a bad bargain for you, but who am I to say?"

"I'm kind of a neat freak, believe it or not. I like organizing things."

"Then you are even stranger than you appear." Vivian sits back and clasps her hands together. "I'll tell you something. By your definition I was orphaned, too, at almost exactly the same age. So we have that in common."

Molly isn't sure how to respond. Does Vivian want her to ask about this, or is she just putting that out there? It's hard to tell. "Your parents . . ." she ventures, "didn't look after you?"

"They tried. There was a fire . . ." Vivian shrugs. "It was all so long ago, I barely remember. Now—when do you want to begin?"